D0249830

Praise for Kat Martin's bestselling Heart Trilogy

"Ms. Martin keeps you burning the midnight oil
as she sets fire to the pages of *Heart of Fire*....
Don't miss this fabulous series! It is definitely a winner."
—*Reader to Reader*

"*Heart of Fire* is a wonderful historical romance....
Kat Martin has created a story that delivers emotion,
steamy romance, and a suspenseful storyline.
This is one you don't want to miss."
—*The Romance Reader's Connection*

"Martin puts a twist on the captive/captor theme
by cleverly combining it with a bit of *Pygmalion*
and a touch of Tarzan for a fast-paced, sensual,
entertaining tale."
—*Romantic Times BOOKreviews*

"With an exciting ending
and a steamy romance, *Heart of Honor*
is a great book to heat up a winter's night."
—*Romance Reviews Today*

"*Heart of Honor* sweeps the reader away on a tidal
wave of emotion, bittersweet, poignant romance and
a tantalizing primal sexuality that are the inimitable
trademarks of multi-talented author Kat Martin."
—*Winter Haven News*

"Ms. Martin always delivers for her readers a romance
that they can sink their teeth into…you can never go
wrong with one of her books. A great winter read!"
—*A Romance Review*

"The happily-ever-after
was a wonderful affair. I really enjoyed *Heart of Honor*.
Its very differences will make it stand out
well on the vast shelves of historical romances."
—*Romance Junkies*

KAT MARTIN

Heart of Courage

MIRA®

ISBN-13: 978-0-7783-2609-0
ISBN-10:   0-7783-2609-8

Recycling programs
for this product may
not exist in your area.

HEART OF COURAGE

www.MIRABooks.com

Printed in U.S.A.

To my dear friend Connie Gartner,
one of life's grand ladies.
Thank you, Connie,
for the joy you brought us all. We miss you!

One

London, England
September, 1844

COVENT GARDEN KILLER STRIKES AGAIN.
Londoners grow nervous.

Thor scanned the front page article in the *London Times*—details of the second brutal murder in the Covent Garden district in the last six months.

Unlike his older brother, Leif, Thor wasn't much of a reader. He figured the best use for a newspaper was to wrap up dead fish. He admitted it was probably important to keep up with what was happening around him, so he struggled through the English words, a language he had only started learning a little over two years ago. Before that, he had lived on an island far to the north, an isolated world only a handful of people knew existed.

With the help of his teacher, Professor Paxton Hart, he

had learned to read and write, how to dress and move about in English society. Leif and his wife helped as well, and life here grew easier all the time. Still, Thor liked being out of doors, not inside reading a book.

"So you're the one who stole my paper!" An indignant female voice snagged his attention. "I've been looking all over." Hands on hips, Lindsey Graham marched across the office like a raven swooping down on its prey.

Holding the evidence of his guilt in one big hand, Thor stood in the doorway of the back room of *Heart to Heart,* the ladies' magazine owned by his brother's wife, Krista Hart Draugr, and her father, his teacher, Sir Paxton Hart. It was Thursday, the day before the paper came out, and the office hummed with activity.

"I did not steal it," he said to the avenging angel bearing down on him. "I borrowed it. I wanted to know about the murder."

Her eyes shot to his, a tawny golden color like the she-cat she was. "There was a second murder?"

He nodded, held the paper so she could read the headline. "Down in Covent Garden," he said. "Same as before."

Lindsey took the newspaper and scanned the article. She was taller than the average woman, yet far shorter than his six-foot-five-inch frame. She was slender, her hair a light golden brown. With her fine-boned, delicate features, she was pretty, but not in the way he preferred.

Like his brother, he wanted his women lusty, buxom and full-breasted, the kind built to satisfy a man. Leif had found Krista, the mate of his heart. Thor was still looking for the female who would be his.

"Another woman killed," Lindsey said, her tawny gaze

glued to the page, "strangled just like the last time. The police believe the same man is likely responsible."

Lindsey was editor of the women's section of the paper and also wrote a gossip column called *Heartbeat*. She was a hard worker, he knew, a quality he admired since he worked so hard himself. Whenever he wasn't down at the docks, bossing the stevedores who loaded and unloaded the cargo carried by his brother's company, Valhalla Shipping, he worked for *Heart to Heart*. He was saving his money to buy a place in the country, far away from the choking air of London.

"Here's something new," Lindsey went on, her fine, straight nose immersed in the printed lines. "It says the women who were killed were 'ladies of the evening.'"

"Whores," Thor said simply.

Lindsey blushed. "That does not mean it is all right for someone to kill them."

"I did not say that."

She sighed. "I feel sorry for the people who live in the neighborhood. Two murders in the last six months. They must be terrified. I certainly hope the police apprehend him this time."

"The paper says they have found clues. They believe they will soon have a suspect. Mayhap this time they will catch him."

"I wonder what they have discovered."

Thor made no reply, since neither of them knew the answer. Engrossed in the paper, Lindsey wandered over to her desk, sat down and continued to read. In the middle of the room, the big Stanhope press sat silent, but soon the next edition would be rumbling off for sale on the streets.

Thor liked to watch the press at work. In truth, he was amazed by the heavy machinery he had seen since his arrival in England, equipment that could spin cotton into cloth, or press glass into various shapes and sizes. There were even powerful steam machines called locomotives that could carry people to distant places in hours instead of days.

There was nothing like that on the remote island of Draugr where he and Leif had been born and raised. People on Draugr still lived as they had hundreds of years ago. They were warriors and farmers, not city dwellers like the people in London.

Flashing a smile at the typesetter, Bessie Briggs, an older woman who mothered him as if he were her son, he went back to work stacking boxes and crates, making room for tomorrow's papers.

It was only a few minutes later that the bell rang above the front door, drawing his attention to a thin man, slightly beak-nosed and dark-haired, who walked into the office. Dressed in an expensive-looking dark brown tailcoat and tan trousers, he carried one of those stupid high hats London men favored and Thor flatly refused to wear.

Returning to his work, he forgot about the man until he heard voices raised in anger. Saying a grateful prayer that this time the object of Lindsey's wrath was someone else, he gazed through the door in her direction and saw the well-dressed man standing next to her desk. They were arguing. Noticing the hard set of the man's jaw, the blood-lust in his eyes, Thor's senses went on alert.

Lindsey clamped her hands on her hips. "I don't give a fig whether you bloody well like it or not. If you hadn't been cheating on your wife, I wouldn't have found out and I wouldn't have written about you in my column!"

"You little bitch! My wife is threatening divorce. I am the Earl of Fulcroft and a Whitfield, and Whitfields do not divorce! You will write a retraction immediately or I will personally see you ruined!"

"And how, may I ask, do you intend to do that?"

A grim smile curved the earl's lips. "I will dig into your past until I find something that will scandalize the very people your column is meant to impress. There will be something—there always is—no matter how young and innocent you seem. And I shall keep digging until I find it! Then we'll see how much *you* 'bloody well like it!'"

Thor had heard enough. Seeing Lindsey's face had turned a little pale, he strode toward Fulcroft, grabbed him by the lapels of his expensive coat and jerked him up on his toes.

"You are finished with your threats to the lady. You will apologize for the name you called her and then you will leave."

"Put me down this instant!"

Ignoring the stunned look on Lindsey's face, Thor shook him like the rat he was. "I said you will apologize. Do it now."

The earl dangled there, his feet swinging, his shiny leather shoes dangling several inches above the floor. "All right, all right. I'm sorry I called you a bitch. Now put me down!"

Thor set the man back on his feet and the earl eased toward the door. He pierced Lindsey with a glare. "Your bulldog notwithstanding, I meant every word. I'll expect to read your retraction in the next edition of the paper."

"Don't hold your breath!" Lindsey called after him as he turned and hurried out of the office.

Thor was feeling well pleased with himself when Lindsey rounded on him. "Don't you ever do that again!"

"What are you talking about?"

"You interfered in my business. I can deal with my problems myself. I don't need any help from you."

Thor clenched his jaw. "You wished for the man to continue his insults? You did not mind that he called you a female dog?"

Her eyes widened. Then a corner of her mouth twitched. "I minded. But I could have handled him myself."

"Fine. The next time a man insults you, I will pretend not to hear. Does that suit you, lady?"

Her eyes held his an instant before she glanced away. "It suits me. I don't need your help or anyone else's."

Thor shook his head. "Stubborn as an ugly horse."

"You mean mule," she corrected.

"Fine. Stubborn as a mule."

Lindsey flashed him a last brief glance, turned and walked away.

Damned woman, he thought, trying not to notice the way her hips swayed beneath her full skirts, to wonder if her waist was really small enough for his hands to fit around it. She was as slender as a boy. Why he should notice her at all he could not imagine.

Still, he had to admit she had a very pretty face and skin as smooth and pale as cream. Her hair, the color of rich, dark honey, shimmered in the sun shining in through the window.

His body tightened. Grinding his jaw against a shot of lust that angered him more than aroused him, he strode back to the rear of the office and began stacking the rest of the newspaper bundles.

He wasn't attracted to Lindsey Graham. She wasn't the sort of woman he found the least attractive. But as she moved across the office in that graceful way of hers, Thor found himself watching her again.

Lindsey finished reworking the notes she had made for this week's column. At the back of the office, she could hear Thor at work loading stacks of bound newspapers, getting ready for the edition that would be on the streets tomorrow.

Lindsey knew Krista was eager for this particular issue to come out. She was campaigning hard against the institution of baby farming, the awful practice of selling illegitimate infants into places that ultimately resulted in their deaths, neatly disposing of unwanted problems.

Their mutual friend, Coralee Whitmore Forsythe, had uncovered the terrible practice during her search for the man who had murdered her sister. While Corrie was away on her quest, Lindsey had taken over writing the society column for the gazette. Though Corrie was currently on her honeymoon with her husband, the Earl of Tremaine, once she returned to England, she and Gray would add their support to Krista's campaign.

Lindsey glanced through the door leading into the back room of the office. She could see Thor at work, his powerful body hoisting and moving the bound stacks of newspapers as if they weighed nothing. It was a laborer's job. Thor was a man who seemed to enjoy physical exertion.

He wasn't obsessed with learning as his older brother, Leif, had been, but considering he had arrived in England only a few years ago, he had educated himself fairly well.

She didn't know much about him, only that he came from some tiny island north of the Orkneys. He spoke English well, with just a slight accent that sounded faintly Norwegian. He could read and write, though not as well as he could speak, and Krista and her father had taught him at least the basics necessary to move about in polite society.

Still, in most ways, the man was a barbarian. He had no interest in the arts, theater, or opera, no desire to attend the soirees, balls, and risottos that Lindsey enjoyed so much. As society editor of *Heart to Heart* and author of the weekly gossip column, *Heartbeat,* it was necessary for her to mingle and mix with the social elite. As the daughter of a baron, Lindsey did it well.

She liked her job, liked the independence it gave her. Of course, in the beginning, her mother and father had been horrified at the notion of their twenty-two-year-old daughter actually *working,* but they were gone a great deal and Lindsey had insisted she needed something to do. In the end, as usual, she had gotten her way.

Once again, her parents were traveling on the Continent, leaving Lindsey in the house under the care of her mother's older sister, Delilah Markham, Countess of Ashford. Lindsey liked her aunt, an extremely forward-thinking woman who, at forty-six, had lived an exciting life and intended to enjoy every moment of the years ahead.

Which meant that basically, Lindsey was on her own.

It was warm in the office this early September day. Lindsey fanned herself with the newspaper she had been reading, then flicked a glance toward the back of the building, where Thor bent down to hoist another bundle. He always dressed simply, never wore a waistcoat, cravat or stock.

Her eyes widened as she realized the man had stripped off his tailcoat and unbuttoned his fine lawn shirt all the way to his navel. She could see his massive chest, a wide V of swarthy skin covered by thick slabs of muscle, even the ladder of muscle across his flat belly. The work was heavy and perspiration ran in rivulets through his dark hair and down his thick neck. It plastered his shirt to his incredible body. His arms bulged with muscle, and when he turned away, slabs of muscle tightened across his broad back.

Lindsey's stomach contracted. The only thing the big brute had going for him was a body that seemed to mimic the Norse god he was named for, and eyes so blue that when you looked into them, you felt as if you might disappear.

It simply wasn't fair that a man should look so good on the outside and have so little of interest on the inside.

It simply wasn't fair.

Still, Lindsey stared at him, unable to look away, fascinated until he turned round and caught her.

His dark head came up and those incredible blue eyes locked on her face.

"I am not decently clothed," he said. "A lady would not look."

Her chin inched up. "And a gentleman would not disrobe except in private!" Whirling her chair around, her pulse hammering far too fast, she jerked her plumed pen from its silver holder, jabbed it into the inkwell and stabbed it down on the paper, leaving a purple stain as she tried to scratch out the first paragraph of her upcoming column.

Thor said something beneath his breath and went back to hoisting bundles.

"Are you all right?"

Her head came up and she flushed guiltily at the sight of her employer and best friend, Krista Hart Draugr, approaching her desk. She started to say that she was just fine before Thor had stripped off half his clothes, but stopped when she realized Krista was referring to the argument she'd had earlier with the Earl of Fulcroft, not Thor.

"Bessie told me about the earl," Krista went on. "I'm sorry I wasn't here." She was tall, taller than most men, except, of course, for her husband and Thor. With her big green eyes and golden blond hair, she was a beautiful woman. And she had found exactly the right man for her in Leif. The pair had a nine-month-old son they adored, and as virile as both brothers appeared to be, soon there would probably be another addition to the family.

Lindsey looked up at Krista and smiled. "I am fine. Fulcroft was just blowing off steam."

"Whatever he threatens, the paper will stand behind you. You don't have to write a retraction if you don't want to."

Lindsey thought of Fulcroft's threat to dig into her past until he found something that would ruin her. He could, she knew. She had always been independent and a bit too reckless. It wouldn't take that much digging to discover her youthful indiscretion with the young Viscount Stanfield. Still, she doubted Lord Fulcroft would actually go through with his threat and she wasn't about to be blackmailed at any rate.

"As I said, he was just spewing hot air. After Thor's not-so-subtle warning, I doubt he will give me any more trouble."

Krista glanced toward the back of the room, caught a glimpse of Thor's perspiration-soaked shirt and the open V where his muscular chest was exposed.

"I hope you aren't offended. My husband and his brother are difficult men to control."

"That is an understatement."

"I can close the door. It's just that it gets terribly hot in there."

"Don't be silly. I have seen a man's chest before."

Krista cast her a knowing glance that said, *not one like that one.* Which, of course, was true.

As her friend returned to her office, Lindsey fixed her gaze on the sheet of paper in front of her and tried to block the image of smooth dark skin and rippling muscles, but there was no way in the world that she could.

It was nearly three in the morning when Lindsey accepted the help of a footman and stepped down from the carriage, waited while her aunt Delilah stepped down, and the two of them made their way inside her parents' Mayfair mansion.

Standing in the marble entry, Lindsey handed her cloak to the butler, a thin, silver-haired man who had been with the family for more than twenty years. "Thank you, Benders," she said.

He gave her a smile then took her aunt's wrap, as well. "Will there be anything more, my lady?"

"That will be all for tonight," Aunt Dee said.

The butler shuffled away and Lindsey made her way into the Rose Drawing Room for a brief recap of the evening, a ritual she and Aunt Dee shared whenever she was in town.

Exhausted, Lindsey sank down on the rose velvet settee, wishing she could simply go to bed.

"My, I can't remember when I've had such a marvelous evening." The Countess of Ashford, widow of the late Earl of Ashford, swept into the room behind her as if it were six in the evening, not numerous hours past midnight. As if they hadn't danced till Lindsey's feet ached and a kink throbbed in her neck. As if they hadn't smiled and made inane conversation until Lindsey thought her face would crack.

Though most of the time she enjoyed herself at affairs like the Marquess of Penrose's ball, tonight she found herself wishing she was somewhere besides a crowded drawing room, somewhere the air didn't smell of too-sweet perfume and shoe polish.

Aunt Dee poured herself a final glass of sherry and offered one to Lindsey, who firmly shook her head. Returning to the settee, Delilah settled herself at the opposite end from Lindsey.

"The Earl of Vardon was certainly attentive tonight." She took a sip of sherry. "I think he is interested in you."

She was tall, like Lindsey, but more robust, her figure still stunning. With her thick black hair and heavily lashed gray eyes, she looked at least ten years younger than her forty-six years, and half the men in London vied for her attention. Only a lucky few were granted the privilege of spending time with her.

"Well, I am not interested in Lord Vardon," Lindsey said. "Or for that matter, any other man. At least not right now."

Delilah sat back on the sofa. "I suppose I shouldn't encourage your independence, but in truth, I couldn't agree with you more. A woman should enjoy her youth while she is able. There is plenty of time later on for a husband and children."

Aunt Dee was a bit of a rebel in her belief that a woman should enjoy the same freedoms as a man. It was amazing Lindsey's parents considered her a proper chaperone. Then again, her father and mother, Baron and Baroness Renhurst, had always been more concerned with their own affairs than those of their daughter.

"I like my life," Lindsey said. "I like being able to do as I wish without some man ordering me about."

"Just as you should, my dear. A woman has to be a bit more careful, more discerning in her affairs, but if she is shrewd enough, she can find any number of ways to enjoy herself."

Lindsey imagined Aunt Dee had often made use of that advice. In a number of ways Lindsey admired her. It took courage for a woman to live exactly as she pleased.

Her thoughts returning to the evening past, Lindsey leaned back on the sofa. "I wonder if Rudy is home yet." Her brother had been at the ball for a bit, but he had left early with some of his friends.

"I doubt he is here. Your brother's late hours are legendary. Odds are he won't be home before noon on the morrow."

Lindsey straightened. "He is merely feeling his oats," she defended. "Every young man goes through these stages." Though Rudy was only a year younger than Lindsey, he was the baby of the family and heir to the barony. As such he had always been indulged.

"Your brother is reckless in the extreme. He is a wastrel who drinks too much and carouses with unsavory people. Your father should have taken him in hand years ago. Now he is grown and it is too late."

"He is young, yet," Lindsey argued. "In time, he'll grow out of it." At least she hoped he would. Since Rudy had been a boy, he had been allowed to run wild. He had a terrible reputation as a rake, and Lindsey wasn't completely sure he was ever going to change.

Aunt Dee finished the last of her sherry. "Well, I suppose it is time we went to bed."

Lindsey breathed a sigh of relief and rose from the sofa. "I believe you're right. Good night, Aunt Dee. I'll see you in the morning."

Wearily she left the drawing room and headed upstairs. All the way there, she thought of Rudy and wondered if her aunt might not be at least partly correct.

Two

Rudy arrived home the next day at ten o'clock in the morning. Lindsey was just finishing breakfast when she heard a noise in the entry. Hoping it was Rudy, she went in to see who had come into the house.

Her brother grinned as he staggered toward her, doffing his tall beaver hat. It fell from his fingers and rolled across the marble floor. "Mornin', sis."

Standing a few feet away, the butler reached down and plucked up the hat. Pretending not to notice her brother's inebriated state, he set the hat down on the side table.

Lindsey marched toward her brother. "Good heavens, Rudy, you are completely and utterly foxed!"

He chuckled, a tall, lean young man with sandy hair and freckles. "You noticed, eh?" He stumbled, fell against the wall, swayed and fell again.

"Benders, will you help me get my brother upstairs to his room?"

"Of course, miss."

The old man started forward, but Rudy lurched away.

"Don't need any help. Just came by for a bath and a change of clothes, then I'm off. Meeting Tom Boggs and the boys at the club."

Lindsey rounded on him, her hands clamped on her hips. "Are you insane? You can't possibly go to White's in the condition you are in. You will make an utter fool of yourself."

Rudy frowned. "That bad, am I?"

"Worse. You can barely stay on your feet."

Her brother shrugged his shoulders. His frock coat was rumpled, she saw, and spotted with heaven knew what in several places. "Maybe I'll lie down for a while, take myself a nap. Room seems to be spinnin' a bit."

"Yes, I imagine it is." Lindsey moved to his side and draped one of his arms across her shoulders, waited while Benders did the same. They headed up the curving staircase, Rudy's feet hitting every other step as they climbed up to the second floor. Benders was wheezing by the time they dumped him like an oversized lump of coal onto his big four-poster bed. The instant he hit the mattress, his eyes closed and he started snoring.

"Young master seems to have put on a bit of an all-nighter."

"Yes, and it is hardly the first time."

"Boy's high-spirited, is all."

"Well, he had better learn to bring those high spirits under control before he winds up getting into trouble."

Benders just nodded. Crossing the room, he summoned Mr. Peach, Rudy's valet, who had the dubious task of undressing him and putting him to bed.

Lindsey sighed as she left the room. Thank heavens Aunt Dee had missed her brother's performance. Though her aunt was all for being independent, she drew the line at behaving like a drunken lout.

Lindsey worked behind her desk on this week's column, penning notes on the Penrose ball. She was in the process of describing the lavish decorations, the huge urns overflowing with chrysanthemums, the ornate columns and gilt mirrors that had been brought in to make the ballroom look like Versailles, when Rudy arrived at the office. He stormed into *Heart to Heart* like a whirlwind set ablaze, his hazel eyes wide and his face a little pale, making his freckles stand out.

"Lissy—I need to talk to you." It was a name he had called her when he was too small to say *Lindsey,* a nickname he rarely used anymore. It brought her head up, her gaze shooting to his face.

"Good grief, what is it? You look as if you are about to swoon."

"I'm a man, Lindsey—men don't swoon. But I—I...I need to speak to you in private."

There was something in his eyes that reminded her of the little boy he had once been. Lindsey rose from her chair and motioned for him to come upstairs to the room Professor Hart often used as his away-from-home study. Rudy followed her inside the high-ceilinged, book-lined chamber and closed the door.

Clamping down on a thread of worry, she turned to face him. "So what has happened to upset you so badly?"

Rudy took a breath, working to calm himself. "This morning, the police came to see me."

"What?"

"A constable named Bertram. He's the lead investigator on the Covent Garden murders."

"What on earth did Constable Bertram want with you?"

As if his legs would no longer hold him up, Rudy sank down in one of the wooden chairs opposite the professor's battered oak desk, leaving Lindsey standing. "He wanted to ask me some questions about this latest murder. About both murders, in fact."

"The police thought *you* might have information on the murders?"

"Not just information. They…um…seem to think I might be involved in some way."

The words chilled her. None of this made any sense. "In what way could you possibly be involved in a murder?"

Rudy looked at her with a face full of misery. Beads of perspiration popped out on his forehead. "They seem to consider me a suspect, Lindsey. They acted as if I might be the man who actually committed the crimes."

Lindsey sank down in the other wooden chair, her heart hammering dully. "What would…" She moistened her lips. "What would make them think you were involved?"

Rudy looked away, staring out the window though he couldn't see anything but a patch of gray, overcast sky. Fall weather had finally arrived. The temperature had dropped and it looked as if a storm might be coming in.

"I knew her," he said, "…the woman who was killed."

Lindsey frowned. "But I thought the woman was a…a lady of the evening."

He looked even more miserable. "She considered herself an actress. We…um…met one night at a sort of party at Tom Boggs'."

Tom Boggs. The spoiled, youngest son of an earl was trouble and always had been. Ever since her brother had begun spending time with Tom and his worthless friends, Rudy hadn't been himself. Now he was involved with a prostitute. She was beginning to see a side of her brother she hadn't known existed.

But then, a young woman wasn't supposed to know about things like prostitution, and a young man was expected to sow his oats in such ways.

"Were you…*involved* with her at the time she was murdered?"

"I'd…um…seen her shortly before it happened."

She was afraid to ask the next question, afraid of what the answer might be. Her brother had been behaving badly for some time. She had worried that sooner or later he would wind up in trouble.

"What about the other woman…the one who was murdered six months ago? Were you…acquainted with her, as well?"

He nodded, long-faced and eyes downcast. "I was only just with her the once, but I think it was somewhere round the time she was killed."

"Oh, Rudy."

"What am I gonna do, sis?"

What indeed? She took a steadying breath, her mind replaying all he had told her, trying to decide on the best course of action. "The first thing we shall do is speak to Father's solicitor, Mr. Marvin. Since he is an attorney, he can advise you as to what you should or should not say to the police."

"I didn't kill those women. I shall simply tell them the truth. I don't see why—"

"I think you do see why or you would not have come to me for help."

He glanced away, cleared his throat. "I admit to being a little worried. It isn't every day I am interviewed by the police."

"Which is why we won't take any chances. Make an appointment with Mr. Marvin. Let us see what he has to say."

Rudy reluctantly agreed. They spoke a few minutes more then returned downstairs. As soon as her brother had left the office, Lindsey went in to see Krista.

"If you aren't too busy, I could use a bit of advice."

"I'm not too busy for you. Come on in."

Lindsey sat down in the chair next to Krista's desk, tucking her full skirts neatly around her. Briefly, she told her friend about her brother and that the police had interviewed him as a suspect in the Covent Garden murders.

"Good heavens."

"That is what I said. I can hardly believe it. My brother might be a little wild, a bit reckless at times, but he is scarcely the sort to kill someone."

"Which the police are sure to discover."

"I certainly hope so." She sighed. "I suppose there is little we can do, at least for the moment. We shall simply have to wait, see if the authorities decide to go further."

"Which is highly unlikely. Rudy is, after all, your father's heir. Baron Renhurst is a highly respected member of the peerage."

"You're right, of course. There is no reason for me to worry."

"None whatsoever…though I am glad you advised your brother to speak to your father's attorney."

It was the smart thing to do, she knew. She told herself the matter would likely disappear and hoped that it was true.

Lindsey returned to the office the following morning. She tried to concentrate on the article she was writing, but her thoughts continually strayed to Rudy. Yesterday he had spoken to Mr. Marvin, whose advice was not to talk to the police unless he was present.

Fortunately, Rudy had not been contacted by the authorities again.

"Still, it worries me," Lindsey said to Krista. "After all, my brother did know both women."

"Knowing them and murdering them are two far different things."

Lindsey sighed. "Indeed, they are."

But later that day when Rudy came rushing in, she couldn't stifle a jolt of fear. He sank down in the chair next to her desk.

"They came to see me again."

"The police? You didn't talk to them without Mr. Marvin, did you?"

"They said they only had a couple more questions. Since I have nothing to hide, I didn't think it would hurt."

Lindsey gritted her teeth. "So what did they want to know?"

"They…um, asked where I was the nights the murders were committed."

Her stomach tightened. The police were seriously considering Rudy as a suspect in the killings. "What did you say?"

"I told them I couldn't remember."

"Rudy!"

"It's the truth, sis. I got drunk with Tom and the boys. That's all I remember until I woke up the next morning with a doozie of a headache in the back room of the Golden Pheasant."

"The Golden Pheasant?"

He looked sheepishly away. "It's a gaming establishment. I go there with my friends."

"Tell me the place is not located anywhere near Covent Garden."

He made no reply, just stared down at his lap.

"Dear God, Rudy. What have you got yourself into?"

He looked up at her. "That's just it, sis. I haven't done anything but drink a little too much."

"And gamble?"

He shrugged as if it were unimportant. "I've lost a few guineas here and there."

But his guilty expression said it was more than a few and she thought how disappointed their father would be to learn the wastrel activities of his son.

"The thing is, I'm not a murderer. I just…I don't know how I'm going to prove it."

Neither did Lindsey. Still, as spoiled and overindulged as her brother was, she loved him. Both of them were a little reckless, a little impulsive. But she knew deep down that Rudy was innocent of the brutal crimes.

And she would do whatever it took to clear his name.

Thor watched young Rudy Graham leave Lindsey's desk and walk out of the office. Though he hadn't meant to listen to their conversation, he had overheard enough to know the lad was in trouble.

He understood how it could happen. When he had first arrived in London and could barely speak the language, he'd had a run-in with the law himself. He had been brawling in the street with a pair of thugs, trying to defend a young woman who was being accosted.

The moment the police arrived, the woman disappeared and Thor was unable to explain what had happened. Instead, he was shoved into the back of a police wagon along with the local riffraff and hauled down to the station. Leif had been forced to come down to gain his release. It seemed to Thor that once the authorities got a notion in their heads it was damned hard to dislodge it.

He looked over at Lindsey, who sat with her head bowed, her plumed pen unmoving in her slim fingers. Apparently the police had decided that young Rudy Graham had murdered two women.

The boy was in serious trouble.

Bracing himself for whatever reaction his offer might get, Thor walked over to Lindsey's desk. She looked pretty today, in her simple printed muslin dress, her honey hair swept back on the sides and held in place with turtle-shell combs. He wondered why he always seemed to notice the small things about her, then cursed himself because he did.

"Do not be angry," he said. "I overheard some of your conversation with your brother."

Her head turned toward him. "You were eavesdropping?"

"I have always had good ears."

Her lips twitched, nice full lips a pretty shade of pink. "I suppose it wasn't your fault," she said. "We should have gone upstairs, but Rudy was so upset…." She shook her head. "I am worried about him."

"He is in trouble with the police."

"They consider him a suspect in the Covent Garden murders. But Rudy would never hurt anyone. He is simply not that sort."

"I know little of your brother, but if there is any way I can help, you only need ask."

Her golden-brown eyebrows drew together. "Why would you help? You don't even like me."

He didn't really *dislike* her. She just had a way of annoying him. "You are Krista and Coralee's friend. They are my friends, so I will help."

She looked up at him with those big tawny eyes and the air in his lungs refused to come out.

"Thank you for the offer, but I don't need your help. My brother is innocent. In time, the police will find the man who is guilty of the crime."

He nodded, hoping she was right. She might annoy him but he wouldn't want to see her hurt, and it was clear how much she cared about her brother.

"He is a good sort," she said. "Lately Rudy has lost his way, but in time, he will find the right path."

"It is good he has you to worry about him."

She managed a smile. "Thank you."

The gratitude in her eyes made his chest feel tight. He had the strangest urge to reach out and touch her, erase the worry lines from her forehead. It was madness. As the lady had said, he didn't even truly like her.

At least he didn't like the sort of woman she was, the kind who worked in an office instead of staying home to tend a husband and family. The kind who believed she was equal to a man. Leif had married a woman like that, and though Thor had grown to care for Krista greatly, still, she was too independent, too outspoken in her views, not the sort he would want to take to wife.

Where he came from, women worked as hard as men, but they always knew their place, knew they were put on earth to serve a man. A lesson Lindsey Graham would never learn.

Unless, of course, some man was fool enough to try to bring her in hand.

He ignored the little thread of interest that stirred, as well as the surge of lust he felt at the notion of her serving his needs. He scoffed. One kiss and she would likely run off screaming. Passion was probably as foreign to her as the notion that a man should be master of his house.

Shaking his head, Thor left Lindsey to mull over her problems and returned to his duties in the back room of the office. The rest of the week, he would be working for his brother down at the dock, unloading the cargo that had just come in, reloading the ships that would sail off to British island ports.

Mayhap tomorrow night, he would pay a call on the ladies at the Red Door, a house of pleasure he visited on occasion.

Across the office, he caught sight of Lindsey. As she bent her head to study the paper on her desk, her honey hair parted, exposing the soft white skin at the nape of her neck.

Thor's groin tightened. For reasons he was at a loss to explain, whenever she was near, the girl left him craving a woman. He thought of the Red Door again and vowed it was time to make a stop.

* * *

Leif Draugr stood on the quay above the dock, watching his brother's crew unloading and reloading the ships that had just come into port. A stiff wind whipped the Union Jack flying atop the masts, and seagulls swooped down, screeching as they soared toward the choppy blue water.

Leif loved the sight, loved the feeling of accomplishment whenever he gazed out over his growing fleet of ships. Since his arrival in England, he had built Valhalla Shipping into an extremely successful enterprise, and though his brother refused to take any of the credit, Leif knew Thor had had a great deal to do with the company's success.

He watched his brother laughing with a couple of the men as they strained to the task of hoisting a cargo net loaded with household supplies for delivery to the northern islands off the Scottish coast.

His brother was amazingly good at handling the men. He had a way of earning their trust and admiration, a way of making them want to do a good job for him. Perhaps it was because he often pitched in to help, no matter that he was the boss, no matter how dirty the job was.

Though Leif and his brother both believed in hard work and accomplishment and both loved the sea, in a number of ways they were as different as their coloring, Leif fair-skinned and blond, Thor swarthy and dark-haired. While Leif had done everything in his power to learn what was necessary to fit into British society, Thor had learned little more than the basics.

He could read and write, of course, and he could speak the language with even less accent than Leif, but he refused to wear anything but the simplest garments, had never attended a ball, and laughed at the notion of what he called prancing around a dance floor.

Though he had no thought of returning to Draugr Island where they had been raised, he didn't like living in the city. Instead, he worked two jobs in an effort to save money to buy a farm in the country. Leif had assured him his interest in the shipping line would eventually earn him enough to get the land he wanted, but Thor wanted to earn the money on his own. He seemed to have something to prove, seemed to be searching for something that remained elusive.

Leif believed at least part of what his brother sought was the very thing Leif had found in the wife and son he adored. Each day he prayed that the gods would bless Thor as he had been blessed and lead him to his life mate. Perhaps then the restlessness would ease and Thor would find the contentment that seemed just out of his reach.

In truth, they were different in a number of ways and yet deep down they were the same, men with strong beliefs in loyalty and duty, honor and courage. Leif would trust his brother with his life and he knew Thor felt the same.

Leif looked toward the dock where his brother stood with his legs splayed, his dark hair blowing in the wind. Thor glanced toward the quay and spotted him, smiled and waved, and Leif waved back.

In time, Thor's mate would appear. His future was surely as fated as Leif's had been. The gods would not fail him, Leif believed. He was only a little worried as he headed down to the dock. Only a little worried as he caught the slightly yearning look on his brother's face.

Three

Lindsey ignored the hum of activity in the office and tried to concentrate on finishing the revisions on her article. The gazette went to press tomorrow and she still had a good bit left to do.

She looked up as the bell above the door rang, saw two sour-faced men walk into the office. The typesetter, Bessie Briggs, a stocky woman with salt-and-pepper hair, walked up to greet them.

"May I help ye?"

The larger of the men reached into the pocket of his dark brown tailcoat and pulled out what appeared to be some kind of credentials. Lindsey realized they were policemen and a jolt of worry spiked down her spine.

"I'm Constable Bertram and this is Constable Archer. We'd like to speak with one of the employees, a Miss Lindsey Graham."

Bessie's eyes widened. She turned and pointed at Lindsey, who stiffened in her chair. "That's Miss Graham. I'll tell her ye wish ta see her."

"That won't be necessary." The men started toward her. The one named Bertram that her brother had mentioned was larger, with piercing black eyes and thinning brown hair. Archer was short and stout, had bushy eyebrows and a pocked complexion. At the back of the room, she caught a glimpse of Thor, who had moved within earshot as the men walked toward her desk.

Like his brother, he seemed to be a protective sort of man. She told herself to tell him to go away, that the policemen were none of his concern, but she couldn't quite summon the will. Instead, he propped his wide shoulders against the wall and simply watched her, making it clear he was there in case she needed him.

It was ridiculous. The man wouldn't know the first thing about British law or what to do with two police constables.

She turned her attention to the men, who arrived at her desk, their hats in their hands. "May I help you?"

"My name is—"

"Yes, constables Bertram and Archer."

"That is correct," Bertram said. "We would like to ask you a few questions, Miss Graham. Perhaps there is someplace we might be private."

She didn't want to be alone with them. She had no idea why. Everyone but Thor was busily working and paying them little attention. Besides, even if someone overheard, the employees at *Heart to Heart* were a close-knit group and nothing that happened ever stayed secret very long.

"You can say what you have to say right here."

Bertram nodded, moving strands of his thinning brown hair. "All right, if that is your wish. As you are surely aware, your brother has fallen under police scrutiny in the matter of the Covent Garden murders. As he seems unable to tell us his whereabouts on the nights of either of the murders, we are hoping that you might be able to shed some light on the subject."

Her pulse kicked up. She told herself to stay calm. "My brother is a grown man. He goes about as he pleases. I can tell you that even if he happened to be in the area those nights, he is not a man with the sort of temperament to commit a brutal murder."

"Are you aware he knew both women?"

"He mentioned it, yes."

"Are you also aware that he was seen in the company of Miss Phoebe Carter, the latest victim, the very night she was killed?"

The blood slowly drained from her face. "That…that isn't possible."

"Your brother's friend…" He glanced down at a scrap of paper he pulled from the pocket of his coat. "A gentleman named Thomas Boggs, says that Mr. Graham left his flat with the woman and did not return to the party."

Dear God, Rudy was with the murder victim the night she was killed? Why hadn't he told her? She tried to remember exactly what he had said, *I had…um…seen her shortly before.* Great heavens, she had thought he meant days, not hours! Lindsey said nothing, just sat there trying to keep her emotions carefully controlled.

"I realize we are talking about your brother," Constable Bertram said, "but the law is the law and if there is something you know that you are not telling us—"

Lindsey shot to her feet. "I know my brother is innocent

of any wrongdoing. In fact…he—he couldn't have been the man who killed Miss Carter because he came home early that night. He must have dropped the woman off somewhere and returned directly to the house."

Constable Archer lifted a bushy eyebrow. "Are you certain of this, miss? Were you awake when he came in?"

"Why, yes, I was. We spoke briefly but he had been drinking and I suggested he had best go up to bed."

"No blood on his clothes? Nothing that might have looked suspicious?"

"Not in the least."

Bertram pierced her with a glare. "What time was it?"

"What time?" she repeated dully.

"That is correct. At what hour did your brother come home?"

Dear God, what time had her brother left the party with the woman? She had no possible way to know. "Sometime after midnight."

"And you remember this particular night because…?"

"Because it was the night of the Kentwells' ball." That much was true. She had come to work the next day and read about the murder in the paper—the one Thor had *borrowed*. Which was probably the reason she recalled. Thor wasn't easy to forget.

"There are laws against aiding a criminal, Miss Graham," Constable Bertram warned. "If you are lying, you will only make matters worse for your brother."

"And extremely difficult for yourself," Archer chimed in.

She straightened. "My brother would never hurt anyone, much less do murder. That is all I have to say on the subject and I would appreciate it if you would now please leave."

She didn't see Thor approach but suddenly he was there, towering over the policemen. "Miss Graham has told you all she knows."

"And who might you be?" asked Bertram.

"I am a friend—one who can see that you have upset the lady."

"If Miss Graham is a friend, it would be wise to advise her to be truthful in regard to her brother."

Thor said nothing. The quieter he was, the more intimidating he appeared.

"Good afternoon, gentlemen," Lindsey said.

"Good afternoon, Miss Graham." Bertram settled his beaver hat over his thinning hair and he and Archer disappeared out the door.

Thor looked at her hard. "Do not tell me you could have handled them by yourself."

"I did just fine, thank you."

"You were lying and they knew it. By the gods, Lindsey, you cannot help your brother by making up tales that are clearly not true."

"I was buying time. In a couple of days, I will tell them I remembered incorrectly, that I got the dates mixed up, but not yet. I need to find out who killed those women. That is the only way my brother is going to be safe."

Thor's blue eyes sharpened. "If the police can't find the killer, how will you?"

"I'm a newspaper reporter, am I not? It is my job to dig up information. That is precisely what I am going to do."

"You are a woman, Lindsey, whether you like it or not. Two women have already been killed."

"I'm going to help my brother—whether *you* like it or

not!" Turning away from him, she picked up her reticule and started for the door.

Thor caught her arm. "You are going home?"

"For now."

"Is your carriage out front?"

"I usually walk to work this time of year."

"You are upset and worried. I will see you get home safely."

She opened her mouth to protest but already he was urging her toward the door, grabbing her cloak off the coat tree, leading her outside and down the front steps. He raised one big hand and a hansom cab jerked to a halt just a few feet away. Thor helped her climb in, settled himself on the seat beside her, and the driver clucked the horse into motion.

"You are a troublesome female," Thor said.

"And you are a meddlesome brute."

His jaw tightened. "An *irritating,* troublesome female."

She cast him a glance. "An *overbearing,* meddlesome brute."

Thor just grunted and leaned back in the seat. Lindsey tried not to notice the powerful shoulder pressing against her, the faint, masculine scent of soap and man. She tried not to be grateful that he was taking her home when she had just lied to the police.

When, instead of her brother, she might be the one who wound up going to prison.

Aunt Delilah was pacing the drawing room when Lindsey got home.

"Lindsey! Thank God you are here! The police just left. What in the name of heaven is going on?"

Lindsey sighed. "I am sorry, Aunt Dee, I should have told you. I suppose I was hoping the entire affair would simply fade away and you would never be the wiser."

"The entire affair? By that you are referring to the murder of two young women, for which the authorities suspect your brother?"

Lindsey caught hold of her aunt's pale hand and they both sat down on the sofa. "He didn't do it. You know Rudy would never do anything like that."

"Of course not. Oh, dear God, I wish your father were here."

Not for the first time in her life, so did Lindsey. From the time she was a child, her parents never seemed to be around when she needed them. "Well, he isn't and so the task of clearing Rudy's name is left to you and me."

"Whatever do you mean?"

"The police can't seem to find the real killer so we must do it for them."

"Are you mad? You don't know the first thing about finding a murderer."

"I imagine it involves digging up information. That is something I know how to do."

Aunt Dee shook her head, moving the glossy black curls on her shoulders. "I don't know, Lindsey…. If anything went wrong, if something happened to you, your parents would never forgive me."

"How do you think they are going to feel when they find out their son has been tossed into prison for murder?"

Aunt Dee groaned.

"I am only going to ask a few questions, see what I can find out. I'll speak to Rudy again, try to discover more about his connection to the women. Maybe I can find out where he was when the women were killed. That would give him an alibi and he would no longer be a suspect."

Aunt Dee pinned her with a glare. "That policeman with the bushy eyebrows told me you said Rudy was here the night of the murder. That, dear girl, is complete and utter rubbish. Sooner or later, the police will discover the truth and you and Rudy will *both* be in trouble."

Lindsey ignored a shiver. "At the time, I couldn't think of anything else to do. In a couple of days, I'll tell them I was mistaken. That will give us a bit of time, at least."

"I hope you know what you are doing, dearest."

"So do I, Aunt Dee, so do I."

Lindsey spoke to Rudy the following morning. He was quite sober and fairly subdued. It was a pleasant change. Rudy had told her he had met Molly Springfield, the first victim murdered six months ago, at a drinking establishment in Covent Garden. He couldn't remember which one. Aside from a brief assignation in one of the rooms upstairs, he'd had nothing more to do with the woman.

"And the second victim—Miss Carter?"

"I told you, I met her at a party at Boggs's town house. She was an actress in Drury Lane."

"Why didn't you tell me you were with her the night she was killed?"

A guilty flush rose in his cheeks. "I told you I'd seen her recently."

"I never presumed you meant *that* recently!"

"At the time, well, it didn't seem important."

Lindsey rolled her eyes.

All in all, the conversation revealed nothing new. Rudy had been so drunk he had no idea what had happened on either of the evenings the women were killed.

She needed more information. She needed to speak to Tom Boggs and other of Rudy's so-called friends to see if anyone might have a clue as to where her brother had been the night of the murders. She needed to find out exactly where the murders were committed and interview people in the area to see if anyone had seen anything that might turn out to be a clue.

In the past several days, she had discreetly been nosing around, trying to ferret out any gossip. Nothing new had turned up. So far no one knew that Rudy was a suspect, or if they did, they were keeping silent about it. In time the information would surface. She had no idea what would happen once it did.

She was sitting behind her desk, making a list of things she wanted to do when Krista walked up.

"Anything new with your brother?"

"I'm afraid not. I'm making a list of what I can do to uncover information. Strangely enough, I think the first thing I need to do is speak to the police."

"The police?"

"I need to know what sort of evidence they have against Rudy. Perhaps it is only that he knew the women, which surely isn't enough to arrest him."

"I see. Actually, I had an idea myself."

"You did?"

Krista nodded. "After we spoke the other day, I sent word to a friend of mine, a private investigator named Randolph Petersen. Mr. Petersen was a great help to me several years ago when we had problems here at the gazette. He also helped Coralee investigate the murder of her sister. Unfortunately, Mr. Petersen is away on business. His office is uncertain when he will be returning to London."

"A private investigator…that is a very good notion. I should like to think that before your Mr. Petersen gets back, all of this will be resolved, but if it isn't, I would certainly be glad to speak to him."

"Perhaps we can find someone else."

"Let's wait for your friend. That will give us time to see if the matter will take care of itself."

Krista nodded. "You were saying that you intend to start with the police?"

"That's right. Tonight the ladies' auxiliary is doing their annual widows and orphans' benefit, a charity strongly supported by the London Police Commissioner. My aunt Delilah has a friend whose son is a police lieutenant. A number of senior officials are expected to attend and Lieutenant Harvey is among them. Aunt Delilah's friend has promised to introduce us."

"This sort of investigation can be dangerous, Lindsey. I can tell you that firsthand."

"I should be safe enough at a ball attended by the commissioner of police and his men."

"Of course. Still…Leif and I were thinking that if you are serious about investigating the murders, perhaps it would be wise to have someone around in case of trouble… a sort of bodyguard, if you would, a person who would be close at hand should you—"

"I hardly need a bodyguard."

"No, of course not, but it might be wise to have some sort of protection just in case you run into trouble."

Lindsey mulled that over. Surely asking a few simple questions wouldn't be a problem. "Who did you have in mind?"

"We were thinking of Thor. He is extremely capable and—"

"Absolutely not!"

"That is what I said when my father suggested that Leif protect me, but one night he saved my life."

"That was a different situation entirely."

"I'm not so sure. You have no idea who the real killer is, no notion as to his social class, which circles he might move in, or if he might somehow learn of your activities. You have already been casting about for information, have you not? You could be putting yourself in danger, Lindsey."

She considered the point. Krista was no fool and Lindsey respected her greatly. "Even if I said yes, I cannot imagine that Thor would agree."

"You're a friend. Of course he will agree."

Which meant, thus far, Thor knew nothing of Krista's outrageous plan. She should have guessed. "Yes, well, I will give the matter some thought. Tonight, however, I shall be perfectly safe in the company of my aunt."

"I am certain you will. Besides, Leif and I were thinking of attending, so you will not be there on your own."

Lindsey felt an unexpected sense of relief. Her friends were overly protective and yet it felt good to know there were people she could count on, people who really cared.

"Then I shall see you tonight," she said.

Krista managed a smile, but Lindsey could tell she was worried.

As for Lindsey, her biggest concern was that she wouldn't be able to prove her brother innocent of murder.

Krista hurried into the house in search of Leif. She had volunteered him to go with her to the benefit tonight and now she couldn't find him.

"Have you seen my husband?" she asked the butler, Simmons, an older gentleman with iron-gray hair and skin so thin it appeared translucent. "I thought that by now he would be home."

"I am sorry, my lady, I meant to give you this when you arrived." He handed her a note with her name scrawled on the back in Leif's bold hand. She popped the wax seal and read the words that told her that he would be late in getting home. He had a meeting with his partners in Valhalla Shipping: Dylan Villard and Alexander Cain. As he had guessed, Krista had forgotten all about it.

"Thank you, Simmons." Tapping the note, she headed upstairs. She had promised Lindsey that she and Leif would attend the party, but Leif couldn't go. It wasn't really important, Krista told herself. Lindsey would certainly be safe with so many policemen about.

Still, her friend would be asking sensitive questions and once she started, word would spread. Someone might already have gotten wind of her investigation, someone who didn't want her sniffing about, prying into affairs that could send a man to the gallows.

Walking over to her writing desk, she set Leif's note aside and penned a quick missive to Thor, asking him to stop by on his way home from the docks. Leif and Thor were close enough in size that Thor could borrow a waistcoat and stock, garments he had heretofore refused to wear, and whatever else he might need. He would grumble and groan but in the end, Krista was sure he would dress appropriately to attend the affair.

Hurrying back downstairs, she handed the message to a footman and sent him off to the docks to find Thor.

Four

~~~~⋘∽⋙~~~~

Walking behind Aunt Dee, who was resplendent in an elegant gown of silver and black, Lindsey made her way through the well-dressed throng. An odd mix of guests were in attendance for the event: society matrons involved in various charities, patrons of local orphanages, judges, barristers, the mayor, wealthy merchants and senior-level police officials.

"Over there," Aunt Dee said softly. "Mrs. Harvey… the woman with the stunning silver hair. She is standing just to the right of the punch bowl." Aside from her gleaming platinum locks, Emma Harvey was a nondescript woman in her early sixties with average features. Nothing at all like Delilah, who outshone women twenty years younger.

Then Mrs. Harvey smiled and her entire face lit up. She was a pretty woman, her features soft and feminine, the sort of person you were sure you would like before you ever met her.

Emma Harvey walked over to where they stood. "Lady Ashford—how delightful to see you."

"You as well, Emma. May I present my niece, Miss Lindsey Graham?"

"I am delighted to meet you," the woman said.

"The pleasure is mine, Mrs. Harvey."

She flashed her amazing smile. "Your aunt said you were doing some research on police work for an article you are writing for your magazine."

Surprised by the fabrication, Lindsey cast her aunt a glance. Perhaps a gift for prevarication ran in the family.

"Why, yes, I am…which is the reason I was hoping to meet your son."

"Of course." She craned her neck to look over the sea of elegantly attired men and women around them, and Lindsey's gaze followed.

She caught sight of Krista, who had apparently just arrived, then searched for Leif. A huge man stood beside her, but he wasn't her husband. For an instant, Lindsey forgot to breathe. Standing next to Krista, elegantly dressed in evening clothes, was the handsomest man she had ever seen.

Beneath his immaculate black tailcoat, he wore a silver waistcoat and black trousers. A frothy cravat teased the dark skin at his throat. He was the same man she saw several days a week and at the same time, a man she had never seen before.

She couldn't stop staring. She knew those fierce blue eyes, recognized the massive shoulders beneath his perfectly tailored coat. Her aunt gave her a not-so-subtle jab in the ribs to remind her where she was and she dragged her gaze away.

"Mrs. Harvey's son is approaching." Aunt Dee tipped her head toward a man in his thirties with light brown hair a shade paler than her own making his way across the drawing room. He walked with purpose, a smile on his face—a very attractive man, she saw as he drew near.

Lindsey flicked a last glance toward the door, just to be certain she had actually seen Thor standing there. He reached up and tugged on his cravat as if it strangled him, and she knew without doubt it was he. Taller than any other man at the gathering, he was stunningly male, yet his features were so perfectly carved, his eyes so incredibly blue, the females in the room couldn't seem to look anywhere else.

Lindsey fought a shot of irritation.

For the first time, she realized she was holding her breath, and just as Lieutenant Harvey walked up, the air whooshed out of her lungs. She managed to compose herself, paste on a smile, and wait for the introductions to be made.

The lieutenant bent and kissed his mother's cheek. "I saw a friend and stopped for a moment to pay my respects. I hope I didn't keep you waiting."

"Not a'tall." She turned to Aunt Dee. "You've met Lady Ashton."

"Why, yes." He bowed over her hand. "A pleasure to see you, Countess."

Mrs. Harvey turned her warm smile on Lindsey, who suddenly felt guilty using the woman to gain information. "And this is the young lady I spoke to you about, Miss Lindsey Graham. She writes for *Heart to Heart,* a fashionable ladies' magazine."

He had the same warm smile as his mother. "I'm familiar with the paper. It's a pleasure to meet you, Miss Graham."

"You, as well, Lieutenant Harvey." They made polite conversation, spoke of the weather, discovered a few mutual friends. It seemed the Harveys were related to the Duke of Linfield, which gave the handsome lieutenant quite an acceptable pedigree.

Little by little, Aunt Dee led Mrs. Harvey deeper into the crowd, giving Lindsey the chance to speak to the lieutenant. Determined not to let her gaze stray to Thor, she approached the punch bowl on the policeman's arm. He fetched them both cups of the fruity drink, then found a couple of empty chairs for them to sit in along the wall.

"My mother says you are doing a research paper on police work. How may I be of help?"

She gave him what she hoped was a winning smile. "I am particularly interested in how the police handle the investigation of a crime. I am using the Covent Garden murders as an example. I was wondering how your department goes about collecting evidence and what sort of things they have discovered about the killings."

He frowned. "A rather unpleasant topic for a young lady."

She kept her gaze on his face. "Yes, it is. Unfortunately, I am also a journalist and at the moment our readers are extremely interested in the murders. I was hoping you would be willing to help."

"I'm afraid the facts of the case, for the most part, are as yet unavailable to the public. Keeping the information confidential helps lead us to a suspect."

"I see. Oh, I do wish I had my notepad. That in itself is interesting information." She gave him a sugary smile, prayed he would be charmed and not revolted. Flirting wasn't really her forte, but she was desperate enough to try it. "I don't suppose there is a chance we could meet someplace for tea and discuss the matter further?"

He nodded, seemed to like the notion. "I imagine that could be arranged, though as I said, much of the information isn't for public consumption."

"I understand, and I would be ever so grateful. There is a coffeehouse in Piccadilly not far from my office... The Pear Tree? It has a pleasant little outdoor seating area. Do you know it?"

"The Pear Tree. Yes, I believe I do. Say one o'clock?"

She flashed a smile wide enough to dimple her cheeks—if she *had* dimples, which unfortunately, she did not. "That would be lovely."

They spoke a bit more and then the lieutenant returned her to her aunt. All the simpering and smiling had exhausted her and she was ready to go home. Instead Thor and Krista walked up just then. Thor was frowning, his nearly black eyebrows drawn together.

"Who was that man?"

"He is a police lieutenant named Michael Harvey. I was hoping to get information that might help my brother."

"Did you?"

"Not yet, but the lieutenant has agreed to meet me tomorrow. Perhaps then—"

"He was looking at you as if he wanted to eat you up."

She shook her head. "You must be mistaken. The lieutenant was merely being polite."

"It is clear he wants you and you encouraged him."

The notion that a handsome man found her desirable

pleased her, even if it probably wasn't true. She wasn't the typical, pale-haired English rose, nor voluptuous like Krista. That Thor believed it was somehow made it even better.

"I told you, I need information. Gaining his cooperation is important."

Thor just grunted.

Lindsey turned her attention to Krista. "I thought Leif was coming with you."

"He had a meeting. I had forgotten about it entirely." She smiled at her brother-in-law. "Thor was kind enough to escort me."

Lindsey looked up at him, into those blue, blue eyes, and told herself it was ridiculous the way her heart was beating. "You dressed up."

He shrugged his powerful shoulders. "Krista said I had to."

"You look very…nice." Now there was an understatement. There wasn't a man in the room who could compare.

"Thank you." His gaze ran over the pale green silk gown that rode low on her shoulders and the light brown curls clustered at the side of her neck. There was something in his eyes, something she had never seen there before. It made a little curl of heat slide into her stomach.

"You look…very pretty."

"Thank you…" she replied a bit breathlessly.

Aunt Dee started talking to Krista and from the corner of her eye, Lindsey caught sight of the lieutenant returning.

"I thought perhaps—if your card isn't full—I might claim this dance."

She loved to dance. And she needed his help. She gave him her dazzling smile. "I would be delighted."

She didn't look at Thor but she could feel his disapproval as if it radiated from his pores. The music of a waltz began. Resting her gloved hand on the sleeve of the lieutenant's coat, she let him guide her toward the dance floor. Over the policeman's shoulder, she caught a glimpse of Thor. He was scowling just as she had imagined he would be.

Lindsey stiffened her spine. So what if she was flirting outrageously with a man? She was a woman. She had every right. What did the big brute know anyway?

More irritated than she should have been, she went into the lieutenant's arms. Keeping her eyes carefully fixed on his face, she smiled at him the entire duration of the waltz.

Thor stood in front of the mirror over the dresser in the bedroom of his flat in Half Moon Street. He had chosen the apartment so he could be near Green Park, an open, grassy area with flowers and trees and ponds, a place he could breathe fresh air and pretend he wasn't in the city.

He went there often. If it weren't well past midnight, he would go there now.

Staring at his reflection, he reached up and jerked the knot on his cravat, then tugged the long white cloth from around his neck. He shrugged out of the coat and waistcoat he had borrowed from his brother and released a sigh of relief.

Free at last. Only for Krista would he wear layers of clothing he did not need. But Krista was Leif's wife and she had become a good friend. He would wear the clothes if it pleased her.

And though he hated to admit it, he had been worried about Lindsey.

Thor grumbled a curse in Old Norse, the language he

had spoken on Draugr Island, the place that had been his home. The woman was nothing but trouble. Still, she was Krista's friend and he had come to feel protective of her.

He thought of her behavior tonight with the handsome policeman and a knot tightened in his stomach. He didn't like the way she had encouraged the man. He didn't like the way the policeman had looked at her.

It was foolish, he knew. Lindsey was too scrawny, too boyish to appeal to him. Still, when he had seen her in her green silk dress, when he had noticed the satin smoothness of her skin, the way the candlelight gleamed on her honey hair, his blood had quickened and he had hardened to the point of pain.

He should have stopped at the Red Door on his way home. Madame Fortier's women were beautiful and always willing to ease a man's needs. The buxom owner of the establishment wasn't really French, one of the ladies had told him, which he thought must be true, because the night he had spent in her bed her lusty cries had clearly been in English. He had intended to pay a call at her establishment tonight, but in the end had returned home instead. Now he regretted his decision.

He needed a woman, had for some time. *Soon,* he told himself as he finished undressing and climbed into his big four-poster bed.

It was quiet in the apartment. Unlike Leif, he didn't have a lot of servants, just a housekeeper, a cook, and a chambermaid, and none of them lived in the flat. He didn't need a fancy valet or a butler. He had learned long ago to take care of himself.

Thor sighed into the darkness. The only thing he needed

was the feel of soft skin pressed against him, the heavy weight of a woman's breast in his hands. His shaft stirred to life and he went hard. Desire burned into him with the force of a blaze. An image appeared of Lindsey, smiling as she danced with the handsome police lieutenant, moving with the grace of a swan.

Cursing himself—and also cursing Lindsey—Thor tried in vain to fall asleep.

Lindsey awakened at first light. She had slept very well last night and felt energized and eager to get out of the house. As was her habit at least three times a week, she dressed in riding breeches, high black leather boots, and a riding coat, stuffed her hair up under a black billed cap, and headed for the stable.

One of her father's hobbies was raising Thoroughbred horses. He kept most of them at Renhurst Hall, the family estate in West Sussex, but the carriage horses as well as a number of saddle horses were stabled at the edge of Green Park, a few blocks from their residence in Mount Street.

Lindsey loved to ride, had been riding since she could walk. For propriety's sake, she rode sidesaddle, but given a choice she preferred to ride astride. She loved the sense of freedom, the feeling of superior control. Which meant she was forced to ride early before most Londoners were awake.

Lindsey made the four-block walk to the stable at a brisk pace, enjoying the slight breeze and the crisp chill in the air. The sun shone overhead, promising relief from the overcast that had darkened the city for nearly a week.

"'E's ready for ye, miss." The groom, Artemus Moody,

a round-faced, stocky man who had been in her father's employ since she was a girl, stood next to a tall, leggy sorrel.

Dancer, a five-year-old gelding and her favorite in the stable, nickered at her familiar scent. The horse pranced at the end of his reins, eager for his morning workout, almost as eager as Lindsey.

"Easy, boy." She patted the animal's sleek neck, and with a knee up from Mr. Moody, swung a leg over the back of the flat leather saddle.

"E's full o' 'imself this morning, miss. A bit of a run is what 'e needs."

"A bit of a run is what we both need."

Artemus smiled as she nudged the tall sorrel forward out of the barn, into the sunlight. The groom knew her well enough not to underestimate her skills and simply stood back as Dancer jumped sideways, then snorted at the rustle of leaves in the bushes along the path.

"Settle down, mister," Lindsey commanded, and as if the horse understood, he obeyed, settling into a steady walk, moving eagerly off toward the open air track around the park.

This early, the place was empty and as soon as she reached the wide dirt path, she increased the pace, urging Dancer into an easy gallop. Several rounds later, they were running full out, Lindsey grinning at the rush of air against her cheeks and the thrill of controlling such a well-bred animal.

As much as she enjoyed life in the city, Renhurst Hall was the one place she would rather be. On her father's twelve thousand acres, she was safe from prying eyes, safe to do as she pleased. She could ride whenever she wished, stay out all day if she wanted.

In truth, she had been restless lately for Renhurst. If it

weren't for Rudy, she would have left last week, carved out some time from her busy schedule to relax and enjoy the country. But until the Covent Garden Murderer was found or Rudy proved innocent, she was forced to remain in the city.

Dancer was sweating, lathering up a bit when she pulled him into a slower gait. She banished thoughts of Rudy and managed to relax in the saddle. It would be foolish to ruin such a beautiful morning with thoughts of murder and intrigue.

Letting her gaze travel over the lovely flowers blooming along the path, Lindsey rode at an easy pace. Before she returned the horse to the stable, she would take him round once more at the brisk pace he seemed to crave, then it would be time for her to resume her city persona and get herself off to work.

Thor leaned back against the wrought-iron bench beneath a sycamore tree, his gaze fixed on the young rider he had been watching. He had seen the lad several times before when he had come to the park this early. The boy was a masterful rider, one he couldn't help but admire.

And the horse was amazing, long and lean, with powerful flanks and legs that ate up the ground at a pace unlike any Thor had seen. In Draugr, he had ridden often. Having won more races than any other man, he was considered the best rider on the island. He even beat his brothers, all of whom were excellent horsemen.

But the animals there were nothing like this one. They were strong but smaller and shaggy-haired, without the beauty of the gelding he had seen racing full speed round the track. His palms itched to trade places with the lad, to hear the thunder of hoofbeats, feel the rush of the wind, the strength of the horse beneath him.

Since his arrival in London, Thor had walked or traveled by carriage. Now as he watched the young man turn the magnificent animal back the way he had come and ride out of the park, Thor vowed that one day he would own a horse like that one.

Five

In a day dress of russet silk, the full skirt flaring out over a printed cream-and-russet underskirt, Lindsey opened her matching silk parasol and made her way along the street to the front of the small café. The Pear Tree was a very respectable coffeehouse that also served an assortment of teas, tiny finger sandwiches, and sweets. It was decorated in yellow and leaf-green, the walls stenciled with pear trees whose branches covered the ceiling overhead.

Lindsey had carefully timed her arrival to be ten minutes late so that Michael Harvey would be waiting. Unfortunately, when she walked inside, the policeman wasn't there.

A young blond hostess seated her at a small, linen-draped table and she ordered a cup of jasmine tea. As the minutes ticked past, she began to wonder if Lieutenant Harvey had forgotten their meeting or if some unexpected problem had come up.

She was halfway finished with her tea when she spotted him walking through the door. The bright smile she gave him slipped at the angry expression on his face.

He stopped right in front of her. "I should apologize for keeping you waiting, but I don't intend to. I just discovered exactly who you are, and I can tell you, Miss Graham, I am not the least bit pleased."

Oh, dear. No wonder he was angry. "Do sit down, Lieutenant. People are beginning to stare."

For several moments, he just stood there, the color high in his cheeks. He sat down abruptly, a dark look on his face. "Rudolph Graham is your brother."

"Yes, he is."

"You are here on his behalf, are you not? Last night was a complete and utter sham. You were hoping to glean information—which is the reason you are here today. You are hoping I will disclose something that might be useful to your brother—the prime suspect in the Covent Garden murders!"

Though inwardly she flinched, Lindsey faced him squarely across the table. "My brother is innocent! I am trying to find a way to clear his name. If your brother were under suspicion of committing two heinous murders, you would do the same!"

The lieutenant studied her intensely, trying to read her thoughts. "I cannot help but admire your loyalty. Not many women would take it upon themselves to try to solve a murder in order to protect someone they love."

She relaxed a bit, managed a tentative smile. "I am sorry for the deception. I did, however, enjoy our waltz. You are quite a good dancer, Lieutenant."

The tension around his mouth began to ease. He was still upset, but perhaps in some way he understood.

"Since all of this is now out in the open," she continued,

deciding to press her luck, "is there anything you can tell me—without giving up police secrets—that might be of help? Sometimes it is difficult to know if what is reported in the papers is correct."

He released a sigh, raised a hand to summon a waiter. "I suppose…since I am already here…I might as well stay long enough to enjoy a cup of tea."

She smiled, grateful he seemed to have forgiven her. "Yes, please do."

A server arrived with a nice aromatic Ceylon, a choice Lindsey approved. She joined him in a second cup and sipped casually, hoping he would answer the question she had posed earlier.

"As I told you last night, I am not at liberty to divulge information. I *can* tell you that if you are providing your brother with an alibi for the night of the latest murder, you are putting yourself in jeopardy, and sooner or later the truth will come out, no matter what you do."

"As I said, Rudy isn't guilty. Since he was drunk that night and doesn't recall where he was, I need time to discover his whereabouts for him. I won't stand in the way of justice, but I need a chance to help him if I can."

"Are you saying he *wasn't* at home that night?"

She hated to lie. She clamped down on an urge to tell him the truth. "I am not changing my story. Perhaps in the future, I shall recall the evening a bit differently."

"They can put you in prison, Miss Graham."

"I shan't wait long, I promise."

He sipped his tea. "You are either quite brave or terribly foolhardy."

She looked up at him. "Perhaps a little of both."

"I will tell you what is public information, some of which may not have been printed in the paper."

She grabbed her reticule and drew out pencil and paper. "Go on."

"Both victims were found within four blocks of each other. The first one, Molly Springfield, was a mother with a six-month-old child. As she had no husband, she sold herself on the street to feed her baby."

Lindsey shivered.

"The second woman was an actress of sorts. She played bit parts, but her dream was to become famous. She liked pretty things and spent time with men who bought her baubles…jewelry and clothes and such."

"Can you tell me exactly where the women were killed?"

"I suppose that wouldn't hurt." He took a sip of his tea. "Molly Springfield lived in a third floor garret above a tavern called the Boar and Fox. She was killed in the alley behind the building. The second victim, Phoebe Carter, lived with two other prostitutes in a flat just off Maiden Lane. She died on the street not more than a block away. It was late, there were no witnesses…at least none we've found so far."

"What about the murder itself? Was there anything distinct about the killings?"

The lieutenant leaned back in his chair. "I'm afraid that is confidential."

"Can you at least tell me if the women were…were violated?"

"No, they were not."

"What about—"

"I'm sorry, I've given you as much as I can."

"And I appreciate it—truly I do."

His mouth edged up. "I have tried to stay angry at you, but I seem to have failed. My great uncle, the duke, is putting together a party to attend the theater. I would ask you to join us but I am afraid that being seen in company with the sister of a murder suspect might put a blight on my career. Perhaps when this is over…"

She was surprised to hear herself reply, "I believe I should have liked to go. As you say, perhaps when this is over…" She glanced up. "Friday next, your uncle, the duke's good friend, Lord Kittridge, is having a ball in honor of his daughter's eighteenth birthday. I was planning to attend. Perhaps I will see you there."

His smile broadened. "Yes, I am certain you will." He rose from his chair and helped her up from hers.

"Thank you for coming, Lieutenant."

"Be careful, Miss Graham. This is murder you are dealing with."

"I'll be very careful."

The lieutenant paid the bill, then walked her back to the front door of the office. As she started up the steps, she noticed a big dark shadow standing at the window. Thor was scowling, she saw, looking at her the way he had last night when she had been dancing with the lieutenant.

For whatever reason, the sight gave her a lift. Lindsey smiled as she opened the door.

"You are behaving like a light-skirt."

"What!"

"Do you truly wish for the company of that man or are you just practicing your womanly skills?"

She shrugged. She liked the lieutenant. But standing beside him didn't make her heart beat the way it was now. The thought sent a jolt of alarm racing through her. It was simply Thor's astonishing good looks, she told herself. Any female under the age of eighty would feel a bit light-headed when Thor looked at her with those incredible blue eyes.

"I like him well enough. Besides, it's a woman's prerogative to flirt with a man if she wants to."

"What is this word *prerogative?*"

"It means I have the right to engage in a harmless flirtation if that is my wish. Besides, you like those sorts of women. You like a woman who acts helpless and simpering. You should be pleased."

"I am not pleased."

She gazed up at him and batted her eyes. "Oh, Thor, would you help me over to my chair. I am feeling a little weak. I am afraid I might swoon."

He snorted.

"I've seen the way women act when they are around you. Perhaps from now on I should behave the way they do."

"He will believe you want him in your bed."

Color rushed into her cheeks. "Well, I don't, so do not concern yourself." Marching over to her desk, she plunked down in her seat and busied herself straightening the papers on top.

Thor walked up beside her. "Did he tell you what you wished to know?"

"Not exactly. He discovered I was Rudy's sister and he was angry...at least at first. I'm hoping that in time, I'll win a bit of his trust and he will be willing to help me."

Thor's dark eyebrows slammed together. "You are seeing him again?"

"I'm sure our paths will cross somewhere."

He looked at her hard. "Just how far are you willing to go, Lindsey, to get this information?"

Her eyes widened at the implication. Angry heat rushed into her cheeks. "You are…you are no gentleman, Thor Draugr, to suggest such a thing."

"No, but mayhap my words will remind you to behave like a lady."

Lindsey bit back a sharp retort as Thor walked away. He was clearly unhappy with her interest in Michael Harvey. For the second time that day, Lindsey found herself smiling.

Feeling a renewed burst of energy, she sat down at her desk and plucked her pen from the inkwell, eager to work on her column for next week.

Lindsey spent the next two days interviewing Rudy's friends. Tom Boggs was a spoiled rich boy, fourth son of an earl, the ringleader of a group of wealthy young dandies who gambled and associated with disreputable women and generally went about looking for trouble. Mothers cautioned their daughters about Boggs and his friends, who were not considered suitable company for a proper young lady.

At least Tom had the decency to stop by the house, as Lindsey's message had requested of all four men in her brother's closest circle of friends.

After briefly greeting her aunt, Tom followed her into the drawing room and each of them took a seat. Lindsey didn't bother to offer him refreshment.

"Rudy says he was attending a party at your town house the night of the murder. He remembers leaving with the victim, an actress named Phoebe Carter. Apparently he was so stinking drunk he doesn't remember dropping her off at her home."

Tom shifted on the sofa. "He left with her. I remember he had his carriage brought round." Boggs was a good-looking man a few years older than Rudy, with dark brown hair and brown eyes. He played on his attractiveness and from what she had heard, had seduced any number of lonely widows and wives.

"Phoebe was a pretty little thing and accommodating… if you know what I mean."

She knew. Thanks to her brother, she was beginning to know a lot more about ladies of the evening than she did a few weeks ago.

"So Rudy took her home in his carriage."

"That was where he was headed. I guess since she was murdered, she never got there."

Lindsey refrained from rolling her eyes. "I guess she didn't. Since we both know my brother isn't a murderer, he must have left her off somewhere else. Do you have any idea where that might have been?"

Tom cleared his throat. "There was another party that night…not the kind you and your lady friends would attend, you understand. This was the sort of place where a man could get…well, whatever he wanted. Phoebe's flat-mates were going. Figured they could pick up a little extra blunt. I thought Phoebe would take Rudy up to her place, but maybe he took her to the party instead."

"Where was this other party being held?"

He got up from the settee, paced over to the window. "I'm not sure I should say. Don't want to make enemies, you know?"

Lindsey came up from her seat. "You listen to me, Tom Boggs. My brother is supposed to be your friend. Do you want to see him hang?"

He turned to face her. "No, of course not."

"Then tell me where the party was held."

"A place called the Blue Moon. It's a gaming hall. The party was in one of the upstairs rooms."

Lindsey frowned. "Rudy said he woke up in the back room of a gaming establishment called the Golden Pheasant. Do you suppose he got mixed up?"

"The Pheasant is just round the block. Could have gone there instead or maybe he went there later."

Lindsey mulled over the information, trying to fit the pieces together. Perhaps Rudy dropped the woman at the Blue Moon then went over to the Golden Pheasant, where he passed out and woke up in the morning. "Is there anything else, Tom, anything at all that might help Rudy?"

He gave her a dopy, slightly embarrassed grin. "We were all pretty well foxed that night. Lucky to remember where I was myself."

Drunk and rowdy. None of them remembered much of anything.

Still, a bit of information here and there was better than what she had before. She would go over all of it with Rudy, see if it might stir his recollections of that night.

As Boggs left the house, it occurred to her that he and his friends were also with Phoebe Carter the night of the murder. They might know Molly Springfield, as well. Why weren't the police dogging Tom's heels the way they were Rudy's?

The interviews with the rest of Rudy's friends went

much the same, confirming the fact that both Molly and Phoebe were fairly well known among the gentlemen who frequented the area. Why had the police zeroed in on Rudy?

Was there something they knew that Lindsey did not?

Or was it enough that Rudy had been the last person to see Phoebe Carter alive?

Determined to find the answer, the following afternoon Lindsey dressed in a simple brown skirt and white blouse and went in search of Elias Mack, one of the footmen. Elias was young and strong and always willing to do more than his share. He was a sensible young man, engaged to one of the chambermaids who worked at the house next door.

"Ye sent for me, miss?"

He appeared in the entry, neatly dressed as she had requested in dark trousers and a shirt instead of his Renhurst powder-blue livery.

"I need your help, Elias. I want you to accompany me on an errand this afternoon."

"Happy to, miss."

Lieutenant Harvey's warning, along with Krista's, rang in her ears. She was involving herself in murder and she needed to be careful. She had considered making Rudy go with her, but she didn't like the idea of him being seen in the area. He needed to keep a low profile. Though the Covent Garden district wasn't the best, during the day she would be safe enough—as long as she had an escort. Elias would have to do.

At two in the afternoon, they left in Lindsey's carriage and headed for the area where the murders had been committed.

The shops and outdoor vendors were open and selling their wares. The taverns in the area were serving libations, but she could hardly go into a drinking establishment. She had located the flat Phoebe Carter shared, but neither of the other two women answered the door. They were prostitutes, after all, and undoubtedly slept during the day.

She asked for directions and found the Boar and Fox, which housed the garret where Molly Springfield had lived, but again, couldn't go inside without attracting attention. It occurred to her to send Elias in to investigate, but she wanted to talk to the people herself, gauge the truth of what they told her. She had her coachman drive past the Golden Pheasant, and also the Blue Moon, but neither of the establishments were open in the afternoon and even if they had been, it wasn't a place a young woman could visit.

Lindsey sighed as the carriage pulled back into the traffic on the cobbled street. Being a woman sometimes had its drawbacks. In a strange way she envied the prostitutes who moved about with much the same freedom as men.

Not that she would want to change places.

She imagined the horror on Thor's handsome face if she said those words to him and found herself grinning. With his old-fashioned attitudes toward women, the man should have lived in the middle ages. Even his speech had an odd, medieval sort of flair.

"Take us home, Mr. McTavish," she called up to the coachman as she settled back against the red leather seat. The day had been an utter failure. She would have to take another tack, figure a way to actually speak to the people in the neighborhood.

Deep down she had known all along it would come to that.

Lindsey imagined how different it would be when she came back wearing men's clothes.

Six

"Are you mad? You can't possibly do a thing like that!"

Standing next to Krista's desk, Lindsey clamped her hands on her hips. "You are supposed to be my friend, Krista, and after some of the things *you* have done, I thought you would understand."

Krista sank back down in her chair. It was impossible to forget the night she had attended the ball given by the wealthy merchant Miles Stoddard. Though she had known very well it could be dangerous, Krista had been determined to confront the man she believed to be behind the vicious attacks on her and the gazette.

"I remember only too well, and if it hadn't been for Leif's unexpected arrival…" Krista let the rest trail off. Both of them knew the danger she had faced that night.

"I won't go alone," Lindsey promised. "I am taking my footman, Elias Mack, with me."

"If you are determined to go, take *Thor* with you. He is a warrior. He knows how to fight and he is big enough to defend you if something should go wrong."

Lindsey eyed her with interest. "What do you mean he is a warrior?" Krista rarely discussed her husband or brother-in-law's background, nor did they. To say that Lindsey was curious was to say the least.

"It is a very long story. Suffice it to say that where Leif and Thor come from, men often fight to protect their families. I would ask Leif to go, but he is out of town. Let me talk to Thor and ask him if—"

"I don't need Thor's help." In fact he was the last person Lindsey wanted to come along. Thor unnerved her in a way other men did not. She couldn't think clearly when he was looking at her with those amazing blue eyes, couldn't concentrate when she heard that deep male voice, laced with its soft Nordic accent.

In truth, she was incredibly attracted to the big, overbearing brute. It was ridiculous, nothing more than the physical pull between a normal, healthy woman and an extremely good-looking man. She would die of embarrassment if he found out, and in this venture, she needed her wits about her.

"I'll be fine with Mr. Mack. I'll go well before midnight and I won't stay long, just time enough to get my questions answered."

"I don't like this, Lindsey."

"Perhaps not, but I am asking you not to tell anyone. Do you promise to keep what I have told you in confidence?"

Krista nodded. Behind her back, her fingers were crossed. She wouldn't tell a soul—except the one man who could protect her friend.

Lindsey came down from the attic carrying an armful of her brother's old clothes. Her mother refused to throw anything away and the attic was filled with everything from baby clothes to musty feather mattresses.

Lindsey had dug through one steamer trunk after another until she found some of the garments Rudy had worn when he had gone to boarding school. He'd been just about her size back then.

The clothes would fit, she was sure as she carted them along the hall toward her bedroom, and would well serve her purpose tonight.

"What on earth are you doing?" Aunt Delilah walked toward her, a frown forming between her black eyebrows.

"I'm…um…I'm cleaning some old clothes out of the attic. I thought I would give them to charity." Which wasn't exactly a lie. She would make a point of giving them away, once she finished using them.

Aunt Dee nodded approvingly. "An excellent notion. The way your mother hoards things, you would think she was raised in a poorhouse."

"She won't miss them. She never goes up in the attic."

"Well, they will certainly do more good being worn by someone needy than up there collecting dust." Aunt Dee continued down the hall and Lindsey breathed a sigh of relief.

She wished she could tell her aunt the truth. But knowing what Lindsey intended would put Aunt Delilah in a precarious position. Even if her aunt were willing to help, in her role as Lindsey's chaperone, it would be a betrayal of her parents' trust.

Lindsey laid the clothes—a brown wool jacket and dark brown trousers—out on the bed. She wouldn't leave until Rudy went out for the evening, as he usually did—though of late he hadn't been drinking the way he was before and he had been coming home at a fairly respectable hour. Perhaps his run-in with the police had made an impression.

Lindsey tried on the trousers and jacket, which were loose enough to hide her slender curves. Checking her image in the mirror she figured that as tall as she was, she could surely pass for a man. Satisfied the clothes would fit, she stashed them out of sight in her armoire. As soon as supper was over and she could escape upstairs, she would call for her maid, undress, and go to bed. Once the household grew quiet, she would get up and change into masculine attire.

She looked again in the mirror. What would she do about her hair? A woolen cap would hide it. A cap instead of a hat might look a bit strange, but where she was going wasn't exactly a fashion-conscious neighborhood.

At precisely eleven-thirty, she set her plan in motion. Dressing in Rudy's old clothes, she stuffed her hair up under the cap and set out for the cab stand on the corner. As they had planned, Elias Mack was already there. The young footman grumbled and tried to dissuade her, but he liked his job and he seemed to like her, and in the end he resigned himself to helping her.

Everything was set.

Lindsey just hoped the plan she had come up with would actually work.

Standing in the shadows at the back of the garden, Thor stood with his shoulders propped against the fence. From his vantage point, he could watch the back door of the house, the exit Lindsey was sure to take. He still had trouble believing she would actually go through with her insane plan, that she would dress as a man and go into one of the seediest districts in London.

He shook his head. He shouldn't be surprised. Lindsey had always been strong-willed and now with the threat against her brother, Thor imagined there was little she would not do.

He had been there nearly an hour when the back door opened and a slender figure walked into the darkness. She was dressed as a lad, just as Krista had said, and silently he cursed.

The little fool was nothing but trouble.

He understood her worry—though he wasn't sure her no-account brother was worth it. Still, there were limits to what a young woman should do and running around in the middle of the night dressed as a man went far beyond that.

He let her get half a block ahead, then started after her, pausing when he realized her destination was the cab stand down at the corner. A man stood waiting, the footman, Elias Mack that Krista had told him about. He looked too young, too inexperienced to be much good in a fight.

If Lindsey got into trouble…

His jaw clenched. Thank the gods, Krista had come to him for help. He might not approve of Lindsey's behavior, but he didn't want her getting hurt. He waited for the pair to climb aboard a hansom cab and set off down the street, then made his way over to the stand and caught another cab.

"Covent Garden," he told the driver. "Keep that other carriage in sight."

"Aye, sir."

Thor watched tensely as the single-horse conveyance ahead of him rounded one corner after another, making its way deeper and deeper into a district of gin halls, gaming houses, and brothels. It was a place a man came for entertainment, certainly no place for a lady.

And Lindsey was one, he grudgingly admitted, even if she was a little reckless at times.

He watched her carriage pull over to the curb in front of the Golden Pheasant, a well-known, slightly disreputable, gaming hall that was hardly a place she should be, no matter how she tried to disguise herself. He fought an urge to storm up and toss her over his shoulder, cart her back home where she would be safe.

He wouldn't do it. She would only return another night and the next time he might not be there to protect her.

Instead, he waited out of sight in the shadows in front of the building until she and her footman came back out fifteen minutes later, then followed them on down the street.

A few blocks farther along the lane, she knocked on the door at the bottom of a three-story walk-up and a woman wearing too much face paint opened the door.

"I'm a friend of Phoebe Carter's," Thor heard Lindsey say. "I am trying to discover where her flat might be located."

She didn't bother to disguise her voice and the woman looked her up and down, taking in the trousers and coat. "Phoebe's dead."

"Yes, I know. I'd like to speak to the women who lived with her."

"Her place was just upstairs, third floor, but her friends ain't home."

"I'll come back another time."

The woman closed the door and Lindsey rejoined the footman, who waited a little ways away. Careful to stay in the shadows, Thor followed the pair who appeared, at first glance, to be two young men making their way along the street. The young footman seemed to have no idea they were being followed and Thor silently cursed. The lad was too green—worthless as a protector.

Lindsey and the footman turned a corner, started along a block Thor knew well, since it was just down the street from Madame Fortier's brothel. In the middle of the block, torches lit the entry to the notorious Blue Moon, the wickedest gaming hall in London. His hand fisted as he watched Lindsey and the footman walk inside.

By Odin, did the woman not have a lick of sense?

Thor resisted the urge to follow her, knowing if he did, he would surely be seen, and instead positioned himself outside the front door.

He would give her this night, but when it was over, he meant to have a very long talk with her.

Making her way through the rowdy, boisterous crowd inside, Lindsey heard Elias Mack's voice, whispering behind her.

"Are ye sure about this?"

She wasn't so sure. This was the worst place they had been so far, the carpet faded and worn, the wallpaper peeling and the air so smoky she could barely breathe.

"This is our last stop," she told him, careful to keep her voice low and gruff. "As soon as I speak to the person in charge, we can go home."

She had learned from her stop at the Golden Pheasant to ask for the manager, but this place looked far less friendly, and she and Elias seemed to be drawing attention. Perhaps it was the fact they had never been in before while most of the crowd appeared to be locals. Maybe it would be better to gamble for a while and try to fit in.

"'Ow 'bout a throw of the dice, mate?" she said in her gruff male voice, feigning a slight cockney accent. "We're due for a change o' luck." She made her way over to the hazard table and Elias walked up beside her. She could feel his mounting tension as they shouldered their way through the crowd, the same tension that was squeezing a knot in her stomach.

She was tall enough to pass for a slender man and the room was dark and shadowy enough to hide her face. Her coat and trousers were wrinkled and plain, and wearing the woolen cap, she hoped to appear nondescript.

Gathered round the hazard table was an assortment of disreputable looking men, several smoking cigars and using foul language, one with thick gray side-whiskers, another with a missing front tooth. As she moved closer to the table, she nearly gagged at the smell of body odor and sour beer and fought to suppress a shudder.

The men roared as someone hit his winning number. It was now or never. She pulled out the pouch of coins in the pocket of her coat and the instant she did, she realized her mistake. Drawing several sharp glances and a whispered word here and there, she ignored the quickening of her pulse and tried to appear nonchalant. There was no turning back, not without drawing even more attention.

Keeping her head down, she shook out a handful of coins, then stuffed the pouch back inside her coat pocket, silently berating herself for not realizing the danger of letting the men know she had money.

She glanced down at the gaming table. She had played

hazard with Rudy—scandalous as it might be for an un-married young woman. Now she was glad. She placed a bet, lost, groaned as if it were more than she could afford, lost again and moved back from the table.

A serving maid in a scandalously low-cut blouse worked her way round the room, encouraging the men's lewd re-marks and allowing them liberties that made Lindsey blush. For the first time, it occurred to her that the Blue Moon was likely far more than a gaming hall. Odds were, it was also a house of ill repute.

The serving maid arrived and Lindsey ordered a tankard of ale. Elias's eyes riveted on the pair of bulging breasts threatening to burst free of the woman's flimsy garment.

"Ye want to touch 'em, luvy?" The wench gave him a lusty wink and Elias grinned.

Lindsey elbowed him in the ribs and he quickly shook his head. "No, thank ye."

"Bring him an ale," Lindsey said gruffly. "We'd also like a word with the manager. Where might we find 'im?"

"Mr. Pinkard's in his office. I'll tell him there's a couple of gents who want to talk to him."

"Thank you."

A few minutes later, Pinkard walked up, a gaunt man with deep-set eyes and black hair. "You wanted to see me?"

"We're friends of Phoebe Carter…the woman what was murdered just down the next block. We was wondering if you or someone here might 'ave seen her that night?"

"Maybe she was here—I wouldn't know. I didn't see her and neither did anyone else."

"There was a party upstairs that night. There's a chance she was there. Maybe you or one of your employees—"

He grabbed her by the front of the coat. "I don't know who you are, but you're through asking questions." He tipped his head toward a couple of men who materialized out of the shadows. One looked like a walking tree trunk, the other was equally tall though not quite as heavy, and bald as a billiard ball.

The bald man caught her arm while the tree trunk grabbed hold of Elias, who tried to jerk free.

"Hey! Whatcha think yer doin'?"

The big man just laughed, tightened his grip and dragged him forward.

"We're leaving—all right?" Lindsey said, fighting against the forward momentum, but the men didn't stop, just hauled them toward a door at the side of the building and out into the alley. It was tar-black outside except for the flickering light of a torch stuck into a holder beside the door.

"Hand over the pouch," the bald man demanded.

Her stomach tightened. So the men had seen her coin purse. Lindsey didn't argue. Her hand shook as she reached into her pocket and pulled out the leather bag of coins. Her heart was racing, trying to pound its way out from between her ribs, and Elias's eyes were big and round.

She handed over the pouch, but as she tried to pull away, the man caught her hand. In the torchlight, her fingers were slender and pale, not the sort that belonged to a man. Lindsey stiffened as the bald man reached up, jerked off her woolen cap, and her hair tumbled down.

"Well, ain't this just our lucky night, Jocko, me boy? A little extra blunt and a piece o' tail to boot."

The blood drained from Lindsey's face. She started to struggle and Elias went wild.

"Let her go!" Straining frantically at the thick arms wrapped around him, Elias fought to break free.

"Take the money and let us go!" Lindsey pleaded, but the bald man just leered and the tree trunk just laughed.

Elias struggled harder, managing to free one of his arms and swinging out wildly, landing a surprisingly solid blow. The huge man growled low in his throat, spun him around and hit him, once, twice. Lindsey screamed as Elias went down. The man hauled him up and pummeled him again and again, until his eyes rolled back and he slumped to the ground unconscious.

Lindsey struggled in earnest as the coat was dragged from her shoulders. Big, callused hands gripped her shirt and ripped the soft lawn fabric apart. A gust of wind chilled the bare skin above the chemise she wore underneath. Another scream and she began a violent struggle as the men jerked off her shoes, then tore off the rest of her clothes. She tried to cry out but a meaty palm slapped her so hard she stumbled and went to her knees.

All she could think was that Krista had tried to warn her but she wouldn't listen. Now she and Elias were paying, perhaps with their lives.

Thor took the corner at a flat-out run. The first cry had been muffled, one of the whores, he had thought, pleasuring a client in the alley. There was no mistaking the second scream, it was female and blood-curdling and it belonged to Lindsey.

Fear clawed at him as he spotted the two big men standing over her prone figure in the torchlight. One held her arms, the other her feet—and she was completely naked.

The instant before he reached her, a single thought

occurred: there was nothing the least bit *boyish* about
Lindsey Graham. She was all sleek curves and lovely
breasts, a tiny waist and the longest, prettiest legs he had
ever seen.

And another man was touching her, stroking a blunt-
fingered hand over her smooth white skin.

Thor let out a cry like a raging bull. He grabbed the first
man and jerked him away from Lindsey. Smashing a fist
into his ugly face, Thor hit him as hard as he could then
hit him again.

With a roar of outrage, the second man lowered his head
and charged, ramming Thor in the stomach, sending him
several feet backward, slamming him into the rough brick
wall. Thor growled low in his throat and drove a fist into
the man's face. Blood spouted like a fountain from the
man's broken nose. He threw a punch, missed, and Thor hit
him again, knocking him into the dirt.

Thor's attention returned to the first man and he started
slamming blows, one after another, into the stout man's
body. The bald man rushed back into the fray and began
throwing punches. Thor almost laughed at the impotent
blows that only enraged him. In minutes, both men were
down, both bleeding, and still he didn't stop. Not until
Lindsey's soft sobs reached him.

Shaking with the effort it took to keep himself from killing the men, he turned to see her huddled against the wall,
her man's coat pulled over her naked body. She was trembling so hard her teeth chattered. There was a bruise on her
cheek and her honey hair tumbled around her shoulders. Her
coat wasn't big enough to hide all of her so he quickly
removed his jacket and draped it round her shoulders.

When he knelt in front of her, she looked at him through eyes glazed with shock and fear.

"Thor...?"

He wanted to hold her, wrap her in his arms and carry her away. Instead, he reached out and gently brushed back her hair. "It's all right, sweetheart. They won't hurt you again."

Tears slipped onto her cheeks. "I can't believe you are here."

"I heard you scream. I came as fast as I could."

Her head jerked toward the wall as she remembered her companion. "Wh-what about Elias?"

"I will take care of him." Though he wanted to stay, reassure himself she was all right, he forced himself to turn away, to search out the boy, who lay moaning in the shadows.

"How badly are you injured?" he asked.

Elias opened his eyes. "They beat me good. I hurt all over." He tried to sit up. "Miss Graham! Is she—"

"Do not worry. She is safe."

The lad struggled to his feet, swayed a bit then straightened. "Who are you?"

"A friend. I followed you here in case of trouble."

The young man nodded. His lip was swollen, his eye an ugly purple-black and swollen nearly closed. "Bloody well glad ye did."

"Can you walk?"

Elias nodded. With a quick glance to make sure that Lindsey was safe, Thor helped him the short distance down the alley to the street. A cab rolled toward them from in front of the gambling hall, a tired old horse in the traces. Thor helped the lad climb aboard and paid the driver to take him home.

"You will not mention Miss Graham."

Elias shook his head. "No, sir. She wasn't even here."

Thor nodded his approval. By the time the carriage pulled away, he was running back to Lindsey. Both men still lay unconscious, facedown in the dirt and refuse of the alley. He fought an urge to finish what he had started but moved away at the soft call of his name.

Lindsey stood propped against the brick wall, barefoot and shivering, clutching his coat around her. It came almost to her knees.

"How badly did they hurt you?"

"I-I'm all right. I just…I just want to go home but I can't…not…not like this."

Beneath his coat, she was naked and the thought of what the men had intended infuriated him all over again. "If you were not here, I would kill them."

Her eyes widened, then filled with tears. "But you are here." She started crying and he scooped her up in his arms.

"I am here. There is no more need to be afraid."

She slid her arm around his neck and clung to him. "You saved me. Oh, God, Thor." Burying her face against his shoulder, she wept as if she could not stop.

"It's all right," he said softly. "I will not let them hurt you again." Whispering soothing words, he held her gently against him as he strode down the street. She couldn't go home—not without clothes—but he knew a place he could take her.

Seven

⌒⌒⌒

Lindsey clung to Thor's muscular neck. Over and over, he spoke to her in a voice so soft and low she could barely hear the words. He told her she was safe, that he wouldn't let anyone hurt her. He said that she didn't have to be afraid, that he would take care of her.

Sometimes he spoke in his native tongue, Nordic sounding words she didn't understand. It didn't really matter. It was the tone of his voice, the rhythmical cadence that calmed her. It was the way he held her, his gentle care of her that told her she was safe.

She had no idea where he was taking her. She should have been concerned, but she was not. Thor had saved her from a fate worse than death, perhaps from death itself. She would never forget the way he had come to her rescue, like a fierce dark angel bringing the wrath of God down on her enemies.

She understood now what Krista had meant. Thor was a warrior, a man skilled in fighting, willing to die for those he protected. She thought of the hard, tough men he had defeated with an ease that was frightening. She had no doubt he could have killed them.

She shivered as he carried her in his arms.

"We are almost there, sweetheart."

The endearment rolled over her. She tried to ignore the soft little flutter in her stomach. Thor was there and she was safe. She should have gone to him for help in the first place.

In truth, she'd been afraid. She had never felt such a strong physical attraction to a man before. Now that attraction was heightened by the gratitude she felt that he had come for her and the care he was taking of her.

She nestled deeper against his massive chest and closed her eyes. She was safe. Elias was safe. For now that was all that mattered.

Lindsey came awake to the sound of female laughter and the clink of glasses. Men laughed and gas lamps, burning low, hissed softly into a low-ceilinged room whose walls were covered with red-flocked paper.

She straightened in Thor's arms. "Where are we?"

"The Red Door," he said simply, setting her carefully back on her feet. "Madame Fortier is a friend."

A woman stood in front of them, with full breasts and a curvy figure, silver-streaked black hair. She was overly made up but she was still a beautiful woman, though she was perhaps in her fortieth year.

"Thor 'as explained what 'as happened," the woman said, her words tinged with a soft French accent that might have fooled someone who didn't speak fluent French. "'E is a very good friend and since you are a friend of 'is, you are welcome 'ere."

Lindsey managed a smile. "It is a pleasure to meet you, Madame Fortier."

"Thor! Is that you, lover?" A red-haired woman started toward him, scantily dressed and smiling.

"It's him!" Two blond women sauntered out of the back in sheer French negligees, one pink and one blue, that barely covered their bottoms. They were clearly twins and equally beautiful. "It's hard to mistake a man that big."

"And he's that big all over," giggled the redhead with a seductive look in her eyes, her gaze admiring Thor from head to toe.

Lindsey just stared. When her shocked gaze found several more scantily clad women in the room, for a moment she thought she was dreaming. Dear God, of all places, it never occurred to her Thor would bring her to a house of ill repute!

"Need company tonight, big man?" The twins came up on each side of him. Long-nailed fingers stroked through his dark hair. "You know how well Greta and Freda can please you."

A flush rose under the bones in Thor's cheeks. "Not tonight."

"How about me?" the redhead asked, her breasts nearly spilling out of a filmy gown Lindsey could see completely through. "It's my night off. You can stay with me and keep your money."

Thor shook his head. "I have other business, but I thank you for the offer."

Good grief! Lindsey knew he was popular with women, but she couldn't have imagined even prostitutes would throw themselves at him! An unexpected surge of what felt oddly like jealousy rolled through her. It was insane. She should be furious that he would bring her to a place like this!

On the other hand, in her state of undress, how many choices did he have?

For any number of reasons, she was grateful when Madame Fortier began to shoo the women away.

"The three of you, leave Thor alone. Can you not see he is otherwise occupied tonight?"

Occupied? Occupied with her?

Great heavens! Lindsey caught a glimpse of herself in the gilt-rimmed mirror above the table in the entry. Thor's coat hung to her knees, but her legs and feet were bare, her hair a tumbled mass around her shoulders. Dear God, did these women think she was one of them? That she was a prostitute in need of Thor's help? That she was one of his bedmates?

She flicked him a glance. Standing there with his shirt torn and bloody, his dark hair mussed and curling over his forehead, he was so handsome her breath hitched.

And yet he felt not the least attraction to her. He had followed her because she was a friend of Krista's. Even though she wore not a shred of clothing under his coat, he hadn't once looked at her the way men looked at the half-naked women at the Red Door.

She tried to tell herself she wasn't annoyed.

"She needs something to wear," Thor said to Madame Fortier. "I will gladly pay whatever it costs."

One of the woman's silver-touched eyebrows went up. "I will be 'appy to provide your friend with clothes, but are you certain you would not rather stay 'ere until morning? I 'ave a very nice room upstairs the two of you could share for the rest of the night."

Thor's gaze swung to Lindsey, ran over her bare legs and feet. The look he gave her wasn't the least bit bland or tinged with disapproval. It was scorching hot, a fierce, burning glance that said he remembered exactly what she looked like under his coat. That she was naked as sin, that taking her upstairs was exactly what he wanted to do.

Lindsey sucked in a breath. It said that Thor Draugr just plain wanted her.

Her pulse started hammering. She couldn't drag her eyes from his face.

Thor glanced away first. "Just the dress," he said a bit gruffly. "That is all we need."

Madame Fortier started walking. "Follow me, dear. I'll see what I can do."

Thor caught her arm. "You are not recovered. Mayhap I should carry you."

For a single, insane moment, she almost agreed, just so he would hold her in his arms again. Good Lord, she was perfectly able to walk. She wasn't under Thor's spell like the rest of his women. She was not!

"I am fine." Abruptly she turned away, refusing to look at him again. Lindsey caught up with Madame Fortier, who led her into a back room of the house. A few minutes later, she was dressed in an orange satin gown that looked exactly as if it belonged in a brothel—which of course it did—the bodice cut so low all but her nipples were exposed.

"I am sorry," the woman said. "This is the best I can do."

"It's better than what I was wearing." *But not much.* Taking a deep breath, trying not to blush, Lindsey followed Madame Fortier back to the main salon.

Thor turned at the sound of footfalls. Crossing toward him was a woman with honey-brown hair and catlike golden eyes. She was slender but not boyish, as he had once thought. Instead, her figure was willowy and graceful—*elegant*—was the English word he might choose.

For an instant he remembered her naked: her tiny waist, the perfect apple-roundness of her breasts, the pale pink crests diamond-hard against the chill night air. He could almost see them now, barely covered as they were by the whore's clothing she wore.

In his mind, he could still see the triangle of soft tawny curls above her sex, the long legs and slim feet. As she crossed to where he stood, he imagined those pale legs wrapped around him, the sweetness of her lips, the taste of her skin, the womanly scent of her in his nostrils as he brought her to fulfillment.

His shaft throbbed and he stifled a groan. By the time she reached him, he was hard as granite, aching to be inside her. He had tried to convince himself she wasn't the woman for him and in his heart he knew it was true.

And yet he wanted her. Had since the moment he had seen her beautiful body—in truth, had wanted her for months before that. But she was Krista's friend, a maiden, daughter of a wealthy aristocrat, as far from his reach as any of the Viking goddesses his people worshipped on the island.

He couldn't have her and so he had convinced himself that she did not appeal to him.

She handed him back his coat and he pulled it on, hoping she wouldn't notice his reaction to her, hoping she wouldn't see his powerful erection. Madame Fortier had a keener sense of such things, and a faint, knowing smile touched her lips.

She stared pointedly at the bulge in his trousers hidden

by the coat and shook her head. "Such a waste. You are certain you do not wish to stay?"

He wanted to stay more than he wanted to breathe. He wanted to carry Lindsey to one of the rooms upstairs, strip away her whore's clothes, and bury himself as deeply as he could. He wanted to cocoon himself in the long silky strands of her hair, feel the hardness of her nipples against his chest, know the tightness of her sweet woman's body, milking him in pleasure.

Thor silently cursed. For months, he had maintained a façade of indifference, fooled her and even himself. Tonight, seeing her naked and vulnerable, attacked by criminals who meant to brutally take what she was unwilling to give, his control had finally snapped.

He couldn't lie to himself any longer. He wanted her as he had never wanted a woman.

Thor vowed he would never let Lindsey know.

Lindsey rode next to Thor in Madame Fortier's private carriage. So much had happened. She and Elias might have died if it hadn't been for Thor. She tried not to think of the Red Door and Madame Fortier, but the image of the beautiful woman kept creeping into her mind.

"You must go to the Red Door often for you and Madame Fortier to have become such good friends."

Thor cast her a glance. "We have taken pleasure in each other's bodies."

Her eyes widened. She tried to hide her blush. She was, after all, the one who had brought up the subject and she knew how blunt Thor could be. Still, she was curious.

"The other women seemed to like you, as well."

He shrugged his powerful shoulders. "A man has needs, and I am not yet married like my brother."

She sat up a little straighter on the seat. "Then Leif doesn't go with you?"

"My brother has found his life-mate. He will not be unfaithful."

So he believed a husband should be faithful. Not a common philosophy among the men of her station. "Are you searching for your own life-mate?"

"If the gods will it, I shall find her."

Thor had the most unusual way of speaking. She wished she knew more about him. She pulled Thor's coat a little closer around her, fighting not to shiver against the cold. She had declined the cloak Madame had offered. She didn't want Thor taking back the cloak, though she was sure, sooner or later, he would return to the women. As he had said, a man had needs and one as virile as Thor must have stronger needs than most.

In the darkness, her cheeks began to burn. She knew what happened between a man and a woman. She had experienced the event firsthand with Tyler Reese when they were just sixteen. She had foolishly believed she was in love with the handsome young viscount, and she was curious.

Being a man, Ty had clearly enjoyed himself, but it had been an utter disappointment to Lindsey.

"You said if the gods will it. Do you believe there is more than one?" she asked.

"Many years before I was born, a priest came to our island. He taught our people about your Christian God, but we also believe in the Viking gods of old."

"Then your island was once the home of Vikings."

He looked at her hard. "We are Vikings, still. It is a way of life that has not changed in hundreds of years."

"You don't mean you're really a—"

"Aye, lady, I do."

She stared at his profile, trying to convince herself she had heard him correctly. She thought of his strength, the fierce way he fought, the ease with which he had vanquished his opponents. "Oh, my."

"Leif and I—we do not speak of it often. It is hard for people in this country to believe. And I do not wish to see it written about in your column."

"Of course not! I would never repeat something you told me in confidence."

Beneath the passing street lamps, he studied her face. "No, I do not think you would. You are stubborn and headstrong and far too outspoken for a woman, but you are also loyal and I believe you are worthy of a man's trust."

She didn't know whether to be complimented or insulted. She decided on a safer subject. "Why did you come to England?"

"To see what lay beyond our island was a dream of my brother's." Thor went on to explain that when a ship had wrecked on the island, providing the timbers needed to build a sailing vessel, Leif had finally gotten his chance to leave. He sailed off with a group of young men but did not return for over a year and they all believed him dead.

Eventually he returned, bringing with him a bride, but he was never meant to stay.

"It was the will of the gods that my brother live here in England. I came back with him. I wanted to learn, see what destiny lay ahead for me."

She mulled that over, trying to come to grips with the things he was telling her. "Do you ever think of going home?"

"There are times I miss my brothers and my sister. I miss the open spaces and the beauty of the land. But it is beautiful here, too, out in the country where the grass is so green and the hills bloom with flowers. One day I will own my own land and then I can be at peace."

She wanted to ask him more but the carriage was approaching Mount Street. She needed to get into the house without being seen. She could imagine Aunt Dee's horrified expression at the sight of the awful orange satin gown.

She spotted the big stone mansion up ahead. She hoped Elias Mack had gotten safely back to his room above the carriage house. She knew she could trust him not to betray their adventure tonight and wondered what wild tale he would concoct to explain his cuts and bruises.

Thor ordered the driver to turn down the alley at the back of the house.

"You are lucky you are not my woman," he said as the vehicle rolled toward an arched wooden gate at the rear of the garden. "I would take the flat of my hand to your pretty behind for risking yourself as you did."

Lindsey ignored him. Thor was not her husband and never would be. As the carriage rolled to a stop, she looked up at him.

"My brother is in trouble. I have to find the man who murdered those women. After tonight, I realize I can't do it alone. Will you help me?"

He studied her for several long moments, then his jaw hardened. "If I say no, will you do something foolish again?"

"Probably."

"You are more trouble than any two other women, lady."

"Is that a yes?"

"Aye, I will help you."

She leaned over and kissed his cheek. "Thank you. I can never repay you for what you did tonight." She started to turn away, but Thor caught her shoulders, holding her in place.

"I will take this as payment."

Lindsey gasped as he hauled her against him and his mouth crushed down over hers. For an instant, time spun to a halt. She could feel the heat of him, the powerful muscles in his chest, the iron-hard strength in his arms. His lips were softer than they looked as they moved over hers, melding perfectly, burning into her. It was a fierce, taking kiss and it completely inflamed her. She was clutching his shoulders, making soft little whimpering sounds when Thor broke away.

Breathing a little too hard, he gave her a last searing glance as he climbed down from the carriage, reached up and helped her down then stepped back out of her way.

"Go inside, Lindsey," he said gruffly. "Before I forget that we are just friends."

Lindsey didn't hesitate, just lifted the skirt of the ugly orange gown and ran as fast as she could through the garden, back inside the house.

Eight

Lindsey sat at her desk, her head bent over the sheet of paper in front of her as she scratched out her column for the week.

Or at least tried to.

Unfortunately, it was nearly impossible to concentrate with Thor in the office. Though she carefully kept her eyes on her work, she could hear him moving about, lifting heavy crates and boxes in the back room. He had been at the office for hours and yet they had only spoken once, merely a strained greeting upon her arrival and an inquiry as to how she fared after her ordeal last night. She had said that she was fine, though every part of her ached from her brutal treatment in the alley.

They hadn't spoken since.

Lindsey sighed. It was clear Thor regretted his impulsive kiss last night. Lindsey wished she felt the same. Instead, that fierce, burning contact refused to leave her mind and secretly she wondered what it would take to get him to kiss her that way again. She reminded herself it was that sort of thinking that accounted for her wicked behavior with Tyler Reese. She had given Ty her innocence and wound up regretting it later.

But part of her argued that this wasn't at all the same. She wasn't in love with Thor, just wildly attracted to him. She was older now, a grown woman no longer susceptible to a man's persuasion.

Not that Ty had needed to do much of that.

In truth it had been more her idea than his. Certainly, it was her idea to refuse the offer of marriage he had felt obligated to make. She wasn't in love with Ty, she had discovered, and she wasn't ready for marriage.

Having done his duty, the young viscount was relieved, and in the end, they had remained friends.

Now, years later, the old curiosity had resurfaced. Kissing Thor had been different than anything she had experienced with Ty or any other man. The hot, mind-numbing sensations, the weakness in the knees, the wild urge to lose herself in the heat and power that vibrated through his big, hard-muscled body was utterly and completely amazing.

She tried not to wonder what it might be like to make love with a man who could set her blood on fire.

She tried not to, but she did.

The bell above the door rang, drawing her attention as the footman, Elias Mack, rushed into the office, bringing gusts of chilly September wind and blowing leaves. Several heads swiveled toward him, but tomorrow the paper went to press and everyone was busy doing his job.

Elias headed straight for her, and Lindsey came out of her chair. "Good heavens, Elias, what has happened?"

He was nearly unrecognizable with his battered face,

swollen lip, and puffy, blackened eye. She hadn't seen him since last night, and a pang of guilt washed through her that her actions had resulted in such a terrible beating.

"The police came to the house, miss. They arrested your brother. They carted him off in a police wagon."

"Oh, my God."

"What has happened?" Thor's deep voice snagged her attention. For an instant she forgot Elias was there.

Mentally she shook herself. "Rudy has been arrested. I have to go down to the police station. I have to find a way to make them understand that he couldn't possibly be the man who killed those women." Reaching over, she grabbed her reticule off the top of the desk, rose and started for the door.

"I will come with you," Thor said, catching up to her in a single long stride.

"I don't need your protection for this. I am going to a police station, for heaven's sake."

"You asked for my help. I am helping. I will come."

She sighed and started walking, stopped near the door to gather her cloak and bonnet, then continued outside in search of transportation.

Elias and Thor followed her out.

"Ye want I should come along?" the young footman asked.

"I think you had better go back to the house," Lindsey told him. "I have gotten you into enough trouble already."

Elias nodded. "Whatever ye wish, miss."

"By the way, how did you explain what happened to your face?"

He grinned. "Mostly I told the truth. I went gambling at the Blue Moon and got me purse pinched by a couple of mugs."

"I feel terrible about the way the evening turned out. I shouldn't have asked you to take that kind of risk."

Elias's grin broadened. "It were some night, weren't it, miss? I woulda' liked to have got in a few more good licks, but I wouldna' wanted to miss it." He waved as he started off down the street, back toward her Mount Street home.

Men, Lindsey thought as he disappeared round the corner. *How did a woman ever understand them?*

Which reminded her of her brother and the trouble he was in.

"What am I going to do about Rudy?" she said to Thor as they made their way to the corner, not really expecting him to know.

"We will have to find the men who killed those women."

Until he said the words out loud, it hadn't seemed such an impossible task.

She took a steadying breath. "We'll speak to the police, try to convince them that Rudy is innocent. Then we'll return to Covent Garden, ask a few more questions."

He frowned. "After what happened last night, you wish to go back?"

She suppressed a shudder at the memory of the men in the alley and their brutal attack. "Going back is the last thing I want. I don't have any choice."

"You must not go there without me."

"You needn't worry about that. Rest assured I have learned my lesson."

Thor did not look convinced.

Lindsey didn't expect to find Aunt Dee pacing frantically in front of the sergeant's desk in the police station when she walked through the glass-paned door Thor held open for her. Though she probably shouldn't have been surprised, since she knew how worried her aunt would be.

"Lindsey—thank heavens you are here! Rudy has been arrested. The fools are convinced he has murdered those two unfortunate women."

"I know. Elias Mack came to the office to tell me."

Aunt Dee sniffed in disdain. "Mr. Mack is lucky to retain his position. Brawling like some sort of ruffian. I have forbidden him to show his face in the house until he is healed. If a guest were to see him…well, I can only imagine the gossip that would stir."

Lindsey glanced up at Thor, who raised a dark eyebrow as if to say, *if you hadn't behaved so recklessly, your footman would not now be on the brink of losing his job, and you would not have been attacked.*

Lindsey merely ignored him. She forced herself to smile. "Aunt Delilah, this is a friend—Thor Draugr. You are acquainted with his brother, Krista's husband, Leif."

"Why, yes, I am." Her aunt looked Thor up and down, taking in his exceptional height and the breadth of his chest and shoulders. "Your coloring is quite different from your brother's, but one can certainly see the family resemblance."

And it was clear her aunt appreciated the younger brother's masculine charms. She was a woman, after all. How could she not?

"Thor is going to help me find a way to clear Rudy's name."

"Indeed." Aunt Dee gave him another assessing glance, trying to determine the level of his intelligence, a question Lindsey had pondered herself. "Let us hope you can."

A man with thinning brown hair walked up just then, Constable Bertram, she recalled, the lead investigator on the murders.

"Lady Ashford," he said to her aunt, "I assume you are here in support of your nephew, Rudolph Graham."

"I am here because of your ridiculous charges. My nephew has had no part in any murder and I demand you release him this instant."

He sighed as if he actually felt regret—which Lindsey was certain he did not. "I wish it were that simple. At the moment, I'm sorry to say there is nothing you can do to secure his release." But he didn't look sorry at all, he looked smugly satisfied as he turned his attention to Lindsey. "I'm glad you are here, Miss Graham. I would like a word in private, if you please."

A trickle of worry slipped through her. She glanced up at Thor, strangely glad he was there. "Whatever you have to say, you may say right here, in the presence of my aunt and Mr. Draugr."

"Then I shall say this. You have given false testimony as to your brother's whereabouts the night of Phoebe Carter's murder. You know it and so do I. I am giving you a chance to withdraw your statement. If you do not and we disprove your brother's alibi—which we will—it will mean that you have willfully attempted to impede a police investigation and I will be forced to file formal charges against you."

"There is no way you can know where my brother was that night. I told you he was with—"

"Tell him the truth," Thor commanded.

Her eyes widened. "What…what do you think you are doing?"

"I am keeping you out of trouble. That is why I am here. Now tell Constable Bertram the truth."

She looked over at her aunt, who was nodding in agreement. Hell and damnation—what she told the police was none of Thor's business. All right, well, maybe after last night it was.

She sighed with resignation. "I am not certain where my brother was that night. I may have mistaken the date. I am no longer sure."

Bertram's lips twisted. "That is what I thought."

"It doesn't mean he was the man who killed Miss Carter."

"I'm afraid there is evidence that he was."

Her chest squeezed. "What evidence?"

"A witness has come forward. The woman identified your brother as the man she saw fleeing the murder scene the night Phoebe Carter was killed."

"But that is impossible! Rudy wouldn't kill anyone!"

Bertram touched her arm in a gesture of sympathy. "In my job I have seen many things, Miss Graham. I have learned that we never really know anyone."

The words stung more than they should have. Rudy wasn't the innocent youth he once had been, the curious boy who collected butterflies and played with toy soldiers. This was a man who consorted with prostitutes and gambled away his money.

Still, she believed him innocent. "Perhaps in some cases that is so, but this is my brother and I know he isn't capable of murder."

The constable made no reply, but his gaze held a trace of pity.

"I want to see him. Where have they taken him?"

"Your brother is occupying a cell on the masters' side of Newgate Prison."

Her stomach knotted. Deep down, she had known that was where he would be taken. Still, she felt a sharp wrenching inside her. Rudy was her brother. When they were children, he was her closest friend. She thought of their shared love of horses, the hours they had spent riding, the pranks they had played.

Wordlessly, she turned and started walking, a thick lump swelling in her throat. As they descended the wide stone steps out to the street, her aunt on one side, Thor on the other, his big hand settled reassuringly at her waist. She was angry at him for making her tell the truth and yet she was glad he was there.

"Tonight," he said softly, bending his head to hers. "Wear the orange dress and I will meet you at midnight at the back of the garden."

Her eyes widened. "The orange dress?"

"The men will think you are mine for the night and no one will bother you."

Lindsey swallowed. The notion of wearing the orange dress brought to mind the awful attack in the alley, the feel of blunt fingers stroking over her skin. It recalled what might have happened if Thor had not come when he did.

The men will think you are mine for the night.

Instead of attending the engagement party for the daughter of the Duke of Pelham as she had planned, she would be playing the role of Thor's doxy. It was ridiculous. She couldn't possibly do such a thing.

And yet there was Rudy to consider.

She was glad she hadn't burned the damnable dress.

* * *

Lindsey, Thor and Aunt Dee left the police station together and headed straight for the prison, a miserable gray stone structure that looked as forbidding as it actually was. Both women and men were incarcerated inside the thick walls, and since its beginning, hundreds of its inhabitants had been publicly executed.

Lindsey had read about the prison and about a female reformer named Elizabeth Fry who had begun the fight for improved conditions. Over the years, some improvements had been made, but it remained a fearful place to be locked away. It was a horrific place for a young man of wealth and position to find himself, and Lindsey's heart went out to her brother.

She shuddered as they walked inside. After they paid the required fee, an overweight guard showed them down a long, damp, dimly lit corridor. The echo of their footsteps accompanied them as they walked along, the flickering light of torches illuminating their way. At the opposite end of the prison, criminals survived in even worse conditions, dozens of people crammed into cells barely suitable for the rats that shared their quarters.

"This is no place for a lady," Thor said, his expression grim. "You and your aunt should not have come."

"My brother is here," Lindsey told him. "We had to come."

He didn't say more, but she could tell he wasn't pleased.

They reached Rudy's cell, a grim, Spartanly furnished chamber behind a thick oak door. Her brother sat at a rickety table with Jonas Marvin, her father's attorney. Both men rose when the small group appeared in the doorway.

"I will wait for you out here," Thor said.

Lindsey nodded. "Thank you." Rudy had enough trouble without worrying about her association with an unacceptable male. Thank God, Aunt Dee had as yet refrained from any comment.

"Hello, sis." Rudy looked so fragile, so frightened that tears sprang into her eyes.

She managed a smile, went over and hugged him. "Are you all right? They haven't mistreated you?"

"I'm fine. Aunt Dee got hold of Mr. Marvin and he came down straightaway. He paid the ease and made the arrangements for me to have a place on this side of the prison."

It was a slightly better area where inmates were kept who could afford to pay for the privilege. The cells were larger and each had a bed, a table and two chairs. Still, it was dismal in the extreme, and Lindsey bit down on an urge to cry for her brother.

Instead, she fixed her attention on the bookish-looking man wearing gold-rimmed spectacles who stood next to Rudy.

"Thank you so much for coming, Mr. Marvin," she said.

"It is good to see you, Jonas," Aunt Dee added. "I wish the circumstances could have been better."

"I had hoped it wouldn't come to this," he said.

"We all did."

"So what are we to do, Mr. Marvin?" Lindsey asked. "How do we get my brother out of here?" Both her aunt and Jonas Marvin had sent word to her parents, but so far had been unable to reach them. Whatever action was taken would be up to the four of them.

"Three days ago, Rudolph and I agreed to hire a private detective, a man named Harrison Mansfield. I am hoping

Mr. Mansfield will be able to find evidence that will prove Rudolph's innocence."

She thought of the investigator, Dolph Petersen, in whom Krista had such faith, but there had been no word of his return to the city.

"Also, I spoke to Avery French about the possibility of acquiring his services should the need arise—as indeed it has. You may recognize the name, since Mr. French is renowned as one of the foremost barristers in London. As soon as I leave, I shall alert him as to what has occurred so that he can begin immediately to formulate Rudolph's defense."

Her stomach rolled. This was really happening. If they didn't find the true killer, Rudy could very well hang.

"Why don't you sit down, dear?" Aunt Dee suggested, noting the sudden pallor of her face.

"I'm all right. It is just…it is difficult to believe any of this is real."

The solicitor nodded gravely. "Unfortunately, I'm afraid it is."

Lindsey took a steadying breath. Now was not the time to fall apart. She turned to Rudy. "Since last we spoke, you've had some time to think. Have you remembered anything more about the night Phoebe Carter was killed?"

Rudy shook his head. "I know I was with her that night. I remember we left Tom Boggs's party together."

"Do you recall who was at the party, aside from your usual friends?"

"Just fellas. I remember seeing Winslow and Finch— you remember them, don't you, sis?"

"Of course." *Edward Winslow and Martin Finch.* More young rakes hardly worth the trouble it took to raise them.

"Who else was there?"

"Mostly they were gents I didn't know."

"Is there anything more you recall?"

"I don't remember where I took her. God, I wish I did."

"There was a party at the Blue Moon that night. Is there a chance you took her there?"

He frowned. "Could have, I suppose." He looked at Aunt Delilah, his face a study in misery. "There is something I didn't tell you. After we left Tom's house, Phoebe took me to a place...I don't remember the name. They smoke opium there, down in the basement."

Aunt Dee gripped the back of a chair. "Dear God, Rudolph."

"I just tried it the once, Auntie. I won't ever do it again."

"Oh, Rudy." The constable's words rang in Lindsey's ears. *You don't ever really know a person.* Was it possible the drug Rudy took could have affected him enough to do murder?

She would find out more about the substance, see if such a thing could occur.

"I was just having fun," Rudy said softly. "I never meant for any of this to happen."

Lindsey forced herself to smile. "You mustn't worry, dearest. We'll figure all of this out. With all of us working together, we'll find the guilty party."

She looked at Rudy, saw the anguish and fear in his face. Her resolve strengthened. Whatever her brother had gotten himself into these past months, deep down, Rudy was the same earnest young man he had always been.

And that young man wasn't a murderer.

Nine

Wearing the orange satin gown, her hair left in loose curls down her back, Lindsey stood in front of the mirror in her bedroom, trying to work up the courage to leave.

"Good Lord!"

She whirled at the shocked tone of Delilah's voice. "Aunt Dee! I—I thought you were asleep."

"I heard you moving about. I knew you were worried about your brother so I came to check on you." Delilah's lips firmed. "Where did you get that dreadful, outlandish dress and why, in the name of God, are you made up the way you are?"

"I'm, ahh…I'm, ahh…"

"I want the truth, young lady, and I want it now."

She let out a sigh. "You are beginning to sound like Thor."

"Thor…yes, well, that is another subject we need to discuss. At the moment I want to know why you are dressed as a…as a…"

"Lady of the evening?" she supplied.

"To put it politely, yes."

"It's a bit of a tale, Aunt Dee. If you are certain you wish to hear it, you had better close the door."

The door firmly closed.

With no other choice but to tell her aunt the truth, Lindsey began to explain as simply and briefly as possible, the efforts she had made to clear her brother's name.

"So you went down to Covent Garden," Delilah confirmed.

"That's right. That was where the murders took place. I wanted to talk to the people there, try to find out if someone might have seen or heard something that might prove useful."

"Did you discover anything?"

"Not that night, which is why I'm going back."

"Going back? But it's nearly midnight!"

"The women who were killed were prostitutes, Aunt Dee. The places prostitutes frequent aren't open in the daytime. I already tried that."

"But—"

"There is no need to worry. I am going with Thor. I promise you I will be perfectly safe."

"I realize the man is as big as a house, but—"

"He saved my life, Aunt Dee. I probably shouldn't tell you, but it's true."

Her aunt sank down heavily on the tapestry stool in front of Lindsey's dresser.

"As I said, I was trying to come up with something that would help prove Rudy's innocence. I went to Covent Garden last night and I took Elias with me."

"Good heavens, is that where he got into a fight?"

She nodded.

"And you have a bruise on your cheek, as well." She sighed. "You had better tell me the rest."

Wishing there were some other way, Lindsey told her aunt about disguising herself in Rudy's clothes. She told her about the run-in they'd had with the awful men at the gaming hall.

"Krista knew what I was planning and she told Thor. If he hadn't come along when he did, we both might now be dead."

"Good Lord." Her aunt shook her head. "Your brother in prison. You running about dressed first as a man and now as a strumpet. I don't know what I am going to do."

"Well, if we don't do *something,* Rudy is going to hang."

Delilah gazed down at her lap. "I know."

"I have to go, Aunt Dee. With Thor I will be safe."

"How can you be sure?"

Lindsey grinned. "I have seen him fight."

Aunt Dee rolled her eyes. "It is my duty as your chaperone to prevent you from putting yourself in danger."

Lindsey opened her mouth to argue.

"On the other hand—you are a grown woman. And I imagine unless I order the footmen to tie you to the chair, there is no way to keep you here."

"None whatsoever."

Aunt Dee's gaze ran over her gaudy, indecent dress. "Perhaps a tucker…?" she suggested, referring to a bit of lace that could be tucked into the low-cut top.

Lindsey laughed. "I'm afraid that might be missing the point."

She sighed. "Yes, I suppose it would."

Lindsey leaned over and kissed her aunt's cheek. "I've got to go. Thor will be waiting."

"Do you have any idea how highly unsuitable that man is for you? He has no title, no wealth of any consequence— why, he isn't even an Englishman. Thor Draugr is the last man with whom you should be keeping company."

"He is only trying to help. Thor and I are just friends."

One of Aunt Dee's black eyebrows went up. "It is difficult to remain friends with a man who looks like that."

Lindsey clamped down on an urge to agree. "Nevertheless…" Grabbing her cloak and reticule, she headed for the door.

Thor would be waiting.

Her stomach lifted at the thought.

Thor paced the darkness outside the arched gate at the back of the garden. It was ten minutes after twelve. Mayhap Lindsey was unable to get away.

Mayhap, gods willing, the girl had come to her senses.

The wooden gate creaked open and a cloaked figure slipped through.

"I'm sorry I am late," Lindsey said. "My aunt came in just as I was ready to leave. She demanded to know why I was wearing this awful dress. I had no choice but to tell her the truth."

"Your aunt let you leave dressed as a whore?"

She shrugged her slim shoulders. "Rudy might hang. Neither of us has a choice."

No choice. He was surrounded by women too bold for their own good. Tonight he escorted a woman who believed she had no choice but to dress up like a doxy and go into one of the roughest sections of the city to protect a brother who seemed unworthy of the risk she was taking.

Inwardly he cursed, but he couldn't suppress a hint of admiration.

Taking Lindsey's arm, he guided her toward the carriage. When she caught a glimpse of the man inside, she halted at the bottom of the narrow iron stairs.

"My brother is coming with us," Thor explained. Lindsey had told Krista about the attack outside the Blue Moon. Krista had told Leif, who insisted on coming along. "I told him he was not needed, but mayhap it is better that he is here."

Lindsey smiled. "Well, I will certainly be safe enough with the two of you." She climbed aboard and settled on the seat across from Leif. Thor's tall, blond brother was even bigger than he was, which left little room inside the carriage.

Thor sat down beside Lindsey, his shoulder touching hers. A spark seemed to leap between them and her gaze shot to his. Thor glanced away, hoping she wouldn't see the lust that simple touch ignited.

As the carriage rolled beneath passing street lamps, he caught glimpses of the orange satin dress beneath the opening at the front of her cloak. She had reddened her lips and cheeks and left her honey hair in long soft curls down her back. She should have looked like one of Madame Fortier's paid-for women but she did not.

With her delicate cheekbones and fine features, she was beautiful. He looked at her and when she smiled, when those ruby lips curved as if in invitation, hunger hit him like a fist. His shaft filled and heat pooled thick and heavy in his groin.

By the gods, he never should have kissed her. He still didn't understand what demon had momentarily stolen his wits. Only moments before, he had vowed not to let her know how much he wanted her. One burning kiss made the fact more than clear.

It was a cruel joke that he had never tasted sweeter lips, never felt such a violent stab of desire for a woman. It angered him that the woman should be Lindsey, a willful female, exactly the sort he disdained.

And it worried him. This wild need for her was something he had expected to feel for the life-mate the gods had chosen for him. But Lindsey could never be his mate. They were completely ill-suited. And yet he ached with desire for her, couldn't get this need of her out of his head. They shared no common destiny and yet he wanted her. More than any woman he had known.

Thor silently cursed.

The first stop was the Golden Pheasant, one of Covent Garden's finer establishments—which wasn't saying much. As they walked inside, Thor took Lindsey's cloak and handed it to a servant who stood next to the door.

"We won't be long," Thor said.

Lindsey glanced around. She had been there with Elias, dressed as a man, but the manager hadn't been in and no one else seemed able to help them. The place was a cut above the Blue Moon, the clientele well-dressed and the establishment clean. Thor started walking, urging her forward with a hand at her waist. She could feel the heat of his touch through the slippery satin, and a little flutter rose in her stomach.

His sideways glance caught her by surprise. She could feel the heat of it moving over her breasts, making her nipples tighten. Her breasts were not large, but the dress fit so snugly they pushed up into the V at the front, exposing the soft white swells and all but her suddenly aching nipples.

Thor glanced from her to Leif, but his brother seemed not to notice.

"Is something the matter?" she asked innocently, knowing full well he was worried about how much of her the dress exposed. Reaching inside his coat, he pulled a crisp white handkerchief from his pocket and stuffed it down the front of her dress.

"Now we can go."

She bit back a grin. Before she could tell him that covering up her bosom was not something a woman who sold her body would do, Leif reached over and plucked out the square of white linen.

"She is playing a role," he said. "Leave her be."

Thor stiffened. "You would not say that if she were Krista."

"Krista is my wife." An odd look came over Leif's face. "So that is the way it is. I should have seen it sooner."

"There is nothing for you to see." He urged Lindsey forward. "Come. It is time we got the answers we came for."

They made their way to the back of the gaming hall, Lindsey walking between the two giant men, one dark, one fair, both with beautiful, crystalline blue eyes. If she had doubted the story Thor told her about the Viking life they had lived on his island, seeing them together this way, she no longer did.

That the men were warriors was clear. It was there in the way they moved, in the confidence that said there wasn't a man in the room who could best either one of them. Any lingering fear from her previous evening dissolved as the people in the room parted to let them pass as if a knife blade cut the crowd in two.

"We wish to speak to Mr. Adams," Leif said to a young man seated at a desk behind the door leading into the office.

Adams was the manager. "Do you know him?" Lindsey asked.

"I used to gamble here. I haven't been back in some time."

Great heavens, how could she have forgot? Before he married Krista, Leif Draugr made a fortune at the gaming tables, enough to win her father's approval and start his shipping business. It was said there was never a card player who was better.

"I'm Mr. Adams. You wished to see me?" The manager smoothed a light-brown mustache. He smiled as he recognized Leif. "Mr. Draugr. It's been a while. It's good to see you. What can I do for you?"

"We'd like to ask you about the night Phoebe Carter was murdered."

Adams shook his head, moving strands of hair he had parted in the middle and carefully combed back on each side. "Nasty bit of business. According to the papers, it happened just a few blocks away. I was working that night."

"Do you know a young man named Rudolph Graham?" Lindsey asked. Her brother's arrest was not yet common knowledge. Tomorrow the story would be in every newspaper in the city.

"I'm sorry, it's our policy to keep our clients' names private."

"He woke up in one of your rooms the morning after the murder," Thor said.

"I see."

"He was here," Thor pressed. "Do you know if the Carter woman was with him?"

"She wasn't here that night. If she had been, after her murder, it would have been the talk of the place. She wasn't here."

"But Rudy was," Lindsey pressed. "Do you know if there is someone who might have seen him?"

She thought Adams wasn't going to answer, but the warning in Thor's blue eyes changed his mind.

"We furnish a room with cots for anyone who drinks too much and needs to sleep it off. Someone on the night cleaning staff might have seen him. They start work at three. If you will follow me, you can speak to Mr. Stubbs."

They followed the manager across the room and out through a door at the back of the club. They found Stubbs hunched over a broom, sweeping the floor, an old man with iron-gray hair and years of hardship etched into his face. The manager left them in the old man's company.

"There was a murder here a couple of weeks ago," Leif began. "Have you heard about it?"

"Who ain't? Kilt her just a few blocks from here."

"Your boss says you were working the night she was killed," Thor said. "Did you see a lad come back here to use one of the cots?"

"Slender, sandy hair?" Lindsey added. "He was extremely inebriated. He woke up passed out on the floor."

Thor handed the old man a coin and his veined hand curled around it.

"I seen him. He were so foxed he could barely stand. Can't remember when he come in…maybe an hour or so after I got here. I seen him back here before."

She didn't like the sound of that. Gambling could become a very bad habit. As heir to the Renhurst barony, it was a habit Rudy could ill afford.

"The lad was alone?" Thor asked

The old man nodded.

"There is a place," Thor said. "The drug—opium—is smoked there. Do you know it?" When the old man hesitated, Thor handed him another coin.

"House of Dreams, they call it. Never been there meself. Bad stuff that."

"Where is it?" Lindsey asked.

When he didn't answer, Thor gave him another coin. "Where," he said simply.

"A basement in the Strand. Place sits on the corner of Strand and Percy. But they won't let you in, not unless you know somebody."

Thor's jaw hardened. "They will let us in."

Stubbs tilted his head back to look up at the man who towered a foot above him. "I'll just bet they will."

"Your brother went into the cot room an hour after the old man got there," Thor said as the carriage rolled toward the Strand.

"Which according to Mr. Adams was around three o'clock," Lindsey said, "which makes Rudy's arrival somewhere near four."

"You need to find out what time the witness claims to have seen Rudy running from the scene of the crime," Leif said. "And you need to find out why she believes it was your brother."

Lindsey thought the handsome police lieutenant who

had helped her before and the ball being given by the Earl of Kittridge, where the lieutenant was likely to be. "I may be able to find that out."

Thor cast her a look, but made no comment. He sat so close she could feel his chest expanding as he breathed. An image of him working in the back room of the office, his shirt open, exposing that same massive chest, made her face go hot and the cool night suddenly warm.

"Your brother and the Carter woman went to the House of Dreams," Leif said, drawing her attention and thankfully Thor's, as well. "Then your brother went to the Golden Pheasant."

"That's right, but Phoebe wasn't with him. Perhaps he dropped her off at the party at the Blue Moon."

"I do not think so," Thor said. "A man that drunk…if he went there, he likely would never have made it to the Golden Pheasant."

"I think you are right."

"You need to know what other men Phoebe Carter spent time with," Leif said. "Perhaps one of them was jealous of Rudy."

"I should have thought of that," Lindsey said, feeling a jolt of excitement. "A jealous man might purposely make it look as if Rudy were the guilty party."

"Her flatmates will know," Thor said.

"But how do we get them to tell us?"

One of Thor's dark eyebrows went up. He dug out his pouch of coins and held it in the glow of the lamp burning inside the carriage. "We will pay them. They sell their bodies. Answering questions is far easier work."

Leif grinned. "Not bad, little brother." He lounged

against the deep velvet cushions of the carriage, his shoulders nearly filling his side of the seat. "I think you may have a knack for this sort of thing."

Lindsey studied both men. It was obvious Leif was intelligent. He dressed impeccably, had perfect manners. He had taught himself everything he needed to know to fit flawlessly into society.

She studied Thor from beneath her lashes as he reclined in the seat beside her. He was different, softer spoken, less driven, well-dressed but in a simpler, more straightforward manner. She had noticed that he always seemed to observe what was happening around him without any conscious effort. He had a way of absorbing and analyzing details other people missed.

The more she got to know him, the more she was coming to believe she had been wrong about him. That she had underestimated his intelligence. That in a different way, he was just as smart as his brother.

"I've read about opium," Leif said. "It's a dangerous, addictive drug when it's misused."

"People take laudanum for headaches," Lindsey said. "There's opium in that."

"That's right," Leif said. "But opium taken through a pipe is a far stronger dose. According to what I've read, it puts the user in a state of euphoria, a dream-like trance so pleasant it becomes addictive. Your brother is fortunate he only tried it once."

"Percy Street!" the coachman called out just then, pulling the carriage over to the edge of the road.

Thor made a sweeping survey of the area while Leif opened the door and jumped down. Thor followed, then turned to help Lindsey down, his big hands reaching out to wrap around her waist. A warm tingle went through her. As he set her on her feet, his gaze locked with hers, the bluest eyes she had ever seen. Something hot and fierce burned in their depths an instant before he released her.

Lindsey's heart pounded. Dear God, when had it happened that the man could merely touch her and all sorts of improper thoughts rose into her head?

Or had it always been that way? Was that the reason she had taken such pains to avoid him?

They made their way round the brick building to a side entrance that led the rooms below. Stone stairs descended to an arched wooden door leading into a basement. A big, beefy man with a small gold ring in his ear stood guard outside the door, his thick arms folded over his chest.

"Is this the place called the House of Dreams?" Thor asked.

"Who wants to know?"

Lindsey moved in front of Thor, parting her cloak, letting the beefy man view the pale swells of her breasts. "We're friends of a client," she said with what she hoped was a seductive smile. "Mr. Rudy Graham? He was a patron several weeks back."

The guard's dark eyes moved over her bosom and beside her, Thor stiffened. She stepped on his foot in warning. Dammit, she was playing the role *he* had suggested.

"Wait here." The guard disappeared through the door, closing it firmly behind him.

A few minutes later, a woman appeared, tall and stunningly beautiful, with thick dark red hair and deep-set green eyes. Her gaze lit for a moment on Leif, skimmed past Lindsey as if she weren't there, and fixed on Thor. It was obvious she liked what she saw.

"So, you're friends of the future Baron Renhurst."

"Aye," Thor answered, since the woman's statement was addressed to him. "Rudy told us about this place. He thought we might enjoy a visit."

Her gaze ran over Thor's perfectly sculpted features and amazing blue eyes, took in his long legs, trim hips, massive shoulders and chest. It was clear there was no padding in his coat. Lindsey ignored a twinge of jealousy she had no right to feel.

"We have certain rules here," the woman said. "I don't allow strangers—but since you are Mr. Graham's friends, I believe I can make an exception." She stepped back out of the way, allowing them entrance. "My name is Sultry Weaver. Welcome to the House of Dreams."

Thor set a hand at Lindsey's waist, urging her forward, and Leif fell in behind them. Lindsey paused just inside the door, her stunned gaze barely able to take in the sight in front of her. The low-ceilinged room was nearly dark, lit only by rows of flickering candles. The fragrance of incense filled the air, along with the soft, sweet smell of pipe smoke.

A dozen cots lined the walls. Only a few were empty. Most held an occupant who either slept or drew on the long, flexible stem of a pipe. The brass bowl, on a table beside the cot, was heated by the flame of a candle, which turned the drug into smoke.

"Would you like to try it?" Sultry asked. "I can guarantee your dreams will be pleasant ones." Her gaze ran over Thor and she looked as if she itched to reach out and touch him, slide her long, slim fingers over his muscular body.

Lindsey's stomach tightened. Sultry was beautiful, her waist tiny, her bosom full and tempting, the sort of figure a man couldn't resist. Lindsey looked up at Thor, dreading to see the same hot look in his eyes she had seen when he looked at her.

Thor seemed unaware of the woman's rare beauty or her obvious interest, and relief filtered through her. It was ridiculous. She had no claim on Thor.

"We are not here to dream," he said simply. "We would like to know about Rudolph Graham. He came here last with a woman named Phoebe Carter. Later that night, she was murdered."

"What our clients do is their business. We protect their privacy and that is the reason they feel free to come here."

"We aren't asking you about what happened here," Leif said. "Rudy Graham has been arrested for Phoebe Carter's murder. We are trying to prove his innocence."

"I am Rudy's sister," Lindsey added on impulse, hoping it might help sway the woman in their favor.

Sultry's brilliant green gaze ran over her, noting the face paint and low-cut, orange gown, guessing the role she played. "You're the daughter of a baron, yet you're willing to go to dangerous lengths for your brother. He must mean a great deal to you."

"I love Rudy. My brother is innocent. We need your help to prove it."

"Would you happen to recall what time Rudy and Miss Carter came in?" Leif asked.

Sultry hesitated, then seemed to make a decision. "They came in around two o'clock, I think, but I am not completely sure."

"Do you know where they might have been going when they left?" Lindsey asked.

"Your brother left by himself. Phoebe remained for a short while after. She came often. She earned her dream-time by bringing new clients."

"How long did she stay?"

"Only a few minutes. We spoke about another client she was hoping to bring in, then she was gone."

"Did she tell you the client's name?"

"I'm afraid not, and even if she had, I wouldn't tell you."

"Do you know where Phoebe was going?"

"She was headed back to her flat. It isn't that far away."

"But she was murdered before she got there," Thor said darkly.

Sultry sighed, moving the rich red curls resting on her bare shoulders. Her gown of striped black-and-gold silk was expensive, low-cut but stylish. "I read about it in the newspaper. That's why I remembered seeing them that night. Poor, dear Phoebe. Such a terrible end."

"Did Phoebe leave by herself?" Lindsey asked.

"I think so, but again, I can't be sure." Sultry turned toward the people on the cots. One stirred, then rose to his feet. Swaying a bit, he staggered toward a door at the back of the dimly lit room and disappeared outside.

"People leave as they wish. They can only come in through the front, but they can go out through the back whenever they desire."

Sultry glanced around, anxious to return to her business. Lindsey took the hint. "You've been a great help, Miss Weaver. We are ever in your debt."

Sultry looked at Thor, reached up and lightly touched his cheek. "Stop by sometime…even if you don't want to dream."

The edge of Thor's mouth faintly curved. "Mayhap sometime I will." But he didn't seem truly interested in accepting the woman's offer.

Then again, perhaps he would reconsider. Sultry was a beautiful woman and Thor was an extremely masculine man.

The thought made Lindsey's stomach knot again.

Ten

"We can prove Rudy left Phoebe Carter at the House of Dreams," Lindsey said to Thor as the carriage rumbled along. "The police will have to release him."

They had dropped Leif off at his town house, the first stop on the route. Thor was escorting her home then returning to his flat near Green Park.

"The police will say he waited for Phoebe down the block and murdered her on her way home."

Lindsey sighed. "Why are they so certain it was Rudy?"

Thor's gaze found hers. "Your brother is heir to a barony. He has power, money, and position. I think Constable Bertram gets satisfaction out of having a man of Rudy's class under his finger."

"You mean under his thumb."

His mouth edged up. "You would know. You also have a knack for wrapping men around your thumb."

She grinned. "In this case, the word is finger." When he opened his mouth, she shook her head. "Never mind." She smiled up at him. "Thank you for helping me."

Thor leaned back against the velvet seat. "We need more answers."

"I know."

"Next time, we will go earlier, talk to Phoebe's flatmates before they leave for the evening."

"How does that work, exactly? I mean, they're prostitutes but they don't live in a house like Madame Fortier's. How do they get customers?"

He shrugged his powerful shoulders. "Sometimes they go to parties, meet men there. Arrangements are made through friends. Sometimes a woman has a protector, a man who is the only one she sees." He straightened, his head going up till he nearly touched the roof of the carriage. "This is not a proper subject for a lady to discuss."

Lindsey laughed. "I am dressed as a strumpet and we just came from an opium den. I think it is a bit late to worry about propriety."

Thor sighed. "You are a vexing female, Lindsey."

She ignored him, toyed with a fold of her gaudy orange satin skirt. "The last time you took me home, you kissed me. Did you like it?"

His brilliant gaze sharpened on her face. "This is another subject we should not discuss."

"Did you?"

A muscle clenched in his jaw. "Aye, lady, you've lips as sweet as honey, as smooth as the petals of a rose. Are you satisfied?"

Satisfied? Those words made her heart hammer like rain on tin and her breasts begin to swell. "I just…I wondered. I've thought about it a great deal and I think you should kiss me again."

His eyes locked with hers. "No," he said flatly.

"Why not?"

He released a long sigh. "Because you are a maid. I am trying to protect you, Lindsey, but I am not one of your saints. If I kiss you, I will want more." He shifted on the seat, adjusted his coat to cover the front of his trousers. "Already I want more and I have not touched you."

Her heart lifted. He wanted her. She wasn't alone in her secret desires.

She studied his handsome profile as he sat on the seat beside her, thought of the amazing kiss they had shared. In that moment, she made a decision. Her aunt believed if a woman was discreet she could enjoy the same freedoms as a man. Lindsey wasn't ready for marriage and even when the time came, odds were it would be a marriage based on practicality, not passion. Her parents would insist she find a suitable husband, a man who would likely turn out to be more companion than lover.

She might never know what it was like to experience the kind of feelings Thor stirred with a single kiss.

"I can only imagine what you will think of me when I tell you this, but I am not a maid."

"What?"

She steeled herself. Once he knew the truth, he might look at her with disgust. He might think she was the same sort of woman as the ones who worked at Madame Fortier's.

It was a risk she had to take.

"I was sixteen when I became a woman. I thought I was in love…and I was curious. One night I let my suitor… I let him have his way with me. It was over in minutes and extremely disappointing—at least for me. It never happened again."

"This man stole your innocence—tell me his name and I will kill him."

She hid a smile. "You needn't kill him—it wasn't his fault. I encouraged him. It was stupid, I know, but at the time I thought I was in love."

"He should have wed you."

"He asked. I refused. I was too young to marry, and by then I knew I didn't want him for a husband."

Thor mulled that over. "Why do you tell me this?"

"Because now that you know you won't ruin me, we can make love." She studied him from beneath her lashes, suddenly uncertain. "That is, if you want to. I mean, you don't have to feel obligated. It just seems we have this mutual attraction and I thought maybe you would want—"

"Stop. Do not say another word."

"But—"

"Not one more word."

She stared down at her lap. He was angry. Somehow she had insulted him. Or perhaps she had read more into his desire for her than he actually felt. She bit down on her lip. Now that he knew the truth, perhaps he would refuse to help her. Tomorrow, Leif was leaving town on business. That left only Elias and he wasn't much good as a protector.

She looked up at Thor. "I am sorry. I didn't mean to upset you. I just…I thought…I don't know that much about making love…I mean, I just tried it the once. I thought with you it would be different and I—"

"Lindsey," he said softly. "You are killing me, sweetheart."

She just stared at him.

"There is nothing I want more than to make love to you. But you are Krista's friend. You are a lady, no matter how much you might wish it were not so."

She swallowed, an odd lump building in her throat. "Even ladies have needs, Thor." She glanced away. "Sometimes I get so lonely. My parents are never at home. Rudy is out with his friends. My aunt is there but it isn't the same. Sometimes at night I lie there, aching to be held, wishing someone were there who truly cared for me."

To her horror, her eyes filled. Frantically, she dug into her reticule in search of a handkerchief, looking up at the touch of Thor's hand against her cheek.

Bending toward her, he very softly kissed her. "You are too beautiful to be lonely. It hurts me to know that you are."

Lindsey slid her hand around his neck and lifted her mouth to his. Thor hesitated only a moment, then claimed her lips as if he owned them. It was a wild, fierce, burning kiss that left no doubt as to his desire for her. Her body softened, heated, turned liquid. Desire tugged low in her belly and Lindsey swayed toward him.

"Thor…" She kissed him sweetly, then deepened the kiss, parting her lips, making a tiny mewling sound as his tongue slid inside to taste her.

Heat and need burned through her. She had never known anything like it. She wanted to feel his skin against hers, wanted his heavy weight on top of her, his massive chest burning into her breasts. She wanted to be joined with him so urgently for a moment she was afraid.

His lips moved to the side of her neck, kissing her softly, nibbling her ear, gentling her as if he read her thoughts.

"I won't hurt you," he said softly. "I would never hurt

you, Lindsey." And then he kissed her again and all she could think of was Thor and how much she wanted him. He opened the front of her cloak and she could feel his eyes on her breasts. Her nipples tightened and began to throb and damp heat slid into her core.

"So lovely," he said, pressing his mouth against the pale swells pushed up in the low-cut opening of the dress. "At night, when I close my eyes, I remember how pretty they were that night when I saw you naked. I remember the hard little tips and I ache to taste them."

The gown, fashioned for a lady of the evening, was made to come open easily and he loosened it with an ease that amazed her. She felt his big hands sliding inside to cup a breast, then he lowered his head and took her aching nipple into his mouth.

Lindsey moaned and slid her fingers into his wavy, dark hair. *Dear God in heaven.* Heat engulfed her. Blood pounded at her temples. She wanted more of him, wanted to rip open his shirt and press her lips against his skin so fiercely her hands started shaking. The thought of stopping made her almost physically ill.

"Thor…" With her eyes closed and hot sensation pouring through her, she was barely aware that the carriage had rolled to a stop and that Thor was pulling her gown back into place.

"If I could, I would make love to you, Lindsey. We both know that cannot happen. But when you are in bed tonight, remember there is a man who wants you above all things, and you will not be lonely."

Her eyes misted. "Thor…"

"Promise me you will remember."

She swallowed past the lump in her throat. "I will remember."

Thor climbed down from the carriage and helped her down.

She took a steadying breath, wishing the beat of her heart would slow. Around her, the night air began to restore her senses. An owl hooted in the darkness above the carriage house. "Will you…will you be working at the paper tomorrow?"

"I am working on the docks."

It was surely for the best, or at least she tried to convince herself. She straightened, forced her thoughts away from Thor, back to the problem of finding a murderer. "We need to speak to Phoebe's roommates again, find out if she was seeing someone special. Tomorrow I have a party I need to attend. Shall we go the evening after?"

"We should not be together, Lindsey. If I had not vowed to help you—"

"But you did."

He sighed. "And I am bound to keep my word. Leif has loaned me his carriage while he is away. I will pick you up at six o'clock Sunday evening. The women will likely be home."

"Shall I meet you in the alley?"

"Aye. It would be best if your neighbors did not see us together."

"Should I wear the orange dress?"

The edge of his mouth tipped up. "The dress has its uses. I can touch you as I please, but since I will not be tasting your lovely breasts again, I think you had best wear something else."

Her stomach contracted and she blushed all the way to her toes. "Well…all right, then. I'll see you Sunday evening." Turning, she started walking toward the gate leading into the garden. Her body still burned, throbbed as it never had before. Thor was determined they would not make love.

But when she wanted something badly, Lindsey could be equally determined.

Leif stood up from behind the desk in his office at Valhalla Shipping. His valise sat at his feet. Outside the window, the *Sea Dragon* bobbed in its berth at the dock. He was packed and ready to leave for his weeklong journey north in the hope of adding additional ports to his packet trading route.

He glanced up as a light knock sounded and the door swung wide. Thor stood in the opening.

"I know you are busy, but I was hoping you could spare a moment before you leave."

"Come in. I've still got a little time." His brother, usually the milder temperament of the two, looked upset and worried as Leif had rarely seen him.

"From the look on your face, I'm guessing this has something to do with Lindsey."

Thor settled into a chair on the opposite side of Leif's desk. "Aye, how did you know?"

"I know because you're my brother and little upsets you. Lindsey can do it without even trying."

"She wants me to make love to her."

"What?" Leif jerked forward in his seat.

"It is hard to explain."

"I think you had better try."

"Your word you will not tell Krista."

"You're my brother. I won't tell anyone. This you know."

Thor sighed. "She is lonely. She needs a man. The woman should be wed and raising a family. Instead she works all the time and sleeps alone."

"There are women who work and also have a husband and family, as Krista does. I have grown used to it. You will, too."

Thor's head came up. "You speak as if we are wed."

"She is your destiny, is she not? Or are you still trying to fool yourself?"

Thor glanced away. "I will admit she makes me feel things other women do not. But I have always wanted a different sort of mate, one who is soft and gentle, one who does not behave as a man. You and Krista—you were perfectly suited from the start. Your wife was clearly meant for you. Lindsey and I, we are two far different people."

"Perhaps it only seems that way."

"I do not think so. I worry about her. I fear for her safety. At night, I ache to have her in my bed. But even if the gods have chosen her for me, it does not mean it will happen. You know this. And even should I wish to wed with her, her parents would not allow it. My earnings are meager. I have no title, no social position."

"You own an interest in Valhalla Shipping that is worth far more than you know. You have saved your money and invested. Your stock in the A&H Railway should earn you a tidy sum."

He nodded. "It appears the railroad is going to be successful. There is great demand for transport in the area. It should be a very good investment. But it is not the money alone. Lindsey is a high-born lady and I am no gentleman.

At least not the sort for opera, or the theater, or to prance about a dance floor."

Leif grinned. "It's an acquired taste, brother. If you give those things a try, you might find you enjoy them."

Thor just grunted.

"So what will you do?"

He shook his head. "I do not know. She would not wed with me, even were I fool enough to ask."

Leif came out of his chair and rounded the desk toward his brother. "I can tell you from experience these matters have a way of working out. Rely on your instincts and your better judgment and you'll be all right."

Thor scoffed. "I cannot rely on my judgment when I am with the lady. My instincts always seem to take over."

Leif smiled. "Who knows, perhaps that is best." He clapped his brother on the shoulder. "Just be prepared to marry the little wench should your *instincts* get you into trouble."

Thor seemed to ponder the words.

Leif wondered if perhaps he was wrong and the girl wasn't meant for his brother. Thor needed a woman to love, someone who would love him in return. He needed someone to share his life as Leif shared his with Krista. But the wrong woman could make a man's life a living hell.

Time would tell.

Leif just hoped Thor could keep his *instincts* under control until his destiny became more certain.

Dressed for the evening in an aqua silk gown and matching kid slippers, Lindsey turned to survey her image in the cheval glass in her bedroom. As was the mode, the bodice rode low on her shoulders and dipped to a V over her breasts. The corseted waistline also dipped into a V, emphasizing the smallness of her waist. Bands of gold silk brightened the full skirt and draped across her bosom, and matching gold ribbon tied back the heavy curls nestled on each side of her neck.

Lindsey turned in the mirror, pleased with her appearance. For an instant, she wished Thor were the man whose attention she sought at the ball instead of Lieutenant Michael Harvey. She chided herself for dreaming. Thor might be the passionate sort of man to inflame her desires but he was hardly a gentleman. He could dress in evening clothes for a night, but she couldn't imagine him making inane conversation just to be pleasant, or sitting through some boring recital merely to be polite.

He was different from other men, more masculine, more virile—more totally *male*. He was the sort of man a woman took for a lover but had no interest in marrying.

The notion disturbed her more than it should have. She couldn't marry a man like Thor. Her family would never approve.

And rightfully so, she told herself, knowing how ill-suited they were.

Still, as she appraised her image in the mirror and thought how well the aqua silk complemented her pale skin and light brown hair, she couldn't help a pang of regret that Thor wouldn't be there to see her in the lovely gown.

With a sigh of resignation, she turned at the light knock on her door. Aunt Dee, her chaperone for the evening, swept into the bedroom.

"My, don't you look splendid."

Lindsey smiled. "And you, as well." In a sophisticated wine silk gown trimmed in dark green velvet and ornamented with tiny seed pearls, her black hair coiled in circles at each side of her long, graceful neck, Delilah Markham was lovely.

Even so, she seemed inordinately nervous, flicking an occasional glance toward the door, and Lindsey couldn't help wondering if perhaps her aunt had dressed for the man who was escorting them this evening, Colonel William Langtree of Her Majesty's Army, recently retired.

The colonel was an acquaintance of Coralee's husband, Gray Forsythe, Earl of Tremaine. Gray had introduced him to Aunt Dee just before he and Corrie left on their belated honeymoon. Since then, Aunt Dee had encountered the colonel on several occasions and always seemed pleased by his attentions.

"Colonel Langtree should be here soon," Lindsey said, just to gauge her aunt's reaction.

Delilah smoothed a nonexistent wrinkle from the front of her wine silk skirt. "I imagine he will. Being a military man, William is always very prompt."

"Considering the circumstances, it was good of him to escort us this evening." Lindsey thought of the headlines in today's *London Times:* Future Baron Arrested in Covent Garden Murders.

The article went on to say that Rudolph Graham, eldest son of the Baron Renhurst, had been taken into custody. The paper relayed the details of the murders, the fact that Rudy had known both victims, and that he had been identified by a witness who had seen him fleeing the scene of the latest crime.

"After what was printed in the paper," Lindsey said, "the evening will be trying at the very least. If I thought Lieutenant Harvey would agree to meet me in private, we wouldn't have to go."

"But you don't think he will."

"He values his career. No, I don't think he will."

"Then we shall have to do the best we can. Besides, it is important we show we are solidly united behind Rudy. We want people to know that we have absolutely no doubt as to his innocence."

"You are right. Besides, I need material for my column. I haven't gone out enough lately."

Aunt Dee raised a fine black eyebrow. "Too bad you can't write about your nightly adventures. I am sure your readers would be quite entertained with the story of your trip to a brothel."

Lindsey flushed. "I'm sure they would. I, however, would never be able to show my face in society again."

Aunt Dee sighed. "Unless we prove your brother's innocence that may well happen anyway."

Hearing a commotion in the entry, Lindsey walked over and pulled open the bedroom door. "I believe the colonel is arrived downstairs."

Delilah's eyes brightened. "Well then, we had better not keep him waiting." Without further ado, the women left the bedroom and descended the stairs to where the colonel stood in the entry.

"Ladies," he said with an appreciative smile, a tall, handsome man with blond hair touched with silver and a very distinguished silver-blond mustache. "What a fortunate man I am to be escorting two beautiful women this evening."

Aunt Dee accepted the colonel's arm. "And you, Colonel, are looking extremely handsome. I shall have to watch myself very closely."

The colonel chuckled. "Not too closely, I pray." The look in his eye spoke volumes.

Lindsey inwardly smiled, hoping her aunt would enjoy her outing with the colonel. As for her, if she got the information she needed, the evening would be worth the strain.

Accepting the velvet-lined cloak the butler draped round her shoulders, she started out the door, hoping Lieutenant Michael Harvey would be as helpful as he had been before.

Eleven

Thor stood in the deep shadows of the garden outside the mansion belonging to the Earl of Kittridge. Through the mullioned windows, he could see into the ballroom, watch the throng of people dressed in fancy silk and lace. An orchestra in silver wigs and blue satin livery played at the far end of the room, and waiters carried heavy silver trays propped on their shoulders, laden with food and drink.

Lindsey stood next to the punch bowl in conversation with her aunt. He had seen her sweep into the room in a pretty silk ball gown some color between blue and green. He had known her instantly, even from a distance. He recognized the way she moved, the way she turned her head, the angle of her chin. There was an elegance and grace about her movements unmatched by any other woman in the room.

He had known she would be there. Worried about the questions she had been asking and the danger she might unknowingly be facing, he had spoken to Krista, whose concerns were the same. His sister-in-law had told him that Lindsey planned to attend a ball at Kittridge House, being given by the earl in celebration of his daughter's birthday.

Thor had arrived shortly before Lindsey and hidden himself away in the shadowy darkness of the shrubbery in the garden, a spot where he could see inside the house.

His gaze sharpened as he spotted Michael Harvey, the police lieutenant, leading Lindsey out onto the dance floor. He watched as the pair stepped into the rhythm of a waltz, the lieutenant holding Lindsey in his arms. As they passed by the window, she smiled at the policeman sweetly, and for the first time in his life, Thor wished he knew the steps of the waltz, wished he were the man holding Lindsey in his arms.

Fool, he told himself. *The woman is not for you.*

But his chest ached as he watched her, and jealousy coiled like a snake in the pit of his stomach.

They danced again a few minutes later, then the lieutenant walked Lindsey out onto the terrace. Thor moved silently closer, knowing he shouldn't, unable to resist.

"People are talking, Lindsey," the policeman said, "whispering about your brother. You should go home. I can see how much it bothers you."

"I don't care what they say. Rudy is innocent. My aunt and I want them to know how certain we are about that. I want them to know it is only a matter of time until Rudy is proved innocent of the crimes."

The lieutenant leaned against the balustrade. "I wish I could help you. You understand the position I'm in."

"I understand. Of course, I do, Michael." She looked up

at him from beneath a thick fringe of lashes. "I hope you don't mind my calling you that—at least when we are alone."

Thor ground his jaw.

The policeman took her gloved hand, brought it to his lips, and pressed a kiss into her palm. It was all Thor could do to remain where he stood in the shadows.

"I don't mind," he said.

Thor's temper heated. *Damned woman.* He wondered if she played a role as she had before or if she was attracted to the handsome policeman.

"After this is over," the lieutenant said, "perhaps I can call on you."

"I would like that, Michael, very much."

Thor's hand fisted. He wanted to drag the man off the terrace and pound him into the dirt. He wanted to toss Lindsey over his shoulder and carry her away from the party.

"As I said, I realize the position you are in, but is there anything you can tell me that might help us in some way?"

"I can tell you the name of the witness, but only because it is going to appear in tomorrow's paper. Some reporter found out. I don't know how. He plans to scoop the other papers with the information."

"I want to talk to her, find out exactly what she saw."

"Her name is Mary Pratt. She lives in the attic of a run-down house in Raven's Court."

"Did she actually see the murder?"

"No. She knew something had happened, but she didn't know what until someone told her. However, apparently, she saw the man as he left the scene of the crime."

"Why didn't she come to the police sooner?"

"She said she was afraid. She thought no one would

believe her. I guess she started thinking that if she didn't help the police catch the man who did it, he would keep on killing women and she might wind up being one of them."

"My brother arrived at the Golden Pheasant around four that morning. Did the woman say what time she saw the man?"

"Sometime around three-thirty. A watchman found Phoebe Carter's body the following morning."

Lindsey reached over and touched his hand. "Thank you, Michael."

Every muscle in Thor's body went tense.

"I wish I could tell you more," Harvey said.

"Lieutenant?" A thin man walked toward him across the terrace. "I'm sorry to bother you, sir, but the chief would like a word with you. He says it's important."

The policeman turned to Lindsey. "I've got to go."

"I'll come inside in a moment. I need a little more air."

The lieutenant squeezed her hand and left her there on the terrace. As soon as he was gone, Thor came out of the shadows. He was angry. Furious, though he had no right to be.

Moving silently, he appeared right beside her. "I see you found your lieutenant."

She whirled at the unexpected sound of his voice. "Good grief—Thor! You scared me half to death! What on earth are you doing here?"

"I am watching you behave like a strumpet. You are getting very good at the role."

Before he could react, Lindsey drew back and slapped him across the cheek. She looked as surprised as he was. Her pretty green eyes filled with tears.

"Just because I told you about what happened when I was sixteen—"

He pressed a finger against her lips, his anger slowly fading. His outburst had nothing to do with her past and everything to do with the present. He took her hand and led her down the steps into the darkness.

"You believe because of what happened I think you are less than pure?"

"You said I was—"

"You are an innocent, Lindsey. That has not changed. What happened when you were a child is unimportant. It does not lessen how much I want you in my bed."

She glanced toward the window. The muffled sounds of a waltz seeped into the garden. She caught a glimpse of Michael Harvey and finally seemed to understand. "I needed information. I did what I had to in order to get it."

He caught her hand, rested it against his burning cheek. "I was jealous. I know I have no right. I am sorry I said those things. You are no whore."

"I didn't mean to hit you. I've never hit anyone before."

His mouth edged up. "I well deserved it."

Lindsey felt the pull of a smile. "Perhaps you did."

"I don't like the way he looks at you. I don't like that he believes you want him."

She cupped his face in her hands. "I don't want him, Thor. The only man I want is you."

He groaned as she went up on her toes and kissed him. Her mouth felt damp and soft under his and she tasted of champagne. Her flowery scent wrapped around him, filled his senses until she was all he could think of.

Do not do this, some foggy part of his brain warned. *She is a maid, no matter her foolish indiscretion.* But when she parted her lips, his tongue slid in to taste her. When she swayed toward him, he eased his hand inside her bodice to cup a lovely pale breast.

Her nipple tightened and Lindsey moaned. "Thor…"

He was hard. So thick and heavy he throbbed with every beat of his heart. He kissed her one last time and reluctantly withdrew his hand.

"We have to stop, sweetheart. Someone might see us." And if they didn't stop soon he would be inside her right there in the garden.

Thor drew her arms from around his neck and eased her a little away. Lindsey stared up at him, a dazed look on her face, as if only now she realized where they were. "Oh, my God."

"Passion is as powerful as any drug," he said, helping her straighten her bodice.

Even in the darkness, he could see the rose that swept into her cheeks. She turned and looked back toward the house. "I have to go in."

"Aye."

"If you came here because you were worried, you needn't be. My aunt and I are escorted by Colonel William Langtree. He was in the army. He is a very capable man."

Capable he might be, but still Thor worried.

"I shall be fine," she said, reading his face.

He sighed. "All right, I will see you at work on the morrow."

"Perhaps we can visit the woman who bore witness against my brother."

He nodded, gave her a gentle shove toward the house. "Go."

Heavy skirts whirling as she turned, Lindsey raced along the path to the terrace and back inside the house. Thor watched her until she disappeared.

He had hurt her tonight, though he had not meant to. Always he had believed that Lindsey was a different sort of woman, the kind who thought she was as tough as a man. But twice he had seen her cry. He had seen that she was as soft and sweet as any other woman. It was just that she hid it from the rest of the world.

Tonight he had been wildly jealous of Michael Harvey.

And so fiercely aroused his entire body still hummed with need.

What he felt for her was different from anything he had felt for a woman before. More and more he was beginning to believe that Lindsey was meant to be his.

Knowing how impossible that would be, Thor prayed to the gods he was wrong.

Sunday morning, Lindsey received a note from Thor. Something had come up, the message said. He would have to postpone their excursion. That *something,* she was sure, was his worry over the passionate kiss they had shared in the garden.

It wasn't until Monday that she saw him.

As she sat at her desk penning her article for the next edition of the gazette, Lindsey carefully kept her mind on the ball she had attended on Saturday night. She described the gala with its lavish bouquets of flowers, magnificent eight-piece orchestra, and glittering decorations. She wrote about the array of wealthy aristocrats and London notables who had attended, and added a bit of gossip.

Lady Marston was *enceinte*—again.

The Duchess of Weyburn had been ill but was now recovering.

A certain Lord F. seemed to have set matters aright with his wife, who no longer threatened divorce.

She smiled at this last. Fulcroft had given her *the cut* last night, but his wife had been quite friendly, grateful, it seemed, that her husband's infidelities had been brought to light and thus had come to an end. It was clear Lady Fulcroft was in love with her husband and that she would rather leave him than share him with another woman.

Lindsey wondered if she would feel that way about the man she married. Unless it was a love match—which she sorely doubted—she probably wouldn't care.

Lady Fulcroft had been friendly, but others at the party had been less gracious. In every corner of the room, there were whispers and speculation about Rudy. Was the heir to Renhurst's fortune and title truly a murderer? Or, as his sister and aunt believed, was the evidence purely circumstantial and pointing in the wrong direction?

Several people had openly asked about her brother's arrest. Each time, Lindsey had firmly defended him.

"My dear brother is completely innocent," she had told Mrs. Marchbanks, a well-known society matron. "It is an utter injustice that he is forced to suffer behind bars as he is."

"How's your brother holding up?" Lord Perry had asked, a longtime friend of her father's.

"He is doing well enough, my lord. It is all an unfortunate misunderstanding, but I'm certain it will be straightened out very soon."

Lord Perry nodded and seemed sympathetic. Still, it had been a trying night, to say the least.

And then there was her encounter with Thor.

Lindsey blushed to think of it. What was there about him that seemed to drive the very wits from her brain? It had to be more than his physical beauty. Surely she wasn't that shallow.

In truth, there was a gentleness about Thor, a kindness and concern she had rarely seen in a man. Twice she had cried in front of him. Lindsey did not allow herself to cry.

With her parents traveling most of the year and much of her life spent in boarding schools, she had learned to take care of herself. She had learned to be strong, to watch out for herself and her younger brother, and rarely let down her guard.

But there was something about Thor that made her feel as if she could trust him, something that made her want to lean on him, allow him to help her solve whatever troubles she might have.

In a way it was frightening.

She was sitting at her desk, pondering the thought, when Bessie Briggs walked up beside her.

"Found this under the door this mornin'. Your name's written on the back."

"Thank you, Bessie." Lindsey looked at the blue lettering on the note, then broke the seal and began to read.

You want to save your brother, look for the killer among his friends.

Good grief! She studied the note front and back, searching for a clue as to who might have sent it, but the paper was blank except for her name on the outside and the words scrolled on the inside.

Look for the killer among his friends.

Her mind went over the possibilities the message posed, but in truth, the words seemed more a jest than a serious attempt to help Rudy. It was the sort of prank Tom Boggs or Marty Finch might enjoy, getting Lindsey to send the police on a wild chase after Rudy's friends.

She tapped the note thoughtfully. Catching sight of Thor in the back of the office, she steeled her mind against those passionate moments in the garden and carried the note in to show him.

"What is this?"

"Bessie found it under the door when she came in to work."

He took the note from her hand and read the contents. He looked up at her, studied her face. "You do not give it credence."

She shrugged. He always seemed able to sense a person's feelings. "Not really. I think it is something one of Rudy's friends might do as a prank. Perhaps whoever wrote it thought it would be funny to have the police tracking down Rudy's acquaintances."

"It does not seem funny to me." He handed the note back to her. "Is there a man among your brother's friends who would do murder?"

"Great heavens, no. They are all spoiled and selfish, but I cannot think of one who is anything but harmless."

"Still, it is something to keep in mind."

She nodded, looked up at him. "We need to speak to Phoebe's roommates, as we had planned."

"Aye, and the woman, Mary Pratt, who accused your brother of the crime."

"Her especially."

"We can go there now. We will take my brother's carriage."

She needed to finish her article, but she still had plenty of time and this was far more important. She made a quick trip to the front of the office to collect her wrap, then preceded Thor out the back door leading into the alley.

Leif's carriage was parked a short ways away. Thor called out to the driver, commanding him to bring the vehicle forward. The driver flicked the reins and the two matched bays leaned into their traces. The shiny black carriage rolled to a stop in front of the alley door.

Thor helped Lindsey climb in then climbed in himself, settling his big frame on the seat across from her. As the vehicle rumbled toward the house occupied by Mary Pratt, Lindsey studied Thor's face, trying for some clue as to what he was thinking. His expression remained inscrutable.

"I…um…I thought we might talk about what happened in the garden."

Thor's dark head came up. His gaze found hers across the carriage. "If you wish for me to apologize, then I will. I behaved badly and—"

"Don't be silly. You did not behave badly. I was the one who kissed you—not the other way around."

Thor sighed. "Fine, then there is naught to discuss. Except that I touched you as I shouldn't have and I will not do so again."

"Why not?"

A muscle jerked in his cheek. "Gods' breath, woman, you

know well enough why not. You are a lady and I am no gentleman. We are not wed and never will be. That is why not."

"You sleep with other women who are not your wife, why not me?"

"The others are whores. It is their job to pleasure a man."

"What if I want to be pleasured? You are extremely good at kissing and touching. I imagine you would be very good at giving a woman pleasure."

His jaw clenched. He moved so quickly she gasped, lifting her off the seat and onto his lap. "You tempt a man, lady. Feel what you do to me?"

Her eyes widened at the thick, hard ridge beneath her skirts, its remarkable breadth and length evident even through the layers of her petticoats.

"Oh, my…"

"I cannot take you, Lindsey. We are not suited—you know this. I would make a poor choice of husband."

"I'm not asking you to be my husband. I am asking you to be my lover." She wriggled a bit and he groaned. "It's obvious you want me. Why can we not make love?"

"By Odin!" He clamped down on his jaw and his eyes glittered like burning coals. With a growl low in his throat, he lifted her again, set her astride his thighs, reached out and pulled the curtains down over the windows.

"What…what are you doing?"

"You wished for me to pleasure you—that is what I am going to do."

Clasping the back of her neck, he pulled her mouth up to his for a deep, burning kiss. His lips seemed to melt into hers and heat tumbled through her. Her heart pounded as if she were running a race and moisture dampened the place between her legs. Lindsey wrapped her arms around Thor's neck and kissed him back with the same fiery passion, then stiffened at the touch of his hand beneath her skirts.

Thor kissed her again, sampling and tasting, gentling her, stroking the inside of her mouth with his tongue. He kissed her until the tension left her body and she melted against him. Warm shivers rose on her calf, her knee as his hand moved higher. He widened his thighs, forcing her legs apart, opening her to give him access, and reached inside the slit in her drawers.

Lindsey gasped at the intimate touch of his fingers, the sound muffled by the crush of his mouth over hers and the deep sweep of his tongue. Long, drugging kisses turned her mind to mush. Fierce, ravaging kisses had her writhing against his hand.

"Is this what you want, Lindsey?" As if in answer, a soft mewling came from her throat. Thor's chest rumbled with male satisfaction. "Just this once, I will give you what you want."

Her eyes closed as he began to stroke her, gently at first, touching her as no man ever had. She hadn't known this was part of lovemaking. Tyler had simply opened his trousers, freed himself, and clumsily plunged inside her. Thor stroked and plundered, touched and caressed, and set her body on fire.

She was drenched and arching against him when he began to tease the throbbing bud of her sex. Desire washed through her, built and heightened. Her breath caught and suddenly she came apart.

Pleasure swamped her, hot and wild, so sweet she could almost taste it. The heavens seemed to open and stars glittered behind her eyes. Thor muffled her passionate cries with his kiss, kept her on the edge of pleasure until she reached the pinnacle again, then held her as she slowly spiraled down.

Lindsey clung to him. She could feel the rapid beat of his heart and knew he was not as unaffected as he seemed. Her own heart refused to slow. *Dear God in heaven!*

Never in a lifetime could she have guessed what it might be like!

He kissed her softly one last time. "I have given you what you wanted," he said. "Once you are wed, you will know this pleasure and more."

Lindsey shook her head, an unexpected tightness in her throat. "No, I won't. I'll marry some wealthy aristocrat like Tyler Reese who won't know the first thing about making love."

"Reese? That is his name?"

"It was a long time ago, Thor. Ty is a different man now. The point is whatever time the two of us have together is all I'm ever going to know of passion."

Thor set her back on the opposite seat. "You cannot know what fate has planned for you. I will not be the man to steal that from you."

Lindsey didn't say more. Her body still throbbed sweetly with the pleasure Thor had given her. And he had said there was more.

Lindsey wanted to know all of it.

And she wanted to know it with Thor.

Twelve

~~~~~∽⟨⟩∽⟨⟩∽~~~~~

The carriage turned into Raven Court, an area of run-down tenements not far from the House of Dreams. It was just off Bedford Lane, the route Phoebe must have taken to go home.

It took two stops to discover which building was occupied by Mary Pratt. Lindsey let Thor guide her toward an outside entrance where wooden stairs, chipped and bleached with age, led up to an attic above the second floor of an old wood-frame house. Filth littered the yard and the stench of sewage and rotting garbage hung in the air.

"I could talk to her for you," Thor offered, his gaze sweeping the dirt and muck on the ground, then going to the hem of her gray wool skirt.

"I wish to speak to her myself."

He didn't seem surprised. He was coming to know her. She wondered if he could ever accept her independent ways. It bothered her, she discovered, to think that he might not.

Thor escorted her up the stairs with a protective hand at her waist. When they reached the landing, he rapped sharply on the weathered door, knocking off chips of peeling paint. It took several more knocks before footsteps sounded on the opposite side and a small woman with dull gray hair pulled open the door.

"Mary Pratt?" Thor asked.

"That's me name." She eyed his huge frame warily then, seeing a woman behind him, seemed to relax. "What can I do fer ye?"

Lindsey came forward. "We'd like to ask you some questions about the murder that happened on your street a few weeks back."

"Who are ye?"

Lindsey summoned a smile. "I'm a reporter with *Heart to Heart* magazine. We're doing a story about the murder." It was as good a reason for being there as she could come up with on the spur of the moment. "We just need a bit of information."

The woman made no comment, which Lindsey took as a sign to proceed. "We'd like to ask you about the man you saw running from the scene of the crime."

"He weren't runnin'…not exactly. 'Twas more like he was saunterin'. Kinda like he was proud o' himself for what he done. Course at the time, I just figured he'd been up to some mischief. Didn't know he'd done murder till I heard talk about it later."

"What did this man look like?"

"He were gentry. Dressed real nice…fancy top hat and fine leather gloves. That's why I noticed him. Seemed so out of place round here."

"I see."

"What else can you tell us?" Thor asked.

"He were tall and slim, had light-colored hair."

"I thought he was wearing a hat," Lindsey said.

"He were carrying his hat when I first seen him. Put it on as he rounded the corner."

"What about his face?" she asked. "What did he look like?"

"Can't say fer sure." She turned, pointed toward a window inside the house then to the lane out in front. "She were kilt right there in that doorway. It's a ways away from me window. Couldn't make out his features."

Lindsey's pulse kicked up. "Then how can you be certain it was Rudolph Graham?"

She shrugged a pair of bony shoulders. "Police said it were him. Same height, same build, same light hair. I figured they must know."

"Thank you, Mary." She reached out and pressed a guinea into the old woman's palm. "You've been a very big help."

The woman grinned, exposing a hole where one of her bottom teeth should have been. "Too bad I cain't read. I'd like ta see me name in the newspaper."

Lindsey left the old woman on the landing and she and Thor made their way back down the stairs. She couldn't hide her excitement as he opened the door of the carriage.

"Did you hear her, Thor? She didn't see the killer's face. It could have been anyone."

"You need to tell this to your brother's attorney. Mayhap it will be enough to get Rudy released."

She looked up at him. "I think we should go there now."

He nodded. "What is the address?"

She gave him the location in Threadneedle Street, and sometime later, the carriage rolled up in front of a three-story brick building. The solicitor, Jonas Marvin, was there in the office. Lindsey introduced Thor as a friend who was helping her investigate the murder, then told the attorney what they had learned from Mary Pratt.

"The woman didn't see his face," Lindsey explained. "The police pretty much convinced her Rudy was the man she had seen leaving the scene of the murder."

Marvin adjusted his small gold spectacles, shoving them up on his nose. "If what you say is true, then the case against Rudolph is built entirely on circumstantial evidence. It's incriminating—without a doubt—but Rudy is a future baron. If your father were here, his release would be fairly easy to obtain."

"I shall speak to Aunt Delilah, ask her to talk to some of her influential friends, see what sort of support we can muster to gain Rudy's release."

"In the meantime, I will speak to Avery French. Perhaps he can work some of his courtroom magic down at the magistrate's office."

"Show Mr. Marvin the note," Thor said.

Lindsey glanced up at him, opened her reticule and pulled out the note she had received that morning. "I think it is probably a prank—one of Rudy's half-witted friends."

Marvin took the note from her outstretched hand and skimmed the words. "I will show it to Harrison Mansfield, the investigator, see what he has to say. We wouldn't want to overlook any possibility."

The meeting ended in a positive vein, Lindsey feeling optimistic for the first time since all this had begun. Since the afternoon was nearly over, she and Thor decided to postpone their call on Phoebe's roommates. Thor returned her to the office, and both of them went back to work.

Two days later, Avery French managed to secure Rudy's release.

Still, it was clear her brother remained the number one suspect in the murders. They had to continue the search, had to find the real killer.

Her brother would not be safe until they did.

His face and chest covered with perspiration, Thor awakened that night from a restless sleep. He was aroused, his shaft hard and throbbing beneath the sheet. He had been dreaming again, another hot dream of Lindsey.

"Blood of Odin," he swore, running a hand through his sweat-damp hair. With a sigh, he lay back against the pillow, his shaft still thick and heavy, pulsing with unspent need. Though the hour was late, he considered getting dressed and paying a call on the ladies at the Red Door. The women would welcome him, as they always did, and his body would certainly welcome their attentions.

His shaft throbbed, craving relief, but his mind wanted something more.

An image of Lindsey in the carriage, her slender hips riding his thighs, her head thrown back in ecstasy as he pleasured her, burned through his mind and he clenched his jaw against a fresh rush of desire. He didn't want one of the women at Madame Fortier's. He wanted Lindsey Graham.

And he could not have her.

Like a sorcerer, the little witch had enchanted him. She couldn't be his, though she had offered herself to him time

and again. She was convinced the man she would wed
could not give her the pleasure she would find with Thor.

*Mayhap I should give her what she wants, what both of
us want, he thought.*

But what if he got her with child? Her hips were slender,
not broad, not the sort to carry a babe the size he would
plant in her belly. Even if she were forced to wed with him,
having his babe might kill her.

Thor punched his pillow, trying to get comfortable on
a mattress that suddenly felt hard as stone. There was no
way around it. He could not take her.

Fighting the demons that tried to convince him he was
wrong, Thor attempted in vain to fall asleep.

Working behind her desk, Lindsey spotted Krista approaching, her blond hair swept into a knot at the nape of
her neck, her simple muslin gown already smudged with
ink. Lindsey straightened as she saw the folded paper in
her friend's hand.

"I found this under the door when I came in this
morning. It is addressed to you."

Lindsey took the note, turned it over and recognized the
handwriting that was the same as before. "I got one like this
three days ago. Some rubbish about one of Rudy's friends
being the Covent Garden Murderer. The handwriting looks
the same." She popped the seal and read the message.

*Can you not see? Not the fools so close at hand. Stephen
Camden is your man.*

"Good grief!"

"What does it say?"

Lindsey handed the note to Krista, who quickly skimmed

the words. "Stephen Camden? Surely it can't mean Viscount Merrick. For heaven's sake, his father is the Marquess of Wexford."

"His country estate, Merrick Park, is in Foxgrove. One of its boundaries borders Renhurst Hall. Stephen is several years older than Rudy but they have known each other for years. They attended the same boarding schools and were also together for a brief time at Oxford."

"I've met Lord Merrick on several occasions. He seemed a pleasant enough fellow. I cannot credit the man is a murderer."

"Neither can I. Living so close, we know each other fairly well. Father has even mentioned Stephen as a possible suitor." She retrieved the note Krista held out to her. "If this is a joke, I find it in extremely poor taste."

"I wonder who sent it?"

"I wish I knew."

"What are you going to do with it?"

"Nothing."

"You got another note?" Thor's deep voice rolled over her as he walked up to her desk, and her heart did a little skip.

"Why, yes. It is as silly as the first. This one accuses an old family friend, Stephen Camden, son of the Marquess of Wexford. The man is a viscount, for heaven's sake. It is completely ridiculous."

"Your brother will one day be a baron and yet he is under suspicion. You should show the note to the investigator, Mansfield, let him look into the matter."

"I will do nothing of the sort. I am not showing this note to another living soul. Rudy would be outraged and it would only embarrass us both."

"But you will keep the note, in case another comes in."

"I will keep it. And when I find out who is sending them, I am going to give him a piece of my mind."

Thor said nothing more, just walked away and went back to work. It wasn't until late that afternoon that they were able to leave the office to visit the two women who had shared a flat with Phoebe Carter. In the carriage ride along the way, Thor was pleasant but distant, clearly intent on ignoring the intimacy they had shared before and putting their relationship back on a formal footing.

Lindsey was irritated and out of sorts by the time they reached Phoebe's three-story walk-up in Maiden Lane. It was late enough in the day that the women would likely be up and moving about—even if their work had kept them awake most of the night—but early enough that they should still be at home.

Thor rapped sharply. On the second series of raps, a redhead in a black satin negligee pulled open the door.

"Stop makin' all that racket! It's early yet, not time for—" Her lips formed an O of surprise as her eyes lit on Thor. Her gaze traveled up his long, muscular legs, over his narrow hips and broad chest, to the face of a beautiful dark angel.

Wavy, coal-dark hair curled over his collar and his brilliant blue eyes took in, at a glance, the woman and her surroundings.

"Maybe I spoke too soon," she said, stepping back to invite him in. "What can Mandy do for you, lover?"

To Lindsey's surprise, Thor paid little attention to the woman's scantily clad form. "We would like to ask you some questions."

"We would like to talk to you about your flat-mate, Phoebe Carter." Lindsey tried not to be peeved that the woman didn't seem to realize she was there. All the redhead could see was Thor. As Lindsey thought on it, in a way she couldn't blame her.

"You don't look like the police."

"My brother is Rudolph Graham. You probably know him. He was accused of Phoebe's murder."

"Yeah, I heard that. Seems to me you got some gall comin' here."

"My brother is innocent," Lindsey said. "If you know him, you know he isn't the kind of man who could murder a woman. That is what we are trying to prove."

Mandy flicked a glance at Thor. "I met him a couple of times. Phoebe liked him. He didn't seem like a killer." She stepped back and opened the door. "Might as well come in." She turned, shouted toward the back of the flat. "Hey, Annie—we got visitors."

The place was fairly clean but the furnishings were sparse, a threadbare rose velvet settee and a matching velvet chair. The floor was covered by a faded Persian rug, and the fringe was missing in places from the lamp shade. Still, it was far above what other residents of the neighborhood possessed. Prostitution paid better than most of the jobs a working woman could get.

"Annie!"

"Relax, I'm coming." A slinky brunette sauntered in wearing little more than Mandy, just a pale pink chemise that flashed when her dressing robe parted as she crossed the room.

She stopped in front of Thor, looked him up and down. "You look familiar. Have we met somewhere before?"

"I do not think so."

"You're right. You're one I would remember." She turned her attention to Lindsey. "So what can we do for you?"

"She's Rudy Graham's sister," Mandy said. "You remember—he was here a couple of times with Phoebe. He's the gent they arrested for her murder."

Annie stiffened. "Get the bloody hell out of here."

"My brother didn't kill your friend. According to the witness—a woman named Mary Pratt—Rudy looks like the man who killed Phoebe, but Mary didn't actually see him, just a man who fit his general description."

"Tall, slim, light hair," Thor added. "Fancy dresser. Do you know such a man?"

"Lot of gents fit that description," Mandy said.

"Your brother was the one who was with her the night she was killed," Annie said sharply.

"He left her at the House of Dreams," Lindsey countered. "She was on her way home when she was killed."

One of Annie's black eyebrows went up. "That so?"

"Phoebe liked to dream," said Mandy. "Thought it made life easier. She brought in clients for Sultry Weaver in exchange for a bit of the drug."

"We know this," Thor said. "Was there a man she saw more often than the others, someone who might have felt she belonged to him?"

"You mean someone who might have been jealous enough to kill her?" Annie asked.

Thor nodded.

"Nobody we know of," said Mandy, getting a look of

agreement from her roommate. "She did her job, never got mixed up with any of her customers. She was smart, was Phoebe."

"Hard to believe she's gone," said Annie.

"If you think of something," Lindsey said, "anything that might be of help, we'd appreciate it if you would send word. I work at *Heart to Heart* ladies' gazette. The office is in Piccadilly."

"We'll keep our eyes open," said Annie. "Nothin' we'd like more than to see the blighter swing."

Lindsey thanked them for their time, and she and Thor left the apartment. Thor helped her climb into the carriage, then took up his silent vigil from the opposite seat.

"We didn't learn much," Lindsey said.

"Mayhap they will think of something later."

"Perhaps." She toyed with a fold in her skirt. "I guess you haven't changed your mind about…you know…us."

Thor just grunted.

"You…um…haven't been back to Madame Fortier's, have you? Recently, I mean?"

Thor shot forward in his seat so fast she gasped. His fierce blue eyes burned into her. "I have not been there. But I am a man and I am in need of a woman. That need grows stronger each time I am with you, Lindsey."

She reached out and touched his cheek, felt the hard curve of his jaw. "What happened the last time we were together… it was wonderful, Thor. I want to know the rest, I want to experience all of it. Let me be the woman you need."

His hand shook as he raked back his thick dark hair. "You make it sound easy, but it is not. What would happen should I get you with child? Have you thought of that, Lindsey?"

"There must be a way to prevent it." She thought of Coralee's husband's Indian valet, a man who brewed all manner of potions. "I have a friend who might be able to help."

"No."

She glanced down. His coat had parted, exposing the hard ridge pressing at the front of his trousers. Knowing she shouldn't, too curious to resist, she reached over and lightly touched him, felt the stiff length leap at her touch.

Thor knocked her hand away. "Gods' blood, woman!"

"You still want me. You cannot deny it."

"I want you. I look at you and I want to tear off your clothes. I want to suckle your beautiful breasts and bury myself inside you. I want to take you until both of us are too exhausted to move."

Her heart pounded and her stomach quivered. Her palms were damp but her mouth felt dry. How could mere words make her feel that way, hot and cold all over, a soft ache throbbing between her legs?

"I know where you live," she said. "Krista showed me once when we went shopping. I shall come to you tonight."

He pinned her with a glare. "I will not be there. I will be busy with the whores at the Red Door."

Pain knifed into her heart. It shouldn't have hurt, but it did.

They rode along in silence toward her home. They had finished work for the day and were out of leads to follow. She looked up at Thor, saw the turbulence in his expression, a mixture of determination and regret. And there was something more, a yearning so powerful it made her breath catch.

She summoned her courage. "I am coming, Thor," she said softly. "I hope that you will be there."

The carriage jerked to a halt before he could come up with a reply.

The coachman jumped down from above and pulled open the door. "We're 'ere, guvner."

Lindsey took the driver's hand and let him help her down. Thor seemed too stunned to move from his seat.

"Lindsey!" he called out to her through the window as the coachman returned to the top of the carriage.

Ignoring him, she collected her skirts and raced along the path to the house.

Thirteen

❧◆❧

The sun shimmered like old gold at the edge of the horizon as darkness began to shroud the city. Lamps burned in windows, casting a soft yellow glow into the street. Lindsey was on her way to the Mayfair residence of the Earl and Countess of Tremaine, only a few blocks away.

Determined not to lose her courage, as soon as the carriage rolled up in front of the house, she descended the iron stairs and quickly made her way up the brick path to the door of the earl's three-story town house. Coralee Whitmore Forsythe and her husband, Gray, had returned just two days ago from their six-week journey across the Continent.

The butler opened the door. "May I help you?"

"I am a friend of the countess. I was hoping—"

"Ah, Miss Graham. Do come in. I'll tell her ladyship you are here. If you will please follow me." He led her into an elegant drawing room done in dark green and gold, with flocked paper on the walls and gilded lamps on the polished mahogany tables. A white marble hearth sat at the end of the drawing room, the painting of a pastoral scene hanging above it.

Coralee walked in a few minutes later, a broad grin on her face. "Lindsey! It's so good to see you!"

"Coralee!" The women embraced then Lindsey stepped away to survey the friend she hadn't seen in weeks. "You look wonderful. I have never seen you quite so radiant."

Corrie was petite and fine-featured, with thick copper hair pulled into curls on each side of a very pretty face.

"I am married to the most wonderful man on earth and I am in love. I suppose it must show."

"Truly, it does." They moved a little farther into the drawing room, walking close together.

"How was your trip?" Lindsey asked.

"Marvelous. I saw such wondrous sights. Paris was… well, it was simply grand. I enjoyed it even more being with Gray."

"It's nice that you both like to travel. My parents are gone so much of the time. Even when Rudy and I were little, they traveled constantly. I suppose that is why I never really cared much about it." Lindsey glanced toward the door leading into the hall. "Is your husband at home? I am not keeping you from him?"

"He had some errands to run. He has not yet returned."

They crossed to the sofa and Lindsey caught both of Coralee's small hands. "I am sorry to barge in this way when you are only a few days home, but my life seems to be taking one unexpected turn after another and I am hoping you might be able to help me."

"You are not barging in. I am delighted to see you after all of this time and of course I will help in any way I can.

Why don't I ring for tea and you can tell me what has happened while I was away."

"I could certainly use a cup," Lindsey said, hoping to fortify her courage. In fact, if she actually went through with her plans for tonight, she would need something far stouter than tea.

Coralee used the bell pull then returned to the dark green velvet sofa and sat down beside her.

"All right," Corrie said, "why don't you start from the beginning? Tell me what has you so upset that you have come so unexpectedly?"

Lindsey took a breath, trying to decide where to begin. For the next half hour, they sipped tea while Lindsey told her friend about the murders in Covent Garden, about Rudy's arrest, and the investigation she had been conducting.

"Good lord, I had no idea." Corrie lifted her gold-rimmed porcelain teacup, but didn't take a sip. "Have you made any progress?" She neatly balanced the cup and saucer on her lap.

"We managed to get Rudy released from prison, but there is every chance the police will come after him again. That is why it is so important to find the real killer."

"That could be dangerous, Lindsey."

"I already learned that firsthand…which is the reason Thor has been helping me."

Corrie's green eyes sharpened. "Thor? I thought the two of you did not get along."

Lindsey glanced down at her teacup, ran a finger around the rim. "We…um…didn't really know each other. Now that we do…well, things have changed."

"Go on."

Lindsey set her cup and saucer down on the table in front of the sofa, reached over and caught hold of Corrie's hand. "You and Krista are my two dearest friends. You are both independent women, the sort to go after what you want. I am hoping you will understand when I tell you that Thor and I…we share a very strong physical attraction. You and Krista were lucky enough to marry men you love, but that isn't going to happen to me."

"You can't know that—not for certain."

Lindsey sighed. "I'm a realist, Coralee. I shall wind up married to some very proper aristocrat with an impressive title and fortune. I shall never know passion—not the sort you and Krista share with your husbands."

"What are you saying, Lindsey?"

"I want to know that sort of passion just once. I want to feel it all the way to my bones. Thor makes me feel things I never knew existed. We cannot marry. We are completely ill-suited. My family would never approve and even if they did, it could not possibly work. We are simply too different."

"But you want him to make love to you."

"Yes."

"I am surprised Thor would agree. He is certainly virile enough, but he is a great deal like his brother. Both men have a very strong sense of honor. If he made love to you, I should think he would feel obligated to marry you."

"That is why I need your help. Thor understands we cannot wed. Which is, as you have guessed, the reason he refuses to make love to me. He is also worried that he might get me with child. That is the reason I am here."

Corrie leaned forward, moving the copper curls clustered on her shoulders. She set her cup and saucer down on the table. "You are speaking of Samir," she said with complete understanding.

"Krista told me about your husband's valet. He is from India, is he not?"

"Why, yes, he is."

"And he makes all sorts of potions and elixirs?"

A slight nod of her head. "He helped Gray save my life."

Her eyes widened. "What happened?"

"It is a very long story and best saved for another time. Tell me what you wish of Samir."

Lindsey smoothed her skirts. "I was hoping…I thought that perhaps he could make a potion for me that would keep me from conceiving a child."

Corrie's gaze searched her face. "You would be taking a very big step, Lindsey."

"Could he do it?"

"I imagine he could."

"How long would it take?"

"In his quarters, Samir has a wall full of potions—bottles and packets of herbs he uses for healing. Odds are he already has such a brew."

Her heartbeat quickened. "I would pay him extremely well." She could go to Thor tonight, as she yearned to do. She reminded herself that he might not be there, that he might be with another woman, and ignored a stab of pain she had no right to feel. Thor owed her no loyalty. In fact, he had done everything in his power to keep her away.

Still, she believed he wanted her as badly as she wanted him.

"Are you certain about this, Lindsey? I can tell you from experience, some of our best ideas wind up being our worst."

"I might never have this chance again."

"What about Thor? He is different from other men, more sensitive, more caring than most. If he makes love to you, he may feel that you belong to him. That is what happened to Krista. Fortunately, she was in love with Leif so, in the end, everything worked out."

Lindsey glanced away, her chest suddenly tight. She told herself she wasn't in love with Thor. Even if she were, she could never marry him.

"Thor has more women than any man has a right. When we part, he will have any number of willing females to take care of him. This brief time is all I will ever have. Will you help me, Coralee?"

Her petite friend rose from the sofa. "I will speak to Samir, see if he has what you need."

Lindsey rose and caught Corrie's hand. For an instant, tears flashed in her eyes. "Thank you."

Coralee just nodded, turned and walked away. She couldn't help thinking of Thor and the sort of man he was, wondering how he had managed to become so entangled with Lindsey.

Love was the only answer.

Clearly Lindsey was in love with Thor, though she didn't seem to know. There had always been something between them, though both had tried to resist the pull of attraction that had been there from the start.

Was it love?

Even if it were, sometimes love wasn't enough.

Corrie had almost lost Gray because of the choices she had made and the games she had played.

She prayed Lindsey was not about to make the same mistake.

Rudy was in the Oak Room with Aunt Dee when Lindsey returned to the house. She had told her aunt that she was going to visit Coralee and wouldn't be home for supper. The meal was now over and Lindsey headed down the marble-floored hall to the drawing room paneled in polished oak that was the most comfortable in the house. She was worried about her brother. Whatever happened in her own life, keeping Rudy from the gallows was most important.

She smiled as she walked in. "Good evening, Aunt Dee…Rudy." She glanced from one to the other, caught the tension sparking between them.

"Hey, sis." Rudy managed a halfhearted smile. "I was just telling Auntie I was thinking of going to the theater. She doesn't think it's a good idea."

"The play happens to be at the Theatre Royale in Drury Lane," Aunt Dee said simply.

Lindsey's attention swung to her brother. "Covent Garden? My God, Rudy, are you mad? You just got out of prison. The police are looking for any excuse to arrest you again. Do you want to hang?"

His face went a little bit pale. He stared down at the toes of his expensive leather shoes. "I just…I been locked up in prison, now I'm cooped up here. I gotta get out, sis."

Delilah stood up from her place on the leather sofa. "I understand a young man Rudy's age doesn't want to spend his evenings at home. I was just suggesting to your brother that perhaps we should spend a few weeks in the country. The gardens at Renhurst are quite glorious in the fall. The change would be good for all of us, and it would give the gossip a chance to die down."

Lindsey felt a wave of relief. It would be wise for Rudy to get out of London, at least for a while. "I think that is a splendid idea."

And there was the added bonus that Merrick Park was the estate next to Renhurst Hall. It was insane to believe the viscount had any part in the brutal murders, as the note she had received suggested. Still, while she was there, she would do a little checking, see if anything seemed out of the ordinary.

"So whatcha think, sis? I'll go if you will?"

Getting her brother away from trouble was her first priority. She could find a substitute to handle her column for a couple of weeks. Perhaps Coralee might even agree to help her, since Lindsey had stepped in so that Corrie could investigate the death of her beloved sister. Coralee might fill in for a while, though she was no longer interested in the job full time.

"I am writing a novel," Corrie had said during their recent conversation. "It's a romantic story of a woman who travels to Paris under a false identity and meets the man of her dreams."

A little like what had actually happened to her, Lindsey thought, though Corrie had traveled only as far as Castle Tremaine and never left English shores before her honeymoon.

Lindsey glanced over at her brother. "As I said, I think it's a marvelous notion. I shall need a couple of days to work out my schedule. Why don't I join the two of you there the first of the week?"

"Excellent," said her aunt. "And I was thinking that once we are in residence, we might have a bit of a house party…just a few close friends, nothing extravagant. It is best to keep up appearances, after all, show that we are not the least concerned about the charges that were falsely made against Rudy." One of her eyebrows lifted as her glance strayed in his direction. "And perhaps it will keep your brother entertained."

Lindsey's gaze followed. "What do you say, Rudy?"

"I say why not? Beats sitting around, waiting for the ax to fall."

"Rudolph!"

He grinned mischievously at his aunt, a hint of the boy he had been. "Sorry, Auntie."

Lindsey almost smiled. Aunt Dee wanted to have a house party and Lindsey would bet Colonel Langtree's name could be found at the top of the guest list. "A house party, it is. As you say, Aunt Dee, we need to keep up appearances until all of this is behind us."

And so it was settled. Delilah would send word ahead to Renhurst, then she and Rudy would travel the following day and Lindsey would join them there a few days after that.

In the meantime, she had plans for the evening that did not include guests.

Her stomach contracted. She was going to Thor. Corrie had provided the potion she needed and though nothing was completely foolproof, she could be fairly sure she wouldn't conceive Thor's child.

The notion was oddly disturbing. She loved children. She

had always wanted a family, perhaps because she had never had much of one herself. It bothered her that she was going to great lengths to prevent the very thing she wanted most.

One day it would happen, she told herself. She would marry a steady, acceptable sort of man and bear him any number of children. Until then, she would take this time for herself.

As she climbed the stairs to her room, she thought of the night ahead. What if Thor wasn't there when she arrived? He had vowed to be absent, to spend the night in the arms of a woman at Madame Fortier's. Should he abandon her for one of them, it would be painful, but if he weren't there, at least he would never know she had come to him and she would never tell him.

She took a deep breath and went into her room. Once the household was asleep, she would leave. It wasn't far to Green Park and the neighborhood was safe enough.

Whatever happened, her decision was made. At midnight, she was going to Thor. Lindsey ignored a curl of heat that slipped into her stomach, along with a little knot of fear.

Thor tossed back the last of his ale and set the tankard down on the bar. He wasn't much of a man for drink, no more than an ale or two when the mood struck.

Tonight he had come to the Thistle and Rose, a tavern on the quay his crew of stevedores favored, determined to drink himself into a stupor. If he got drunk enough, mayhap he would not be tortured by images of Lindsey in his bed.

"Hey, Thor—how 'bout we head down to the Pig and Garter? Hear tell they got a couple o' fine new wenches. Maybe we can find ourselfs a bit o' entertainment."

It was Johnson, a big strapping dockworker with bushy blond hair and a ready smile. Benders and Schofield were also there, keeping him company.

He tried to muster some enthusiasm for the idea, but wound up shaking his head. "Mayhap next time." He had drunk more ale than he was used to but, unfortunately, still felt completely sober. He pulled the watch his brother had given him at Christmastime from the pocket of his trousers and checked the hour.

Twelve-thirty. If she had been insane enough to go to his flat, surely she would be back in her own bed by now.

The thought made his stomach tighten. He tossed a couple of coins on the bar, waved to his co-workers, and headed out the door. As he walked along the darkened street, he thought of Lindsey and the vow she had made. He knew how reckless she could be, but neither was she a fool.

Once she'd had time to consider the consequences, he was certain she would have come to her senses.

He raised his arm to hail a cab, more than ready to go home. He felt tired in a way he couldn't explain. Every step seemed a burden, every movement weighed him down. The thought of facing his empty bed seemed an impossible feat. He didn't want to be alone tonight. He didn't want to think of the woman he had turned away, no matter the reason he had done it.

You had no choice, he told himself, and he knew it was true. He had done what was best for Lindsey, what was best for both of them.

A hansom pulled up in front of him. Wearily, he climbed into the seat, dreading the night ahead and the hours he would lie abed—thinking of Lindsey, unable to fall asleep.

Fourteen

It was well after midnight, the moon no more than a sliver in the sky, the stars obscured by the glow of lights in the city. Climbing out of the carriage she had hailed at the corner, Lindsey paid the driver and turned to make her way up the outside staircase leading to Thor's apartment.

Her heart was pounding, her hands clammy with perspiration. She thought of turning back but she had come this far and it seemed impossible to think of leaving. She lifted her hand to knock, then decided to try the latch. Perhaps he had left it open so that she could come in.

The door was indeed unlocked, a hopeful sign that he was expecting her. She entered the house on legs that wobbled only a little. It was dark, but the fingernail moon and the gas street lamp below the window gave her enough light to see. She glanced around, curious about the place Thor lived, saw that the parlor was clean but sparsely furnished, saw that he kept his quarters very neat.

There was a sofa and chair in front of a small coal-burning hearth. Next to it, a leather shield hung on the wall, and a huge sword leaned against the wall beneath it. She itched to examine the items more closely, but she was too nervous, too anxious to see Thor.

Praying he would be waiting for her in his bedroom, she crossed the parlor to the door, her heart hammering with a mixture of uncertainty and anticipation. Turning the knob, she quietly eased it open. The room was also neat and clean, the bed carefully made. Her heart squeezed hard as her worst fear was confirmed.

Thor was not there.

A sob caught in her throat. As he had vowed, he had gone to the Red Door. He would rather spend the night with a paid-for woman than make love to her. Tears gathered in her eyes. She was a fool. A complete and utter idiot. Thank God he wasn't there to witness her shame. Thank God he would never know the lengths she had gone to so that they could be together.

She had wanted him so badly, enough to humiliate herself by coming to a man who would rather make love to a whore.

Her heart twisted inside her. Perhaps that was how he saw her. A soiled woman, the doxy she had portrayed the night she had gone with him to Covent Garden. The tears in her eyes spilled onto her cheeks. Pulling her shawl a little closer around her, Lindsey turned and ran out of the bedroom. She had to escape before he returned, had to get away before he found her there and her shame would be complete.

She had almost made her escape when the front door swung open and Thor's massive silhouette appeared in the opening.

Dear God in heaven—he had returned from Madame

Fortier's! He had taken his pleasure and now he would find her there in his rooms, just another of his foolish, besotted women. She ducked her head so he wouldn't see the tears on her cheeks and tried to rush past him.

Thor blocked her way. "By the gods—you came."

"Let me pass," she demanded, praying he wouldn't hear the tremor in her voice. "Get out of my way!"

But he didn't move and when she tried to squeeze past, he simply reached out and encircled her in his arms. "Lindsey…"

Humiliation washed over her. He had just left another woman's bed. She couldn't endure it. She simply could not.

"Get your hands off me!" She tried to twist out of his hold, managed to free one hand and swung at him. Thor ducked her useless effort and pulled her against his chest.

"Lindsey…sweetheart."

She was crying in earnest now, making a complete and utter fool of herself. "Please let me go," she whispered between ragged breaths. "I just want to go home."

But instead, he lifted her into his arms and carried her over to the sofa, sat down and cradled her in his lap. "I am so sorry," he said, pressing soft kisses against the side of her neck. "Forgive me for being a fool."

"I am the fool." Aching deep inside, hurting as she never had before, she shoved her hands against his chest in a futile effort to escape. "I thought I was special. I thought I meant something to you."

Thor kissed her temple. "You mean everything to me. Do you not know?"

She looked at him through her tears. "If you care, why did you go? Why do you want them and not me?"

"I did not go to the Red Door."

"I don't believe you."

"I do not lie, Lindsey. This you know."

She did know. In fact he was often too truthful. "I thought you wanted me."

"I was trying to protect you."

She glanced away, swallowed past the lump in her throat. "I want to go home."

He traced a line down her cheek. "It is too late for that, sweetheart. It was too late the moment you stepped through that door."

She felt his fingers beneath her chin, gently turning her to face him, then his mouth settled softly over hers. His kiss was warm and moist and tasted faintly of ale. *A tavern, then, not the Red Door.* The lump in her throat began to ease.

Thor deepened the kiss and her stomach contracted. Her heart was hammering, beating with wild anticipation.

Still she pulled away.

"I can't…can't do this." She shook her head, a tightness building in her chest. "I thought I could, but I can't."

"What is wrong?"

"You need a woman to ease your needs. I thought I could be that woman. Now I…I see that I can't be like the others, no matter what you make me feel."

Thor's blue eyes burned into her. "You are nothing like the others. I have never met a woman like you. Day and night I think of you, ache for you. There is no other I want, Lindsey, only you."

She looked at him, read the sincerity in his face. She meant more to him than just a woman to warm his bed. How much more she couldn't say, but for now it was enough.

"Thor…" Cupping his face in her hands, she brought her mouth to his for a trembling kiss. His lips claimed hers, swift and sure, moved over them with burning need, and desire rose up inside her.

She was the woman he wanted, she and no other.

And dear God, she wanted him.

Thor kissed her again, deeply, slowly, his tongue sliding in, tangling with hers, setting her body aflame. He nibbled and tasted, teased and coaxed until she was writhing on his lap, pressing herself against the thick ridge of his sex.

Thor groaned.

Lindsey kissed him again and Thor kissed her back, kissed her until her mind had turned numb and her body seemed to melt into his. One last kiss and he set her on her feet and slowly began to undress her. His hot blue gaze ran over every inch he exposed and her breath froze in her lungs. She trembled as he removed her bodice, loosened the tabs on her skirt and petticoats, and urged her to step from the fluffy folds.

Lindsey did as he bade, filled with a mixture of anxiety and longing, basking in the appreciation she read in his brilliant blue eyes. He reached up and drew the pins from her hair, laced his fingers in the honey brown curls and spread the heavy mass around her shoulders.

She held her breath as he untied her corset strings, removed the garment and tossed it away, turned her to face him in her chemise, drawers, garters and stockings.

"So sweet," he said, "so much a woman. How could I not have seen?"

She didn't have time to consider his words before he was kissing her again, long deep kisses that had her stomach floating up beneath her ribs. He peeled down her chemise and filled his hands with her breasts, stroked the tips until they hardened and throbbed, then settled his mouth over an aching nipple.

Lindsey's head fell back, giving him better access. She clutched his head, slid her fingers into the silk of his thick dark hair. She moaned as he suckled and tasted, gently bit the rigid tip, circled the tight pink crest with his tongue. Pleasure washed through her, deep and pure, and heat and need and something else she could not name.

"Thor," she whispered, wishing she could touch him as he was touching her.

As if he read her mind, he stepped away from her and stripped off his tailcoat, drew his full-sleeved shirt off over his head. Naked to the waist, he turned back to her, the most magnificent man she had ever seen.

She rested a shaky hand on his powerful chest, felt the muscles there contract. "I want to touch you," she softly admitted. "I want to know the taste of your skin, feel the texture of your muscles. I want to kiss you as you kissed me."

Bending her head, she pressed her lips to the place above his heart, circled a flat copper nipple with her tongue, felt the slide of liquid heat into her core. She inhaled the heat and masculine scent of him and desire made her legs go weak.

Thor lifted her into his arms and started striding toward his bedroom as if he couldn't wait a moment more. An instant later, she was naked and lying in his big four-poster bed. Thor kissed her fiercely, kissed her until she was mindless with need, aching for the pleasure he had shown her before.

He left her only long enough to remove the last of his clothes. Her cheeks burned as she watched him walk toward her, the male part of him long and thick, riding high and hard against his flat belly.

She thought of her own slight frame and how the two would join and though she had known a man before, he was nothing at all like Thor.

"Do not be frightened," Thor said gently. "There is no need to hurry." His hand found her wetness, began to stroke her. "I will not take you until you are ready."

Her breath hitched, came faster. She remembered the pleasure he had given her that day in the carriage and closed her eyes, allowing him to take her to those same thrilling heights again. In moments, she was trembling, her skin hot and burning. She barely noticed when he joined her on the bed, when his hard length replaced his hand and he began to slide his thick shaft inside her.

He was long and heavy, so big she feared he would tear her in two.

"Thor…?"

"Easy, sweetheart. You were made for me. This I now know. We will find a way." And then he kissed her and his big hands stroked her and she forgot the tightness, the stretching, forgot her fear.

Instead, she marveled at the feel of his massive chest against her breasts as he surged forward, the smooth muscles teasing her rigid nipples. She reveled at the warmth of his long legs rubbing against her calves, the weight of him pressing her down in the mattress.

Thor kissed her deeply, his tongue sliding in, his mouth hot and coaxing over hers. Through a haze of need, she realized his hard length was fully impaled inside her. She had expected the same pain as the first time, but there was only a delicious fullness, the glorious feeling of being one with him.

She wriggled a little beneath him, testing the weight and thickness, the unusual sensation of his body joined with hers.

Thor hissed in a breath. "Do not move."

But Lindsey couldn't help herself. She liked the way he felt inside her, needed to move so badly she could not possibly stay still. Arching upward, she took him even deeper, and Thor softly cursed. Then he was driving hard, his hips pumping, moving in and out with deep penetrating strokes that sent wild ripples of pleasure spearing through her. Something tightened inside her, clenched with a need so strong she cried out.

Thor drove into her again and again, his heavy thrusts driving all conscious thought from her head. Pleasure engulfed her. Bright searing light and great waves of sweetness had her arching upward to receive his deep penetration, digging her nails into his broad, muscular back.

For long moments, they clung together as each of them spiraled down. Thor's dark head nestled against her shoulder, her arms round his powerful neck. It took a moment to realize the burning in her eyes was tears. For so many years she had fought them. With Thor, it seemed to happen without conscious thought. Still, she had cried enough this night and she blinked them away before he could see.

Thor kissed her softly, then eased himself from her body, lay down beside her and nestled her in his arms.

"I did not hurt you?"

Lindsey shook her head. "You were wonderful, Thor. Everything I imagined and more."

The edge of his mouth faintly curved. "I am glad you are pleased."

She rolled onto her side to face him, found his beautiful blue eyes on her face. "You don't have to worry about… you know…a baby. I went to see Coralee. Her husband's manservant is from India. He gave me a potion so that you would not get me with child."

He glanced away. "I suppose that is best."

But suddenly she wasn't so sure. She couldn't think of anything more wonderful than having Thor's baby. "I suppose."

He said no more and neither did she. Perhaps tomorrow she would regret her decision to come here.

But tonight she was with Thor and it was the place she most wanted to be.

It would soon be dawn. Exhausted from the lovemaking that took up most of the night, Lindsey slept peacefully. Awake and watching her, Thor ran a finger along her bare shoulder, looked down at her and thought how beautiful she was. He had taken her thrice last night, and each time she had responded with innocent abandon. It was clear her single experience with a man had done nothing to further her education.

And yet she was a woman of great passion, he had discovered, something he had guessed the first time he had kissed her.

He looked over at the clock on the wall. It was past time she returned home. He leaned over and gently shook her, rousing her from a restful slumber, wishing he could make love to her again.

She opened her eyes and yawned. "Is it morning?"

"Aye, close enough."

She glanced toward the window. "What time is it?"

"Time for you to leave. You do not wish for your aunt to discover you gone."

"No." But instead of getting up, she burrowed against him, pressed a soft kiss against his chest.

His body stirred to life. She had only to touch him and he wanted her. "Do not tease me, little fox. You will get more than you bargain for."

She laughed. "A fox? That is what I am?"

"Aye, lady, as coy as any fox, as sleek and beautiful."

She sat up in bed. "If I am a fox, then you are a big dark wolf." She made a growling sound and laughed, and he smiled.

"On Draugr, I was called Thorolf the wolf. Ulfr is our word for it."

"Truly?"

"Aye." As if to prove it, he came up over her, caught both of her wrists in one hand and dragged them above her head. "It is time you learned how dangerous it is to tease a wolf." And so he kissed her deeply and began to devour her as if he truly were one.

After another passionate round of lovemaking, Lindsey reluctantly climbed from her warm place beside Thor and began to put on her clothes. Thor followed her from between the sheets, magnificently naked, making her cheeks turn pink as she watched him approach.

"I will see you home," he said, beginning to pull on his clothes.

She had gotten there without his help; she didn't need

it now, but when she opened her mouth to argue, he gave her one of his warning glances and Lindsey simply nodded.

"Will you be working at the office?" she asked as he turned her around and began to fasten the buttons at the back of her gown.

"I am working on the docks."

"I'll be in the office for a while today and again on Monday. Then I will be leaving for the country."

His head came up. "What do you do there?"

"My aunt wishes to get my brother out of the city for a while. I thought it was a good idea."

He started to frown. "Your home, Renhurst Hall, lies next to Merrick Park. That is what you said, is it not?"

"Yes, but if you are worried about Lord Merrick, there is no need. It is nonsense to think Stephen had any involvement in the murders."

"Still, you will ask questions and not be satisfied until you know for sure. I do not like this, Lindsey."

He was beginning to know her too well. She leaned over and pressed a quick kiss on his mouth. "I will be fine."

"If you were my woman, I would forbid you to go."

She glanced away, an odd tightness in her chest. "But I am not your woman and even if I were, I would not obey such a ridiculous command."

"Then I would have to beat you."

Lindsey grinned. "I do not think so."

Thor grumbled a curse. She was beginning to know him also. And she didn't believe he would ever harm a woman.

"I would never hurt you," he admitted, "but should you put yourself in danger as you did before, I will take the flat of this hand to your pretty little bottom."

Lindsey blushed. All too clearly, she remembered him kissing her there, remembered the feel of his big hands running over the naked globes as if they were some sort of treasure.

She ignored a tendril of heat that slipped into her stomach and finished putting on her clothes. A few minutes later, they were hurrying along the street toward the cab stand, boarding a hansom carriage and riding through the darkness toward the alley behind Lindsey's house.

Thor said little when they arrived at the wooden gate at the back of the garden and for the first time, Lindsey felt uncertain.

"Do you…do you wish me to come to you tonight?"

He scoffed. "Do I want to make love to you again? That is what you are asking?"

She nodded.

"Does the moon rise every second fortnight?"

She smiled. "Then I will come to you as I did."

The carriage rolled to a halt in the alley and Lindsey threw open the door. Before she could rise from her seat, Thor caught her wrist.

"I would walk you to your door, but I cannot. I do not like the way this makes me feel, Lindsey. I cannot wed with you and so we must hide what we do as if it is wrong."

"I'm your mistress, Thor, not your wife. We have no other choice."

Pulling her back into the seat, he stepped down from the carriage, then turned and lifted her down. "I will wait for you on the corner at midnight."

She smiled, pleased he had so easily agreed. "All right."

"Send word if you come to your senses."

She laughed. Leaning toward him, she brushed a light kiss on his lips. Thor caught her against him and kissed her long and deep.

Lindsey reached up and touched his cheek. "My senses fled the first time you kissed me that way." Turning, she ran for the house.

Fifteen

◦⨾⊙⨾◦

Thor knocked on the door to his brother's town house, then stepped back as the butler welcomed him into the entry.

"Mr. Draugr. It is good to see you."

"You as well, Mr. Simmons."

"If you will please follow me into the drawing room, I will tell your brother you are here."

"Thank you." Thor followed the butler into the formal sitting room his sister-in-law had hired someone else to decorate. Though it was far too cluttered to suit his tastes, he made himself as comfortable as possible on a horsehair settee. Thankfully, it was only moments before Simmons returned.

"Your brother is in his study. He wishes you to join him there."

Thor nodded, followed the butler down the hall. Leif stood up from behind the desk as Thor walked in.

"Good to see you, brother." He motioned toward a seat in front of the fire burning in the hearth. "My wife is not yet home from work and my son is asleep, which makes your company doubly welcome."

Thor walked over to join him and the men sat down in front of the low flames in the hearth.

"What brings you out on a rainy Saturday afternoon?"

"We finished early at the dock. I was hoping I would find you at home."

"And glad to be here. It's a good day to spend at home. I know you don't care much for brandy but it's damned cold outside. A brandy might—"

"I will join you in a glass."

One of Leif's blond eyebrows arched up. He poured them both a drink, handed one of the crystal snifters to Thor, then sat down in a deep leather chair across from him. "Since you are here and drinking brandy, Lindsey must still be a problem."

Thor nodded. "Aye."

"Woman trouble is always the worst."

Thor sighed. "You were right. She is the one."

Leif grinned, lifted his snifter. "Congratulations, little brother."

Thor took a drink of his brandy, made a face as the amber liquid burned down his throat. "She came to me last night. I could not turn her away." For an instant, he closed his eyes, feeling a flush of heat at the memories of what had happened between them. "It was unlike anything before. She is the one meant for me and yet I cannot claim her."

"She wouldn't have given herself to you if she didn't care for you greatly."

"Lindsey is the daughter of a baron. That cannot change. She is used to fine clothes and fancy houses. I cannot give her those things."

"You are not poor. You own a portion of Valhalla Shipping and there is the railway stock you purchased."

"She is used to living in a mansion. My money would not be enough."

"Perhaps those things aren't important to her."

"She loves parties and balls. She loves to dance. I do not enjoy those things. I do not fit into her world and I never will."

"I learned to fit in. You could too if you put your mind to it."

He only shook his head. "You are different. You like life in the city. I do not. I could not make her happy."

Leif released a slow breath, leaned back and rested his arms on the leather arms of his chair. "The point you make is a good one. I tried to force Krista into a life that didn't suit her. If you do that to Lindsey, I don't believe either of you will be happy."

"What should I do?"

"I can't tell you what to do. But I believe if the gods have chosen her for you, you must not give up too soon. Perhaps a path will open, as it did for me. If time passes and that does not happen, then you can decide what you need to do."

It was good advice. And it helped ease his troubled mind. Lindsey wished to come to him. Thor wanted nothing so much as to have her in his bed. For now, he would close his mind to the guilt he felt in taking her, along with thoughts of the future, and enjoy the time they had together.

Thor took a drink of his brandy, the taste less offensive with the second sip. Soon Lindsey would be leaving for Renhurst. Thor intended to follow. Digging for information about a murder could be dangerous. He would find a way to be near her, a way to protect her if her questions got her into trouble.

One day he would have to give her up, but for now—whether the words had been spoken or not—Lindsey belonged to him.

Thor intended to keep her safe.

Lindsey left for Renhurst early Tuesday morning, though only part of her wanted to go. The other part wanted more than anything to stay in London with Thor.

She sighed as the carriage jolted along the muddy road, the wheels dropping into one pothole after another, and Renhurst Hall was yet a half day's travel away. At least today it wasn't raining.

Leaning back against the seat in a futile effort to get comfortable, her little maid, Kitty, asleep on the seat across from her, Lindsey thought of the nights she had spent with Thor and wished again that she didn't have to leave the city. That she could spend more time in Thor's bed, experience more of the incredible pleasure he had shown her.

Lindsey smiled at the memory of his lovemaking last night, the passionate hours she had spent in his bed, the intimate things they had done. It was truly amazing and yet, by the time Thor dropped her off at the gate at the back of the garden, his mood had turn sullen and dark. It bothered him, she knew, that he was not welcome as a suitor. He was a man of honor and he saw it as his duty to wed her, though both of them knew it would never work.

The situation wasn't good for either one of them and yet she refused to give him up until circumstances forced them to part.

Which might not be so far away.

According to Aunt Dee, her father and mother had finally been located in Rome. Word had been sent of Rudy's arrest and that, though he had been released, he remained a suspect in two brutal murders. A reply would soon be forthcoming.

Lindsey sighed. It was one thing to carry on a scandalous affair while her aunt was in residence, quite another to attempt to fool her father. He would be furious if he found out. God only knew what steps he might take—none of which involved a marriage to Thor.

Cutting off her monthly stipend, perhaps. Strongly suggesting she spend time in a convent contemplating her sinful ways. She shuddered to think of the lengths he would go to in order to separate her from Thor. Though she had always considered herself an independent woman, the salary she earned at *Heart to Heart* wouldn't pay the bill for the fancy undergarments she wore, let alone the gowns and jewelry she had always taken for granted.

She could give them up, of course. But could she ever really be happy as the wife of a man who cared nothing for the sort of life she enjoyed? A man who would never be accepted by her family or her peers, a husband with whom she shared nothing more than a physical attraction?

And what of their children? Would she want them to miss out on all the things a more suitable marriage could provide?

Lindsey sighed. Fortunately, she wasn't in love with Thor nor he with her, and she intended to keep it that way. They enjoyed making love. It was all they would ever have, but it would have to be enough.

As the carriage rolled toward Renhurst, Lindsey ignored a pang of regret that throbbed deep in her heart.

* * *

Thor knocked on the door of the offices of Capital Ventures, the group that handled, among other investments, the A&H Railway stock he had bought. With the money he had saved from his two jobs and his dividends from Valhalla Shipping, he had purchased the stock nearly a year ago, when the railway was only half finished and a new stock offering had just come out.

Before he had invested, he had carefully researched the company that was building the line, what sort of management the railroad would have, and the demand for services along the route. All the information he had collected led him to believe the A&H Railway was a solid investment that would make him a good deal of income.

Now, months later, according to the newspapers, his instincts had been correct. The line was finished and operating, and taking in record amounts of money.

Which made him wonder why he hadn't heard from Capital Ventures—the reason he was standing at the front door of their office.

Thor pulled open the door and walked into an elegant wood-paneled reception room that looked far nicer than when he had come to them with his money nearly a year ago. He walked up to the front desk where a young blond man worked writing letters and filing papers.

The lad looked up at him and smiled. "May I help you, sir?"

"I am here to see Mr. Wilkins."

"May I please have your name?"

"Thorolf Draugr."

"What may I say this is in regard to, Mr. Draugr?"

"My A&H Railway stock."

"Very well. If you will excuse me, I'll find out if Mr. Wilkins can see you." The young man disappeared through an ornate mahogany door that replaced the plain wooden door there last year. He returned a few minutes later.

"I'm terribly sorry. I thought Mr. Wilkins was in, but apparently he had a meeting." His smile looked slightly pained. "He must have gone out the back way."

Thor frowned. The lad's expression said something was amiss. "You are certain, he is not here?"

"I'm sorry—no, he isn't. He'll be back tomorrow, however. Perhaps you should make an appointment."

If Wilkins was gone, he must have just left. Thor needed to be on his way to Renhurst no later than the morrow. "I will be here at eight o'clock in the morning. I will expect to see Mr. Wilkins then."

The lad hurried over to the desk. "Just let me check his schedule—"

"Tell him to be here."

The young man opened his mouth but Thor was already heading for the door. He had a feeling Wilkins was avoiding him and he didn't like it.

Tomorrow morning he would speak to the man, ask the questions for which he had come.

And Wilkins had better have the right answers.

Lindsey arrived at Renhurst late in the afternoon. As she passed through the nearby village of Foxgrove, she could see the massive three-story mansion built of Cotswold stone perched on a gently sloping hill. It was fashioned in the Georgian style, with a slate hip roof and two symmetrical wings that extended toward the rear of the house.

Lindsey smiled, always pleased by the beauty of the structure. Her father had told her his great-grandfather had built the mansion in the early seventeen-hundreds as a gift for his wife on their fifteenth anniversary. The couple had enjoyed the house for thirty more years before the old man had passed away. Six months later, his wife had followed him to the grave. Rumor was she had died of a broken heart.

It was a romantic tale, the sort that made Lindsey yearn for the kind of love her great-grandparents had shared. It wasn't going to happen, not for her, and Lindsey was resigned to the fact.

Exhausted from the long, bumpy coach ride over a road still muddy from last night's rain, she leaned back in the deep velvet seat, her gaze on the rolling green landscape. A flight of ducks passed overhead, and in a distant field, two young boys flew a pair of long-tailed kites. Lindsey smiled, thinking how much she had missed the country.

The carriage rolled to a jolting halt in front of the big stone house and a footman rushed forward to open the door. Though a brisk wind whipped her cloak, the sun shone through the clouds, illuminating a patch of green here and there. The leaves formed a pallet of rich golds, vibrant reds, and bold oranges that collided with the deep green shrubs and foliage.

As she climbed the wide front steps, she glanced off toward the stables. Horses were the other thing she missed. Her father owned a string of blooded stock that nearly rivaled those in Lord Merrick's impressive racing stable next door.

A shiver of anticipation went through her. Riding in the park simply could not compare with galloping wildly across open fields, jumping hedges and fences, and splashing through frothy streams.

The front door opened before she reached it. The butler, a thin man with bushy gray eyebrows, smiled as she walked into the house. "Welcome home, miss."

"Thank you, Creevey. It's good to be back."

"Your brother has gone riding but your aunt is in the Red Drawing Room. She asked that you join her there as soon as you arrived."

"Very well."

"I'll see to your luggage."

She nodded, and headed down the hall. In the Red Room, Aunt Dee sat at an ornate gilded French writing desk, her head bent over the inlaid leather top.

She stood up at Lindsey's approach, a wide smile on her face. "You are here and safe. How was your journey?"

"Damp and bumpy."

Aunt Dee laughed. "The roads can be miserable this time of year." She looked down at the stack of invitations she had been addressing. "I hope the rain won't pose a problem for our guests."

Lindsey followed her gaze to the rather formidable pile of engraved, gold-embossed cards. "I thought you said only a very few people would be coming."

"There are only fifteen or so. The house has sixty bedrooms. I don't think we shall be overcrowded."

Lindsey smiled. "I suppose not." She picked up the invitations, began to leaf through them. "I see Mr. Langtree is among those invited."

"Why, yes, he is."

"He seems a very pleasant man."

Delilah glanced away, a bit of rose appearing in her cheeks. "The colonel is quite good company."

Lindsey made no reply. It would be nice if her aunt found someone to replace the husband she had lost ten years ago. Her marriage to the Earl of Ashford, a much older man, had been arranged. She deserved a love match the second time around.

Lindsey shuffled through a few more names. "You've invited the Earl and Countess of Tremaine. I do hope they can come."

"Grayson is quite an intriguing man. I have met him several times. I look forward to getting to know him better."

"As do I." Lindsey flipped to the next card. Stephen Camden, Viscount Merrick. "I hoped you would include Lord Merrick."

"He won't be an overnight guest, of course, since he lives next door, but it will be nice to see him again."

Lindsey nodded. And it would give her an opportunity to talk to him, see what might be happening in his life. See if there was any reason his name should be mentioned in a note regarding murder.

She moved on to the next invitation. "I hope Krista and Leif will be able to come. They have the baby to think of and of course the running of their businesses."

She couldn't help wishing Thor's name was on the guest list, but he didn't like social affairs. She remembered how handsome he had looked dressed in evening clothes at Lord Kittridge's ball. He could certainly play the role of gentleman if he wished—at least on the surface.

Still, it wouldn't be fair to expect him to change himself merely to please her. Thor was his own man and that was one of the things she liked best about him.

There were other things, as well, she realized. She liked

his protectiveness, though at times it could be most annoying. She liked his sensitivity and the gentleness that ran beneath the surface of his very formidable exterior. She liked that he was a man—a real man, not some overblown dandy.

Lindsey blew out a breath. "I think I shall go up and unpack, if you don't mind. I find I am a bit tired after my journey."

"Of course." Her aunt sat back down at the desk, picked up her plumed pen and dipped it in the inkwell. "Supper is at eight. Your brother will be dining with us. I will see you then."

Lindsey nodded. Rudy was here, safe, at least for the present. Still, the threat of arrest hung over him. As she climbed the stairs, she thought of the notes she had received and how she might discover if there was the least bit of truth to what had been written inside them.

At eight o'clock the next morning, Thor went to the offices of Capital Ventures only to find a CLOSED sign on the door. Furious and even more determined to discover what was happening with the stock he had purchased, he left the office. His business would have to wait until his return from Renhurst. Traveling satchel in hand, he made his way to the nearest coaching station for his trip out of town.

For now, he had more important business than confronting Silas Wilkins, but soon the time would come.

Since the interior of the mail coach was confining for a man of his size, he found a seat on top where he could enjoy the fresh air and the passing landscape. The coach rolled along at a steady pace, arriving in the village fifteen minutes ahead of schedule at four o'clock in the afternoon. Spotting a sign that read Foxgrove Tavern, he went inside and inquired of a serving maid the directions to Renhurst Hall, which, the maid pointed out, he could see atop a distant knoll.

"There it be, luvy. Just a good walk up the hill."

He handed the woman a coin. "Where will I find Merrick Park? It is also near, is it not?"

"Merrick is farther down the same road. The viscount's land sits side by side with Renhurst."

"Thank you." Thor took his satchel and headed up the hill. The road was still muddy from last night's rain. He wove his way in and out of a string of puddles until he came to a well-maintained gravel drive. Two huge stone pillars marked the entrance to Renhurst Hall, though he couldn't see the house from the road. Instead of turning down the lane, he continued to his destination, Merrick Park.

Before he had left London, he had decided to do a bit of investigating on his own. The best approach, he figured, was to go directly to the source. Turning down the gravel lane that led to Merrick Park, he rounded a corner and spotted the red brick mansion and the huge timber-roofed brick building that housed the stable behind the house.

In the checking he had done so far, he had learned that Stephen Camden was a breeder of horses, the owner of a fine string of racing stock. Thor knew horses and hoped he might use his knowledge to find temporary employment. A great deal could be learned about a man from his servants. And he would be close enough to keep an eye on Lindsey, in residence less than a mile away.

As he neared the stable, Thor watched with admiration

as half a dozen of the viscount's horses raced over the field, prize animals, indeed. They were the same lean breed as the one he had seen in the park. It would serve his own purpose, as well as Lindsey's, should he be able to study the horses he someday hoped to own.

His blood pumped with excitement as he walked up to a stocky, balding man giving orders to the stable boys, the head groom, it would seem.

"You have some fine-looking livestock," Thor said, his gaze returning once more to the horses racing across the rolling green field.

The bald man looked up, then up some more, till his gaze lit on Thor's face. "What can I do for you, mister?"

"I have worked with horses for a number of years. I was hoping you might have a job for a man who knows how to handle such fine animals."

The bald man studied him closely. "You're lookin' for a job?"

"Aye, that I am."

"There's always a place here for a man who knows horses. In fact, we just lost one of our trainers. That's a pretty big job. You think you could handle it?"

"Aye, I could."

The bald man nodded. "Me name's Horace Nub."

"Thor Draugr."

"All right, Draugr, follow me."

They made their way inside the stable, which was swept so clean there wasn't a loose bit of straw on the floor. Bays, sorrels, and blacks of the highest caliber filled the stalls, nickering as grooms tended their water buckets and carried them bags of oats. Thor followed Horace Nub out the rear stable door to a large pen on the opposite side.

Nub pointed to a big black stallion prancing around inside the ring. "That black devil is the King's Saber. Should have named him Satan. Ain't a man been able to stay in the pen with him more'n ten minutes. Last trainer what tried left here with a broken arm."

Thor looked at the magnificent creature snorting and stomping on the other side of the fence. The stallion was larger than most of the other horses the viscount owned, but the lines of his body were the same as the others, the long sleek neck, the lean, powerful muscles in the hindquarters and long sinewy legs. His mane and tail floated like banners of silk as he darted and pranced round the ring.

He was the most beautiful horse Thor had ever seen.

"His lordship bought him to race, but he don't have the temperament for it. Can't even breed the bastard. Damned near kilt the last mare he mounted. Head trainer—that'd be Harley Burke—advised his lordship to put him down afore he kills someone."

Thor's chest tightened at the thought. "I will take a look at him."

"Any harm comes to you, that's your problem. But you get him to let you stay in there, you got a job."

Thor just nodded. The animal captured his full attention. He wanted nothing so much as to touch him, to feel the smooth, inky blackness of the stallion's coat, to harness the power of his long, lean stride as he raced around the pen.

Thor started for the gate, moving slowly but with confidence. They had to see each other as equals from the start.

He opened the gate and just stood there in the opening.

In the middle of the ring, the horse jolted to a halt. His ears shot back and his nostrils flared. For several seconds he pawed the ground, danced and reared and made a low, shrill whinny of warning. An instant later, he charged, teeth bared, ears flattened back against his head.

Thor did not move.

The animal slid to a halt just inches away from him. He went up on his hind legs and pawed the air, a fearsome sight that would drive any sane man away.

Thor did not move. "Saber of the King," he said so softly only the horse could hear. "*Brandr fra dat Konungr* would be your name where I come from. It is a good name."

The stallion snorted, reared again, then came down on his front hooves almost on top of Thor.

"You are angry, *Brandr*. I can see this. Someone has hurt you. They did not understand how strong you are, how much you need your freedom."

The horse turned his head to the side and studied him with a wild, dark eye. He snorted his displeasure and tossed his satiny mane while Thor continued speaking softly. In Norse and in English, he told the stallion that he would not hurt him, that in time he would be granted his freedom.

The animal backed away, went up on his hind legs but did not charge again. Instead, he raced around the ring in a fury, making the entire circle, then sliding to a halt in front of Thor, who had moved a little farther into the ring.

Saber snorted and pawed.

Thor did not move.

The stallion reared and charged, but stopped a little farther away.

Thor did not move.

The animal turned and thundered away, slid to a stop at the back of the ring. He whirled and stood with his long legs braced apart, his dark eyes fixed on Thor, who still did not move.

Thor had no idea how much time passed, how many times the horse charged threateningly, then turned and raced away. It did not matter. If the gods were willing, he would find a way into the heart of this magnificent creature, a way to get him to accept whatever fate lay in store for him.

From the corner of his eye, he caught sight of the head groom, Mr. Nub, watching him through the fence. Two other grooms stood watching, pitchforks unmoving in their hands.

"If I hadn't seen it with me own two eyes, I wouldna' believed it."

At the sound of the other man's voice, the horse charged the fence like a madman, shrieking wildly, sliding to a halt in front of where the three men stood. Thor used the moment to leave the ring.

Horace Nub backed away, rubbing a hand over his shiny bald head. "Bloody horse is a killer."

"He is angry. Someone has hurt him. Do you not see the scars on his neck and flanks?"

"Burke took a whip to him. Tried to break him but it didn't work. Stallion ought to be put down."

"Give me a chance to work with him. In time he will give you what you want."

The head groom eyed him with speculation. Again he rubbed his head. "Worth a try, I guess. Just remember what I said—you get hurt, it's your problem."

Thor just nodded. He couldn't wait to get started. Saber of the King was a name the stallion well deserved. Such a fierce beast must carry the blood of champions. It would take a good deal of time, but such a magnificent animal was worth it. In the end, Thor had no doubt he would succeed.

And once he gained a bit of trust from the men in the stable, he would begin to ask questions. He would find out if there was any reason to believe the viscount had some role in the Covent Garden murders.

And each day he would check on Lindsey, make certain that she was safe.

Sixteen

Lindsey sat next to Aunt Dee in the Renhurst carriage. They were on their way to visit Stephen Camden at Merrick Park.

"It was kind of Stephen to ask us to luncheon," Aunt Dee said.

"Why, yes, it was," said Lindsey, feeling a thread of excitement at the prospect of speaking to Merrick, anxious to begin some sort of dialogue that might tell her why the viscount's name had been mentioned in connection to the murders. She wasn't yet certain how she would approach the problem, but sooner or later, the chance would come.

The carriage pulled up in front of the huge brick mansion and a footman rushed up to help them down.

"Lady Ashford…Miss Graham," the young man said. "His lordship is expecting you. A matter came up at the stables. He'll join you in the drawing room in just a few minutes. If you would please come with me—"

"Why don't we go down and see what's happening?"

Lindsey suggested, always appreciative of Merrick's blooded stock.

Aunt Dee glanced in that direction. It was a lovely day with no hint of rain and better enjoyed out of doors. "All right." Lifting their skirts out of the way, they wandered along the brick path leading down to the barns and pens where Stephen kept his prize racing horses.

"His lordship is out in the back," one of the grooms said, showing them the way through the barn to the pen behind the building.

"Over there." Lindsey pointed toward a tall, blond man she recognized as Lord Merrick, handsome, in an elegant, refined manner that made him seem older than his years. Next to him, a man of his same height, bulkier through the chest and shoulders, stood with his legs braced apart and a frown on his ruddy face.

It was the third man, the one who worked a magnificent black horse in the ring, who brought her feet to an utter standstill.

"My heavens," said Aunt Dee, her gaze following Lindsey's. "Isn't that your friend, Thor?"

Knowing the man as she was beginning to, she shouldn't have been surprised to see him. "Clearly, it is," she admitted since Thor wasn't a man her aunt would likely forget.

"What do you suppose he is doing here?"

There was no choice but to tell the truth and perhaps she should have done so before. Lindsey glanced round to be certain no one could hear. "He is here because of a note I received last week. It was similar to an earlier note, accusing one of Rudy's friends of being the Covent Garden Murderer. This note specifically named Stephen Camden."

"Why, that is preposterous. Surely you gave the note no credence."

"None whatsoever, which is the reason I didn't mention it to you or to Rudy. But Thor is extremely protective. He was sure I would not rest until I knew for certain Stephen was innocent of any wrongdoing. He was afraid my questions might put me in danger. I suppose that is why he is here."

The women stood on the path, watching man and horse in the arena. "They are both quite magnificent," Aunt Dee said. "I don't believe I have ever seen a finer specimen of man or beast."

It was true. Lindsey stood transfixed, her gaze locked on the huge man and massive horse facing each other in the pen. It was as if neither saw aught but the other, just a man and a horse, locked in some inner battle of wills.

The stallion was spectacular, as black as a moonless night, powerfully sleek and majestic. The man was equally impressive, thick dark hair curling softly over his collar, eyes as blue as the sea. In a pair of breeches that clung to his long, muscular legs, his broad shoulders and powerful back stretching his full-sleeved white shirt to the limit, he was the most beautiful man Lindsey had ever seen.

"If that man is here for you," Aunt Dee said, "you are in very serious trouble, my girl."

Lindsey moistened her lips, which suddenly felt as dry as an autumn leaf. "We are merely friends. I told you that before."

"Impossible," said her aunt.

Lindsey didn't argue. Even now as she watched him, memories arose of the last time he had made love to her, the feel of him inside her, his big hard body moving above her. Her lips burned at the memory of his kiss and her body wept in anticipation of the next time they would be together.

She swallowed. "Even if...if you were right, there can't ever be more. You know that, Aunt Dee."

Her aunt stared at her from beneath winged black eyebrows. "I hope you remember that when the time comes."

Lindsey said no more. She prayed when the moment came, she would have the courage to leave him, but each time she was with him, the notion grew more painful. Pasting on a smile, she made her way down the path toward the place where Stephen and the ruddy-skinned man watched the goings-on in the ring.

"I hope your friend will be wise enough not to mention your acquaintance," Aunt Dee said before they reached the two men.

"I'm sure he will be." Whatever he was, Thor was no fool. He was there to help her find the truth about the viscount and he would do whatever it took to make that happen.

Stephen spotted the women approaching and returned the smile of greeting on Aunt Dee's face.

"My dear Lady Ashford, it is so good to see you." He turned that same smile on Lindsey. "And you, Miss Graham, as well. You both look lovely, as always. I apologize for not being at the house when you arrived. I heard there was something of interest going on down here. I seem to have let the time escape me."

"That's quite all right, Stephen," said Aunt Dee. "We were enjoying the show."

He turned, frowned at the man and horse in the ring. "That stallion is quite beautiful, but also completely unmanageable. My trainer, Mr. Burke, has advised me to have him put down before he hurts someone badly—or worse."

There were horses that simply could not be broken. Perhaps something had happened when they were colts, someone had abused or mistreated them, or their minds were not right from birth.

"Draugr is a fool," said the trainer to Stephen. "He just stands there talking—as if that killer actually understands what he is saying. It's only a matter of time until we're carrying the lackwit off to the surgeon's."

Lindsey looked at Thor. Though he was speaking so softly she couldn't hear what he said, she could see his lips moving. A little tremor went through her as she remembered the night the men had attacked her outside the Blue Moon, the whispered words Thor had spoken that calmed her as nothing else could have.

She remembered the way he had soothed her with his tender words and gentle touches before he made love to her that first time. Perhaps he was a fool to believe a horse would respond to that same gentle treatment, but Lindsey didn't think so.

As she watched him working the stallion, reaching out slowly to run a hand along the animal's glistening black neck, she thought that Thor was the most amazing man she had ever known. She thought that she would never meet another man like him and suddenly her heart throbbed with longing.

Lindsey bit her lip, forcing the unwanted emotion away.

Stephen's voice caught her attention. "Well, ladies, I invited you for luncheon. I understand Cook has prepared quite a feast." He offered his arm to her aunt. "Why don't we leave the stallion to the men and enjoy Cook's delicious fare?" Offering his other arm to Lindsey, he led the women back up the path to the house.

Only the prospect of discovering some clue about the murders kept Lindsey from peeking over her shoulder for a last glance at Thor.

Thor worked with the stallion until late in the evening. Before dawn, he was up and working with the animal again, making a good deal of headway, he believed.

Still, the business he had come for was Lindsey, and after seeing her yesterday with Merrick, he wanted to be sure she was safe.

Several of the horses needed exercising. He saddled a white-faced gelding and rode off toward the Renhurst lands to the west. He had just topped a knoll when he spotted a horse and rider in the early morning light, moving at breakneck speed across the landscape. Thor pulled the gelding to a halt, watching as the pair approached a tall hedge and cleared it with ease. There was something familiar about the rider, something that stirred a memory of the lad who had ridden with such skill and grace in the park.

Horse and rider cleared a high stone wall and landed smartly on the opposite side. Thor smiled at the young man's ability, at the bold way he approached the next obstacle in his path, a wide stream that required the horse to stretch out in front of it in order to clear a small hedge on the near side of the water.

Horse and rider cleared the stream, the animal's hooves spraying drops of water into the air. They were almost out of sight when the rider's hat blew off, exposing a long thick braid of tawny hair. For an instant, Thor couldn't believe what he was seeing. Not a lad, but a woman in men's riding breeches—a woman who belonged to him!

Clenching his jaw, he set his heels into the gelding's ribs, urging the horse to give chase. What before he had seen as skill he now saw as wild, reckless behavior and he was determined to stop it before Lindsey got hurt.

He had nearly caught up with her by the time she spotted him. When she did, instead of drawing rein, she grinned and bent over the sorrel's neck, urging the animal to a faster pace. She took a hedge, clipping it neatly, and Thor's fury increased. She was no man, even if she rode like one. Sooner or later she was going to get hurt!

She took a stream, clearing it completely, and landed neatly on the opposite side. Thor cleared the stream right behind her, his anger driving him on.

Lindsey slowed as he neared, but Thor did not stop. Instead, at the last minute his arm shot out, hauling her out of her saddle onto his, landing her neatly upside down across his lap. His palm came down hard, once, twice. Lindsey shrieked in outrage and began to struggle against his hold. If he hadn't been afraid she would fall, he would have landed a couple more blows.

Instead, he stilled the gelding and lowered her to her feet, then swung down from his saddle beside her.

"How dare you!" she spit at him like the angry little she-cat he had called her before. "I have been riding since I was three years old! I can manage a horse just as well as you, Thorolf Draugr! You've no right to treat me as if I am a misbehaving child!"

"You are a woman, not a man! You could get killed!"

"So could you! So could anyone!" She stomped away, her cheeks burning as hotly as he imagined was her bottom. "I did not deserve that! I am a very good rider." She turned a venomous glare in his direction. "Perhaps you are jealous. Perhaps you don't like it that a woman can ride as well as you."

"You are my woman, Lindsey. I will not see you hurt."

"I am *not* your woman! We are lovers—that is all! I demand an apology! You were wrong in this. The only question is, are you man enough to admit it."

Thor stared down at her. Strands of honey hair teased her cheeks and her lips were plump and pink. She was beautiful—and one of the finest riders he had ever seen. It was his duty to protect her, and yet, like the stallion, she deserved her freedom.

He blew out a breath, knowing she was right. "Your riding is equal to that of any man." He shook his head, amending the words. "In truth, you are as good a rider as any I have ever seen. I was afraid for you. I let my fear turn to anger. I am sorry."

She was still angry. The color remained high in her cheeks. Stiffly she nodded. "I accept your apology. I suppose I can forgive you—this once."

He moved toward her, reached out and ran a finger along her cheek. "I know no woman like you. It is hard for a man like me to accept a woman who is his equal."

Surprise flared in her eyes. And something else he could not read. She stepped toward him, went into his arms. "I've missed you."

He kissed the top of her head. "Aye, as I have missed you."

She held onto him for several long moments and when she stepped away, he didn't want to let her go.

"The black stallion is beautiful," she said. "Merrick says Burke wants to put him down."

"Burke is a fool."

"Can you tame him?"

He ran a hand along Lindsey's jaw. "You, little fox, are the only creature I cannot seem to tame." He tipped her head back and kissed her, tasting the sweetness of her lips, taking her deeply with his tongue. He was hard in an instant, aching to be inside her.

He felt her slender hand on his chest, unbuttoning the front of his shirt, parting the fabric and reaching inside, her palms smoothing over the muscles across his chest. His groin tightened and he deepened the kiss, inhaling the scent of her, unable to get enough. His sex throbbed, pressed painfully against the front of his breeches. He felt her hand there, tentatively touching, testing the hardness. Thor hissed in a breath.

Lindsey broke the kiss and looked up at him, turned toward an ancient cluster of stones, the remains of an old stone abbey.

"There…let's go over there so no one will see us."

When she tugged on his hand, he didn't resist. For now she belonged to him and he meant to take what was his.

In the ruins of stone, he kissed her long and thoroughly, ran his hands inside her blouse to cup her breasts. They were as round and plump as ripe peaches, as smooth as the petals of a rose. He ached to taste them, to feel the pink crest tighten against his tongue.

He parted her blouse and set his mouth to a tempting mound, laved her nipples until they tightened into diamond-hard peaks, then unbuttoned the front of her breeches and eased them down over her hips.

Turning her back to him, he bent her over till her hands flattened on one of the lower stones.

"What are you…?"

"I will take you this way, as the wolf takes his mate."

He nipped the side of her neck while his hands smoothed over the lovely white globes of her bottom, feeling a twinge of guilt at the pink mark left by his palm. He bent and pressed his mouth there, a series of soft butterfly kisses to tell her he was sorry, that from now on he would grant her the respect she deserved. Lindsey trembled beneath his touch and his body hardened to the point of pain.

"Please…" she whispered, her breath coming faster at his probing touch.

She was wet and ready. He eased himself inside her tight passage, pushed forward until he filled her completely, settled his hands around her waist and slowly began to move. Heat and need rolled through him, stronger than anything he had ever felt before. With each deep stroke, he claimed her, grew more certain she was meant to be his, and yet he knew it could not be.

Still, he took her with a need he seemed unable to control. Took her and took her, until he was blind to all but Lindsey, all but the feel of her slender body gloving him so sweetly, of her soft moans of pleasure, of the ripples of fulfillment coursing through her.

His own release came swift and hard, his muscles turning to steel, his seed spilling hotly inside her. He wondered if her potion would work and worry gripped him. She was too slight to bear a child he sired, too slender to carry his babe.

He prayed the potion would work and yet deep in his heart, he wanted nothing so much as to plant his seed and watch it grow, to know the child in her womb would be part of them both. It was wrong to feel that way when he could never be the man she needed.

He withdrew himself from the warmth of her body and she turned and went into his arms. After a time, he let her go. Silently waiting while she freshened herself, when she had finished, he helped her refasten her clothes.

"I have to go," she said.

He nodded. "As do I." He cupped her face in his hands. "Promise me you will be careful—with the horse and with Merrick."

"I learned nothing when I was there yesterday. He seems a very unlikely murderer, but—"

"But it is something you cannot know for sure."

She nodded. "Stephen is coming to the house party my aunt is giving. Perhaps we'll discover something of his activities while he is there."

"I will keep my ears open. The men talk of him. I will see what they have to say."

She turned away, walked over and collected her horse. "We could meet somewhere tonight."

The temptation was nearly overwhelming. Thor shook his head. "We should not have done what we did here. The risks are too great."

"I don't care."

"I think you do."

She glanced away, toyed with the horse's reins. "Leif and Krista will be here in a couple of days."

"Good. Mayhap between the three of us, we can keep

you out of trouble." Turning her toward the horse, he caught hold of her waist and swung her up on the flat leather saddle. "Behave yourself, little fox."

She grinned. "I promise not to do anything a wolf wouldn't do."

Thor shook his head, fighting a smile as she rode away.

Horse and rider disappeared over the top of the hill and his smile slipped away. It was wrong, what they were doing. If they could not wed, he should leave her alone.

He told himself he would.

He just wished he could make himself believe it.

Seventeen

The cool October days slipped past. Rudy was becoming moody and bored, consoled only by the fact that next week the guests would begin to arrive for the house party Aunt Dee was giving. Delilah had a number of activities planned, everything from cards and afternoon outings, to a traveling theatrical group she had hired as entertainment and even a small soiree with a number of the neighbors invited.

The week would conclude with the Foxgrove Derby, a local event, an annual steeplechase people came from miles round to see.

"It should make quite a spectacular conclusion to our party, don't you think?" Aunt Dee said to Lindsey. "You know how men like to gamble. I thought this year we might enter a Renhurst horse and, of course, Lord Merrick will be racing."

Merrick. The man never strayed far from her thoughts. In the village she had quietly asked questions about him, but the locals seemed reluctant to speak of him. He was an important member of the community, his estate and horse breeding operation provided a number of people with jobs. They didn't wish to risk losing them.

Though frustrated by how little she had learned, Lindsey was enjoying her time in the country and especially the chance to ride. She had done so every morning, breathing in the cool, moist air, absorbing the pleasure of being out of doors, away from the noise and congestion of the city.

Each day as she rode out of the stable, she hoped to see Thor, but if he were somewhere about, he did not show himself. He had not made himself known since their heated encounter among the ancient stones.

Her stomach contracted at the memory of that morning, of his mouth on her breasts, of his hard length moving inside her. She couldn't help wishing he would come to her again, couldn't help wondering what other pleasures he might show her.

Instead, he was avoiding her. Thor wasn't the sort of man to carry on an affair with an unmarried young woman he could not wed. She was tempted to send him a note, invent some dire emergency in the hope he would come to her rescue, but she was afraid it would only make him angry. Still, she had a feeling he was often there at Renhurst, making certain she was safe.

It was the following week that the guests began to arrive. Most were people she had known would be coming. Others were unexpected.

Along with Colonel Langtree, Aunt Dee had invited the Marquess and Marchioness of Penrose, both her aunt's longtime friends. The Earl and Countess of Kittridge and their two daughters, Elizabeth and Sarah, were also on the guest list. Sarah had just turned eighteen. At one-and-twenty, Elizabeth had been in the marriage mart for several years but rumor was she enjoyed the young men's attention far too much to accept a proposal.

The second day of the week, Leif and Krista arrived.

"I am so glad you could come," Lindsey said, stepping up to hug her friends.

"It took a bit of persuading," Leif said. "This is the first time we've been away from our son. At least farther away than the other side of town."

"I hope Brandon will be all right," Krista said worriedly.

Leif leaned over and kissed her cheek. "He'll be fine, love. Mrs. McElroy is a genius with babies."

Krista sighed. "I know you're right. I shall do my best to relax and enjoy myself."

Coralee and her husband, Gray Forsythe, Earl of Tremaine, arrived that same day. "You look marvelous," Lindsey said to Corrie. "I swear you are lovelier each time I see you."

"Married life agrees with me." She leaned over and whispered, "And I think I may be carrying Gray's child—though I cannot say for certain and I haven't told him yet."

"All right, ladies—no secrets," Gray said. He arched a sleek black eyebrow at his wife. "I thought you had learned your lesson." His thick black hair, tied back with a ribbon, was hardly stylish, yet seemed to suit him perfectly, giving him the look of a pirate.

"I've learned, my darling, I promise." But she grinned at Lindsey and Lindsey grinned back. "We need to talk," Corrie mouthed.

Lindsey reluctantly agreed, certain her friend was concerned about Thor and the potion Samir had made for her.

Aunt Dee joined them and the group chatted amiably for a while. Lindsey found Gray to be intelligent and interesting, and he was incredibly handsome—and obviously in love and devoted to his wife.

Other guests arrived. Rudy had invited Tom Boggs and Edward Winslow, and the two young men showed up at Renhurst together. Lindsey had hoped her brother had finally outgrown his rich, spoiled, rakehell friends, but apparently he had not.

She thought of her brother and the viscount and wished she could discover who had sent her the notes. She vowed that she would find out, and the following day managed to break away for a ride to Merrick Park. Perhaps Thor had unearthed something useful. Finding out was as good an excuse as any for her to see him.

Mounted sidesaddle and dressed in a smart green velvet riding habit and a jaunty little matching green hat, she headed down the lane to the viscount's home, trying to decide how best to speak to Thor without giving away their relationship. As luck would have it, Stephen was on his way to the stables when she rode in.

He smiled at her as she pulled her tall bay mare to a halt in the gravel drive in front of his house.

"Why, Lindsey, what a nice surprise." Sunlight shone on his thick blond hair, making it gleam like new gold, and she thought how handsome he was and how unlikely it was that a man with his money and charm would consort with prostitutes—let alone murder them.

"Good morning, my lord."

He shook his head. "Stephen, please. We are friends too
long for such formality." The smile reappeared. "To what
do I owe such a pleasant surprise?"

"I was out riding. I thought I would drop by, see how
your trainer is doing with that marvelous black stallion."
After considering her options, she had decided to stay as
close to the truth as possible. She did want to see the
stallion and she particularly wanted to see his trainer.

"What a coincidence. That is exactly what I am about
this morning." He reached up and lifted her down from the
sidesaddle, handing her horse's reins to the groom who
rushed up to lend his assistance.

They walked down the brick pathway together, into the
cool shadows of the barn and back out into the sunlight on
the opposite side. She spotted Thor immediately, at work
with the stallion in the ring. Another man stood some
distance away, tall, barrel-chested and ruddy complex-
ioned. She remembered he was Stephen's head trainer, a
fellow named Burke.

"You've been at it almost two weeks," Burke was saying
to Thor. "Near as I can tell, the horse still can't be controlled."

"It takes time." Thor released the stallion from the rope
round his neck, then headed for the gate leading into the ring.

As he walked past Burke, the man caught his arm. "Lord
Merrick has been patient long enough."

Thor straightened. "The horse was mistreated. It takes
time to repair the damage."

"And I say you are wasting his lordship's money."
Burke caught sight of Merrick just then, turned his atten-
tion in that direction, and for the first time Thor realized
Lindsey was there.

His features tightened, then turned carefully bland.

Lindsey managed to keep her expression equally un
readable though her heart was beating too fast and he
cheeks felt a little too warm.

"What's going on?" Stephen asked the two men.

"Nothing," Burke said. "That's the problem—nothing
is going on. That black devil is as mad as he was the day
he arrived. It's clear that isn't going to change."

"Mr. Draugr, have you anything to say in the horse'
defense?"

"Saber is worth the time it will take to gentle him."

"I don't think so," Burke disagreed. "I don't think tha
stallion will ever be worth a fiddler's damn." He turned to
Merrick, a cunning smile curling his lips. "I've given the
matter a good deal of thought. The Foxgrove Derby is com
ing up the end of the week. I say the stallion should run o
be put down. It's time to face the facts and cut our losses."

People came from all over to watch the annual steeple
chase. Both locals and gentry participated, riding an array
of livestock from saddle horses to Thoroughbreds. Stephen
always entered one of his prize racers and he hadn't lost i
years.

"Saber is not ready," Thor said.

"That horse will never be ready," argued Burke. "He'l
never be more than the devil he is now."

As if to prove the point, Saber caught the man's scen
just then and charged the fence like a creature from hell. H
reared up on his hind legs and let out an unearthly scream
his teeth bared and his ears flattened back against his skull
He stomped the ground, whirled and charged again, and fo
an instant, Lindsey thought he was coming over the fence

"He does not like you," Thor said to Burke.

"I don't give a bloody damn what he likes. That spawn of Satan ought to be destroyed." He glanced up at Lindsey. "Sorry, miss, but that horse is going to wind up killing someone."

Lindsey gave him a tight-lipped smile. "He seems to do all right with his trainer."

Burke scoffed. "You think so? Then let the pair of them ride in the derby."

"Burke has a point," Stephen said to Thor. "You believe that horse can be managed. Exactly how certain are you?"

"In time, he will be all you wish him to be."

"I've owned him for more than a year. He's already injured three trainers, including Mr. Burke, and I haven't been able to get anywhere near him without putting myself at risk. We can't even put him out to stud—he's too rough with the mares. As far as I can see, he's just as violent and out of control as he was when he arrived. I won't have that kind of animal on the premises. I agree with Mr. Burke. Either he races or his days are over."

Thor flicked a glance at Lindsey. "If that is the choice, then he will race." His jaw hardened. "But if he wins, he is mine."

Burke burst out laughing. "You think that beast can win the derby? He'll have you on the ground before the first fence."

"Mayhap you are right. If that is so then you have lost nothing."

Stephen smiled coldly. "If you win, you want the horse. What do I get if he loses?"

Lindsey heard the sound of footfalls on the path. A familiar feminine voice spoke up from behind them.

"If the stallion loses," Krista said, "Thor will forfeit two thousand pounds."

Stephen's gaze sharpened on the beautiful blond woman standing next to her even taller blond husband, an impressive couple whose attractiveness rarely went unremarked.

"Make it three thousand and you have yourself a bet."

Thor opened his mouth to protest, but Leif gave a faint shake of his head.

"The bargain is struck," Krista said. "The stallion races—and if he wins, he belongs to Thor."

Thor left the group, rounding the barn and striding off into the trees. He was furious at himself for speaking out as he had, and even more furious at his brother and sister-in-law for betting such an outrageous sum. *Three thousand pounds!* If he risked his own money it would be one thing. To risk Leif and Krista's money was unthinkable.

He had to win—or find a way to pay them back.

Which made him think of his A&H Railway stock. Even selling it would not be enough. Thor sighed as he sank down in the grass and leaned back against the trunk of a tree.

He could only imagine what Lindsey must be thinking. She knew he didn't have money enough to provide for a woman of her station, but he didn't want the fact thrown in her face.

He looked up just then, surprised to see her approaching, the skirt of her green velvet riding habit rustling around her long legs. He remembered those legs in snug men's riding breeches, remembered sliding them down over her hips then gripping her tiny waist and riding her to fulfillment.

His shaft thickened, went rock-hard. By the gods, the woman drove him mad with lust for her.

"You should not be here," he said, rising to his feet, ignoring the hot burn of desire rushing through his blood. "What will Lord Merrick think?"

"He will think that you are Leif's brother, as he now knows, and therefore a friend. Your relationship was clear the moment Leif arrived, since the two of you are of an unusual height and build, and though you are dark where Leif is fair, you look a great deal like him."

"What is my brother doing at Merrick Park?"

"Krista has known Lord Merrick for some time. As you just found out, Stephen likes to gamble. Apparently Leif met him during his gaming days. At any rate, since Leif and Krista were enjoying a carriage ride round the countryside, they decided to pay him a visit."

"I suppose it no longer matters. I found nothing that would tie Merrick to the murders."

"I never really believed he was involved."

"The grooms do not like him. He is hard on the horses, but he pays well and they need the work."

She glanced back toward the barn, caught a glimpse of Saber prancing around the paddock. "What about the race?"

Thor shrugged. "It was a foolish bet. There is no way Saber can win."

"Has he let you ride him yet?"

He nodded. "In the mornings, before anyone is up. He loves to run and he is as fast as the wind. He takes the fences as if he has wings. It is only the way he's been treated that makes him the way he is."

"You think it was Burke?"

"Burke and men before him. Saber is angry. He wants to punish those who hurt him."

She gave him a teasing smile. "Is that what he told you when you talked to him?"

Thor grinned, making him look so handsome she sucked in a breath. "That is what I learned when I spoke to the grooms. Burke talked Merrick into buying the stallion. He bragged about how he could ride him when others could not. Saber threw him, made him look like a fool in front of the viscount. Burke beat the horse and he became even harder to handle than he was before."

"If he's so fast, why can't he win?"

"Merrick's entry will be a champion and his rider will be small and light. As fast as Saber is, the disadvantage in carrying a man of my size is too great."

Lindsey pondered the problem, recognizing Thor's words as true. Then her pulse took a leap as an idea popped into her head. "Do you think…? Would he let someone else ride him?"

Thor gazed back at the pen where Saber snorted and danced. "Mayhap in time he would. If the man won his trust. Even so, there is no one who would take the risk."

"I would."

Fierce blue eyes locked on her face. "That is not possible."

"I could do it. If you helped Saber get to know me, I could ride him. And I could win."

Thor shook his head. "It is too dangerous, Lindsey. I will not see you hurt."

"You know how well I ride. If Saber allowed me on his back and he is as fast as you say, I could win—you know I could. If that happened, the stallion would belong to you. That's what you want, isn't it? You want to own the King's Saber?"

She could read the temptation, his overwhelming desire to own such a magnificent animal.

He sighed. "As much as I might wish it could be so, I will not risk your life."

"We wouldn't try it unless Saber accepted me. If he did, then there would be no greater risk than with any other horse."

"Do not ask this of me, Lindsey."

"I'm not asking for me, Thor. I'm asking for Saber. They'll put him down if he doesn't win that race. Are you willing to stand by and let that happen?"

"Mayhap I could find a way to buy him."

"I don't think Merrick will sell him to anyone and especially not you."

He turned away, his jaw iron-hard. He paced away from the tree, stood there for several long moments with his long legs braced apart. It was all she could do not to go to him, try again to make him see.

Thor turned and paced back to the place in front of her. She could see the turmoil in his face. "How can I allow this?"

"You said once that I was your equal. If you meant it, then you have no choice."

His gaze held hers.

"Let me do this, Thor. For you and for Saber."

A resigned breath slipped from his lips. "We will see what Saber has to say."

Lindsey grinned, excited by the prospect of the race, barely able to keep from releasing a whoop of glee. It didn't matter that she would have to dress like a boy and that if she won, no one could ever know she was the rider. "When do I meet him?"

Thor looked back at the magnificent horse. "Tonight. Come to me at the ruins of stone. Saber will be the one to decide."

Lindsey strode into the house, followed by Leif and Krista. They had shared a luncheon with Lord Merrick, who had been both gracious and charming, then returned home together, tying Lindsey's mount to the rear of the carriage. On the brief journey, they had talked about the derby at the end of the week and Thor's plans to race the huge black stallion, but Lindsey kept silent about her intention to participate in the event.

Both Leif and Krista were excellent riders, but she couldn't take the chance they might disapprove and do something to try to stop her.

They arrived at the house and went inside.

"I hear laughter in the card room," she said as they crossed the entry. "And I imagine you'll find my aunt and some of the others out on the terrace."

Leif cast his wife a burning glance. "I think we'll go up and take a nap before supper." His hot look said sleep was the last thing on his mind.

Krista actually blushed. "That sounds like a very good notion. A little rest should be just the thing."

Lindsey hid a smile. If Leif was nearly as virile as his fiercely passionate brother, Krista wouldn't give a fig about sleep.

Leif took hold of Krista's hand, and husband and wife headed up the stairs. Intending to get a bit of rest herself, Lindsey turned to follow, then noticed the butler lurking in the hallway.

"What is it, Mr. Creevey?"

He came forward, silver-haired and a bit stoop-shouldered. "A message arrived for you, miss. One of the lads from the village brought it 'bout an hour ago."

She looked down at the silver salver the butler held out to her, saw her name scrawled on the folded, wax-sealed square of paper. As she recognized the writing, her hand paused midway to the tray. It was the same as the notes she had received in London, and a little shiver went through her.

Irritation overrode her trepidation and she plucked the message off the tray, wondering if the sender would continue to malign the viscount, or if, perhaps, he had some new mischief in mind.

Walking a few feet away, she cracked open the red wax seal and read the words scrawled in blue ink.

Since you are now in the country, you must be starting to believe. Ask about a young woman named Penelope Barker. Find her and you will discover the truth about Merrick.

Lindsey crushed the note in her hand. Thanks to her brother, both Tom Boggs and Edward Winslow were guests at Renhurst for the house party. Odds were, one of them was the culprit responsible for the note. If he was, Lindsey was going to give him a piece of her mind.

As she climbed the stairs, she recalled the words in the message. She had visited Merrick's estate several times and asked as many questions as she dared, but Stephen was a man of impeccable reputation, a longtime family friend, and she had never seriously entertained the notion that he might be responsible for two brutal murders.

She had come to Renhurst to get her brother out of London and enjoy herself.

Or had the trip merely been an excuse to examine the information in the notes she had received?

Whatever the truth, another accusation had been made against Stephen, this one even more specific.

Lindsey sighed as she walked into her bedroom and crossed to the bell pull to summon her maid for help changing out of her riding clothes. Whoever had written the note had left her no choice but to find out about Penelope Barker and locate her whereabouts.

Lindsey tried not to think what she might discover if a woman named Penelope Barker actually existed, and if she did, what might have happened to her.

Eighteen

An elegant supper of roasted pheasant accompanied by a filet of turbot in a light lemon cream sauce had finally come to an end, and the ladies and gentlemen of the house party now engaged in various evening activities.

Colonel Langtree sat next to Aunt Dee on the gold brocade sofa in the Gilt Drawing Room. Near the hearth, the Earl of Kittridge sipped a glass of brandy and conversed about India with the Earl of Tremaine while other of the guests played cards in the game room.

Lindsey and Coralee sat in the circle with Colonel Langtree and Aunt Delilah, Lindsey trying not to glance at the ormolu clock on the sienna marble mantel. She had been trying to find a polite means of escape for nearly an hour, so far to no avail.

"So, Miss Graham, your aunt tells me you are an extremely proficient rider." Colonel Langtree smiled, introducing talk of a sport he enjoyed.

Lindsey returned the smile. "I refuse to play coy and deny it. I have been riding since I was a child. It is a joy to be here at Renhurst where I have access to my father's purebred horses."

"She's a marvelous rider," Coralee added. "It's a talent I find myself sorely lacking, but Gray has assured me in time I shall improve."

"It is mostly a matter of practice," Lindsey said. Her glance returned to the colonel, then moved to Aunt Dee, resplendent in a gown of burgundy silk trimmed with pale peach lace. "My aunt also rides very well. I imagine she would be willing to give you a tour of the estate."

Delilah smiled brightly. "A marvelous notion, my dear." She turned to the colonel. "If you like, we could go sometime on the morrow."

"I would like that very much, indeed." It took the colonel a moment longer than it should have to glance away from Aunt Dee's lovely gray eyes. He cleared his throat and returned his attention to Lindsey. "So what do you think of the upcoming derby? I image you've watched any number of them over the years."

"I can tell you it is quite an occasion and certainly a great deal of fun. It should be a fitting end to the week."

"I hear you are entering one of Renhurst's Thoroughbred horses," Coralee said to Aunt Dee.

"Indeed, we are. Though we have not yet decided which horse to run."

"I pray you choose well," the colonel said, a mischievous twinkle in his eyes. "I plan to bet on the Renhurst entry and I am counting on winning."

"Lord Merrick's horse will be difficult to beat," Coralee warned. "From what I've heard, the viscount trains all year for this event."

"Still, our horses are all first-rate," said Aunt Dee, "and we have very good trainers. You may be certain we will give the race our utmost effort."

Lindsey thought of the beautiful black stallion, the King's Saber. With any luck, she would be riding in the race herself. If that occurred, the colonel would be wise to place his bet on the black—for Lindsey was determined to be the winner.

She yawned behind her hand. "It's getting late. I am afraid I am a bit worn out. If you don't mind, I think I shall retire for the evening."

"Of course, dear," Aunt Delilah said.

"Sleep well," said the colonel, rising as she left her seat and started for the door. She imagined he was hoping the rest of the guests would leave as well—all but Delilah.

The colonel and her aunt were extremely well-suited, Lindsey thought as the man returned to his seat beside Aunt Dee—unlike she and Thor, who were so completely ill-suited. She ignored a twinge of regret. Some things were simply not to be and there was nothing one could do about it.

Still, she couldn't keep her pulse from speeding in anticipation of their meeting tonight. Lindsey hurried up the stairs to her room.

Thor paced nervously back and forth at the edge of the stone ruins. If Lindsey didn't arrive soon, he was going in search of her.

He swore a soft oath. He never should have let her come out here at night, never should have agreed to this meeting in the first place. He knew she had been asking questions in the village. If there was any truth to the notes, Merrick might well be disturbed by her interest in his affairs. Mayhap he had sent someone to watch her. Mayhap she was being followed.

He tried not to think of the men in the alley and what they had intended to do. He took a deep, shuddering breath.

Five more minutes and he would go after her.

He glanced toward the grassy area where the stallion grazed contentedly, happy to be out of his pen. Today had been a day of accomplishment for the horse—Thor had convinced the animal to stand under saddle. According to Horace Nub, before Saber had been mistreated, he had been trained to accept both saddle and bridle.

Then he had been sold to a man who treated his horses cruelly. After that, a string of trainers who believed in using brute force couldn't bring the stallion back under control and three of them had been seriously injured.

Thor had managed to win the horse's trust, but that didn't mean that Saber would allow Lindsey to ride him—or even if he did, that Thor should allow it. What if the stallion threw her? What if she were injured or killed?

Worry had him pacing again. He was about to collect the stallion and ride in search of her when he heard the soft whicker of an approaching horse. Relief flooded through him. And a sweet yearning to see her that he did not wish to feel.

Thor steeled himself. How many times had he vowed to leave her alone? What was it about her that made it so difficult a promise to keep?

She rode up to where he stood and he reached up to lift her down from the saddle. She was wearing the velvet riding habit she had worn earlier that day, the soft cloth warmed by her body where his hands wrapped around her small waist. He inhaled her scent, the fragrance of flowers and woman, and his body tightened. His shaft turned to steel inside his breeches. She was nothing like the voluptuous women he had always desired and yet no other woman had affected him so strongly.

"The house is still swarming with people," she said with a smile just for him. "I figured Saber and I would simply be getting acquainted tonight so I wore this in case someone saw me go out to the stable."

Her hair curled loosely down her back, held in place on the sides with turtle-shell combs. He wanted nothing so much as to slide his fingers into the tawny mass and drag her mouth up to his for a deep, burning kiss.

Instead, he caught her hand. "Come. We will see if Saber thinks you look as pretty as I do."

She laughed and followed him toward the stallion, who grazed at the end of a long rope tether. The horse's head came up when he saw her and his nostrils flared.

"Not too fast," Thor warned, tugging on Lindsey's hand to slow her down. "Give him time to get used to your presence."

Saber snorted and began to paw the ground, his senses on full alert.

"Easy boy," Lindsey said softly as she slowly approached. "I am not going to hurt you."

He danced a moment, lifted his front feet off the ground, and whinnied sharply.

"Keep talking," Thor said.

"Such a pretty boy, you are. I hope you will let me ride

you. I would like that ever so much." She kept moving closer, talking softly all the way. Thor walked beside her, prepared to step between them, should the stallion decide to charge.

"I bet you can run," Lindsey said. "Thor says you are as fast as the wind."

The horse began to still. His ears twitched and he fixed his attention on the sound of Lindsey's voice.

"I've never seen a horse like you," she said. "You could sire the finest Thoroughbreds in all of England."

To Thor's amazement, the horse nickered softly, lowered his head, and came trotting toward her as if they were old friends. By the gods, it was the last thing he expected. There was no confrontation in the stallion's approach, nothing that signaled the horse considered her a danger.

"I cannot believe it." Just then he caught a hint of Lindsey's soft perfume. Her voice was equally soft and infinitely feminine and he realized that was the difference.

Lindsey reached out and scratched the stallion's ears, received a whiffle of gratitude for the gesture.

"You're a woman," Thor said. "He doesn't like men but you—you are a female. He must have known a woman in his past, someone who cared for him."

Lindsey pressed her cheek against Saber's, drew her fingers through his thick, silky mane and stroked his gleaming coat. "We're going to be great friends, you and I—aren't we, darling?"

She turned to look at Thor. "He doesn't feel threatened the way he does with men."

"So it would seem."

"He's going to let me ride him—I can feel it."

"It is too soon to know that for certain."

But by the end of the session it was becoming more and more clear. Lindsey pressed a kiss on the stallion's forehead. "We're going to ride in the steeplechase, Saber, and we are going to win."

Thor didn't argue. All evening he had felt the bond growing between Lindsey and the stallion. There was no hostility. In truth, the stallion seemed eager to please her.

Thor's heartbeat quickened. If Lindsey rode Saber, they might just win the derby. The horse would be saved and the stallion would be his.

For years he had been searching, trying to find his rightful place in the world. For the first time he saw it clearly. He would find a way to buy the land he had dreamed of. The stallion would be the foundation of a string of Thoroughbred horses to equal those belonging to Lord Merrick or any man in the country.

If Saber could win…

Thor looked at Lindsey and his heartbeat quickened with worry. As good a rider as she was, any steeplechase was dangerous. How could he allow her to risk herself?

"You've got that look again," she said, beginning to know him too well.

"What look?"

"That *I'm-a-male-you're-my woman-and-it's-my-duty-to-protect-you* look."

He almost smiled. "I should not let you do it."

"We've been through this before and I'm telling you right now—if you don't let me ride Saber, I'm going to ride one of my father's horses. I'm riding in that race—with or without your permission. Will it be Saber or some horse you don't know?"

"I swear, Lindsey, you are the most—"

"Vexing creature. I know."

He did smile, then. "All right. If Saber allows it, you will ride the stallion. I will not try to stop you again."

And so he spent the last few hours before dawn working with Saber and Lindsey, Lindsey walking him, feeding him lumps of sugar, talking to him and petting him.

"Why don't we see if he'll let me sit on his back?" she suggested.

Thor was only a little uneasy at the notion. The stallion seemed more relaxed just being near her. When Saber appeared to be ready, Thor lifted Lindsey sideways up on the animal's bare back, careful to keep a tight hold on the lead. He walked them in a small circle, then a larger one.

Never once did Saber do anything threatening. In fact, he seemed happy to carry her about.

Thor shook his head. The woman had a way of capturing a man's affections. It seemed the stallion was no less susceptible than he.

It was late in the evening, dawn less than two hours away, when they decided to call it a night.

"I'll come again tomorrow evening—earlier if I can."

Thor nodded. "I do not like you riding out here by yourself. I will wait for you at the edge of the woods east of the stable."

She opened her mouth to protest, caught his warning glare and nodded. "All right."

He walked her over to where she had hobbled her horse.

"There's something I should mention before I leave," she said. "When I got back to the house this afternoon, another note was waiting. The writing was the same as before. One of the boys from the village brought it."

"What did it say?"

"That I should find a woman named Penelope Barker. If I did, I would learn the truth about Lord Merrick."

"I will ask around, see what I can find out."

"The men you work with…they didn't give you any trouble about being Leif's brother?"

"I told them I was not rich like Leif. I had to work just like any other man."

She nodded. "There's one more thing."

"Aye?"

"Before I leave, I need you to kiss me. I've been thinking about it all night."

"Lindsey…"

"You want to, don't you? It isn't just me."

He shook his head. His entire body ached for her. He'd been hard off and on all evening. "There is nothing I would like more than to kiss you. I ache to be inside you, Lindsey—this you must know. But we are not wed and never will be. We cannot—"

She went up on her toes and pressed her mouth to his, cutting off his words. He groaned at the feel of her soft breasts pressing into his chest, the way her lips trembled then parted, inviting his tongue inside to taste her. His arms went around her, hauling her hard against him, and his erection strengthened to immense proportions.

By the gods, he couldn't resist her, couldn't turn away from the tempting butterfly kisses she pressed against his mouth, his nose, his cheeks, couldn't deny himself the feel of her plump little breasts teasing his chest.

"Go now, Lindsey, before it is too late."

"I don't want to go, Thor. Not yet." And then she was sliding her hands inside his coat, shoving it off his shoulders.

With a sigh, he gave in to his fierce desire, reached around to unbutton the back of her gown, moved the fabric aside and filled his hands with her lovely pale breasts. He caressed the tips, turning them to hard little buds, eased the gown off her shoulders and bent his head to taste them.

In minutes, she was lying on the ground beneath him, her riding habit askew, his hands inside her drawers. She was unbelievably wet as he stroked her, stretched and prepared her to take him, slid himself deeply inside.

Mindless with need, he began to move, driving wildly toward release, barely able to hang onto his control yet determined to give her the same burning pleasure she gave him. She reached her peak and cried out his name, and a few minutes later, he allowed himself to follow.

As he lay in the soft grass beside her, he tried to tell himself this would be the last time he touched her.

But he refused to make another vow he could not keep.

Nineteen

❧❧❧

Pleading a headache, Lindsey slept all afternoon in preparation for another late night with the stallion. As she lay in the middle of her deep feather mattress, she couldn't help smiling as she thought of Thor and the way they had made love. It was as if he couldn't get enough of her, as if she were some drug he simply had to have.

Lindsey felt the same—without the guilty conscience that seemed to burden Thor. Whenever the chance arose, she intended to make love with him. She was faithfully taking the potion Samir had made and it seemed to be working. There wasn't much time left before her parents arrived back in London and her affair with Thor would have to end, but until then, she meant to enjoy every moment.

The late afternoon sun shined through the windows, warming her as she lay in her chemise, dreamily imagining her rendezvous with Thor that night.

Then her little maid, Kitty, burst into the room. "You've a visitor, miss. That big handsome brother of Mrs. Draugr's husband is here. He says he needs to see you."

"Great heavens, Thor is here?"

"That he is, miss." She grinned and rolled her eyes. "Not that you could mistake him for anyone else."

Lindsey laughed. "No, certainly not." Jumping up from the bed, she reached for the robe Kitty held out to her. "Fetch my apricot silk gown, will you, Kitty? Hurry—I need to get dressed."

As fast as possible, she stepped into her gown and waited impatiently for Kitty to tie back her hair. "You can curl it before I go to supper," she said. "I don't have time for that now."

If Thor was here, it must be important. She grabbed her pretty fringed shawl off a chair in case they went outside, and headed downstairs, anxious to see what he wanted.

She found him waiting in the Red Salon. As she walked into the room, he rose to his feet, his incredible eyes seeking her out, sending a little curl of heat into her stomach.

"What is it, Thor? What's happened?"

He flicked a glance at the door and she walked over and pulled it mostly closed, leaving it open just enough to spare them from gossip.

"Tell me."

He caught her hand and led her toward the sofa, waited for her to sit, then sat down beside her. "It is the girl, Penelope Barker."

A thread of uneasiness slid through her. "What…what about her?"

"She was a chambermaid at Merrick Park."

Her unease heightened. "What do you mean, *she was?*"

"She worked there for several years. Then one day she disappeared. No one knows where she went. The grooms say she was with child. The old man, Horace Nub, says the babe she carried belonged to Lord Merrick."

For several moments, Lindsey just sat there. "Perhaps Stephen gave her money and sent her away somewhere to have the child."

Thor looked down at his feet.

"What? What are you not telling me?"

"There were rumors…the people in the village believe… they think she was murdered."

The breath she had just taken stalled in Lindsey's lungs. "No. It can't be true."

"As you say, mayhap he gave her money and she just went away."

"But you don't believe it."

"I do not know what to believe. I know Merrick's name has been linked with murder. Now there is the chance of a murder at Merrick Park. It seems a strange coincidence."

Lindsey bit her lip. "It does, indeed. We need to find out who is sending those messages. Someone knows the truth. We need to know who that someone is."

Thor rose from the sofa, big and dark, and completely out of place among the delicate porcelain vases, crystal prisms, and lace doilies in the drawing room. "I will see what more I can find out."

Lindsey rose as well. "I assume we're still meeting tonight."

With obvious reluctance, he nodded. "I will be waiting for you in the trees."

She glanced toward the door, turned back to him, went up on her toes and kissed him. He smelled of horse and man, a virile combination that sent soft heat into her belly.

Lindsey parted her lips and his tongue swept in. Her heart-beat quickened, began to pound loudly in her ears. For an instant, she forgot she stood in the drawing room, that someone could walk in at any moment.

It was Thor who ended the kiss. His eyes were dark with heat and promise, and this time she knew there would be no need to coax him into making love to her.

Lindsey ignored the little tingle of warning that said perhaps she had finally unleashed the wolf, and she was no longer the one in control.

It was late in the evening before Lindsey was able to excuse herself from the guests downstairs and make her way up to her bedroom. A waxing moon rose over the landscape, lighting her way to the stable to saddle a horse. The grooms were all asleep in their quarters upstairs. All but one, it seemed.

Tobias Dare approached, a sleepy-eyed groom with a worried frown on his youthful face. "Miss Graham! I wasn't sure who it was."

"Just me, Tobias. I have business to attend to. I hope I can count on you not to tell anyone I was here."

"Of course, miss." He was used to her wearing men's riding clothes, as she did so quite often. "I'll saddle Buddy Boy for you."

She was on her way a few minutes later, riding out the back door of the barn, heading Buddy Boy off toward the copse of trees at the east side of the house.

As she knew he would be, Thor was waiting in the shadowy darkness of the grove. He said nothing as she rode up beside him, just whirled the stallion, and they set off in the direction of the ruins. She had never seen him astride the powerful black and she thought what an incredible pair they made. Thor rode bareback, using only a bridle, handling the horse so easily they seemed fused together.

Saber should be his, she thought, and silently vowed that she would do everything in her power to make it so.

They reached the stone ruins and Thor pulled the stallion to a halt. He slid off the animal's back, walked over and helped Lindsey down from her saddle.

"I wasn't sure if I should wear men's breeches, but I wanted to be able to ride astride. I hope he'll still know I'm a woman."

Thor assessed her from head to foot and she couldn't miss the heat in his eyes. "You are a woman, sweetheart, of that there is no doubt."

The hunger was there, though he tried to hide it. She wondered if he would act on it, as she had imagined in the drawing room, or if he would be reticent, as he had been before.

Saber nickered a greeting. Thor took her hand and walked her over to where the horse stood. Lindsey spoke to him softly, rubbed his ears, and fed him a lump of sugar, then Thor lifted her up on the animal's bare back.

Saber's head came up. His ears twitched an instant before he settled back down for another few bites of grass. For the next two hours, Lindsey worked with the horse, climbing off and on, rubbing his neck and flanks, walking him in circles then mounting him again, walking, trotting, increasing his pace until she was able to ease him into a canter.

"Even with such a bright moon, it is too dark to run him

or take any jumps," Thor said. "Do you think you could get away sometime during the day tomorrow?"

"It won't be easy with so many guests, but I'll find a way. I shall meet you here at noon."

Thor nodded. "In the daylight, I suppose you will be safe. You haven't seen anyone following you? No one out of the ordinary paying you any sort of interest?"

"No, of course not."

"There is still the matter of the murders. You need to be careful, Lindsey."

He was probably right. At least two women were dead. Perhaps three—and one of them might have died somewhere very near here.

She watched Thor lead Saber over to a grassy area to graze. All evening he had carefully kept his distance, though she hadn't missed the heated glances, the scorching desire in his eyes when he thought she couldn't see. She wondered if she had been wrong, if the wolf would remain carefully leashed and again she would have to coax him into making love to her.

She was trying to decide how best to approach the matter while he finished tethering the stallion. As soon as he was through, he began striding toward her. He didn't stop when he reached her, just bent and scooped her up in his arms.

"Great heavens!" Lindsey gasped.

His eyes locked on her face, smoldering with the hunger he no longer tried to hide. "Our work for tonight is done. The rest of the night is ours."

Her heart jerked, then set up a clatter. The wolf was free. Anticipation roared through her as he carried her inside the cluster of ancient stones and set her on her feet. Moonlight reflected on the hard line of his jaw and glinted on the wavy dark hair that curled at the nape of his powerful neck.

With efficient yet unhurried movements, he untied her braid and spread the heavy mass of hair around her shoulders, then began to strip away her clothes.

"Tonight we will take our time," he said, kissing each new area of skin he exposed. "I will make love to you as I should have done before."

As he should have done? Sweet God, each time had been better than the last. She couldn't image what he could possibly do to give her more pleasure.

He turned her, kissed her slowly and deeply. His lips felt like hot moist silk as they moved over hers, nibbling, teasing, coaxing, his tongue sweeping in to taste her, his kisses deepening until her mind spun away and she was trembling.

She moaned at the feel of his mouth moving over her bare shoulders, of hot, damp kisses trailing down to her naked breasts. He took each one into his mouth, laved and suckled until her legs felt too weak to hold her up.

Thor seemed to know. Lifting her into his arms, he carried her over and settled her on a bed of yew branches covered by a soft woolen blanket. He had planned this. There would be no need for seduction tonight.

Stripped of her clothing, lying languidly on the blanket, she watched him undress in the moonlight. He drew off his full-sleeved shirt and her pulse increased at the bands of muscle across his powerful chest. She held her breath at the sight of his flat belly and narrow hips, exposed as he slid off his breeches. His legs were long and supple, and his male anatomy—dear God in heaven—the man was built like a stallion!

He strode toward her with eyes full of purpose, kissed her deep and thoroughly, then knelt between her legs. Lindsey shifted restlessly, eager to feel that hard length inside her, craving the wild release he could give her.

Thor seemed in no hurry, just leaned down and pressed his mouth against the inside of her thigh, bent her knee and kissed the sensitive skin underneath.

"Thor…please…"

"Not yet, sweetheart. I would taste you first." And though for a moment she didn't understand his meaning, as his mouth settled over her most feminine part, she knew.

Great heavens!

Sensation poured through her. The velvet claws of desire sank into her, gripped her, and held her in thrall. Thor tasted and suckled, used his hands and his mouth to pleasure her as she never could have imagined. Her body tightened, spun into a taut, quivering thread and finally broke free. She arched upward, crying out his name, but Thor did not stop. Not until a second climax shook her, stirring wild, fierce spasms of pleasure.

She was trembling when he entered her, surging deeply, his hard length filling her at last. He slid his hands into her hair, held himself still as he kissed her, then slowly began to move.

She heard the whisper of his deep voice in her ear. "By the gods, Lindsey, you belong to me. No matter the future, for tonight you are mine and I mean to make certain you know it."

When the passion rose again, when the pleasure overwhelmed her and her body crested and tightened around his hard length, Lindsey knew it all the way to her soul. When

he thrust deeper, took her harder, stirred her to climax, she
knew there was no other man who would ever take his
place, no other man who would ever fulfill her as he could.

The hard truth hit her like a fist. *Dear God, I've fallen
in love with him!*

Lindsey thought of all the pain that would mean, all the
heartbreak, all the grief. As she reached another shuddering release, it was all she could do not to weep.

As promised, the following day, Lindsey left for the
ancient ruins just after luncheon. She hadn't slept in the few
hours left last night or early that morning, her mind too full
of Thor and the terrible situation in which she found
herself. In the hours since she had left him, no matter how
she tried to convince herself she had been wrong—that it
was lust, not love she felt for him—she knew it was a lie.

She was in love with Thor and losing him was going to
break her heart.

She loved him, and because she did, she wanted to give
him the gift of the beautiful horse.

As Thor had urged, before she rode out that morning, she
carefully checked to be certain no unknown person watched
the stable or the house. It might be foolish, but sometimes
caution was the wiser course. As expected, Thor waited for
her in the copse of trees east of the house and they rode
together to the ruins.

Lindsey steeled herself against the turbulent emotions
she felt as he lifted her down from the saddle and tried to
control the soft thudding of her heart. She wished she could
turn and ride away, never have to see him again, put an end
to these feelings that would only grow more painful.

"Are you ready to try the fences?" he asked, saying nothing of the fierce night of passion they had shared.

Lindsey was grateful. She could do this—she could pretend nothing had changed between them. But she would have to gird herself against the powerful feelings she had finally come to realize she held for him.

"I am more than ready." She approached where Saber grazed peacefully at the end of his tether and her eyes widened in surprise. "You saddled him!"

He nodded. "He was used to it once. It wasn't so hard to convince him."

She gave him a lighthearted smile. "I suppose you just asked him and he agreed."

The edge of Thor's mouth faintly curved. "It took a bit more than that."

Turning to the stallion, hoping to build on the bond they had been forming, Lindsey approached the horse. Saber's head jerked up as he caught sight of her in masculine clothes, but at the sound of her voice, he calmed. They repeated the procedure they had used each night, letting him get used to her, riding slowly then increasing the pace, exercising in the meadow for more than an hour.

"I think he is ready," Lindsey said as she returned to where Thor waited.

"Horace Nub says Saber has raced before. It was one of the reasons Burke wanted to buy him. I have worked with him on the hedges, but he will take them much easier with your lighter weight on his back."

And so she set off, putting him through his paces, trotting then cantering, galloping, then running flat out. Excitement built as she settled him into a rhythmical canter and aimed him toward the first fence, a low hedge with flat ground on both sides, an easy, confidence-building jump. Saber took the fence with ease and she couldn't stifle a grin.

She moved him on to a harder target, a hedge that sloped down on the opposite side, then to a wide water jump, a low stone wall, then a higher wall a little ways away.

By the end of the afternoon, she was elated. The horse was a natural, the kind of animal who focused his entire attention on the obstacle in his path and took pleasure in conquering whatever lay in front of him. She was sure the stallion would give all he had in the race he must win to save his life.

Saber was glistening with sweat, Lindsey's muscles sore, by the time horse and rider rode up to Thor. Grinning, she jumped down from the saddle before he had time to reach her and handed him the reins.

"He is wonderful—a true champion, Thor. He is everything you believed he would be."

He nodded, a wide smile on his face. "He wants to please you. He will run his heart out for you, Lindsey."

She slid her hand along the animal's sweat-damp neck. "I'll come tomorrow and the day after that. I told them here was a sick child in the village whose mother was a friend and needed my help. So far it seems to be working."

Thor just nodded. All afternoon, she had managed to keep her distance. Thor must have sensed her effort to put some space between them for he made no move to approach her. From the start, he had tried to make her see it could never work between them. Perhaps he believed she had finally realized he was right.

"I wish I could stay," she said, not meaning a word of

it, eager to escape her unwanted feelings for him. "I have to get back before my aunt begins to worry."

He glanced away. When he looked at her again, his fierce blue gaze was guarded. "I appreciate what you are doing."

She only nodded, turned away from him with a heavy heart and started for her horse. Thor lifted her into the saddle and she ignored a tremor of longing.

She cleared her throat. "You didn't mention Penelope Barker. You didn't find out anything more?"

"Not yet. You will remember to be careful."

"I will remember." She wanted so much to touch him, lean down and kiss him, knew what would happen if she did. After last night, she understood as she never had before. She had a different future ahead of her, a different life to live—one that did not include Thor. It was time to end their affair.

"I have to go," she said, the words thick in her throat.

His beautiful blue eyes moved over her face but he made no move to stop her.

Lindsey glanced away, unable to look at him a moment more. Wheeling her horse, she rode off across the meadow.

Remember to be careful, he had said. She wished she had remembered before she had fallen in love with him.

Twenty

Holding onto Saber's reins, Thor stood some distance away from the crowd, anxiously awaiting Lindsey's arrival. The riders were taking their places at the starting line. Still, she had not come.

Mayhap it is for the best, he told himself, then felt a wash of relief he should not have felt as he spotted her running toward him in her man's riding clothes, her hair stuffed up under a black billed-hunt cap.

"I am sorry I am late," she said breathlessly. "I had to wait until everyone else left the house."

"So you did not change your mind."

She shook her head, smiled. "I told them I was a bit under the weather. I said I would join the group later if I began to feel better."

"And your aunt and the others believed you?"

"They know I love the derby. I wouldn't miss it unless I was ill. Krista offered to stay with me but I told her I planned to return to bed and that she and Leif should go on and enjoy themselves."

He scowled. "I do not know if I like that you are such a good liar."

Lindsey grinned. "It will be worth it if I win the race."

Hidden from view behind the wide trunk of a tree, he cupped her face in his hands. "Promise me you will not take any chances."

"Of course not," she said flippantly, making him even more fearful. He gave her a quick, hard kiss, and lifted her up on the horse. He walked the pair around for a bit, while Lindsey petted and spoke to the horse.

Then he watched with his heart in his throat as she waved and rode off to the starting line to take her position among the other entries, who seemed stunned to see the big black stallion among the contestants. The starting pistol fired before Saber had time to grow nervous, and Lindsey and the stallion jolted into motion, bolting off the starting line, setting a ground-eating pace that would separate the true contenders from the rest of the pack before they reached the quarter turn.

Thor watched horse and rider take the first hedge in third position, Saber completely focused on the obstacle in front of him, Lindsey giving the stallion just the right commands to clear the hedge and land neatly on the opposite side. Another few jumps and the pack disappeared out of sight, leaving Thor staring after them, terrified something would go wrong.

The horses were off and running, thundering around the makeshift two-and-a-half-mile racecourse that had been laid out for the event. His heart was pounding, hammering away inside his chest. Thor said a silent prayer that Lindsey would come back unharmed.

He glanced at the cheering crowd around him. The entire village and dozens of people from around the countryside had turned out for the race. Lindsey's aunt and her friends watched from a few feet away, while Leif and Krista, Coralee and her husband, Gray, stood next to Thor. The tension was thick in the air, the excitement almost tangible. A lot of money had been bet on the race, most of it on Merrick's champion bay stallion, Fleet Journey.

Thor turned his attention to his brother and Krista, his worry, now that Lindsey was out of sight, continuing to build. How could he have let her ride the stallion? What had he been thinking? And what of the vast amount of money his brother and Krista had wagered?

"If we lose," he said to Leif, staring off toward the place where the horses would eventually reappear, "I will find a way to pay you back."

"It's a wager," Leif said. "Sometimes you win. Sometimes you lose. That is the risk you take. Besides, Saber made an excellent start. The race isn't over until the first horse crosses the finish." He surveyed Thor's worried expression. "So tell me again who this young man is you convinced to ride in your stead."

Thor glanced away, hating to lie to his brother. He never should have agreed to Lindsey's mad plan. Even now, she could be out there, injured or even— He broke off the thought, swallowed against an image of her lying beside a stone wall, her beautiful body battered and broken. "The lad is a friend."

Leif continued to assess him. "Whoever he is, he seems an excellent choice. A fine rider, light and skillful, and Saber appeared to accept him without a problem."

Thor just nodded. It wasn't his place to reveal Lindsey's secret. It was her decision to make should she wish her friends to know. "Do you see any sign of them yet?"

"Not yet, but it won't be long. Whoever is left in the field should be coming over that rise any minute."

Thor stared off in that direction. Inside his chest, his heart beat dully. Worry tied a knot in his stomach.

What have I done?

At the sound of a taunting male voice, he looked up to see Harley Burke sauntering toward him. "You really think that black devil will make the finish?"

Thor's jaw hardened. "Aye."

"I'm betting the fool you convinced to ride him is lying out there somewhere in the dirt. Want to wager a little extra on it?"

Thor felt sick to his stomach. Lindsey lying hurt or dead. He couldn't bear the thought. To say nothing of gambling more money he couldn't afford to lose.

Still, he couldn't stand the smug expression on Harley Burke's face. "I will match whatever—"

"Here they come!"

The words ended the discussion, and Thor's gaze shot to the group of horses and riders who were just now cresting the hill, the pack less than half the number of those who had started the race. He strained to see Saber and Lindsey but couldn't spot them and his insides churned with fear.

The pack drew closer and his heart took a leap. The huge black stallion and its slender rider thundered into view, pulling out of the group that included the Renhurst entry, a sorrel named Sweet Vengeance; and Fleet Journey, the viscount's prized Thoroughbred hunter.

"It's her, isn't it?" This from Krista, who was jumping up and down with excitement. "It's Lindsey!" She grinned as if she wished she were the one in the saddle.

Thor cast her a glance. "She was afraid you would try to stop her."

"Are you kidding? I just wish I could—"

"Not a chance," Leif said.

The stallion began pulling ahead, and Thor caught Burke's foul curse.

"She's winning!" Krista exclaimed. "She's going to win Saber for you!"

Thor couldn't breathe. He had never seen anything so beautiful as the magnificent black stallion and the woman who risked herself to win him, riding full speed toward the finish line. Both of them were champions of the highest caliber and he had never felt so proud.

Horse and rider pounded full speed across the finish and Krista let out a yell. "She did it! She won!"

And done it a good half length ahead of Merrick's horse, Fleet Journey, who came in second, followed by the Renhurst entry. Fourth place was a tie between two horses entered by residents of the village.

Lindsey rode up to Thor, Saber sweating and prancing beneath her, still full of fire after his victory. Her grin was wider than Thor had ever seen it. "We did it!"

"Aye, that you did. I would haul you down and kiss you but I do not think it would look right for a man to be kissing his jockey."

She laughed and the sound filled his heart.

"He needs to be cooled down, but I've got to get out of here before someone sees me and figures out who I am."

"I will cool him down."

Lindsey swung a leg over Saber's neck and jumped down like a man, grinned up at him and let out a whoop of glee. Everyone was moving toward them, beginning to form a circle around the prancing black stallion. Saber spotted the approaching crowd and snorted in protest, whinnied, and went up on his hind legs.

"Stay back," Thor warned. "He is not used to so many people." One look at the wild-eyed stallion sent them all backing up several paces. Lindsey took the moment to slip away, pausing a moment when Krista caught her hand.

"You were wonderful! You both were!"

Lindsey grinned. "Winning feels really good!" She glanced around, saw people coming toward her. "I'll be back as soon as I change." She disappeared into the woods, and Thor walked the stallion in circles for a while, then led him a safe distance away and tethered him to a tree. When he returned to the cheering revelers, they began to pat him on the back and congratulate him on winning the race. He was smiling when he spotted Harley Burke stalking toward him.

Thor straightened. "I claim the horse, as is my due."

"That isn't going to happen since you cheated. You didn't ride the horse—someone else did."

Leif stepped up beside Thor. "The bet was whether or not the horse could win and he did. The stallion belongs to my brother."

"And I say he still belongs to Merrick and we put the bastard down."

The crowd parted around them and from the center of the circle, Stephen Camden, Viscount Merrick emerged, immaculately dressed as always, his blond hair perfectly combed and not a strand blowing in the slight afternoon breeze.

"The man won the horse," Merrick said. "I made the bet and I lost." Thor felt a grudging respect he didn't want to feel, considering the viscount might be a murderer.

"Thank you," Thor said.

Merrick speared Burke with a glare that said, *he handled the stallion, why couldn't you?* Then he turned and disappeared into the crowd.

Thor felt a burst of elation. Saber belonged to him. His dream had become a real possibility and all because of Lindsey.

More well-wishers surrounded him. Lady Ashford, Lindsey's aunt, made a point of seeking him out. "Congratulations. Your stallion was amazing, Mr. Draugr. Of course, my niece is quite a good rider."

Thor looked up in surprise. He couldn't help a grin. "I guess she is not so good a liar as she believes. For this I am grateful."

"Yes, well, she has always been a marvelous rider and I have seen her dressed as a man before. For everyone's sake, I hope this is the last time."

"I am afraid you will have to discuss that with Lindsey. Your niece has a mind of her own."

Lady Ashford sighed. "I can't imagine where she gets that." But it was clear from the look her escort, the colonel, cast her way the lady was of a similar disposition.

Thor took a deep breath. The victory felt good, but in truth, he just wanted to be with Lindsey.

And yet he was no fool. In the past few days, she had begun to put up barriers, finally realizing, he was sure, how poorly they were suited. It was time to end their affair and though it was the last thing he wanted, he had known from the start this day would come. In this he would respect her wishes.

Still, he needed to speak to her. In the village this morning, he had discovered some interesting information, gossip that might concern Lord Merrick. Thor prayed what he had found out would not turn out to be true.

Lindsey did not see Thor until late in the afternoon. Though she wanted nothing so much as to celebrate their victory together, she had gone out of her way to avoid him. Thor seemed to have guessed the reason. Though he couldn't know she was in love with him, he always seemed able to read her thoughts.

Which was the reason she was surprised when he sought her out toward the end of the celebration.

"I need a word with you before you leave."

She glanced away, then back to him, her heart thudding painfully. "What is it?"

"In the village before the race, a man approached me. I have not seen him before and he would not give me his name. He said I should go to the town of Alsbury. I should seek out a woman named Martha Barker, Penelope Barker's mother. He said I should ask what she knows of her daughter's disappearance."

"Do you think he was the man who wrote the note?"

"I do not know. I had been asking questions about the girl. The man may have heard and wished to provide information."

"We must go to Alsbury right away."

"I can go alone if—"

"I want to be there."

He just nodded.

"Some of the guests have already left for the city. Those who remain will be leaving early in the morning. I will meet you at the edge of the village on the road leading to Alsbury at ten o'clock tomorrow morning."

He agreed to meet her but didn't say more, though she sensed he wanted to. He understood what was happening, realized she had decided to end their affair. She knew he would not press her to resume their relationship—not unless she wanted him to.

Dear God, she wanted that so much.

Instead, she lifted her skirts and hurried back to her friends, her aunt, and their guests.

The village of Alsbury nestled in the hills a three-hour journey away. In the Renhurst carriage, Lindsey arrived at the appointed meeting place just outside Foxgrove. Wordlessly, Thor climbed in and settled his big frame on the seat across from her. Only a few days ago, he would have sat beside her, perhaps pulled her into his arms.

That time was past. Lindsey ignored a sharp stab of pain and ordered the driver to continue on to their destination.

They spoke little along the route. Lindsey tried to concentrate on the book of poetry she was reading, with very poor results. Thor mostly watched the scenery passing by outside the window. A few autumn leaves still clung to the branches of the trees, and yesterday's turn in the weather had chased the clouds away and made today a pleasant one.

Eventually, they reached the town of Alsbury, which was smaller than she had imagined, mostly built of stone, with a pretty little market square, a church on a nearby hillside, and a rippling stream that meandered through the middle of the town. A few stops along High Street to ask directions yielded the location of Martha Barker's cottage, a thatched-roof, white-walled structure on the far side of the village.

"I hope Mrs. Barker is at home," Lindsey said, beginning to grow anxious as the carriage rolled up in front of the house.

"Someone is there. I see movement on the other side of the window."

The carriage drew to a stop and Thor jumped down, turned and helped Lindsey alight. Together, they made their way up the few steps to the porch. Several sharp raps and a stoop-shouldered woman with drab gray hair mostly hidden beneath a mob cap opened the door.

"Mrs. Barker?" Thor asked.

"Yes, that's right."

"We are here about your daughter," Lindsey said. "We were hoping you might be willing to tell us a little about her."

Her eyes misted. "Yer friends of Penny's?"

Lindsey managed a smile. "In a way, I suppose we are."

Mrs. Barker stepped back into the cottage and Lindsey took the move as an invitation to come inside.

"Would ye like a cup of tea?" the woman asked, grateful for the company, Lindsey imagined, or perhaps the chance to talk to someone about her daughter. "I've got water hot on the stove."

"Thank you, that would be very nice."

Tea was made and served and they drank it seated at a small wooden table in the kitchen. They spoke pleasantries for a while, then the conversation turned to Mrs. Barker's daughter.

"We were wondering…" Lindsey said gently, "we would like to know if you've heard from Penny. Perhaps you saw her or received a letter from her after she left Merrick Park."

The woman seemed to wither before their eyes. "She were a good girl, was Penny. But he were so handsome, such a fine gentleman. She were young and sweet and he wanted her." Mrs. Barker's lips trembled. "Poor little fool was in love with him. She thought 'e would marry her."

"Who was Penelope in love with, Mrs. Barker?"

"Why, his lordship…Lord Merrick."

A chill whispered down Lindsey's spine. She flicked a glance at Thor, saw that he was scowling.

"We know Penny left his employ," she said. "We'd like to find out where she went after she left Merrick Park."

The older woman shook her head, her features grim. "She were supposed to come home. Sent me a letter…said she wanted to come back to have the babe. She was supposed to leave on Monday, be home that afternoon, but she never got here." A glazed, faraway look came into the older woman's eyes. "No one knows what happened, but I do. I know that fancy viscount kilt her."

Lindsey stiffened.

Thor leaned forward in his chair. "Why do you think that, Mrs. Barker?"

"'Cause after he got her with child, the way he treated her changed. Penny were afraid of him…told me so herself." She lifted the mug of tea growing cold in front of her but set it back down without taking a sip. "A week after she was s'pposed to come home, I got a letter. She must have mailed it before she left his house. She said he'd threatened her, told her to keep her mouth shut about the babe. Said if she didn't, he'd make sure she kept quiet forever."

"Do you still have the letter?" Thor asked.

The woman looked up. "What?"

"Do you still have the letter your daughter sent?"

She seemed to collect herself, slowly shook her head. "I burnt it. I knew what he'd done and just havin' it in the house gave me a fright. I thought about takin' it to the constable, but Merrick's name weren't actually mentioned and I knew no one would believe me. They'd think Penny just run off to have the babe."

Lindsey mulled over the words, thinking that the woman was right. No body had ever been found, no evidence of foul play. Penelope was just a young woman who had turned up missing. But someone knew what had happened. The person who had written the notes. The same person, Lindsey was sure, who had approached Thor in the village.

"Is there anything more you can tell us?" Thor asked.

The woman looked up, her eyes a dull, listless blue. "She were all I had…all I had."

It was clear there was nothing more to say and with a quiet thanks, they left the cottage. Inside the carriage, Lindsey rode in silence. Neither she nor Thor said a word all the way back to Foxgrove.

"Do you think he did it?" Lindsey finally asked.

"Mrs. Barker believes he did. Whoever sent the note believes he is guilty."

"Merrick is going back to London. He told my aunt he would be leaving in the morning." She turned to look at

Thor, who apparently still meant to help her. "We need to find out exactly where Stephen Camden was on the nights of the Covent Garden murders."

Twenty-One

A bleak sky hung over the crowded London streets, flat gray clouds that promised rain. A chill wind whipped leaves and papers into the air as Thor stepped out of the hansom cab in front of Capital Ventures. He turned and paid the driver for his time, then started up the brick steps leading to the impressive front door.

He had returned to the city three days ago, leaving on the same day as Lindsey, her aunt and her brother. She was determined to discover more about Stephen Camden, which meant she might yet be in danger. Though she had made it clear their physical relationship had come to an end, Lindsey meant a great deal to him. Thor intended to see that she remained safe.

In the meantime, he had found a place to stable Saber, not an easy business since the stallion was extremely high-spirited and still not used to people. A large stall in one of the barns at the edge of Green Park was the best he could do for now, and fortunately, he had also found a young groom named Tommy Booker who seemed to have a way with horses.

After a lengthy introduction and a few hours of working with the lad and the horse, Thor had been satisfied that the youth would be able to handle Saber's basic needs.

And Thor planned to continue his daily routine of working the horse in the early morning. In time, the stallion would be as biddable as he had been before he had been mistreated. Thor thought of the stallion and the plans he had for the beautiful Thoroughbred. Most of those plans depended on the stock certificates he had purchased from Capital Ventures.

His thoughts strayed for a moment to Lindsey and the viscount, but he shook his head, driving them away. At present he had business that did not involve murder—at least not yet.

Turning the heavy brass knob, he shoved open the office door and stepped into the elegant interior of Capital Ventures. He was there to see Silas Wilkins about his A&H Railway stock. He wanted answers and this time he meant to get them.

The slender young male behind the desk turned toward him, recognized him as the man who had been there before, and a pasty smile appeared on his face. "May I help you?"

"I am here to see Silas Wilkins."

"Mr. Draugr, is it not?"

Thor nodded. "Is he in?"

"Give me a moment and I'll just go and see…"

"Do not bother. I will go myself."

"B-but you can't just—"

"Aye, I can." Thor walked over to the door the secretary had gone through the last time he had been in the office. He turned the knob and shoved it open to see a man with fine, mouse-brown hair parted neatly in the middle rising from behind his desk.

"Mr. Wilkins," Thor said.

Wilkins managed a smile. "Mr. Draugr. It is good to see you. What can I do for you, sir?"

"I came to find out about my A&H Railway stock. I have been reading the newspaper. The railroad seems to be a great success, but I've had no word about my stock."

Wilkins smile turned into a frown. "Your A&H Stock? You aren't referring to the Alberton and Hollis Railway, are you?"

"I am. If you have forgot, I invested a good deal of money in that company."

Wilkins nervously cleared his throat. "Well, now, that isn't quite correct. The company you invested in was a secondary branch of the railroad, the A&H Railway of Chillingwood. I'm afraid that line has done very poorly. In fact, I am sorry to say, your stock is nearly worthless."

Angry heat rose at the back of Thor's neck. "I gave you the money to buy A&H stock. I know nothing of any A&H of Chillingwood."

Wilkins tittered nervously. "Well, then, perhaps I am mistaken. Perhaps you should go home and check your certificates. If they are indeed original A&H stock—"

Thor pinned him with a glare. "They had better be. You sold me those stocks. You knew exactly what I wanted to buy when I came in here."

Wilkins coughed behind his hand, his eyes shifting back and forth from Thor to the door, as if he wished to escape. "As I said, before we go any further, you need to look at your stock certificates, make sure exactly what it is you own."

"I will do that—have no doubt. And then I will be back."

Wilkins tried for a smile, but it never appeared. Thor turned and stalked out of the office. Nearly all of his savings had gone into the Alberton and Hollis Railway Line. When he had come to Capital Ventures, there had been no doubt as to what he wished to purchase.

By rights, he should already have made a good deal of money. He didn't know how much, but he hoped it would be enough to buy the property he wanted, a large enough piece of land to begin his horse breeding farm. Now that he owned Saber, he would need capital to buy broodmares, to build a proper stable and make the necessary improvements to run a successful business.

Thor's hand fisted. For Wilkins's sake, those stocks the man had sold him had better be the right ones.

Dear God, how she missed him. As hard as she tried to put Thor out of her mind, he was firmly rooted there and Lindsey could not seem to push him away.

She wanted to be with him. She had never wanted anything so badly. She wanted to hear the slow, deep cadence of his voice, bask in his soft smile, feel the strength of his powerful arms around her. She had never felt so safe, so protected as when she was with Thor.

She told herself it was better this way, that it was time she gave him up and got on with her life. Yesterday, her parents had arrived back in London, returned from their journey to the Continent, and frantic with worry over Rudy. They were terrified for their only son, who was still a suspect in the murders. They were happy to see their daughter, of course, but Rudy was their main concern, as clearly he should be.

So far the Covent Garden Murderer had not been found. Lindsey wanted to know where Stephen Camden had been the nights of the murders, but aside from straight-out asking him, she had no idea how to find out.

She sat down at her desk at *Heart to Heart*, glad to be back to work after three weeks in the country. She had written several articles before she left. Coralee had penned several in her stead while she was away, and Lindsey had sent in an article on the house party at Renhurst Hall given while the Countess of Ashford was in residence.

She was home now, back in the office, listening to the familiar sound of the big Stanhope press chugging away in the middle of the room, inhaling the smell of paper and ink, listening to Bessie Briggs railing about a missing piece of type needed for the next edition. She was glad to be back, and yet after all that had happened, it was difficult to concentrate on her work.

Instead, she thought of the viscount and the murders and tried to tell herself that by now the police had surely figured out that Rudy was innocent of any wrongdoing and she could forget about involving herself any further.

Then she would think of Martha Barker and her missing daughter, Penelope, and she knew there was no way she could simply let the matter drop. She had to know if Stephen was responsible, if he was a murderer, as the notes implied.

She bit her lip, considering several different ways she might approach the matter. Then an idea suddenly struck. *His valet!* The man who laid out his evening clothes would be privy to his movements, or at least have some notion.

"I can see the wheels turning in your head." Krista stood

beside her. Lindsey hadn't heard her approach. "What are you up to now?"

"I was thinking about Lord Merrick and the notes I received. I was thinking about poor Penelope Barker and her mother." Lindsey had told Krista about the message that had been sent to Renhurst Hall, the accusations made against the viscount, and her meeting with Martha Barker.

"And…?" Krista asked.

"Well, it occurred to me that the viscount's valet might know something of his whereabouts the nights of the murders. We don't even know if Stephen was in London. Perhaps he was in the country when the murders were committed or has some other alibi that would assure us of his innocence. If I could speak to his valet, perhaps I could—"

"So you are still digging—still determined to put yourself in danger."

Her heart sputtered then jerked to life at the sound of Thor's familiar deep voice. She looked up at him, into those blue, blue eyes and wondered if he could see how much she missed him, how deeply she had fallen in love with him. His gaze met hers. For an instant, his nostrils flared and she glimpsed the heat, the hunger that always sparked between them.

Then his expression turned shuttered and he fixed his attention on Krista. "The woman is always looking for trouble," he grumbled.

Lindsey spoke to Krista as Thor had done—as if she weren't there. "That didn't seem to bother him when I went to the trouble of winning that race for him."

His jaw firmed. They were back to their sparring, the

only way they could be together without touching, without wanting. Lindsey was grateful.

"I was a fool to let you ride," he said. "You are a woman and you could have been injured. I never should have—"

"But I wasn't injured and because of me you are now the owner of a very valuable horse!"

"You are the most—"

"Stop it, you two." Krista's voice rang with authority. She was, after all, their employer as well as their friend. "Arguing won't solve anything. And I will not tolerate it in here." Turning, she led the way into her office, waited for them to follow her inside and firmly closed the door.

"Now...Lindsey, your idea is a good one. Why don't we send a note to Lord Merrick's valet? We'll ask him to meet us, tell him he'll be well compensated for his time. We'll say the rendezvous is of a private nature and ask him to keep his silence."

"If he is loyal to Merrick, he will tell the man what we discuss," Thor said.

"Perhaps he will," Lindsey agreed. "Perhaps not. Besides, you said yourself most of the viscount's employees don't like him."

Thor didn't argue. "I have been thinking about this, as well. I will speak to his coachman. The driver should know something of Merrick's movements the nights of the murders."

"An excellent idea," Krista agreed.

For the next few minutes, they worked to come up with a plan. They had just chosen a rendezvous spot to set up the meeting with the valet when a light knock sounded at the door.

A second, tall, incredibly handsome man walked into the

room, and Krista smiled at her husband, obviously pleased to see him. "I thought you were busy down at the docks."

"One of the men said my brother came looking for me. I knew he would be working at the office today. I thought it might be important."

Lindsey glanced up at Thor. She could tell by the set of his jaw that it was, indeed, important.

"There is a matter I wish to discuss."

Leif tipped his blond head in the direction of the stairs outside Krista's office. "Let's go up to the professor's study. We can talk there."

Lindsey watched the two big men walk out the door. She wondered what Thor wanted to discuss with his brother and wished they were still friends enough that he would discuss it with her.

"What is it?" Leif asked Thor as they walked into the professor's makeshift office and closed the door.

"Before I came in search of you, I went to see Silas Wilkins at Capital Ventures. He is the man who sold me the A&H Railway stock."

"Yes, I remember."

"Wilkins claims the railway stock I bought was for a different line than the one that has been so successful. He says the stocks I bought were A&H of Chillingwood. He says they are nearly worthless."

Leif's jaw hardened. "I helped you with that purchase. Everything was completely aboveboard. There was no mention of a second railway line, none but the one whose stock you bought."

"I went home and examined the certificates. They look

the same but slightly different, with the word Chilling-wood printed on the paper. I think someone took the original certificates and put different ones in their place."

"Where were they?"

"A chest at the foot of my bed." On the island where he and Leif came from, the certificates would have been safe. It should have occurred to him that things were different in London.

Leif swore softly. "Have you confronted Silas Wilkins?"

"I went back to his office this morning. Wilkins wasn't there. His secretary says he doesn't know exactly when the man will return."

"I'll bet he doesn't." Leif paced over to the window. "By Odin, that man is not going to cheat you out of your money. You worked too damned hard to get it."

Thor clenched his jaw. "I do not intend to let him cheat me. I came to you because you are a better businessman than I am. I wanted to be sure that I was not wrong."

Leif reached over and clamped a hand on Thor's shoulder. "You are not wrong, brother. We'll figure out a way to get the money you invested—along with the money you've earned."

Thor just nodded. He was furious with Wilkins and his treachery, but that problem could be solved.

It was losing Lindsey that tore at him.

"There is more," Leif said. "I can tell by the look on your face. What is it?"

Thor sighed. "It is Lindsey. It has ended between us. She has finally come to her senses."

"And by that you mean she believes the two of you do not suit."

Thor paced over to the small, coal-burning hearth, though there was no fire lit there now. "I have told myself it is for the best and deep inside I know it is true. I could never give her the things she deserves. I am not the man she needs and I could never make her happy. Still, I…"

"I have been where you stand, brother. Losing the woman you love is not an easy thing."

Thor's gaze swung back to Leif. "I did not say I loved her."

Leif smiled sadly. "You did not have to. It is there in your eyes whenever you look at her."

Thor stared into the dead coals in the hearth. "She is trouble. I am lucky to be rid of her."

Leif made no reply, but when Thor looked back, he caught a trace of pity.

Thor said no more. Even he did not believe the lie. He wanted Lindsey as he always did, but she no longer belonged to him and never would again.

It was a pain that would not go away.

They waited for Stephen's valet, Simon Beale, at the Quill and Dagger Tavern, just two blocks from the viscount's stylish residence in Grosvenor Square. The promise of money seemed to have convinced the valet to agree to the meeting.

Lindsey sat next to Thor at a table not far from the door, watching anxiously to see if the man would actually appear. Krista and Leif sat at a table nearby, not wanting to make the man uneasy and also providing a chaperone for Lindsey, now that her mother and father were home.

Of course, her parents had no idea Thor would be with her. They would be horrified at the thought of her with a man who was not her social equal.

They need not have worried. Thor remained carefully distant, respectfully playing the gentleman he was not. Every minute Lindsey was near him was pure agony—surpassed only by the hours she spent without him.

She forced her mind away from him, back to the business at hand. "Do you think Beale will come?"

"You offered him a good sum of money," Thor said. "It is likely he will come."

"We don't even know what he looks like." She searched the soft light of the tavern, only half full tonight. Situated in a wealthy neighborhood, the place was spotlessly clean, with low beamed ceilings and dark-oak-paneled walls polished to a glossy sheen. Just the faintest smell of tobacco marked it as a spot where men came to drink and converse.

"He is here," Thor said, his eyes sharpening on a lean man with black hair who had just pushed through the heavy front door, the top half brightened by colored glass.

Lindsey leaned toward Thor, her gaze riveted on the stranger. "How do you know it is he?"

"He is the man who approached me in Foxgrove—the one who sent us to see Martha Barker."

"I thought he was probably the one."

Thor rose from his chair as the black-haired man came near. In the light of the candle flickering in the center of the table, Lindsey could see fine threads of silver in the black hair at his temples.

"Mr. Beale?" Thor asked.

He took a quick glance around. "Simon Beale." He had a thin face and a bladelike nose, but his features were pleasant. "I believe we met before."

Thor's mouth faintly curved and that simple movement made Lindsey's stomach float up under her ribs.

"Aye, that we did."

Beale sat down and introductions were made all round. "We spoke to Mrs. Barker, as you advised," Thor said. "It was an interesting conversation."

"Ah, so you begin to see the sort of man Merrick is."

"It is too soon to know for certain."

"Perhaps," Beale said. "But I believe Lord Merrick may be the man responsible for the murders of the women in Covent Garden—as well as that of Penelope Barker. I have no proof. I had hoped when you read the notes—and considering your brother had fallen under suspicion—you might be moved to involve yourself in the search."

"How did you know about my brother?"

He shifted in his chair, nervously glanced toward the door. "Rumors travel among the staff of any big household. Word has a way of getting round."

A tavern maid approached just then. Thor ordered Beale a tankard of ale, and she brought it quickly, smiling at Thor as she set the mug down on the table. Lindsey ignored a trickle of jealousy that skittered along her spine. Thor was an extremely virile man. Sooner or later he would seek out another woman. She had to resign herself to that, but dear God, she didn't want to.

"We've been searching," Thor said. "So far we have found nothing of substance that points to Merrick."

"Since you believe him guilty," Lindsey said, "you must know he was in London the nights of the murders. Did he go out of the house both nights?"

"He goes out quite often." Beale took a sip of his ale. "On those particular nights he said he was going to his club. I helped him dress in the appropriate manner."

"We need to know why you believe the viscount is a murderer," she said. "Surely it isn't solely because of Penelope Barker's disappearance."

"I have worked for Lord Merrick since he was a youth. I know his habits, his proclivities better than anyone. I know that he frequented houses of ill repute—though I am not certain he still does. I know that in the past when he returned home after such a night, on occasion there were bloodstains on his clothes."

Lindsey sucked in a breath. This was certainly not the Stephen Camden she knew!

"Go on," Thor urged.

"I know what he did to Penelope Barker after she told him she was with child, that he used a horsewhip on her, that he might have killed her right then if one of the grooms hadn't stumbled upon them. I know he disdains women without morals, that he is repulsed by whores and at the same time attracted to them. He once recounted the punishment he meted out to what he called 'a particularly sinful whore' at the Red Door. I believe there is something not right in the viscount's head that might make him capable of murder."

"Why do you not go to the police?" Thor asked.

Beale scoffed. "I am a servant. Do you really believe the police would take my word over that of a viscount? And as I said, I have no real proof."

"If you believe the man is a murderer, why do you continue to work for him?" Lindsey asked.

"I stay because I wish to see justice done for Penny. In that I am determined."

Lindsey flicked a glance at Thor, read the thoughts swirling round in his head. "Thor spoke to Merrick's coachman. The driver said he took the viscount to White's the nights of both murders."

"The driver said he heard about each woman's death the next day," Thor added, "and thus he recalled."

Lindsey straightened in her chair, a notion popping into her head. "Rudy is a member at White's! I shall convince him to ask around, see if he can discover if Stephen was actually there and if he was, what time he might have left the club."

Although convincing her brother might not be easy. He and Stephen had both gone to Oxford. Stephen was nearly four years older and Rudy had always looked up to him. There was no way he would believe the viscount was capable of murder.

"It's been six months since the first woman was killed," Beale reminded them. "I doubt if anyone will recall much about it."

"Perhaps not," Lindsey said, "but there is always a chance. And the second murder wasn't all that long ago."

They talked a little longer, exploring different avenues, going over anything that might be valuable in their search for some sort of proof. At the end of the meeting, Lindsey shoved a pouch of coins across the table toward Beale.

He reached out a thin-fingered hand and shoved it back. "I was in love with Penelope Barker. I was too old for her, I suppose, but I loved her just the same. I want justice for her and the others. If I find out anything useful, I will be in touch." With a last glance round the room, he rose from the table.

Lindsey watched him walk across the room and disappear out the tavern door, her mind running over bits and pieces of their conversation, wondering if it were possible that Stephen was actually guilty of murder. When she turned, she felt Thor's fierce blue eyes on her face and all thought of Merrick fled.

"Thor…" At the sound of his name, his features closed up. His expression turned guarded, but a hint of longing remained. Her heart swelled with love for him. "Thank… thank you for coming," she said, just to break the awkward silence.

He shook his head, ran a hand through his wavy dark hair. "We should not be together, Lindsey. When we are, I remember the way it felt when we made love. I remember the feel of your beautiful body moving beneath me and I can only think of having you that way again."

A soft little whimper escaped her throat. She swallowed. "Perhaps…perhaps we could meet…just one more time. Perhaps…"

His jaw firmed. "Our time together is over, Lindsey. You know this."

Her eyes filled with tears and she looked away. It was over. She was the one who had ended the affair. She had done the right thing, she told herself.

A few feet away, she saw Leif and Krista rise from their table and begin moving toward them.

"They'll want to know what we have learned," Thor said.

"Yes…yes, of course." Lindsey told herself she was grateful when they arrived and Thor began filling them in on what the valet had said.

But she couldn't quite convince herself.

Twenty-Two

〰〰◦〰〰

Lindsey slept poorly that night. Her dreams were filled with images of Thor, memories of them laughing together, of riding his magnificent stallion, of him holding her, kissing her, making love to her.

"Time to get up, miss."

She groaned, unable to believe it was already morning. Her eyes slowly opened to see her maid, Kitty, hovering over the bed.

"Are you feeling unwell, miss?" She rarely slept late, wouldn't have today except for her restless night.

"I am fine." She threw back the covers and slowly swung her legs to the edge of the bed.

"Your mother wishes you to join her. She said to tell you that once you are up and dressed and have had your morning cocoa, she will see you in the Blue Drawing Room."

"Did she mention what this is about?"

"No, miss."

Stretching to work the kinks from her neck, Lindsey walked over to the bowl and pitcher on the dresser, poured in some water and washed her face. Feeling a little better, she finished the cocoa and biscuits Kitty had brought up, then chose a velvet-trimmed, chocolate-brown wool gown in deference to the chilly, late-October weather, dressed and made her way downstairs.

In the Blue Drawing Room, her mother sat waiting, the full skirts of her rose silk gown spread out around her, an embroidery hoop in her hand. She set the hoop aside as Lindsey approached.

"Good morning, dearest."

"Good morning, Mother."

"Did you sleep all right? You look a little tired."

"I am fine," she lied.

"Would you like a cup of tea?"

"Yes, thank you, I would." Lady Renhurst was an attractive woman in her late forties, with thick brown hair a darker shade than Lindsey's, lightly streaked with silver. They were of a size, both tall and slender, though her mother appeared to have put on a bit of weight during her latest travels on the Continent.

She poured a fragrant cinnamon tea into two gilt-rimmed porcelain cups then set a cup and saucer down on the table in front of Lindsey. Her mother seemed in no hurry to begin whatever discussion she wished to have, but Lindsey had never been much for wasting time.

"You asked to see me. Does this have something to do with Rudy?" She picked up the silver tongs, snared a lump of sugar and dropped it into her cup.

"Your brother has his own set of problems. This has to do with you, dear—you and your future."

Lindsey felt a sliver of alarm. Nervous now, stalling for

time, she added an extra lump of sugar and carefully stirred until it had dissolved.

Her mother pinned her with a knowing stare. "I can see you would still prefer to avoid the subject. Unfortunately, your father and I have shirked our duty where you are concerned far longer than we should have. That is about to change."

Lindsey took a sip of her tea. "I'm afraid I don't understand."

"I believe you do, but in case you truly do not, I shall not beat about the bush. It is past time you married, dearest. You are two-and-twenty. You have enjoyed your youth long enough. Now it is time to look to the future."

Her stomach was churning. She wasn't prepared for this conversation. "I like things the way they are, Mother. I have a job I enjoy. I have friends, a life of my own."

"You are still living at home, dear. It is time that changed."

"You and Father are rarely in London. I didn't think you minded."

"Of course we don't mind! This house is your home. But that can't go on forever. You want children, don't you? You want a family of your own?"

There was a time she hadn't been entirely certain. That time was past. In the months she had come to know Thor, she had discovered a good deal about herself. She wanted children, she had learned, wanted a husband and family. Thor's beautiful face popped into her head.

If only the man in her life could be Thor.

Her throat tightened. "Of course, I want those things... someday."

"But that is the point, darling. If you wait, you may miss out on the very things you want. You are in your prime, dearest. The time to act is now. Your father and I have discussed this. We believe it is time you accept a proposal of marriage and begin to plan your future."

"That may sound good, Mother, but in case you haven't noticed, I haven't received a proposal of marriage."

Her mother smiled. "Do not fret, dear. Your father and I have been looking into the matter and we have come up with several interested suitors. You will merely have to choose which one you want."

Her uneasy stomach clenched into a knot. "I cannot believe this. You are saying you have chosen the man I am to wed?"

"Of course not. We have merely put together a list of suitable men, all of whom have expressed an interest in making a match."

This couldn't be happening. "H-how many are there?"

"Three, so far. We can probably come up with another one or two if you are truly disinclined toward all three of them, but I think you may be surprised at the quality of the candidates we've come up with."

It was madness. She was an independent woman—for the most part. She didn't need her parents to find a husband for her.

"I appreciate your concern, truly I do." She tried to smile, but her lips felt stiff and unwilling. "But you see I am simply not ready to wed."

Her mother set her saucer down on the table with enough force to rattle her cup. "Perhaps I have not made myself clear. As our daughter, it is the responsibility of your father and me to provide for your future, and we believe it is in your best interest to marry. Though you have never been one to take advantage of our generosity, should you decide not to wed any of the men we approve, you will be cut off completely. You will be asked to leave the house and you will not be welcome here again."

Lindsey just sat there.

"I realize this has come as a shock but perhaps when you see how well we have chosen—" She broke off, reached over and picked up a sheet of paper lying next to her on the sofa. "These are the names of the men your father has interviewed. Each of them was excited at the prospect of making you his wife."

Embarrassment flooded her, along with a rush of anger. "I cannot believe Father would do such a thing! Those men must think I am desperate. They must think I can't get a husband on my own!"

"Not a 'tall," her mother soothed. "You are a lovely young woman and the daughter of a baron. Mostly they were flattered that you would consider them as a potential mate."

Lindsey's hand shook as she reached out and took hold of the list, looked down and read the first name.

William Johnston, Earl of Vardon. She had danced with the earl on numerous occasions. He was always attentive, always tried to be charming, though he had never completely succeeded. His interest in her came as no surprise. The man had money and social position. But Lindsey hadn't the least bit of interest in *him*.

"Vardon would be quite a good catch," her mother said, "though your aunt seemed to think you might prefer Michael Harvey."

Her gaze shot to the second name on the list. Great heavens, her father had spoken to Lieutenant Harvey? Had he dangled her pedigree in front of him, knowing that marriage to the daughter of an aristocrat would help his career? With Rudy still a suspect, she was surprised Michael would even consider the notion of marriage, no matter the benefits it might bring him.

"Mr. Harvey hasn't Vardon's fortune or title, of course, but he is extremely well-connected, his uncle being a duke and all."

"Great-uncle," she corrected.

"Yes, and according to what we've found out, he is quite well situated financially. His father inherited a great deal of money and Michael is in line for the fortune. He can provide for you very well and if he is more to your liking—"

Her eyes widened at the third name on the list. "*Stephen Camden?* You talked to Stephen about marrying me?"

"The man is in need of a wife. He requires an heir and the two of you are well acquainted. His property connects with ours and our families have been friends for years. Stephen was pleased to be approached. Of course, none of the men know there are others who are being considered so we must be careful how this is handled."

Lindsey stared down at the list. "I cannot…cannot believe this."

"Perhaps not, but as you can see, your father and I are quite serious. You may take some time, of course. We want you to be happy with whatever choice you make. And as I said, we believe we can enlist another one or two names, should those three be unacceptable."

Lindsey said nothing. She couldn't believe her parents were selling her off as if she were a prize piece of livestock, a wife with the proper pedigree who would suit each man's purpose.

Lindsey lifted her chin, facing her mother squarely. "This is all quite unexpected. I'll need some time to think it over."

"That is certainly to be expected."

She set her cup and saucer down on the table and rose to her feet. "I have a few things I must do. If you will excuse me, Mother…"

"Of course, dearest."

Lindsey left the drawing room on legs that felt wooden. She made her way up the sweeping staircase, went into her bedroom and closed the door.

Her parents were determined she should marry. It should have come as a shock and in a way it did. But in another way, she had known this day would come, that she couldn't live with her parents forever, that if she wanted to continue the sort of life she was used to living, she would have to wed.

It was strange, but the notion of marriage no longer seemed distasteful. In truth, over the past few months, the idea of a husband and family, of children and a home of her own had been stirring at the back of her mind. The trouble was, the man she wished to marry wasn't on her parents' list. He had no fortune. He didn't fit into the society in which she and her parents lived.

Lindsey tried to imagine herself wed to stuffy Lord Vardon, not unattractive, but twenty years her senior and utterly bland.

She thought of Lieutenant Harvey. Michael was handsome and charming, but his job would always come first and she wasn't in love with him and never would be.

For the first time, she realized there was only one man she wanted. Only one man she would ever want.

She wanted Thor Draugr and it didn't matter how much money he had or that he was different from other men. She wanted him to be her husband, wanted him to be the father of her children.

Instead of the worry and fear she expected to feel as she gazed at her parents' list, Lindsey felt a jolt of exhilaration. She had never been good at taking orders—though in this she had just decided to accept her parents' edict.

They wanted her to wed—then wed she would!

But when she married, it would be to the man she loved.

Lindsey's thoughts centered on Thor the following morning—as they had for most of the night. Discarding one idea after another, she had tried again and again to figure out the best way to approach him. She was sure he would agree to marry her. He felt guilty for making love to her when they were not wed. He would feel it was his duty.

She considered that. What if he married her out of obligation? What if he didn't really love her?

As she made her way downstairs to the breakfast room, Lindsey cast the notion away. Thor loved her. She was sure of it—well, almost sure. And if he didn't love her quite yet, once they were married and he realized how much she loved *him,* he would surely grow to love her in return.

And she had discovered that—contrary to what she had believed— the two of them were very well suited. Thor's soft-spoken, thoughtful manner complemented her more impulsive nature. They both loved horses and the country. He could be stubborn and demanding, yes. But she had always had a tendency to run over the men in her social circle. Thor would not let that happen.

She smiled to herself as she continued along the hallway and shoved open the door of the breakfast room. A sunny chamber that overlooked the garden, the room was empty except for Rudy, who lounged in a high-backed chair consuming eggs and sausage collected from a row of steaming silver dishes along the sideboard.

"Mornin', sis." He smiled at her but his nose remained buried in the morning edition of the *London Times*.

"Good morning." Lindsey walked over to the sideboard, lifted the lid off a silver chafing dish and scooped a spoonful of eggs onto a plate for herself.

Thinking that now might be a good time to speak to her brother in regard to Stephen Camden, she joined him at the table. A footman brought her a cup of tea and she took a sip, her gaze running over the young man immersed in the newsprint. His sandy hair was mussed and he looked a little sleepy-eyed, but not dissipated and lackluster as he used to after a night of carousing.

"Out late last night?" she asked, nibbling on a slice of toast.

Rudy shrugged. "Not so late. Went to the club for a bit, then stopped by the Golden Pheasant for a few hands of cards."

She paused as she lifted her teacup. *The Golden Pheasant.* She supposed he couldn't stay away from Convent Garden forever. It was, after all, one of London's main centers of entertainment. "I thought you had decided to give up gambling."

Since his arrest and the days he had spent in prison, he seemed a little more mature, a little less bent on self-destruction. She hoped his return to the city hadn't changed that.

"You don't have to worry, sis. I played a bit, but mostly

just for fun. I'm not as stupid as you think. I know I've got responsibilities. I'm not going to shirk them."

She flashed him a smile filled with relief and approval. "Good for you." She ate a few bites of her breakfast and sipped a little more tea, thinking he had given her the perfect opening. "You mentioned the club. I believe Stephen Camden is a member. Do you ever see him there?"

Rudy swallowed a mouthful of sausage. "He's there quite a lot. Second home of sorts when he's in the city."

"He's in London now, I believe. He said something about returning when we were at Merrick Park."

"He's here. Seen him last night."

She tried to hide her interest, shoved her eggs around on her plate then took a bite. "You wouldn't happen to recall whether you went to the club the night Phoebe Carter was murdered."

He glanced up. "I was there…early on. Only bit of the evening I recall."

"Do you remember if Stephen was also at White's that night?"

His head came up and he studied her closely. "He was there. I saw him that night. Like I said, I don't remember much after that, but early on, I remember he was there."

"Any idea what time he left or where he might have gone from the club?"

Rudy's gaze sharpened with suspicion. "Why the sudden interest in Merrick? And what's he got to do with Phoebe Carter?"

Lindsey released a breath. "There's a chance Stephen may somehow be involved in the Covent Garden murders."

"What are you talking about?"

"When I was at Renhurst there were rumors, gossip that Stephen had murdered a young woman named Penelope Barker. Rumors have also surfaced connecting him to the women who were killed in Covent Garden."

Rudy yanked the white linen napkin off his lap and slammed it down on the table. "*Rumors.* It is rubbish, is what it is. Merrick is the son of a marquess, for God's sake, and a viscount on his own. He is a friend and hardly the sort to do murder. What's gotten into you, sis? You saw Stephen's name on Mum's marriage list and you're trying to discredit him?"

"This has nothing to do with Mother's list."

Rudy shoved back his chair and stood up. "Stephen and I went to university together. We've been friends for years. I know the sort of man he is and so do you. You ought to be ashamed of yourself." Casting her an angry glance, he turned and stalked out of the breakfast room, a portion of his breakfast uneaten.

Damn and blast. She should have known her brother would defend the man. He had always looked up to Stephen. At least now she knew the viscount had actually gone to his club, as his coachman had said, the night of the latest murder.

But what time had he left?

And where had he gone from there?

Twenty-Three

The office buzzed with activity. It was nearing the end of the week, the Stanhope press chugging, printing copies of the next edition. Lindsey sat fidgeting in the chair behind her desk, though she had already turned in her weekly article. She was there to see Thor. She needed to talk to him, relay the conversation she'd had with her mother and convince him to marry her.

The door swung open, emitting a flash of sunlight accompanied by the sound of heavy boots on the wooden floor. Her heart took a leap at the sight of Thor's tall, muscular frame filling the opening, his nearly black hair slightly ruffled by the breeze. He ducked his head and stepped into the office and Lindsey rose from her chair as if lifted by invisible wings. She moved toward him, stopping him midway across the room.

His gaze swung to hers and her stomach contracted, began to hum with nerves. "Krista said you would be working today. I…um…I was hoping… There is a matter of importance I wish to discuss with you."

"As you wish. We can go upstairs."

She glanced away. They were no longer seeing each other and he meant to keep his distance. How could she have imagined this would be easy?

"I spoke to Krista. I asked if we might leave a little early. I thought we might take a walk in the park." Green Park wasn't far away. The day was surprisingly warm for this late in the year and she couldn't imagine discussing this sort of topic in the room upstairs or even in a restaurant or coffeehouse.

Besides, Thor's apartment wasn't far from the park. If he agreed to marry her, perhaps they could seal the pact with an hour or two of lovemaking. The thought sent a little quiver of heat into her stomach.

Thor was watching her closely. "You have news of Merrick?"

"No, I... This is about us, Thor."

He shook his head. "I do not think our being together is a good idea. This I have said before."

"Perhaps you will change your mind...when you hear what I have to say." After her decision had been made, she'd had time to do a great deal of thinking herself.

Money wasn't so important. Thor worked hard; Lindsey had her job at *Heart to Heart*, as well as a small monthly stipend she had inherited from her grandmother. They would manage.

Society wasn't so important, either. They could save enough to buy a small place in the country. Thor preferred country living and she enjoyed it herself. Thor owned the magnificent stallion. Once the stallion was completely tamed, Saber's stud fees would be extremely valuable, and in time they could raise a colt of their own. She didn't really need society to make her happy. As long as she was with Thor, it didn't matter.

"I will leave at four and wait for you on the corner," he said. "You will talk and I will listen. That is all."

She nodded. He was tired of their illicit relationship and, in truth, so was she. She couldn't wait to see his face when she asked him to marry her.

Lindsey worked at her desk through the afternoon, going over notes she had made for her next *Heartbeat* article, but it was difficult to concentrate. The hands on the clock seemed frozen in place and each time she looked at them, they only seemed to move more slowly.

Finally four o'clock came. Thor quietly left the office, disappearing out the door. Lindsey left Bessie arranging type and Gerald Bonner and his apprentice, young Freddie Wilkes, working to get ready for the next edition. Lindsey waved goodbye to Krista, grabbed her woolen cloak off the brass hook on the wall and headed out the door.

It wasn't such a bad day for a walk. The sun lingered above the horizon and the temperature was still bearable, though a brisk wind whipped the hem of her cloak and in the distance, clouds had begun to collect at the edge of the city.

"A storm is coming," Thor said, walking up beside her. "Mayhap we should walk another day."

"We need to talk and it isn't something that can wait. Besides, the storm is still off in the distance. What I have to say is important. And it shouldn't take all that long."

He nodded, reached out and drew her hood up over her head against the breeze, took her hand and led her along the street toward the park. They reached a pretty spot next to a small, quiet pond and sat down on a wooden bench in front of it.

Thor turned to face her and she noticed the faint shadow of afternoon beard beginning to darken his jaw. She wanted to run her fingers over the roughness, wanted to bend her head and press her lips against the faint indentation in his chin.

"What is it you wished to say?"

Lindsey banished her musings and took a steadying breath. "Several days ago, my mother asked to see me. She believes it is time I married."

The muscles across his shoulders tightened but he made no comment.

"She and my father have spoken to several men they believe would suit and—"

"They mean to choose your husband for you?"

"It is commonly done in the upper classes."

He nodded. "As it is where I come from."

"I wasn't certain I ever wished to marry—not until I met you."

She thought he might say something that would make things easier but he didn't. "What I am trying to say is that I do not wish to marry some proper gentleman my parents choose for me. I wish to marry you, Thor." *I am in love with you.*

His eyes widened in shock. He stared at her as if she had completely lost her wits. "You cannot think to wed with me? I have no fortune, no title. My future yet remains uncertain. I cannot take a wife—any wife—and especially not you."

"Money isn't that important. When you love someone—"

"Do not say you love me."

"Why not? Surely you know that I do."

"I know you are not thinking clearly. We cannot wed. This you have known from the start."

Her heart was beginning to pound. She had thought that he might be resistant at first, but only until he understood. She thought that once he did, he would be eager to marry her.

She sat up a little straighter on the bench. "We have to marry, Thor. You took my innocence. It is your duty to wed me."

His eyes searched her face, but his expression remained carefully guarded. "You must listen to me, Lindsey. You know we cannot marry. I am not the man for you. I never have been."

"But—"

"Do not do this. Do not make things more difficult between us than they are already."

She swallowed, truly beginning to worry. "I thought you would wish to wed me. I thought you would be glad to make me your wife."

He glanced away. When he looked back at her, his eyes were dark and turbulent, filled with some emotion she could not read. Rising from the bench, he paced off toward the pond, stood with his back to her, his long legs splayed as he stared into the water. A pair of mallards skimmed the surface, the male's green head glinting in the fading rays of sunlight, but Thor didn't seem to see them.

Lindsey held her breath, praying he would realize she was right, that they belonged together, no matter the obstacles ahead of them.

Instead, when he turned and walked back to her, his features looked carved in stone.

"You believe I am obliged to wed you, yet you told me

yourself you were no longer a maid. What I took was given freely. Do you deny this?"

A vise was beginning to tighten around her heart. "I do not deny it. I was not…not a maid. You said it did not matter."

His jaw hardened even more. "I am not the man for you. You need a proper husband, a gentleman, and that I will never be."

Panic made her breathing shallow. "I don't care. I love you. I want us to be together."

He leaned toward her, his blue eyes fierce. "Do you not understand? I have had you. I have enjoyed the use of your beautiful body but now I am tired of you. I am not a man to settle for only one woman. You must know this. Do what your family believes is best for you. Marry the man your father has chosen."

She couldn't breathe. Her eyes welled with tears. "You…you don't mean it. You're just saying that because you think it is the right thing for me to do."

"It *is* the right thing. The right thing for both of us." He urged her up from the bench and began guiding her firmly back toward the office. Her carriage was waiting. She was fighting not to cry when Thor opened the door and thrust her firmly inside.

"Your future is ahead of you. Mine is yet to be determined."

She stared at him through the window. "I need to know the truth—is it really other women you want?"

Thor shrugged his powerful shoulders. "We enjoyed each other. It was good between us. But I am a man of strong appetites. This you know, Lindsey."

She leaned back in the seat, closing her eyes to block

the sight of him. Her heart was aching, breaking into a thousand pieces. As the carriage jerked into motion, tears rolled down her cheeks. How could she have been so wrong? How could she not have seen?

Fresh pain stabbed into her heart—for the love she had never really had and the dreams she had lost.

Lindsey began to weep.

It was two days later that Thor stood in front of the offices of Capital Ventures, pounding fiercely on the door. Pain and fury lashed at him, fired his temper until he could barely see. If Wilkins hadn't cheated him…

But it wasn't only the money that had forced him to drive Lindsey away. He had told her the truth. He was not the man she needed and he never would be.

His fists made another fierce assault on the door and it finally opened. The young blond secretary stood there, his eyes bulging with fear.

"Where is he?" Thor demanded. "Where is Silas Wilkins?"

The lad swallowed hard. "I am to tell you that he is away on business. I am not certain when he will return."

Thor reached out and caught the young man by the lapels of his brown tweed coat, lifted him clear off his feet. "Where is he?"

"I'm not…not supposed to tell you."

Thor shook him—hard.

"H-he has a house in Kent. He left the day after you were here the last time."

"Tell me where to find this place in Kent."

The young man spit out the directions to a country house at the edge of the village of Westerly. Thor released his grip and the secretary settled back on his feet. "Please don't tell him I told you."

Thor grunted. "I do not intend to do much talking." He meant to get the money he was owed and leave.

"If I didn't need this job, I would quit," the lad said. "Wilkins is a dishonest man."

Thor just nodded. Wilkins was a charlatan. He had stolen the valuable stock certificates and replaced them with worthless pieces of paper.

Turning away, he descended the steps and stalked off down the street. Since his conversation with Lindsey, his fury was all that kept him going. He had lied to her, disdained the love she believed she felt for him, and hurt her very badly. It was the last thing he wanted to do.

As he approached his flat, his anger slowly faded, leaving him completely drained. He would get his money—of that he had no doubt. But he would never have Lindsey.

Climbing the stairs seemed a Herculean task; opening the door took every ounce of his strength. He had destroyed whatever feelings Lindsey might have held for him and in doing so, had destroyed part of himself. His heart ached as it never had before. His brother was right. He was in love with her.

Looking back, he realized he had loved her even before he had seen her riding the hills of Renhurst, taking the jumps with the skill of a man, like a Valkyrie, a female warrior, strong and brave, woman enough for a Viking chieftain.

He would gladly give his life for her and in saying the awful things he had said to her, that was exactly what he had done.

Something stirred in the faint light inside the sitting room. "How could you?"

His head snapped toward the sound of the feminine voice coming from out of the shadows. In a chair next to the sofa, Krista leaned forward, outlining her lovely face in the weak light streaming from the street lamp on the corner.

"How could you say those terrible things to her?"

He sank down on the sofa across from her. "I had no choice."

Krista came up out of the chair. "You had no choice? You had no choice! You crushed her, Thor. You broke her heart into little pieces and I don't think she will ever be the same."

"She will marry a proper gentleman. She will have the life she deserves."

"You are a fool, Thor Draugr. I never would have guessed how big a fool you are."

His throat felt tight. He had said those same words to himself. "I could never make her happy. We are not the same."

Krista stormed toward him from across the room. "And you think that if she marries another man that will make her happy? She loves you. She will never be happy with another man. She isn't that sort and neither are you. Surely you are not too blind to see that."

"You are not saying I should have agreed to wed her?"

"Of course I am!" She knelt in front of him, reached out and took hold of his hand. Hers felt warm while his was icy cold, just like the lump inside his chest that was his heart.

"I know you love her," Krista said. "And because you do, you will find a way to make her happy."

For an instant, hope stirred inside him. Could it work between them? Could he truly make her happy? That hope quickly faded. Lindsey needed a gentleman, a man of her own social class.

"Have you thought what might happen if I got her with child? The potion she took kept her safe, but if we were married, sooner or later my seed would take root in her belly."

"So...?"

"Lindsey is too slight to bear the babe of a man my size."

Krista scoffed. "Don't be ridiculous. A woman's body grows to accommodate the child inside her. And if you haven't noticed, Lindsey has nice womanly hips, not so narrow as to be a problem. Besides, those are decisions God makes, not you."

He felt a moment of relief. At least his lovemaking had not put her in danger.

"I hurt her," he said. "I could not think of another way."

"Well, I can. You can go to her, tell her you didn't mean those awful things you said. Tell her you love her and want to marry her."

He looked up at her, wishing he could, knowing he could not. "I must do what I think is best for Lindsey. I am not the man for her."

"She's your life-mate! She belongs to you! Do you deny it?"

Thor said nothing.

Krista made a sound of frustration, turned away from him and headed for the door. "Think about what I've said. And don't wait too long. She thinks you don't want her. I believe she will marry whichever man her parents choose." She jerked open the door. "One of them is Stephen Camden. Perhaps you think he will make her happier than you can." Krista slammed the door behind her, leaving him alone in his misery.

Camden.

He knew Lindsey would never marry a man who might be a murderer, a man known for his cruelty to women. Still, the point was well made. Who could say which man would make Lindsey happy? The only one he could be sure would try his very best was him.

But even if he wanted to undo the mess he had made, he could not.

He knew his woman well. After the things he had said and the way he had hurt her, Lindsey would never trust him again. And she would never forgive him.

Twenty-Four

$\mathbf{P}$leading ill health, Lindsey stayed home from work—as she had done yesterday and the day before.

Worried about her, Krista had stopped by that first day and the whole ugly tale had spilled out.

"I thought…I thought he would want to marry me," Lindsey had told her, swallowing past a lump of tears. "God, I was such a fool."

"He loves you, Lindsey, no matter what he said. He just doesn't believe a marriage between you would work."

"You didn't see his face. H-he…he needs other women to make him happy. That is what he told me. And Thor doesn't lie."

Krista hadn't pressed the issue. There was no use discussing a matter that wasn't going to change.

Thor wasn't going to marry her.

Instead, her mother was pressing her to make a choice from among the men on her list.

A knock on Lindsey's door signaled her mother's return

again this morning. She smiled as she floated toward the bed. "How are you feeling, dearest?"

Lindsey glanced guiltily away. She was being a coward and she knew it. Still, she wasn't ready to leave the sanctuary of her bedroom. "I'm sure I will be fine in another few days."

Her mother rested a hand on her forehead, checking for fever. "You don't feel hot."

"I told you I will be fine. It is probably just a mild ague of some kind."

Instead of leaving, her mother sat down in the chair beside her bed. "You've been home for the past several days. Have you given the matter of your marriage any more thought?"

Lindsey shrugged. Now that she understood Thor's true feelings, she no longer cared whom she wed. "I'm leaning toward Lieutenant Harvey. He seems a nice enough fellow."

Her mother's eyes widened with glee. "Indeed! I think the handsome lieutenant would make an excellent choice. You would make a lovely couple. Your father and I were both quite impressed with the man."

Lindsey's chest squeezed, began to feel leaden. "I need to get to know him, Mother. I need to spend time with the lieutenant before I can be sure."

"Of course, dearest—that goes without saying."

"Unfortunately, at the moment, I am simply not feeling well enough to go out in society."

Her mother smiled and patted her cheek. "Of course not. We won't make any plans until you are completely recovered. Lieutenant Harvey must see you at your very best." With a triumphant smile, her mother left the bedroom, so thrilled at the prospect of Lindsey finally agreeing to marry, she was willing, for the moment, to let the matter rest.

Lindsey was grateful. She was ready to get on with her life, but she was still wounded, her heart still painfully sore. In time, she would be able to get past the awful blow Thor had dealt her, but not yet.

Not yet.

She tried to hate him for what he had done, but since she was the one who had started the affair, the one who had always pressed him to continue—it would hardly be fair. When she thought of those times, shame engulfed her. She had behaved like a wanton. She remembered the women at the Red Door. No wonder Thor had been attracted to her. He was a man who enjoyed his whores.

Lying in bed, Lindsey told herself she had cried enough, but when Kitty set a tray of chocolate and biscuits down on the beside table and quietly left the room, Lindsey's heart seemed to shatter all over again.

She turned and wept into her pillow.

Thor knocked on the door of the large, slate-roofed manor house at the edge of the village of Westerly. He had ridden the stallion hard to get there. He wanted his stock certificates returned. He wanted this business over and done.

He rapped again and a doddering old man pulled open the door. The butler leaned toward him, staring at him through the quizzing glass he held up to a rheumy old eye.

"May I help you?"

"I am here to see Silas Wilkins."

A bushy gray eyebrow arched up. "Mr. Wilkins is working in his study. Whom may I say is calling?"

"Thorolf Draugr, but I will tell him myself." Thor brushed past the old man, careful not to knock him over as he walked into the entry. "Which way?" he asked.

Staring at him in amazement, the butler pointed a bony finger down the hall.

"Thank you." Thor strode off in that direction, looking into several rooms before he reached the study. The door was open. Wilkins sat behind a big oak desk. His eyes widened in shock at the sight of Thor striding toward him.

"Wh-what are you doing here?"

"I came for my money. I want it now."

"I—I told you…the stock you bought is—"

Wilkins squealed like a pig when Thor leaned over, grabbed hold of the lapels of his coat, and jerked him halfway across the desk.

"You stole my certificates and we both know it. I want them back." He shook the man, then released his hold, strode round the desk and leaned over Wilkins's chair. "They are here, are they not? You would not have left them in London."

"But…but I did! They are in my office safe. We'll have to go back there and get them."

"So you admit to stealing them."

"No, of course not, but—"

Thor wrapped a hand around the man's skinny neck and lifted him out of his chair. "I want to hear you say it. Tell me the truth."

Wilkins sputtered and tried to speak, but the words came out hoarse with Thor's fingers gripping his throat. "Let me…go!" He gagged and tried to break free, but there wasn't the slightest chance.

"The truth!"

"All right…I—I paid…paid a man to take them."

Thor slammed him back down in his seat but didn't let go. "And if you wish to live, you will give them back. Now."

Wilkins nodded, his neck bent back as he stared into Thor's angry face. "Let…me…go and I will…get…them for you."

Thor released his hold and Wilkins sat there panting. When Thor moved toward him again, he scrambled out of his chair and backed away. Shaking all over, he turned round and reached for a painting that hung on the oak-paneled wall behind his desk. He lifted it off to reveal a hidden safe.

"Open it."

"Yes, yes…all right, I'll open it. But before you do anything rash, perhaps there is a way we could both—"

"No more talk. Open the safe and give me back what belongs to me."

Wilkins's watery blue eyes darted around the room in search of help, but it was clear his butler, the ancient old man, was the only help available and even that would not be forthcoming. He turned and opened the safe, took out a pile of stock certificates and set them on the desktop.

"I'll have you arrested for this. No one will believe your story. The police will come after you."

Thor ignored him, checked the certificates to be sure they were the correct ones, counted out a large stack—the number he had purchased—and shoved the remaining few back across the desk.

"You will not involve the police. If you do, they will investigate. If you stole from me, you stole from others.

Unless you wish to spend the rest of your miserable life in prison, you will say nothing."

Wilkins opened his mouth to argue, but only a sputtering sound came out. On shaking legs, he sank weakly back down in his chair.

Thor stalked out of the house, slamming the front door behind him. Tied to the rail out in the yard, Saber's head came up at Thor's approach. The stallion nickered a greeting as Thor stuffed the certificates in his saddlebags, took the reins and vaulted into the saddle.

"Time to go home, my friend," he said, leaning down to pat the animal's shiny black neck. He whirled the stallion and started back to London at a much more leisurely pace, his mission completed, the stock certificates riding safely behind him.

He had achieved his goal, secured his future. But nothing seemed able to fill the hollow place in his heart.

It was dark by the time Thor reached London. He returned Saber to the stable near Green Park, leaving him in the care of young Tommy Booker. The stallion nickered softly as the boy took the reins, fond of the gangly blond youth.

"Give him an extra ration of oats," Thor instructed, "and see he's well rubbed down before you put him away."

"Aye, sir."

Thor left the stable. Hailing a carriage at the corner, he headed straight for his brother's town house. It was late to be calling, but lamps still burned inside, glowing through the windows of the three-story brick residence. Both Leif and Krista were home, the butler told him as he led Thor along the hall toward the family sitting room.

He caught sight of Krista on the sofa, cuddling his nephew, little Brandon Thomas; then he spotted Leif, who came out of the chair where he had been reading.

"Good evening, brother." Leif smiled. "What brings you here at this time of night?"

Thor walked over to the sofa and looked down at the baby in his sister-in-law's arms, a robust, towheaded child who was certain to be the image of his father.

"How is my nephew?" he asked, fighting to ignore a pang of longing.

Krista flicked him a glance. "He is well, though he certainly has a good set of lungs." But he was fast asleep at the moment. She rose from the sofa, gave Thor a brief look at the blanket-wrapped child, then carried the babe over to his nurse, a young woman with big green eyes and dark hair who stood in the doorway.

"We'll be up to check on him before we go to bed," Krista told her, kissing the baby's cheek.

The young woman nodded and disappeared down the hall, and Thor turned back to Leif.

"I just got back from the country. I paid a visit to Silas Wilkins. I retrieved the stock certificates he stole from me."

"You got them back?" Krista said. "You make it sound easy, but I don't imagine it was. How did you do it?"

"*Honing,* you don't want to know," Leif said. *Honing* was the word for honey in Old Norse, and a warm look passed between them.

"Why don't we all sit down?" Krista suggested. "Would you like a brandy, Thor, or perhaps something else?"

He merely shook his head. Crossing to the sofa, he sank down wearily. "It was a tiring journey."

"Even so," Leif said, "I'm glad you stopped by. After our last conversation, I did some checking. You say you've got your stock back, the certificates you originally purchased?"

"Aye."

"Do you have any idea what those certificates are worth?"

Thor released a breath. "Enough to buy a place in the country, I am hoping."

Leif grinned. "You're a wealthy man, brother. Those stocks doubled and split, then split and doubled again. They're worth a hundred times what you paid for them. Add to that your interest in Valhalla Shipping, and your finances are in extremely good condition."

Krista smiled. "Your future is secure, Thor."

"That is good news, I suppose."

"It is very good news," Krista said. "It means—if you chose to do so—you could marry Lindsey."

His heart jerked. Since the moment he had retrieved his stock, wedding with Lindsey was all he could think of. Now that Leif had discovered their worth, he knew he could take care of her, give her the things she deserved. And yet it was not enough.

He studied the swirls in the Persian carpet at his feet. "You say I have plenty of money. I can provide for her, but that is not enough. I am no gentleman and that is what Lindsey needs."

"You could learn," Leif said gently.

"It isn't really so hard," Krista added. "And if you truly love her, the price would be worth it."

He stared at his two best friends, a ray of hope expanding in his chest. "Do you truly believe I could do it?"

"My father taught you the basics," Krista reminded him.

"You already know most of what you need, and I could teach you the rest."

Sir Paxton Hart had taught him a good deal, enough to move about comfortably in this country he now called home. In exchange for his help, the professor had bargained with Leif to be taken to Draugr Island. He was there now, studying the people and the Viking way of life. Sir Paxton would remain a year before Leif returned to pick him up and bring him back to London. Thor inwardly smiled to think of the professor trying to turn his sister, Runa, into a lady.

He looked over at Krista. "For me to become a gentleman…how long would it take?"

Krista glanced at Leif, who cast her a knowing look in return. "We would have to work fast. Lindsey's mother is pressing her hard. If you're serious about this, we could start first thing in the morning."

Thor glanced away. "Even if I am able to learn what is needed, there is another problem."

"Which is…?" Leif asked.

"Lindsey will not marry me."

"You, my dear friend, are entirely correct," Krista surprised him by saying. "Which means you will have to win her trust and love all over again."

Thor said nothing. His heart was pulsing, his chest tight with building hope. Learning had always come easy for him. He could speak English almost as well as his brother, who had lived in England longer. He absorbed information well—when he put his mind to it. Surely he could learn to dress a bit more fashionably, memorize a few silly rules—and learn to dance.

But could he convince Lindsey to forgive him? Could he convince her to marry him? It was a question he could not answer.

"I will be here early tomorrow morning. First I am going to the bank. I am going to sell half of my stock and put the money and the rest of the certificates in the vault."

Leif grinned. "Good idea. You're learning already, brother."

"I must speak to an estate man, begin looking for a place in the country. Saber chafes to be free of his stall. He needs a place in the open—as I do."

"And Lindsey?" Krista asked.

His chest tightened. "She is my life-mate. If she will have me—I will marry her."

Krista smiled broadly. "Tomorrow, then."

Thor just nodded. If he hadn't been so stubborn, he would have already learned the things he needed to know.

He might even now be married to Lindsey.

Instead of trying to find a way back into her heart.

Twenty-Five

An inky blackness seeped from the alleys and crept into deserted corners. The faint light of a distant street lamp couldn't penetrate the all-consuming pitch-dark gloom. Walking along the street ahead of him, a woman hurried toward home, her satin-lined cape floating out behind her. Every few steps, she turned and looked back over her shoulder, checking to be sure no one followed.

The man smiled to himself. His reputation preceded him. The woman was as wary as a cat and yet it would not matter. He had practiced hunting, stalking his prey, and he was good at it. Whatever her destination, she would not reach it.

Soon now, she would be his to deal with as he saw fit.

He watched her round a corner up ahead and slipped into an alley that would shorten his path, careful to walk in the middle, staying clear of the refuse and foul-smelling offal that lined the walls of the old wooden buildings, not wanting to soil his fine new Spanish leather shoes. He came out of the alley and spotted her ahead, ducked into the shadows out of sight, then resumed his deadly path.

He had followed her from the Golden Pheasant, where she had been gambling and drinking with men of wealth and position. She wore a blue silk gown one of them had bought for her, a high-class whore but a whore just the same.

Men were fools when it came to women, especially a practiced doxy like this one. Her name was Rose McCleary. The Red Rose, they called her because of her fiery hair. They lusted after her, degraded themselves by having sex with her.

He smiled grimly. A whore was a whore by any name.

After tonight, there would be one less of them to darken the face of humanity.

And at the same time, an old debt would be repaid. Among her companions for several hours this evening was his old friend, Rudolph Graham. The police would be convinced that a man who had consorted with each of the victims the nights they were killed had to be guilty of murder.

And this time he meant to give them a reason to be sure.

Lindsey sat in the breakfast room staring at the headlines of the *London Times*.

COVENT GARDEN KILLER CLAIMS THIRD VICTIM.

Her father sat at the head of the table, the newspaper in front of him. Her mother sat at the opposite end. Across from Lindsey, Rudy stared down at his untouched plate of food, looking pale and shaken.

"This happened night before last," her father said. "There wasn't time for the murder to make the papers until today."

Rudy looked up, worry lines etched into his face. "I cannot believe he killed another woman."

"They've got to catch him," Lindsey said. "Surely this time the police will find some sort of clue."

Rudy swallowed so hard she could hear it. "I...um... knew her."

Her mother's head came up. "The woman in the paper?" Her voice went up a notch. "The woman they called the Red Rose?"

Rudy nodded.

"But she was a...she was a..."

"A prostitute," the baron said to his wife. "The girl was a prostitute, my dear. A young man needs to sow his oats."

"I wasn't with her that way. I stopped by the Golden Pheasant that night with Tom Boggs. Rose came in later with Martin Finch. We played a few hands of cards. Finch backed her at the Hazard table and Rose won. He meant to...to take her home but we got to playing. When Marty went to look for her, Rose was gone."

Her mother's hand trembled where it rested beside her plate. "Dear God, the police will be asking questions. They're sure to find out you were with her that night."

"I told you—I wasn't with her. She was there with Marty Finch."

"Still, it is a matter of some concern," her father said.

More than some, Lindsey thought. The police would be certain her brother was involved. They would question him at the very least. She fixed her attention on Rudy. "Where did you go after you left the Golden Pheasant?"

"I came home."

"What time?"

"I'm not sure…'bout four o'clock, I guess."

"What did you do between the time you left the Golden Pheasant and the time you got home?"

"I was feeling a little light-headed, so I went for a walk. I wasn't gone that long, maybe half an hour or so."

Oh, Rudy. He wasn't drinking the way he had been, or gambling nearly as much. And yet it was clear this could only mean more trouble for him.

A sudden thought occurred. "Did you go to your club last night?"

"I was there for a bit."

"Was Lord Merrick there?"

Rudy features tightened. "Stephen goes there often, same as me. It don't mean anything."

"Was he there?" she pressed.

"He was there. He was still there when I left. So what?"

"Did you see him at the Golden Pheasant?"

"No," he said darkly.

"What is all this about Lord Merrick?" her father asked.

"Nothing—at least not yet." She had no idea whether or not Stephen was truly involved, but she was beginning to think that whoever was committing the murders was singling Rudy out to take the blame. Perhaps Stephen had followed him from the club, seen him go into the Golden Pheasant. Seen the woman—Rose—go in, as well. Perhaps he had waited, watched the woman come out alone, followed her—and killed her.

But why?

"If you will all excuse me…" She shoved back her chair and stood up. "I am afraid I have to leave. I am running late for work." It was time she returned to the office, time she faced her demons—or in this case it was only one. Though she hoped Thor would not be there. Besides, she wanted to do a little more digging, see what she could come up with before the police arrived at the house—which she was certain they would.

At the door of the breakfast room, she stopped and turned. "One more thing. Rudy, are you still planning to go to Lady Paisley's ball tomorrow night?"

"I was until now."

"Good. I think you should keep up appearances. We can discuss it later." And then she was gone.

She was going to the ball. Her mother was also attending, in company with Emma Harvey. Her son, Michael, would also be there. Lindsey's parents were in favor of a match with the lieutenant and this was a chance for them to get better acquainted.

Lindsey's stomach knotted.

She didn't want to get better acquainted with Michael. She didn't want to marry him. But he might have information she could use. And if she had to marry someone, she would rather it be Michael than some other man her parents might come up with.

A memory of Thor popped into her head, tall and unbearably handsome, eyes as blue as the sea. He was smiling at her so sweetly for a moment she forgot to breathe. A knifing pain stabbed into her heart, but Lindsey ignored it. Gritting her teeth, she forced the pain and the memory away.

It was Michael who wanted to marry her. It should be Michael she was thinking of, Michael's image she should be seeing. And it would be, she told herself.

Tomorrow night she would make a start.

* * *

Krista reached out and took hold of Thor's hand, rested it lightly at her waist. "Now the other." He laced their fingers together. "Ready?" she asked.

Thor nodded. Krista turned to the slight, silver-haired man seated at the pianoforte, Mr. Pendergast, her childhood music teacher. She gave him a nod and he began to play a waltz. As her husband watched from the sofa, Krista and Thor stepped into the mesmerizing rhythm of the music.

She was only a little surprised at how graceful her big, strapping brother-in-law had turned out to be. He was solid and tough, and yet both brothers carried themselves with an easy confidence that translated well to the graceful movements of the dance.

"One-two-three, one-two-three. *Ouch!*"

A flush rose beneath the bones in Thor's cheeks. "Sorry."

Krista smiled. "You are doing better than your brother did at first. I have every confidence you will be a very fine dancer."

And he had been working equally hard to memorize all of the little rituals that went into becoming a gentleman. Since time was short, Thor was staying at their town house. The clothier had come by yesterday to fit him, tailoring a few items from Leif's extensive evening wardrobe, garments purchased when he had been gaming almost every night. And Krista had demanded he order garments of his own.

The barber had come and neatly clipped his thick dark hair. Though he had always kept his nails cut short, they had been carefully filed and buffed to a glossy sheen. Thor had grumbled only a little.

With time so short, they had decided to act swiftly. When

Krista had spoken to Lindsey at the office, she had mentioned that tonight she planned to attend Lady Paisley's ball. Lieutenant Harvey would be attending and after this latest Covent Garden murder, Lindsey was worried about her brother. Tonight she planned to speak to the lieutenant, see if she could glean any useful information. Lindsey had also said that Michael Harvey was the man she would mostly likely wed, though nothing had yet been formally decided.

Still, time was running out for Thor and tonight seemed the perfect opportunity to begin his campaign.

Thor stepped wrong, throwing Krista off balance and jolting her thoughts back to the task at hand. Mr. Pendergast ended the waltz and Thor released a breath.

"Dancing is not so easy as it looks."

Grinning, Leif stood up from the sofa. "It gets easier with practice. Besides, I think you'll like it a great deal more if the woman in your arms is the one who belongs to you."

Thor's blue eyes darkened. He was determined in this as Krista had never seen him. Once he had realized there was truly a way for him and Lindsey to be together, he had set out to achieve that goal like a man driven by demons.

"I will learn to dance," he said. "It is the rest I worry about. I only hope I will know what to say to Lindsey when the time comes."

So did Krista. Telling a woman you love her and asking her forgiveness wasn't something she could teach him. Thor would have to do that on his own.

Twenty-Six

⊶⊷⊷⊶

The Countess of Paisley's ball was held in the fashionable Arunedale Rooms in Arunedale Street. The building was an elegant structure, formerly the residence of the Count du Lac, whose original opulence had been added onto and restored. The rooms had opened two years ago, providing a place that could be leased for particularly large, stylish affairs.

The ballroom, big enough to accommodate some four hundred guests, was lavish, with a row of crystal chandeliers burning brightly down the center and mirrored walls lit by ornate gilt sconces. Huge potted palms had been brought in for the affair, and a twelve-piece orchestra played at the far end of the chamber.

The dancing had already started by the time Lindsey and her brother arrived, along with her mother and Emma Harvey. A silver-wigged waiter in satin livery approached just moments after she had shed her fur-lined cloak and walked into the ballroom with the others.

Lindsey took a glass of champagne off the waiter's silver tray and next to her, Rudy did the same.

"Let's just hope the police don't come after me here," her brother said darkly.

"Let us pray they have another suspect." And Lindsey hoped that if they did, Michael Harvey would tell her.

In a gown of emerald-green silk that rode low on her shoulders, dipped far enough in front to hint at the swells of her breasts, and nipped in snugly at the waist, her tawny brown hair pulled into ringlets nestled against her shoulders, she walked beside Rudy as they began to mingle with the guests. Michael had not yet arrived and Lindsey was grateful for the time to compose herself.

According to her mother, the lieutenant had been clear in his intentions. He had told her father that he was interested in making a match. Lindsey needed a husband—or at least her parents believed she did—and she had agreed to see it done. Tonight, she wanted to give Michael her utmost attention, see if she might be able to build some sort of future with him.

Convince herself she could be happy as his wife.

Her dance card began to fill. She danced a reel with Lord Vardon, forcing herself to smile at his bland, uninteresting conversation, knowing she was right to cross him off her mother's list.

Aunt Dee danced beside her, partnered with Colonel Langtree. They made a handsome couple, Lindsey thought. The colonel asked Lindsey to dance and she found him to be as charming as he had been in the country. And obviously taken with her aunt.

"She looks lovely tonight, doesn't she?" Spots of color appeared in his cheeks as he realized he was staring at the woman in purple and black at the edge of the dance floor.

"Not that you don't, of course. Because you look quite lovely yourself, Miss Graham."

Lindsey smiled. "Thank you, Colonel. And I couldn't agree with you more—Aunt Dee is a beautiful woman."

His gaze drifted once more in that direction. "A woman like Lady Ashford has any number of admirers."

"She does."

"I wonder what she would do should I propose she put an end to her long list of suitors and agree to entertain just one." He looked down at her, awaiting an answer to his not-so-subtle question.

"I know she greatly enjoys your company. I suppose you will have to discover the answer to that for yourself."

He nodded, said nothing more as he returned her to the group. She nudged Rudy as she spotted the Earl of Fulcroft walking their way, the man whose infidelities she had exposed in her column. He cast her a fulminating glance and marched past her without a word.

"I am not one of his favorite people."

"So it would seem," her brother said dryly.

She spotted Krista and Leif not far away, standing close together, staring at each other as if there were no one else in the room.

Something tightened in her chest. They always seemed so happy. She wished she hadn't seen them, wished seeing them together didn't make her think of Thor.

She started to turn away when a man of Leif's same size moved into her line of vision. In his perfectly fitted black evening clothes, his dark hair neatly trimmed and immaculately combed, she almost didn't recognize him. His gaze caught hers, held her like a rabbit mesmerized by a cobra.

He walked toward her, stopped directly in front of her. "Good evening, Miss Graham."

She moistened her lips, which were as dry as the starch on his snowy cravat. "What…what are you doing here?"

"I knew you would be here. I wanted to talk to you."

Her insides knotted. Talking to Thor was the last thing she wanted. "We've already spoken. You had your say and it was more than enough."

His eyes never left her face. "I lied to you. I need to tell you the truth."

Lindsey swallowed. She told herself to ignore him, but it was impossible to do. "You don't lie. Not ever."

"I lied that day. I did it for you."

Her stomach churned. "I don't want to talk to you, Thor—not now, not ever—and especially not here."

"It must be here. Now."

She took a deep breath. If she refused, he would make a scene. On the outside he might look like a gentleman, but inside he was a warrior, a man used to being obeyed.

"Fine, but this had better not take long." She ignored the arm he gallantly held out to her and walked stiffly over to one of the potted palms. It provided little privacy, but enough to keep their conversation from being overheard. "What is it you wish to say?"

Thor reached out to touch her, but Lindsey moved away.

"The day we spoke…I lied about the women. Since the day I met you, there has never been another I wanted."

"I don't believe you."

"I lied because I wanted to protect you. I believed that I was the wrong man for you, that I could not make you happy. I no longer believe that is true."

She ignored a little pang and steeled herself to leave. "I have to go." She tried to brush past him, but he stepped in front of her and it was as if she had collided with a wall.

"I have become a man of some means, Lindsey. I have enough to take care of you as you deserve."

"I told you money wasn't important."

"I don't want you to marry the man your father chose for you. I want you to marry me."

Pain seared through her. Tears burned but she refused to let them fall. A brittle laugh escaped her throat. "After the way you treated me, do you really believe I would even consider it?"

Thor's blue eyes turned dark and intense. "I do not expect you to forgive me. I do not expect you to trust me the way you did before. Not until I prove myself. But I promise you this—if you marry me, I will do everything in my power to make you happy. I will be the man you deserve."

She just stood there staring, her heart squeezing so hard she thought it might break into pieces.

"Until the day comes that you can believe in me again, I only ask one thing."

She arched an eyebrow, trying to pretend nonchalance, ready to say no to whatever he asked.

"Dance with me."

Her breath caught. Of all the things she might have expected, this was not one. Thor did not dance. He was no gentleman and he did not want to be. And yet as she looked at him standing there in his evening clothes, so handsome he drew a sigh from every woman in the room, she thought that he was doing a very good job of pretending.

"You wish to dance with me?"

"Aye, lady. More than you will ever know."

She glanced toward the crowd of elegantly dressed men and women, to the couples moving in perfect rhythm to the music. She cocked an eyebrow, still unconvinced. "Out there on the dance floor along with the others."

"Aye."

A grim smile curved her lips. He was certain to make a fool of them both and yet she could not resist. "Fine. Then we will dance." She turned and started walking ahead of him, looked back over her shoulder to be certain he wasn't making some sort of joke, and found him right behind her. A little tremor of awareness went through her she did not want to feel.

They reached the dance floor and, as if on cue, a waltz began to play. She caught sight of Leif walking away from the musicians on the platform and realized Thor had an ally in his cause.

He took up his position among the other dancers and turned her to face him, one of his big hands settling at her waist. His other hand captured hers. His fingers felt warm through her white cotton glove, and she fought not to tremble as she took her place in front of him, still not certain he actually meant to go through with it.

She fixed her eyes on his chest instead of his face then gasped as Thor swung her into the dance as if he feared she might bolt. Lindsey stumbled. For an instant he looked stricken, but he didn't release her, just righted her and kept moving, guiding her into the rhythm he set.

In tune with the sweeping music, they made their way round the dance floor. He wasn't as good a dancer as Michael Harvey or any number of other men she had partnered, but he wasn't that bad, either.

"I didn't think you knew how to dance," she said tartly. "Or was that another lie?"

"I only just learned."

For the first time she realized he was counting the steps, trying his best not to make a mistake. "Why?"

His gaze captured hers, his eyes blue and intense. "I wished to please you. And I wanted to hold you again."

Lindsey swallowed, found it impossible to look away. He had learned to dance for her, learned in order to please her. Lindsey found it so endearing, so impossibly sweet that for an instant, she gave in to the wondrous sensation of being back in his arms.

But learning to dance wasn't enough to make up for the terrible things he had said. And after the way he had treated her, how could she believe he truly wished to marry her?

Before the waltz came completely to a close, she left him there on the dance floor, turned and made her way back to where her mother stood next to Emma Harvey. Her heart was throbbing, beating a painful cadence in her chest. Dear God, why had he come to her now? Why couldn't he just leave her alone?

She had time for a single glance over her shoulder to find him staring at her from beside his brother, before Michael Harvey arrived at her side. He was perfectly groomed and completely at ease, an interesting, attractive man her parents approved, the perfect match for her. If only she could fall in love with him.

"Miss Graham, you look lovely this evening." He lifted her gloved hand to his lips, pressed a kiss against the back. "But then you always do."

She forced herself to smile, refused to let her gaze go

in search of Thor, and instead appraised Michael's tall, lean frame, light brown hair and refined features, thought again how attractive he was. "Thank you, Lieutenant."

They made pleasant conversation—the weather, what an elegant affair the ball had turned out to be, her trip to the country. She tried to imagine what Michael would say if she told him she had dressed as a man, ridden a magnificent black stallion in the Foxgrove Derby—and won. He would scarcely approve, she was sure, but then how many men of her acquaintance would?

Michael asked her to dance, but she declined. She had come in search of information about the murders. She refused to let Thor's presence distract her. "I think I would rather have a glass of punch, if you don't mind."

"An even better idea." He smiled and offered his arm and they made their way toward the refreshment table.

Michael filled two crystal cups with fruit punch and since it was too cold to go out on the terrace, they carried the cups into the long gallery. Several other couples stood talking at the far end of the elegant but sparsely furnished chamber where paintings of war heroes hung on the walls. She recognized General Cornwallis and, of course, the Duke of Wellington. There was no sign of Thor and she began to relax, to focus her thoughts on the problem at hand.

She took a sip of her punch. "I imagine you are working on the latest murder."

Michael nodded. "We've all been putting in long hours."

"I cannot believe that monster has killed another woman."

Michael started to frown. "This is not a good subject for us to be discussing."

"Why not?" she asked innocently.

"You know very well why not."

She sipped her punch. "Actually, I was hoping that by now you might have come up with a suspect other than my brother."

"Your brother was seen with the latest victim the night she was killed—which you probably know. Which means, I'm afraid, he remains at the top of the list."

A sick feeling settled in her stomach. "Rudy wasn't with Rose McCleary. He was merely in the same place at the same time."

"Even so, it doesn't look good for him."

"I realize you are not at liberty to discuss the crime and especially not with me, but I am asking—if you have any real interest in me beyond friendship—that you tell me as much about what happened as you can."

Michael sighed. He set his empty punch cup down on a rosewood table along the wall next to a bust of the queen. "I can tell you that we think we know how the women were murdered. At first we believed the killer had strangled them with his hands, that he was likely wearing gloves at the time. But the bruised area on the neck was wide and there were no separate finger markings. We've come to the conclusion that perhaps the killer used a scarf. That would account for the width and evenness of the bruising."

"A scarf?"

"It would seem likely."

"And again there was no...ravishment of the victim's person?"

"No. We believe he derives his pleasure from the act of the murder itself."

Inwardly she shivered. "Do you think he picks his targets randomly or does he have a particular woman in mind?"

"I'm not sure." He turned her, caught her bare shoulders in his hands. "I know you love your brother and I wish I could spare you this, but the truth is, the police are convinced Rudolph Graham is the killer. They're assembling the evidence they need to prove it. I am just hoping that when this is all over, you will be able to consider my role in the investigation separate from my feelings for you."

And then he bent his head and kissed her.

Lindsey stiffened, but only for a moment. She had kissed Michael before and the warm pressure of his lips felt familiar and not unpleasant. But there was no stirring inside her, no hot need pouring through her. She tried not to think of Thor but he was there as if he stood beside her.

Michael ended the kiss, which didn't last long, since he didn't wish to stir up gossip. "There is little we can do to further our relationship until this is over. But I will be thinking of you, Lindsey. I hope you will be thinking of me."

Lindsey managed to smile. At the moment, all she could think of was that soon the police would be coming to arrest her brother. From what Michael had said, this time they must have found some sort of evidence they believed would prove Rudy guilty. She thought about mentioning Stephen and his possible involvement, but she hadn't the slightest proof—and she wasn't completely sure herself. She needed to find the killer.

And she needed to discover who might have reason to want her brother to take the blame for a crime he didn't commit.

* * *

"It went fairly well, don't you think?" Krista stood near a potted palm, looking up at Thor. "At least you convinced her to dance with you." The crowd had begun to thin as the evening began to wane.

Thor shook his head. "I do not think she will ever forgive me."

"In time, she will. She loves you. All you have to do is remind her how much."

Thor thought of the last time he and Lindsey had made love. He had used the skills he had learned at the Red Door to give her the greatest of pleasure. In doing so, he had gained great pleasure for himself.

"She let him kiss her. I saw them in the gallery."

"She doesn't love Michael Harvey, she loves you. After what you said to her, she is confused."

Thor looked back to where Lindsey stood with her brother and her family near the front of the ballroom. The police lieutenant was gone. He supposed that was something. He wondered what would happen if he asked her to dance again.

Krista caught his arm. "You can't give up, Thor—not yet."

His features hardened. "I will not give up. I was a fool before. Lindsey is mine and I mean to claim her."

Krista's shoulders relaxed and she smiled. "Of course you do." She flicked a glance at her husband, so like his younger brother, then looked back at Thor. "She belongs to you—of course you mean to claim her. I can't imagine what I was thinking."

Twenty-Seven

Lindsey paced back and forth across the floor of Krista's office, the full skirt of her gray wool gown swishing around her ankles. She stopped and looked back. "I've got to go back to the Red Door."

"What?"

"I don't know why I didn't think of it before. The night we spoke to Simon Beale, Stephen's valet, he said Stephen has been known to frequent houses of ill repute. He even mentioned the Red Door. I need to go back there, see if any of the women remember him, find out if they know something that might tell us if he is a murderer."

"You can't go to a…a house of pleasure, Lindsey. And certainly not by yourself."

"I know, I know." She walked over to Krista's desk. "Perhaps Leif would be willing to take me."

"Leif is out of town." Krista's pale eyebrows drew down pensively. "But I think you are right about going." She sighed. "Leif is going to be furious, but it cannot be helped. I am going with you. We'll go tonight."

"Oh, Krista, you are the best!" Lindsey leaned over and hugged her. "I shall bring the orange satin dress. Returning it will give us an excuse to be there."

"We had best go early. The later it gets, the more dangerous the area becomes."

"So what time do you think?"

"I'll bring my carriage round at eight. That should be late enough for the place to be open and early enough that we won't run into trouble."

"Perfect." Lindsey left Krista's office and went back to her desk. Thor was working at the docks today and Lindsey told herself she was glad. She didn't want to see him, no matter that he had tried to make amends. No matter that now he was willing to marry her.

Still, she couldn't get him out of her head. Sweet God, why had he changed his mind?

She wished she knew the answer, but she certainly wasn't going to ask him. She still felt humiliated every time she remembered the hard look on his face when he had reminded her that she wasn't an innocent and now that he'd had her, he was no longer interested.

An ache throbbed beneath her breastbone. It was too late to go back to the way things were, too late to take back the hateful words.

She left the office a little early, taking her carriage instead of walking. Once she reached the house, she went straight up to her room, declining supper and asking that a tray be sent up later. Wearing her simple gray wool gown, she prowled nervously till the clock struck eight. Her parents had gone out for the evening so there would be no problem leaving the house. She packed the gaudy orange dress in an old hat box and as soon as the clock began to chime the hour, hurried downstairs.

"Shall I fetch your cloak, miss?" the butler asked.

"Yes, the black wool, if you please."

She accepted the plain woolen wrap he draped round her shoulders. "Thank you, Benders." Then she stepped back so he could open the door.

As promised, Krista's carriage waited out in front. The coachman helped her climb into the dark interior. Lindsey squeaked in surprise as she sat down across from Krista and found herself perched on the hard thighs of a man's lap.

Thor's arms closed around her waist. "I like you sitting there, sweetheart. I have missed you."

Apparently he had. Her cheeks heated as she felt his maleness hardening beneath her skirt. "Damn you, Thor, let me go!" As the carriage lurched forward, she broke free, turned and plopped down on the seat next to Krista.

She cast her friend a glare for her treachery, though it was too dark inside for Krista to see. "What is *he* doing here?"

"Thor stopped by the house looking for Leif. I was just leaving. He asked me where I was going and I could hardly lie to him."

She arched an eyebrow. "Why not? He's gotten very good at it himself."

Thor just grunted.

Lindsey sat up straighter on the seat. "I've changed my mind. Please take me home. I shall go to the Red Door another night."

In the light of a passing street lamp, she saw Thor lean forward, bracing his elbows on his knees. "I will wait outside if you wish. But you are on your way now and you were right in deciding to go. Mayhap…*perhaps* one of the women will know something about Lord Merrick that will help your brother."

She clamped down on her urge to escape. Thor was right. There was no time to lose. Even now the police might be on their way to arrest Rudy. "Fine, I shall go."

"Thor is good to have along when you are going somewhere like this," Krista added.

"Oh, he makes the perfect bodyguard," Lindsey said tartly. "As long as the body he is guarding is not mine."

Thor crossed his arms over his massive chest. "We will see," he muttered darkly.

It occurred to her that his repentant attitude had already disappeared. The old Thor had returned, a domineering, demanding male, taking care of her whether she wanted him to or not.

Sweet God, why did she find the notion so appealing?

Lindsey stiffened her spine, trying not to bump her legs against his, trying not to feel his gaze burning into her through the darkness, knowing she could not possibly, yet certain that she did.

They rode mostly in silence, the driver doing a masterful job of weaving the conveyance through the traffic in the busy cobbled streets. Eventually, he turned into a quiet lane in Covent Garden and pulled up in front of the Red Door. Thor jumped down from inside the carriage, reached up and swung Lindsey then Krista to the ground.

"We'll be all right," Krista told him. "We won't be long."

"No more than a quarter hour," he commanded. "Then I come in and get you."

Lindsey rolled her eyes at his high-handedness. And yet it felt good to know Thor was out there in case they needed him. They made their way up the steps to the big brick house with the front door painted red. Krista knocked, knocked again, and the door swung open.

Lindsey plastered on a smile for the brawny man who stood in the opening. "Good evening. We'd like to speak to Madame Fortier, if you please. We have something of hers that we are returning." She held up the hat box and smiled as if being there were an everyday occurrence.

The doorman stepped back, allowing Lindsey and Krista to walk inside. "Who should I say is here?"

Lindsey looked at Krista, then back to the brawny man. "Friends of Thor Draugr."

The doorman nodded and walked away. In the background, Lindsey could hear a pianoforte being played, accompanied by the soft strings of a harp. Men's voices came from another room, along with the high-pitched laughter of women.

"Interesting place," Krista said, taking in the ornate surroundings, the gilded mirrors, crystal lamps and red-flocked paper on the walls.

"Isn't it? Perhaps women should have a place like this to escape to whenever they feel the need."

Krista's blue eyes widened.

"I am jesting…though as I think on it, it is not such a bad idea."

Krista laughed.

Madame Fortier returned, hips swaying, moving her saffron silk skirts. The bodice of the gown was extremely low-cut, perfectly displaying the swells of her voluptuous breasts. When she recognized Lindsey as the woman who had been there with Thor, her dark eyebrows arched up.

"I am surprised to see you again," she said in her fake but accomplished French accent. She glanced around, looking for Thor.

"Thor isn't here at the moment." Lindsey handed over the hatbox. "This is the orange gown I borrowed. I've been meaning to return it."

Madame eyed her with suspicion. "You came 'ere at this 'our to return a gown that 'as already been paid for?"

"That and another reason."

"And what reason would that be?"

"My friend and I have been trying to find the man they call the Covent Garden Murderer."

Madame made the sign of the cross. *"Mon Dieu."*

"We need to ask you some questions about a man we believe may be one of your clients. His name is Stephen Camden."

"I do not give out information about my clients."

"We understand that. But this is different. Women are being murdered right here in your neighborhood. Three of them have died so far. We have reason to believe Lord Merrick might be involved."

Madame cast a glance toward the salons where her ladies were entertaining. "You will please follow me." The skirts of her gown swayed with each of her steps as she led them into her private quarters and closed the door.

Her accent mostly faded. "Lord Merrick hasn't been here for some time."

"I see."

"He was asked to leave."

"Why was that?" Lindsey asked.

"He was cruel to some of my girls. He mistreated them, even beat them. There are men who gain pleasure from such things, but Merrick went to extremes. The girls were frightened of him. In the end, I told him he was no longer welcome."

Krista spoke up just then. "Is there one of your ladies who might tell us about him? Perhaps she might know something that could be useful."

Madame seemed hesitant, then she sighed. "I will let you speak to Silky. She used to be his favorite." The buxom woman disappeared, returning a few minutes later with a redhead Lindsey recognized from when she had been there before.

"Ziss is Silky Jameson," Madame said, her accent returning. "She will tell you what she can."

Silky was beautiful, with big blue eyes and the kind of body men imagined in their dreams. Her gaze assessed both Lindsey and Krista. "So it takes two of you to please him. I am not surprised."

Embarrassed heat burned into Lindsey's cheeks. She started to tell the redhead that neither of them were Thor's women—at least she wasn't anymore—but considering she had used his name to get in, she swallowed her pride and simply smiled.

"We need to know what you can tell us about Stephen Camden. We have reason to believe the viscount may be involved in the Covent Garden murders."

Silky made a sound of disgust. "*Merrick.* He paid me well, but he was one of those men who could only get satisfaction by being cruel. He liked to tie me up and then he would whip me with a little buggy whip. At first, it was mostly just play, but then he got more and more brutal. He wasn't happy unless he made me cry. I used to hide when I saw him coming. Finally, Madame asked him not to return."

Lindsey flicked a glance at Krista, both of them thinking the same thing. "He tied you up?"

Silky nodded. "He tied me to the bedposts. He used these long pink scarves he always brought with him." She tossed her head, flipping her long red hair over one shoulder. "Like I said, at first I didn't mind. He wasn't the only man who liked to play rough. But Merrick was different. The more he hurt me, the more he enjoyed it." Her russet eyebrows drew together. "And there was another odd thing."

"What was that?"

"A couple of times, he called me Tilly. He used to say, 'It's your turn now, Tilly. How do you like it?' I think he was punishing her and not me."

"*Tilly.* Did he ever say her last name?"

"No. It only happened once or twice, as I recall."

"Thank you, Silky," Lindsey said. "We appreciate your honesty."

She shrugged her shoulders, left bare in the low-cut gown. "Women are dying. Someone needs to stop it."

"Perhaps what you've told us will help," Krista said.

Lindsey left the Red Door bursting with excitement. They had gained what might be valuable information, as well as a lead to follow. The trip had truly been worth it.

Then she spotted Thor standing next to the carriage, his long legs braced apart, his gaze hot and possessive, and Lindsey wasn't so sure.

* * *

The following morning, Rudy was arrested. Constable Bertram came to the house with three other policemen and took him away in manacles.

Lindsey's mother was nearly hysterical. "Do something, William! You can't just let them come in here and take our son!"

"You mustn't overset yourself, my dear. This is just some dreadful mistake." He accepted the greatcoat Benders handed him. "I am off to see Jonas Marvin. He will know what to do. We will have our son home by the end of the day."

But as Lindsey watched him leave, she knew it wasn't going to be that easy. From what Michael Harvey had said, the police had enough evidence to find her brother guilty of murder.

Michael!

She would go to Michael, make him tell her what the police had discovered. Michael would have the answers she needed.

Ignoring the noisy weeping in the drawing room, Lindsey retrieved her cloak and raced out the door, leaving so fast she forgot her bonnet. There wasn't time to ready her carriage and have it brought round. At the cab stand on the corner, she spotted a hansom and climbed onto the worn leather seat. "Police headquarters, if you please."

"Aye, miss."

The horse plodded off, the wheels of the rig bouncing over the cobbles as the cab wound its way through the heavy traffic. It seemed to take hours, but finally the conveyance arrived. Lindsey paid the fare and a little extra and departed the carriage. Unfortunately, when she dashed up the wide brick steps into the station, Michael wasn't there.

"I'm terribly sorry, Miss…?"

"Graham," she told the bulky sergeant who manned the front desk. "I should like to wait for him, if I may."

"It might be a while, Miss Graham."

"That's all right. I shall just take a seat over there." She pointed toward a wooden bench along the wall. Perching on the edge of the seat next to a long-faced woman in black, she waited anxiously for the lieutenant's arrival.

It was nearly two hours before Michael walked into the station, his expression weary, his hair wind-tousled. Exhausted herself from worry, Lindsey rose the moment she spotted him and hurried in his direction.

"Michael!"

He stopped and turned.

"I need to speak to you. It is important."

He nodded, but he didn't look happy. It was clear he knew why she was there and also obvious he wished she hadn't come. He wanted to remain as neutral as possible in the matter of her brother, and her appearance at the police station wouldn't look good.

Michael escorted her down a long narrow hallway, into a room furnished with a wooden table and four wooden chairs.

"I wish I could help you, Lindsey. You know I can't."

She clasped her hands in front of her to keep them from trembling. "I didn't come to ask for your help. I came to tell you that I believe I may have found the man who killed those women."

He arched a light brown eyebrow.

"It wasn't my brother—it was Stephen Camden, Viscount Merrick."

Michael looked stunned. "Merrick? Why in the world would you think Lord Merrick killed them?"

"It's a long story, Michael. I pray you will give me the chance to explain."

He tipped his head toward the table, indicating she should take a seat, and both of them sat down.

For the next half hour, Lindsey poured out the information she had collected: beginning with the notes she had received, how she had followed the clues that led her to Merrick Park, led her in search of Penelope Barker. How the young girl had disappeared and her mother was convinced Lord Merrick was the man who had killed her.

When she finished, Michael sighed. "Listen to me, Lindsey. The proof you have is nothing more than gossip. This girl, Penelope Barker, you say she disappeared, but her body was never found. You don't even know if she is actually dead."

"Her mother believes she is." She went on to tell him about Silky Jameson and his cruelty to the women at the Red Door. "Silky says that Merrick likes to hurt women—that he ties them up with *scarves. Scarves,* Michael—surely that means something."

"It means the man is a sexual deviate." His gaze fixed on her face. "Tell me you didn't personally go to the Red Door."

She glanced away. "One of my friends went with me."

She could read the disapproval in his face. "That is hardly appropriate behavior, Lindsey, for a young, unmarried woman—and especially not one who may well become my bride."

Her chest squeezed. As attractive as Michael was, she couldn't imagine being married to a man so concerned with the dictates of society.

"My brother's life is at stake. That is more important than any chance of scandal my actions might cause. Besides, I was extremely careful. No one there knows my name."

He sat back in his chair. "Well, I guess that is something." He released a slow breath. "I'm sorry to say this, Lindsey, but all the information you have given me is moot. The police have irrefutable evidence that Rudy is the man who killed those women."

She came up out of her chair. "That is impossible. My brother is not a murderer."

"This time a clue was left at the scene of the crime. Constable Bertram found the button off a gentleman's greatcoat. This morning, when the police arrived at your house, they found the coat with the same missing button. That coat belongs to your brother, Lindsey. I am sorry."

"No…" Her legs began to tremble. "It isn't possible."

"I'm afraid it is. As I said, I am sorry."

"Stephen must have planted it. Rudy saw him earlier in the evening. He must have somehow taken the button. He must have left it at the scene of the murder."

"Why would he do that?" Michael asked gently. "What reason could the viscount possibly have?"

"I don't know." Lindsey gathered her strength and with it her resolve. "But I intend to find out."

Lindsey left the police station and headed straight for Newgate Prison. Her brother had already been checked into the master's side. She handed a pouch of coins to one of

he guards, then followed him along a narrow corridor that
ed deep inside the dismal stone walls. When she came to
a crossroads, she heard the sound of weeping. The smell
of sewage filled her nostrils and she fought down a wave
of revulsion.

Dear God, poor Rudy!

When she reached his cell, she found him sitting on the
edge of his narrow bed, unshaven and dressed in the same
trousers and shirt, wrinkled now and stained, that he had
been wearing when they brought him in earlier that day.
He looked wan and pale and utterly distraught. He glanced
up at her as she entered the stark, wood-floored chamber
but didn't bother to rise.

"You don't believe I did it, do you, sis?"

She hurried to where he sat on the bed, knelt in front of
him and took hold of his pale, icy hands. "Of course I
don't believe it! I know you would never hurt anyone, especially not a woman."

He swallowed, his Adam's apple moving up and down.
"What am I going to do?"

She rose and tugged him up from the bed, over to the
rough-hewn table, and urged him down in one of the chairs.

Lindsey sat down across from him. "The first thing you
are going to do is listen to what I have to say. You are going
to keep an open mind and then you are going to tell me
what you know about Stephen Camden."

"But—"

"No buts, Rudy. Your life is at stake."

Rudy nodded, propped his elbows on the table and
rubbed a hand over his unshaven face. "All right, I'll listen."

Lindsey started from the beginning, telling him about

the notes, about what she had learned in Foxgrove, about Penelope Barker and what Silky Jameson had said.

"God's teeth, sis, Silky works at the Red Door, don't she? Tell me you didn't go in there."

"I found out Stephen frequented the place—or used to. I wanted to ask the women about him."

"God's bones! Isn't there anything you won't do? No wonder you can't find a husband."

An instant of hurt went through her, followed by a thread of irritation. She was getting extremely tired of condemning males. "Actually, at the moment, I have more potential husbands than I can handle."

The breath rolled out of him. "Sorry, sis, I didn't really mean it. I'm just so…" He shook his head, unable to put words to his despair.

"It's all right. I can only imagine the way you must be feeling."

Rudy inhaled deeply, sat up a little straighter in his chair. "So what did Silky tell you?"

Lindsey's thoughts returned to the reason she had come. "Silky said Merrick enjoyed hurting women. She said he liked to whip them. She said he tied them up with scarves—and the police think that is what was used to murder those women."

"I can't believe you're talking about the same Merrick I know. Stephen always seemed disinclined to any sort of violence. Tried to get him to box a couple of times, but he wasn't interested."

"Well, perhaps he is interested in a different sort of violence. I want you to tell me about him, anything at all you remember."

Rudy shrugged. "Not much to tell. Stephen was always kind of a loner. He was four years older, you know. I was just starting university when he was finishing up."

"Did the two of you ever have an argument, something that might have stayed with him, something that might have made him angry enough to want revenge?"

Rudy shook his head. "As kids, we played together whenever I was at Renhurst, but he was never allowed to stay out very long. I used to feel sorry for him." He looked up. "I got to tell you, sis. I think you got the wrong man."

"You saw him at White's the night of the latest murder, right?"

He nodded. "He was there at the club like he usually is."

"Is there a way he could have taken the button off your overcoat?"

"What?"

"The police found a button at the scene of the murder. They found the same button missing from your greatcoat."

He looked even more defeated. "I left my coat in the cloakroom. Anyone could have taken the button."

"Did you go straight to the Golden Pheasant after you left?"

"I did."

"And afterward…you said you walked around for a while before you came home. Did you stop anywhere else?"

He shook his head.

"That means that the button had to have been taken at the club or by someone at the Golden Pheasant."

"I kept my coat with me at the Pheasant. Didn't intend to stay very long."

"Then it had to be Stephen or someone else at White's that night."

Rudy mulled that over. "Merrick ain't a killer."

"Maybe he is, maybe not. Right now I'm leaning toward he is." She stood up from the chair. "I've got to go. In the meantime, I want you to think back, try to remember anything you might have done that would make Stephen want you to take the blame for murder."

Twenty-Eight

Thor rapped on the front door of Baron Renhurst's big stone mansion, which took up half a block in Mount Street. A second series of knocks and the door swung open to reveal a thin, silver-haired butler panting from his efforts to reach the door.

"May I help you?" he asked, tipping his head back to look Thor up and down.

"I need to speak to Miss Graham. Tell her Thor Draugr is here about her brother."

"Yes, sir, I'll just be a moment. If you would like to wait in the drawing room—"

"Great heavens—Thor!"

Lindsey stood at the top of the stairs, slender and feminine, elegant in that way she had, and so womanly it made his chest hurt. She started down the stairs and her skirts fluffed up, exposing her trim little ankles, and a jolt of hunger stabbed sharply into his groin.

By the gods, his need of her would have to wait. He conquered the surge of lust and started striding toward her. He hadn't quite reached her when a tall man with her same fair coloring, tawny hair and eyes stepped into his path.

"And just whom, may I ask, are you?"

Thor looked over at Lindsey, who had paused near the bottom of the stairs. He felt a surge of possessiveness so strong he fought an urge to haul her over his shoulder and carry her off as his captive, as the men of his island would have done.

"You are Lindsey's father?"

"I am."

"I am Thor Draugr—the man who is going to marry your daughter."

"What!"

"Now is not the time, but soon we will talk. For now, I need to speak to Lindsey. I have found information that might help your son."

The baron just stared, his eyes bulging in shock. As Lindsey hurried forward, he seemed to regain his senses. "This man, Lindsey—what on earth is he talking about?"

"I'm not quite certain myself, Father, but if he is here, it must be important."

"I am not about to let that man get anywhere near—"

"Lindsey and I must speak, Baron," Thor said. "Now."

Lindsey rested a hand on her father's arm. "It is all right, Father. I have known Mr. Draugr for some time. We work together at *Heart to Heart.* He has been helping me try to find the Covent Garden Murderer."

"Good God! Have you lost your mind, girl? Murder is no business for a woman."

Lindsey looked at him as if she had heard those words

too many times. "Give us a moment, Father. I need to hear what he has to say."

The baron cast a hard glance at Thor. "All right, you may have just that—two minutes in the drawing room. And leave the doors open."

Thor made a slight inclination of his head. "As you wish, my lord." Following Lindsey, he let her lead him into an elegant drawing room and they sat down on the sofa, careful to keep an acceptable distance between them.

"If this is about anything other than my brother—"

"I know you have not yet forgiven me. I am here with information that might help."

She eyed him with a hint of suspicion. "What have you learned?"

"I went to see Simon Beale. I thought he might know this woman, Tilly, that Silky Jameson told you about." On the carriage ride home, he had demanded to know what she and Krista had learned from the women at the Red Door and reluctantly she had told him.

"What did Beale say?" she asked.

"He said the only Tilly he knew was Tilly Coote, Stephen's nanny. He said she was already out of the marquess's employ by the time he took the job as young Merrick's valet."

"Did he remember anything else?"

"Only that he didn't think Merrick liked the woman. During Beale's years as valet, the viscount had few good things to say about his childhood."

Lindsey stood up from the sofa. "I've got to find her. I've got to talk to her."

Thor felt a surge of triumph. He had known what Lindsey

would wish to do and the first part of his plan had just fallen into place. "I have found her. I will take you to her."

She started shaking her head. "Just tell me where she is."

"I will not do that, Lindsey. It is too dangerous. If you wish to go, I will go with you."

"Damn you!"

"That is the way I have felt since the day I said those awful words to you. Come, I will take you there now."

He reached out a hand, held it there, hoping she would take it. Lindsey cast him a long, hesitant glance. But she took hold of his hand and let him lead her toward the door.

"I have borrowed my brother's carriage, but soon I will have one of my own."

She looked up at him, let go of his hand as they stepped into the hallway. Her father still stood in the entry, his legs braced apart, his hands clasped behind his back.

"I was just about to come for you," he said to Lindsey. "It is past time for your friend to leave."

"He is going, Father. But I have to go with him. Thor may have found the proof we need to save Rudy."

"Thor? You call this man by his first name?"

But Lindsey was already hurrying out the door, heading down the steps to the carriage.

"Come back here, Lindsey!" the baron shouted, striding after her out the door.

"Don't worry, Father—" she called back through the open carriage window. "I shall be back very soon."

Thor settled himself in the seat across from her and the driver whipped the team of bays into a steady trot. They pulled away from the house and Lindsey assessed him from the opposite seat of the coach.

"You told my father you were going to marry me. How could you do something like that?"

"Because it is true. You belong to me. Deep inside, you know this, Lindsey."

Her chin went up. "I don't belong to any man and especially not you!"

Thor said nothing. Lindsey was there with him and that was a start. She was determined to speak to the woman named Tilly Coote and he meant to help her. Lindsey was certain her brother was innocent of murder. Thor had learned to trust his woman's instincts.

May…*perhaps* this would give them the evidence they needed to prove Rudy Graham's innocence.

Then he would deal with the matter of making her his wife.

Tilly Coote lived in a tumbled-down, wood-frame house at the edge of the city. Grass grew up through the boards in the porch and the wooden steps were cracked and broken. Tilly came to the door in a worn, printed muslin dress beneath a moth-eaten sweater, an older woman with blond hair turning gray and teeth that were beginning to yellow. Once she might have been pretty, years ago when she had been Stephen's nanny. Not anymore.

"Good afternoon, Mrs. Coote," Lindsey said pleasantly.

"Afternoon. What can I do for you?"

"My name is Lindsey Graham. This is Thor Draugr. We came to talk to you about the years you worked as a nanny for the Marquess of Wexford. Do you think you might have a moment to speak to us?"

"It's *Miss* Coote, and I suppose I've got time. Not much else to do these days." She stepped back to allow them into the house, which was cluttered with bric-a-brac collected over the years, stacks of yellowed newspapers, and too much furniture for the size of the house.

Miss Coote offered them tea, which Lindsey and Thor declined, and instead they all took seats in the sitting room.

"I worked for his lordship for nearly thirteen years," Miss Coote said proudly. "Good man, he was, always kind to his employees. When little Stevie reached the end of his thirteenth year, the marquess figured my job as his nanny was done."

"He fired you?"

"Retired me. Gave me my severance plus a bonus for doing such a good job. That's what he said... 'You did a fine job of raising my boy, Miss Coote.' Said I'd done right, teaching little Stevie to mind his manners."

"Was Stephen a hard child to handle?" Lindsey asked.

"Not so hard, once we came to an agreement." She shook her head. "But he was a terror in the beginning. Wouldn't mind a thing I said, always running off to play when he should have been doing the schoolwork his tutor, Mr. Barnes, gave him."

"What did you do about it?"

She chuckled. "I fixed the little devil. Tied him up, I did. Borrowed a couple of nice silk scarves from his mum so it wouldn't hurt him. Tied him to the bed when he wouldn't behave."

Her heart was pounding. "You tied him up?"

Tilly smiled, showing her yellowed teeth. "He calmed himself right away."

"And his mother knew what you were doing?"

"Lady Wexford, she was glad for it. You see, Stevie

wasn't really her son. He was born to the first Lady Wexford, who died. Her ladyship and little Stevie didn't get along."

"How did you and *little Stevie* get along?" Thor asked darkly, his tone catching Lindsey's attention.

"We were fine. I had a nice stout birch rod, you see. Kept it right there in the nursery. Took it to his little arse when he misbehaved. Didn't take long for him to figure out he was supposed to do what I said."

"What about when he was older?" Thor asked. "What did you ask him to do for you then?"

Lindsey turned toward Thor, not sure what he meant. When she looked back at Tilly, the woman was sweating.

"Didn't do anything he didn't appreciate. He was growing up, wasn't he? Needed to learn things about women. I just helped him learn."

Lindsey just sat there, trying to digest what Stephen's nanny was saying. Surely it didn't mean she had pressed herself on the boy in an intimate fashion. But from the dark look on Thor's face, Lindsey realized it must be true.

She stood up from the sofa, a little shaky on her feet. "I think it is time for us to go, Miss Coote. We appreciate the information."

"Like I said, I just taught him what he needed to know."

"I'm sure you did," Lindsey said. But she was thinking that no wonder Stephen hated Tilly Coote. And she thought she had just found out why he had murdered those women.

"Are you all right?" Thor's voice reached her from the opposite side of the carriage.

"I am all right." She looked up. "How did you know what she had done to Stephen?"

His jaw hardened. "There was something in her face… the kind of need a man recognizes in a woman, no matter what is her age. She had no man—not now or then. It was a good guess she had satisfied her need with the boy."

More instinct than guess, Lindsey thought. One thing she had learned, Thor was a man with keen instincts.

She sighed. "It makes me sad to think what Stephen must have gone through as a child."

"A lot of people have troubles when they are young. It isn't an excuse to do murder."

There was something in his voice that alerted her. She had always been curious about his past. "What about you? Did you have a troubled childhood?"

He shrugged his powerful shoulders, lifting the fabric of his dark brown tailcoat. He wore a stylish waistcoat, as well, and a perfectly tied cravat. If she didn't know better, she might actually believe he was a gentleman of the highest order.

"My mother died when I was eight," he said, surprising her since he rarely talked about his life before he came to England. "I barely remember her. Leif was oldest so he was closest to our father. In a way it was good, I suppose. It forced me to grow up early, learn to take care of myself. It is a good thing for a man to know."

But she thought that he must have missed having the love of a mother. As she looked back on it, thought about his independent nature and the distance he kept from others, she realized that perhaps what Thor needed most and never had was a woman's love.

Her heart squeezed. There was a time she wanted to give him that love more than anything on earth.

"I have not thought of my mother in some time," he said. "My father said I was born with her more gentle nature. I do not know."

But Lindsey thought it was true. She thought that although he was the most masculine man she had ever known, there was a side to him that was sensitive and caring. The combination was lethal. It was the reason she had fallen in love with him.

Her heart pinched. Things were different now.

Weren't they?

Lindsey glanced out the carriage window, saw a stray cat dart into an alley, heard the sound of a trash barrel turning over.

"You had better take me home. I need to talk to Lieutenant Harvey, give him this new information. And my father will be wondering where I am."

"I will take you back, but not yet."

She looked up at him. "Then where are we going?"

"We need to talk. I am talking you to my apartment."

She remembered the last time she had gone to his flat, remembered their heated lovemaking, and a flush rose in her cheeks. "I am not going to your house, Thor. Not now, not ever again. I am asking you to please take me home."

He crossed his arms over his chest. "Not yet."

"I am not going, Thor."

He simply ignored her.

"Stop the carriage this minute or I swear I will start screaming." When he made no move to comply, she opened her mouth, but before a sound came out, he hauled her across his lap and smothered her cry with a kiss.

His lips were hot and possessive, familiar and oh, so seductive. It was a hard, taking kiss that gentled and turned coaxing, a kiss that reminded her of the way it had been the times he had kissed her before.

He parted her lips with his tongue and the taste of him filled her senses. His male scent mingled with his fragrant cologne enveloped her. She told herself to break free, but the heat of his big, hard body surrounded her. The muscles across his chest pressed into her breasts and the pink tips puckered and began to throb.

Thor cupped her face between his palms and kissed her, tenderly yet fiercely.

"I have missed you," he said softly, between small, nibbling kisses. "I am not happy without you." Another deep, mind-numbing kiss.

Lindsey couldn't think, could barely breathe. She knew she should stop him but her body was responding, heating, melting into his, and the last thought of struggle slowly faded. Recalling all they had shared, Lindsey kissed him back with all the hot need boiling inside her. The heat of desire scorched through her and when he drew away to kiss the side of her neck, she tilted her head back to give him better access.

"You loved me once," he whispered against her ear. "This you said. Do you deny it?" He claimed her mouth in a long, drugging, breath-stealing kiss. "Do you?"

Another hot kiss left her trembling.

"Do you?"

"I...loved you."

He ran his tongue over her trembling bottom lip. "You wished for us to wed."

"Yes…"

He ran a finger along her cheek, tipped her head back so that he could look into her eyes. "Then you will marry me."

She shook her head, but he trapped her face between his hands and kissed her again, deeply and thoroughly, a reminder and a promise all at once. She was limp and pliant in his arms by the time he had finished. For the first time, she realized he had pulled the shades on the windows. Vaguely, she heard him tell the driver to keep going until he was told to stop.

She didn't resist when he opened the back of her gown and slid it off her shoulders, didn't fight him when his hand slid inside the cups of her corset to caress each of her breasts. He stroked each one tenderly, until the taut peak throbbed beneath his fingers. She didn't stop him from bending his dark head to taste them, to suckle and lick until she was squirming in his lap, fighting not to beg for more.

"We will wed," he said between soft, nibbling kisses, "as we should have done before."

Lindsey swallowed. She was so hot, burning hot, and aching with hunger for him. Yearning for him to touch her all over, longing to feel him inside her.

"Say it," he softly coaxed. "Say you will marry me." She felt his hand beneath her skirts, stroking her gently, skillfully, then more insistently. Pleasure washed through her, fierce and sweet. She was on the verge of climax when he stopped.

"Say it."

Lindsey whimpered, tried to find her voice. She would say whatever he wished if he would only continue.

"Say it!" he demanded, stroking her deeply again.

"I will...I will marry you." But instead of giving her what she wanted, he drew his hand from beneath her skirts, lifted her up and set her astride his thighs. Lindsey moaned as he opened the front of his trousers and freed himself, lifted her again and impaled her to the hilt.

Her head fell back and her eyes slid closed. "Sweet God in heaven." She looped her arms around his neck as he eased her down on the velvet carriage seat and began to thrust deeply inside her. Long, powerful strokes turned her insides to flame. The heavy thrust and drag of his shaft stirred pleasure so intense she trembled all over. Nothing had ever felt so good or so completely right.

In that moment she realized, no matter the awful things he had said, no matter that he might not love her, it was Thor she wanted.

And whatever his reason for wedding her, she was going to marry him.

"Lindsey...sweetheart..." he whispered, kissing her again, taking her to that place that seemed so easy to reach when she was with him.

She cried out as she crested, broke free and soared among the stars. Thor followed a few minutes later, the muscles tightening across his massive chest, his thighs like iron where they spread her open to receive him. In a corner of her mind, it occurred to her that she was no longer taking Samir's preventive potion, but she was past caring. And in truth, she wanted Thor's child.

They floated down together, finally settled back to earth.

He brushed a tendril of tawny hair back from her cheek, bent his head, and very softly kissed her. "I will talk to your father."

Her sweet languor fled. Lindsey bit her lip as she tried to imagine the scene with her father. "Not yet. I—I need to… I've got to prepare him a little." *If there was any such thing.*

Great heavens, her parents were going to be furious. They wanted her to marry a gentleman, a man from her own privileged class. They wanted her to marry Michael Harvey, or one of the other men on their list.

But Lindsey didn't love Michael. She loved Thor and she was determined. She didn't know why Thor was equally determined they should marry. Perhaps it was lust, perhaps something more. In time she would discover the truth.

She ran a hand over his cheek, felt the slight roughness of a beard beginning to form along his jaw. She wished they could talk, begin to plan their future, but there would be time for that later. For now, there was Rudy to think of and finding a way to save him.

Lindsey sat up on the seat and began to straighten her clothes. "I have to talk to Michael," she said. "Tell him what we found out from Tilly Coote."

She saw Thor's deepening scowl and realized too late that in using the man's first name she had made a big mistake. Instead of turning the carriage around and taking her back to her house, he started kissing her again. Then he was pressing her back down on the seat, pulling her beneath him, filling her a second time.

The sweet surge of pleasure washed away thoughts of any other man.

Twenty-Nine

He should have told her. He should have said the words he knew a woman wished to hear. He should have told Lindsey he loved her.

Thor cursed himself as he swung up on Saber's back and rode out of the stable into the grassy open spaces of Green Park. At this early hour, there was no one to disturb them. Weak yellow rays of sunlight barely visible above the horizon lit the gravel path around the park.

Thor came every day at this early hour to work the stallion, to ride him, gentle him, and make certain of the animal's care. Though young Tommy Booker was an excellent groom, Thor also stopped by in the evenings as often as he could. Saber was his future, the foundation for the blooded horses he intended to raise once he owned a place in the country. A future he intended to share with Lindsey.

As he rounded the park, urging the horse into a canter, he thought how much he had yet to do in that regard. Once he had finished riding, he would head for his brother's town house for his daily morning session with Krista, lessons on how to become a gentleman.

He was doing well at that, he thought. Working hard to learn the subtle little rules he would need to know if he meant to be accepted by Lindsey's family. Thor held no illusions about that. It might take years before they welcomed him as their daughter's husband. It didn't matter. She belonged to him and there was no changing that now.

Nor did he want to.

He leaned forward, reached down and slid a hand along Saber's sleek neck. The wind was rising, blowing the brown grasses in the park that had fallen victim to a heavy frost. He urged the stallion a little faster then gave him his head, and the horse stretched into a ground-eating gallop.

Thor knew a moment of pride, ever amazed by the magnificence of the animal beneath him. He knew that in the entire span of years ahead of him, he would never be able to repay Lindsey for the precious gift she had given him.

Her image returned.

I should have told her. I should have said the words.

He should have told her he loved her, for it was the truth. She meant everything to him. *Everything.* Without her, his life meant nothing.

But where he came from, in a world dominated by warriors, where a woman mostly served to satisfy a man's hunger, men didn't speak of love. It was a rare thing for a man to feel, an emotion seldom acknowledged.

He knew his brother loved his wife.

Perhaps his father had loved his mother. Now that he understood what it was to love, he thought that may...*perhaps* the faraway look he had glimpsed in his father's eyes was a yearning for the woman he had loved and lost.

Thor steadied the stallion, reined him into a cooling walk, and they continued round the gravel track that circled the park. Soon he would tell Lindsey the way he felt, that he loved her beyond all reason. When the time was right, he would say the words.

Thor sighed as he turned the stallion back toward the stable. He didn't understand why, but it seemed a challenge more daunting than any he had ever faced before. Even fighting the Berserkers on his island, men with little conscience who left a trail of warriors dead in their wake, seemed a far less fearsome task.

He would tell her, he told himself, and soon.

He just wasn't exactly sure when.

An early sun shone the next morning when Lindsey went in search of Thor at the stable where he kept his big black horse. She knew he spent as much time there as he could, went there in the mornings, and in the evenings, as well. The stallion was his most valuable possession and Lindsey knew how much the horse meant to him.

She had almost reached the barn when she spotted him, riding along the path in her direction. He looked up, surprised to see her, then his eyes turned a deeper shade of blue, burning with the familiar heat she always seemed to spark. Lindsey smiled as he rode into the open space in front of the barn, a breathtaking sight atop the stallion in his black riding breeches and full-sleeved shirt, his shoulders so wide they blocked the sun.

Thor reined Saber to a halt. "Good morning," he said in

near-perfect English, followed by a smile so sweet her stomach lifted as if it had wings.

"Good morning," she replied brightly.

"What are you doing here?" he asked as he swung a long leg over the horse's rump and dismounted. Just then Saber caught wind of her and his ears perked up. He tossed his beautiful head and nickered a greeting, obviously glad to see her.

Pulling a lump of sugar from the pocket of her skirt, Lindsey walked over and held it out in the flat of her hand. She scratched the stallion's ears. "Such a pretty boy, aren't you?" Saber tossed his head as if he agreed.

She turned back to Thor. "I came to talk to you. I hoped I would catch you before you left for work. I figured this would be a good place for us to speak."

"I've missed you." Bending his head, he gave her a very soft kiss. Lindsey parted her lips, allowing his tongue to sweep in, and Thor groaned. He straightened to his full height and his massive chest expanded. "What is it you wish to discuss?"

Knowing every contour of his incredible body, Lindsey forced away the memory of him naked in the circle of stones.

She cleared her throat. "I've been thinking about Tilly Coote. This afternoon, I am going to the police station." She cast him a pointed look, thinking of their heated lovemaking in the carriage and trying not to blush. "As I intended to do yesterday."

He gave her a hot look in return, which Lindsey determinedly ignored.

"I need to tell Constable Bertram what Tilly Coote said about Stephen."

"Do you really believe that will convince him Merrick is guilty of murder?"

Lindsey glanced away. "I doubt it. The man has his mind made up that Rudy is the one who is guilty. Until we have solid proof, nothing is going to make the police believe he is innocent."

Thor eyed her with growing suspicion. "So what does this have to do with Tilly Coote and the reason you are here?"

"It isn't exactly about Tilly. It's about the scarves she mentioned. If Stephen is truly the Covent Garden Murderer, there's a chance the scarf or scarves he used to strangle those women are somewhere in his house. Or maybe we might find some other sort of evidence. I was thinking that if we could get inside—"

"No."

"We need to go there, Thor. We need some sort of physical proof."

"Even if you were lucky enough to find the scarves, there is no way to prove they belong to Merrick."

She pondered that. The police refused to believe anything she told them. They would have to be the ones to find the evidence. But how could she convince the police to search the viscount's house? And what if they found nothing there?

"You are right. We need to talk to Simon Beale. Maybe he has seen the scarves. I mean, they wouldn't be the sort a man would normally have in his possession. Beale might even know where Stephen keeps them. He could lead the police right to them."

Thor led Saber into the shadows of the barn, Lindsey walking beside him. "I, too, have been thinking of Beale and what else he might know. Yesterday, I sent him a message. The note I received in return came from Merrick's housekeeper. It said Simon Beale is no longer in Lord Merrick's employ."

Lindsey's eyes widened. "Mr. Beale has worked for Stephen for years. Why would he leave? And especially now, when he is trying to see justice done?"

Thor shook his head. "I do not like to think it, but I am afraid something might have happened to him. After I got the note, I stopped by the viscount's house. According to Mrs. Woodruff, the housekeeper, Merrick said Mr. Beale had to leave the city unexpectedly, that important family matters had come up. Beale regretted ending his employment on such short notice but he had no choice."

Lindsey bit her lip. "Dear Lord, you don't think…you don't think Merrick killed him?"

"If the viscount discovered his valet was giving us personal information, there is no telling what he might do."

Lindsey swayed a little and Thor caught her round the waist to steady her. "The man is dangerous, Lindsey. This you know."

She nodded. But she was thinking that it was more important then ever to get inside his house. Perhaps this time Michael or Bertram would listen.

Time was running out for Rudy. Something had to be done.

Though the hour was not late, this time of year darkness came early. A gas street lamp burned on the corner, but a few feet away the circle of light dimmed and faded.

Stephen stood in the shadows outside the offices of *Heart to Heart*. Lamps still burned inside, glowing through the windows, but soon they would all be snuffed out. The workday was over, the employees leaving one by one. Lindsey's carriage waited in front, there to carry her from Piccadilly to her parents' Mount Street mansion.

Lindsey. The name tasted foul on his lips. When her father had come to him asking if he might be interested in making a match with his daughter, Stephen had been intrigued. He didn't know the girl that well, but as neighbors, their encounters over the years had always been pleasant. His own father was getting old. Soon Stephen would be Marquess of Wexford. He would need an heir, and Lindsey, the daughter of a well-respected baron, would do well enough.

He knew she was an independent sort of woman and in an odd way that suited him. She would require little attention, just enough to get her with child. He figured he could manage that, though the notion of bedding her did not stir him. Unless, of course, she proved even less tractable than he imagined. He liked a woman to fight him. He found his pleasure in the conquest.

He looked back through the windows of the office. Only a single lamp burned. Lindsey remained inside but soon she would leave. Stephen meant to follow her, as he had been doing for the past several nights, ever since he discovered his valet had betrayed him.

Discovered that Lindsey Graham was trying to prove him guilty of murder.

Stephen thought of all he had discovered since that day. He had found out the woman he thought to wed was no innocent. That she was a sinful little whore who eagerly shared her body with the big dark-haired man who had worked for him in the stable.

The bile rose in his throat. The urge to wrap his hands around her throat was so strong he could taste it in his mouth. She had duped him—duped them all. She was a whore and he wanted her dead. And he wanted to be the man who killed her.

And yet if he did, if he took her life in the way that pleased him, that satisfied his need as nothing else ever had, Rudy Graham would go free. It would be clear, since he was in prison at the time of the latest murder, that another man must have killed the whores in Covent Garden.

Stephen wanted Rudy to take the blame. An old debt would be repaid, the moment of his humiliation washed from his mind once and for all. In the beginning, he had told himself that after Rudy was dead, he would stop. No one would ever know the truth and he would never be suspected of the crimes.

After all, he hadn't set out to do murder. It had started with the girl, Penny Barker, the little slut he had gotten with child. He hadn't meant to kill her, but then she had told him about the babe, said she expected they would wed and that if he didn't agree, she would go to his father. Something inside him had snapped. He had strangled her there in the woods and buried her beneath an old yew tree.

He hadn't meant to continue, but after Penny, the lust had continued to grow. The need to cleanse the world of the filthy little creatures who lured men into sin was simply too strong.

He gazed toward the office, watched another employee leave. He thought of the little whore he might have married, thought of how it would feel to slide his scarf around her neck and squeeze. He would have to wait, but not for long.

Once Rudy was dead, he could start again. He had never come close to being caught. He could have it both ways, he believed.

He watched as the door opened up and Lindsey walked out of the office, descended the brick steps to her carriage, climbed inside and closed the door. Time grew short for Rudy Graham. He was certain to be found guilty and hanged. Stephen told himself to wait, see the matter finished.

But as the carriage rolled away, the urge to watch the life drain from the little whore's treacherous body became nearly unbearable. Sweat broke out on his forehead and his gloved hands unconsciously fisted.

He started walking along the darkened street, the cape of his greatcoat billowing in the sharp evening breeze. He followed the coach lights toward the house where she lived. Sooner or later a time would come when she would be alone and unprotected.

Then he would have to decide.

His palms itched. It would not be a difficult decision.

Another day passed. Lindsey left the office early and went back to her house. Thor was working at the docks so she hadn't seen him, not since the morning she had gone to the stable, though she had dreamed about him at night, hot, lurid dreams of her breasts being fondled, of his big, muscular body pressing her down into the mattress, of his hard length moving inside her.

As she walked down the hallway to the drawing room, she waved her hand back and forth in front of her face to cool the heat that had risen in her cheeks. Dear Lord, the man could make her mad with lust for him when he wasn't even there!

She blew out a breath. Her parents were in the drawing room. She needed to speak to them, inform them of her decision to marry a man who was definitely not on their list. She wished she could wait. Her mother was sick with worry over Rudy and her father walked around in a sort of impotent rage that he hadn't been able to clear his son's name. She didn't want to upset them any more than they were already, but she knew Thor would not wait.

He was determined they should wed and he was probably right. Since she no longer took Samir's potion, there was a chance that even now she carried Thor's babe. The idea should have frightened her but it only made her smile. She would love to have Thor's child. And although he was a big man and the birth might be difficult, there were other large men in her family and their wives seemed to do just fine.

Though they couldn't possibly wed while Rudy faced a hangman's noose, the matter of her marriage needed to be resolved. If she had to, she would wed Thor against her parents' wishes, but she hoped, in time, they would accept her decision.

Lindsey steeled herself to face them and continued along the hall to the drawing room. In a rose silk tea dress, her mother sat on the brocade sofa while her father rested in a chair not far away. An embroidery hoop lay in the baroness's lap, but the needle in her hand wasn't moving. Her father tried to read, but stared at the hearth instead of the pages of his book.

Knowing how worried they were, Lindsey's heart went out to them. Still, she had important matters of her own to address.

She forced herself to smile. "Good evening, Father. Mother. I am glad I found you both here together."

Her father set his leather-bound book down on the table beside his chair. "You wished to speak to us?"

"Yes, I did."

He smiled, seemed pleased. "About your decision to marry?"

She nodded. "I know the timing is wrong. Certainly it isn't something that is going to happen until Rudy's... situation has been dealt with, but I wanted you to know what I have decided."

A hint of color seeped into her mother's pale cheeks. "We could all use a bit of good news." She smiled. "I am guessing you've chosen the handsome Lieutenant Harvey. Am I correct?"

Lindsey bit her lip. "Not exactly. What I mean is, if it weren't for a particular problem, Michael would likely be the man I would choose."

Her father frowned. "What exactly is this problem?"

Lindsey lifted her chin. "I'm not in love with Michael. In fact, I am deeply and irrevocably in love with someone else."

Her mother smiled as she came up off the sofa and started toward her. "Lord Merrick! You've chosen to marry the viscount! An excellent choice, my darling."

Lindsey held up a hand, stopping her where she stood. "I am sorry, Mother. The man isn't Stephen. Lord Merrick is the last suitor I would choose. The man I love is Thor Draugr."

Her father's eyes narrowed. "You don't mean that over-bearing hulk who stormed in here the other day?"

"Thor is the kindest, gentlest, most wonderful man I have ever known. Once you get to know him, you will see it is true. I love him and I am going to marry him."

"But…but what are his circumstances?" her mother asked. "The man has no title, no social position—"

"How will he provide for you?" her father demanded, coming out of his chair.

"Thor is hardly destitute and I would marry him even if he were. He wishes to speak to you of these matters, Father. I only wanted to prepare you."

"If you think for one moment I am going to allow you to—"

"I am two-and-twenty, Father. With or without your permission, Thor is the man I intend to wed." She walked over and captured his hand, felt the tension running through him. "But I am so hoping you will give him a chance. I truly believe that if you do, you will see what it is I love about him. You will see the qualities in him that I see, and you will both know that he is the only man who could ever make me happy."

Her mother walked back to her place on the sofa and sank down heavily. Her father just stood there staring.

"As I said, this isn't the time. For now, we must focus our attention on Rudy. Proving his innocence is all that matters."

Her father cleared his throat. "Rudy…yes. We'll discuss the matter of your marriage once your brother is free."

Lindsey said nothing more, just turned and walked out of the drawing room. She prayed that soon her brother would be released from prison.

And that somewhere deep in his heart, Thor loved her.

Thirty

Lindsey left the drawing room, her thoughts torn between worry for Rudy and the future she had chosen to make with Thor. As she walked along the hallway toward the stairs, she looked up to see the butler hurrying toward her, a frown on his thin, aging face.

"What is it, Benders?"

"A note, miss. The boy who brought it said to tell you it was important."

A tremor of unease went through her. Wondering if the note could be from Simon Beale, she was surprised to see her name scrolled in Rudy's familiar handwriting. Lindsey flipped over the message and broke the seal.

Sis—
I think I may have remembered something. Come as soon as you can.
Ever in your debt,
Your brother, Rudy

Her heart squeezed, then began to pound. Rudy had remembered something about Stephen. Perhaps it would be the information they needed to prove his innocence.

"Please tell my parents a matter of importance has come up and I won't be joining them for supper."

"Yes, miss. Shall I order your carriage brought round?"

"There isn't time. I shall catch a cab at the corner."

Used to her independent ways, he nodded and went to retrieve her fur-lined cloak. He settled it round her shoulders.

"Thank you, Benders."

She left him standing in the entry, raced down the steps and along the street to the corner. It didn't take long to hail a cab.

"Newgate Prison," she ordered the driver, a white-bearded man who flicked her a disinterested glance and slapped the reins against the bony old horse's rump.

It seemed to take forever. At last, the conveyance pulled up in front of the prison and Lindsey climbed down from inside. "I will pay you double your normal fare if you will wait until I come out."

He rubbed the whiskers along his jaw and nodded. "I'll be here."

Hurrying toward the gate, she spoke to the guard, gave him a handful of coins, and he led her inside the courtyard, then into the chilly interior of the prison.

The sound of their footsteps echoed along the stone corridor and a shiver slipped down her spine. Pity for Rudy brought tears to her eyes. Lindsey blinked them away as she reached her brother's cell at the end of the passage. The door creaked as it swung open and Rudy came up off the lumpy mattress on his narrow bed.

"Sis! I say, I'm glad to see you."

She hurried to his side and gave him a hug, and unusual for Rudy, he returned it, holding onto her as if she were his only hope.

Lindsey swallowed and managed to smile. "I thought Mr. Marvin might be here."

"He was here earlier…him and that detective he hired."

"Mansfield? Has he learned anything useful?"

"I told him what you said about Merrick and that missing girl and he went to Foxgrove right after. Apparently, he talked to a man in the village who claims to have been there the night Penelope Barker disappeared. He said he saw Merrick arguing with the girl outside the stable that night. Merrick was angry, furious, I guess, that she was pregnant. The girl was never seen again."

"That proves he was with her the night she disappeared."

"But it doesn't prove he killed her."

Lindsey unfastened her cloak and swept it off, laid it over the back of a rickety wooden chair. "Your note said you remembered something. What was it?"

Rudy released a breath. "I don't know if it means anything. Didn't mean much to me at the time. In fact, I had completely forgot until you were in here talking about the Red Door and the women Merrick liked to tie up."

"Go on."

"It happened one night after I started university. A bunch of us sneaked out and went into the village. There was a tavern, a place we'd heard about. There were women there… you know, the kind men pay for their favors."

"Prostitutes."

He flushed.

"So you and your schoolmates went to the tavern. Did Stephen go with you?"

Rudy shook his head. "He was older. We didn't chum around together."

"So what happened that night?"

Rudy stared down at the bare wooden floor. "I don't know if I can do this, Lindsey. This ain't the kind of conversation a man has with his sister."

"I need to know, Rudy. Just pretend I am a man."

He looked up and his lips curved. "I've seen you dressed like one when you sneaked out to go riding. I guess I can pretend."

She almost smiled. "You were saying that you went to the tavern."

"A place called The Goose. There was a wench there named Molly. At least I think that was her name. She was a little older, buxom and kind of pretty. Rumor was she really knew how to please a man. My chums were making bets, goading me into paying for her favors, betting I wouldn't have the nerve to do it. I thought she was alone upstairs so I went up to find her."

"What happened?"

"There was a room at the end of the hall. I tried the knob and it wasn't locked. I pushed the door open and there was Stephen, naked, spread-eagle on the bed, his hands and feet tied to the bedposts. I was so shocked I just stood there. Molly was pointing at him, laughing, making fun of him because he wasn't…he couldn't seem to…" He looked away, his face flaming.

"Go on, Rudy. Tell me the rest."

He shoved a hand through his sandy hair, causing

several strands to fall forward. "I started laughing, too. I mean, it was kind of funny, I thought…being tied up and all. It was the sort of thing a young fellow did, experimenting, you know. I mean, once I let a woman—" He broke off, his face turning an even deeper crimson. "The point is, to me it was just funny. Maybe to Stephen it was more than that."

"Did you tell the other boys what you saw?"

"I don't think so. I might have. I was a little drunk at the time."

Lindsey turned away from him and walked over to the table. Would a man carry a grudge for years over an incident like that? True, it would have been humiliating. Perhaps Stephen connected it in some way to what he had suffered as a boy. But would it be enough to make a man go to such extremes?

"So what do you think?" Rudy asked.

"I don't think he murdered those women because you walked in on him in an embarrassing situation. But I think, once he started committing the crimes, it might have occurred to him that he could pay you back for humiliating him by making you take the blame."

"That's kind of what I was thinking."

"This whole thing with the scarves and being tied up…I don't think it's a coincidence." She told Rudy about Stephen's nanny and how Tilly Coote had punished him and used him for physical gratification when he was just a boy.

"I remember her. I never liked her and I don't think Stephen did, either." He looked up. "If you're right, how do we prove it? My trial's coming up in just a few days. How do we prove he's the one?"

Lindsey shook her head, a lump beginning to form in her throat. In just a few days, Rudy could be sentenced to hang. "I don't know." She walked over and took hold of his hand, felt a slight tremor run through it. "I don't know, Rudy, but as God is my witness, I promise we'll find a way."

It was dark when Lindsey left the prison. Even so, the weather-beaten cab sat in front of the building, the driver asleep in the back as she approached.

He snored so loudly he woke himself up then sat up in the seat, blinking like an owl. "'Bout time you come back."

"Thank you for waiting." He climbed out of the back seat and she climbed in, settled herself against the cracked leather while he took his place in the driver's seat and picked up the reins.

"There's a flat in Half Moon Street," she told him. "I can show you where it is. I would like you to take me there."

"Aye, miss." He clicked the reins and the old bay horse, looking as sleepy as the driver, raised its head and began to plod off down the street. She wanted to see Thor, to tell him what Rudy had said and see if together they might figure out what to do.

And she simply wanted to see him.

The cab finally reached its destination and Lindsey paid the driver. She was about to climb out when she glanced up at Thor's apartment and realized no lamp burned inside. The sun had set long ago, but it was not really that late. If he wasn't at home, there was a chance she would find him with Saber.

"There's a stable at the edge of Green Park. I want you to take me there. It's only a few blocks away."

He nodded, happy with the additional fare. Lindsey fidgeted as the cab rolled along, anxious to tell Thor about the incident with Stephen and Rudy at The Goose.

The cab arrived a few minutes later and she felt a sweep of relief at the sight of a lantern burning in the window of the barn. It cast only a small amount of light, yet she was sure Thor must be inside. Even if he wasn't, it was only a short walk back to her house.

"Thank you again," she said, handing him several more coins. Turning away, she hurried along the path to the big wooden building at the edge of the park, not far from the stone one where her father kept his horses.

She stepped inside, her gaze searching for Thor, but the building was empty, and disappointment filled her. Then the stallion nickered a greeting and she smiled. Lindsey lifted her skirts and walked toward him.

"Hello, pretty boy. Where's your master tonight? I thought for certain I would find him here."

Saber whinnied softly.

"I guess I'll have to wait until tomorrow." She glanced round the stable. The other horses stood quietly in their stalls, but even the young groom, Tommy Booker, was gone. She was alone in the barn and for the first time, a thread of unease slipped through her.

So much had happened, so much intrigue swirled around her. Women were dead. Simon Beale might well have been murdered. She thought how angry Thor would be if he knew she was roaming about by herself. She should have asked the driver to wait, but it was too late for that now.

Still, the neighborhood was the safest in London and she didn't have far to walk to reach her home. Lifting her skirts off the earth-packed floor, she started for the door. She was halfway there when the lantern in the window went out, leaving the barn in total darkness.

Lindsey froze. Her heart slammed hard inside her ribs and a ribbon of fear snaked down her spine. She told herself it was only the wind that had blown out the flame, that there was no reason to be afraid. But the breeze was quiet tonight, the leaves unmoving on the trees.

Something stirred in the darkness. A mouse, she told herself, or the barn cat who kept the mouse population at bay. She ignored the uneven thudding of her heart and continued toward the door, her eyes beginning to adjust to the darkness. Through the entrance, she could see a sliver of moon beginning to rise over the row of buildings to the east, giving her enough light to find the door she had come in through.

And outline the shadow of a man.

Lindsey gasped and bit back a scream. The shadow was too small to belong to Thor, too large to be young Tommy. "Who is there?" she called out, hoping her voice didn't quiver, hoping whoever it was would identify himself and she could laugh at her worry.

"You know me…" the man said in a voice that sent chills down her spine. "I might have been the man you married— if you hadn't turned out to be such a little whore."

Thirty-One

~~~❦~~~

The inside of Lindsey's mouth went dry and it was suddenly hard to breathe. The night seemed eerily silent. The darkness inside the stable seemed to press in on her. She knew that voice—Stephen's voice. He had followed her to the stable. It was clear he had discovered her relationship with Thor. And perhaps through Simon Beale or Tilly Coote, he had learned that she was trying to prove him guilty of murder.

There was only one reason he was there in the stable.

Stephen meant to kill her.

Lindsey trembled as he stepped out of the shadows, a tall, blond, handsome man, a man of wealth and position who had chosen evil instead of good. Tilly Coote might have turned him down that path, but as Thor had said, the choice remained his.

Lindsey watched as he moved closer and a shaft of moonlight illuminated his face. Malice distorted his features. Pure evil glinted in his eyes. She almost didn't recognize the man who blocked her path to safety.

"What do you want?" she asked, her stomach churning with fear, stalling for time as she mentally ran over her options. The shutters on the barn were closed to keep out the cold, except for the window where the lamp had been burning and that was too near the front door. There was no back entrance, only one way to escape. And Stephen blocked the way.

Lindsey glanced round, trying to control her trembling limbs, searching for some kind of a weapon, some way to defend herself. In the stalls, the horses began to stir. Saber must have heard the tension in her voice for he snorted and started pawing the earthen floor of his stall.

"You know what I want," Stephen finally answered, easing closer. "I want to rid the world of another worthless whore."

Lindsey swallowed, tried to hang onto her courage. "Is that what Tilly was, Stephen? Is it Tilly you murdered when you killed each of those women?"

He made a harsh sound low in his throat. "Tonight it will be you I kill." He disappeared into the darkness and her pulse jerked into high gear. She couldn't reach the door. There was no way Stephen would allow it. She spotted a row of tools in a rack on the wall, ran over and grabbed a pitchfork. Keeping her back to the wall, she braced her legs apart and waited. Her ears strained into the darkness, listening for sounds that would tell her where he was.

The only sound she heard was the wild thudding of her heart and the shuffling of the horses, uneasy now, moving around in their stalls.

A noise came from the corner and she whirled in that direction.

"Over here," Stephen said softly. "You want to fight me? I'd like that. Why don't you come and get me?"

Why didn't she? If he was going to kill her, she wasn't going down easily. Coming away from the wall, she moved toward the sound of the voice. Perhaps she could circle round him, reach the door, and make a run for it. Gripping the pitchfork, her palms so sweaty it was hard to hold onto the long wooden handle, she whirled at the sound of Stephen's voice coming from behind her.

"Put down the weapon," he softly commanded. "You don't want to make this any harder than it has to be." On the opposite side of the barn, Saber began to rear and snort and kick the boards in his stall. Shrill neighs filled the barn.

"I'm not letting you kill me, Stephen." Her fingers tightened on the handle. "Come any closer and you will be the one who is dead."

He chuckled, a soft rumble in the darkness. "You think I mean to strangle you? I am sorry, but this time I must forgo the pleasure."

Hooves pounded against the boards in the stall but Stephen didn't seem to hear. He stepped out of the shadows, into a ray of moonlight, and the hatred in his features sent a cold shiver down her spine.

"There is nothing I would like better than to put my hands round your lovely pale neck and squeeze the life from your treacherous little body. But then Rudy would go free and that would spoil my plan."

"You're paying him back for what happened at The Goose?"

"So he told you about that, did he? Rudy never could keep his mouth shut about anything." He raised his hand and she gasped at the sight of a pistol barrel glinting in the light streaming in through the open barn door. "You would satisfy my needs very well, little whore, but alas it is not to be."

Though the air felt icy cold, a trickle of sweat rolled between her breasts. Stephen moved closer, moved the pistol and aimed it at her heart. In seconds she would be dead.

Gripping the pitchfork, Lindsey let out a piercing scream and charged, turning away as she thrust the pitchfork toward him with all of her strength. The blast of the gunshot echoed through the barn and Stephen grunted in pain as the iron prongs dug into his side. Swearing a violent oath, breathing hard, he jerked the pitchfork free, and an instant later, a second pistol appeared in his hand. He aimed the gun at Lindsey.

"You did better than I thought." He reached down to touch the blood oozing from the holes in his side that hadn't been deep enough to kill him. "Now let's make this end." He moved closer, the weapon pointed at her chest.

"Lindsey, is that you?" Thor's deep voice reached her through the darkness, his tall silhouette outlined in the moonlight streaming into the barn.

"It's Stephen!" she shouted. "He has a gun!"

"Stop right where you are!" Stephen commanded, the pistol still pointed straight at Lindsey.

Thor jolted to a halt.

"Move a muscle and she's dead."

He took in the scene at a glance and in the faint rays of moonlight, his jaw looked hard as steel. "You think I will let you kill her? You have only one shot and you will need that for me."

The pistol swung toward Thor. "Fine, I'll shoot you first

and deal with your whore when I'm finished." Stephen took aim, then froze as a loud crash rent the air and Saber streaked like black lightning out of his stall. The stallion thundered toward Stephen, who jerked his pistol in that direction and blindly pulled the trigger. Saber reared up on his hind legs and his hooves slammed down with murderous force, sending Stephen crashing into the dirt. The stallion's hooves slammed down again, cutting into Stephen once more.

"Saber, hold!" Thor rushed forward. "Saber!" But by the time he brought the animal under control, Stephen Camden, Viscount Merrick lay in a bloody heap, dead on the floor of the barn. The stallion backed away, shaking all over, his black coat glistening with sweat.

"Thor!" Lindsey ran toward him and he caught her up in his arms.

"By the gods, Lindsey!"

She buried her face in his shoulder and his hold tightened around her. "Are you hurt? Lindsey—are you injured?"

Tommy Booker ran into the barn just then. "Sweet Jesus!"

"St-Stephen followed me here," Lindsey tried to explain, her voice shaking. "He—he tried to kill me and I—I stabbed him with the pitchfork. He would have killed you, too—if…if it hadn't been for Saber." She started crying then, deep racking sobs she couldn't seem to stop.

Thor's hold tightened even more. Tommy Booker retrieved the lantern, lit the wick, and the stable filled with golden light.

"Easy boy," said Tommy, moving closer to Saber, reaching out a hand to stroke him, then jerking back in horror. "He's been shot! Saber's been shot!"

Lindsey cried out and she and Thor raced toward him. Lindsey bit back a sob as she reached the spot where the stallion stood trembling. Blood oozed from a wound in his chest. The animal whinnied softly, nudged her with his nose, then went down on his knees and lay down heavily on his side.

"Saber!" Tears rushed into Lindsey's eyes as Thor knelt beside his beloved horse. "Oh God, oh God!" She bit down on her lip, trying to pull herself together, knowing now was not the time to fall apart. "We have to get help. We have to do something!" Blood darkened her skirt as she knelt beside Thor, whose hands shook as he worked over the horse.

"There's an animal doctor," she said, fighting to steady her shaking voice. "He takes care of all the livestock my father keeps in the city. His name is Carlton and he lives close by...in...in Kinsey Street...at...at the end of the block off Richman Lane."

Thor turned to the groom. "Go get him, Tommy, and fetch the police."

"Use my father's name," Lindsey added. "Tell the doctor that Baron Renhurst said for him to come."

"I'll bring him, miss!"

"Hurry, Tommy!"

The lad raced out of the barn, leaving them to care for the stallion. Saber nickered softly and tried to lift his head, but he didn't have the strength.

"We've got to stop the bleeding," Thor said.

Lindsey ran to the tack room in search of a blanket, her heart aching for Thor as well as Saber. Kneeling next to Thor, she handed him the blanket, which he tore into strips and stuffed into the hole where the lead ball had entered. Folding another strip, he pressed it over the bleeding wound.

"He can't die," Lindsey said, the tears in her eyes beginning to slide down her cheeks. "He saved our lives."

Thor made no reply, but his jaw clenched and unclenched in helpless fury. Lindsey looked at Saber. It was clear the injury was grave, perhaps fatal. Lindsey knew Thor was hurting nearly as much as Saber.

She stroked the stallion's neck, smoothed his silky cheek. "You have to get well, boy. You have work to do for Thor."

The horse made a soft sound in his throat and Lindsey's heart squeezed. His eyes were a velvety brown and they seemed to be saying farewell.

"I won't let you die," she whispered, "I won't." But dear God, she wasn't sure what more she could do, what anyone could do to save the magnificent horse.

Thor stroked the stallion's neck and whispered soothing words, some in his own native language. As Lindsey pressed the cloth over the horse's bleeding wound, Thor left them for a moment, retrieved another blanket, and walked over to where Stephen lay dead on the floor. Taking note of the bloody pitchfork, flicking a glance in her direction, he unfurled the blanket and covered the man's lifeless body.

"You did not deserve such a quick death," he said darkly. "Hanging would have been too good for you."

Lindsey thought of the women Stephen had brutally murdered, thought of the beautiful horse whose sides heaved with each labored breath, and believed that Thor was right. Merrick had gotten less than he deserved.

Thor returned to Lindsey's side, traded places, and pressed his big hand over the blanket-covered hole. All the while, he spoke to the stallion in that gentle way of his, calling the horse *Brandr fra dat konungr,* Saber of the

King, soothing him and promising that help would soon come, asking him to fight like the champion he was, asking him not to die.

"You cannot let a man like that steal your life," he said softly, stroking the horse's side. "Your veins run with the blood of champions. You were meant to sire sons that would rule for generations." His voice broke on this last and he glanced away, his throat moving up and down.

He swallowed. "Where is that doctor?" he said gruffly after what seemed hours but wasn't nearly that long.

"He'll come," Lindsey said, reaching out to touch him, aching for him deep inside. "We have to believe that. Saber just has to hang on until he gets here."

A quarter hour later, the sound of footfalls drew Lindsey's attention to the door. Tommy Booker appeared in the light of the lantern, breathing hard and perspiring. At the sight of the gray-haired doctor who walked in behind him, Lindsey felt a stirring of hope.

"Dr. Carlton!" She rose to her feet and hurried toward him. "Thank God you are here. Saber has been shot. He desperately needs your help."

Carlton, a man in his fifties, wore rumpled clothes and the sleepy-eyed look of having been summoned from his bed. He knelt at the stallion's side, lifted the bloody square of wool, and frowned. He gently examined the wound and Saber made no attempt to stop him.

"What can you tell us, Doctor?" Thor asked anxiously.

The doctor continued his work, then looked at Thor. "There is no frothy blood coming out of the wound, which means the ball didn't hit a lung."

He did a bit more probing, trying to discover the angle

the lead ball went in. Saber lifted his head and tried to avoid the doctor's touch, then lay back down, weak from loss of blood. "I can't tell if the ball is still in there or if it might have gone out through his side."

Since the horse was too heavy to move, Thor reached gently beneath him, feeling for the telltale sticky wetness. Saber jerked as he touched the exit wound, which was also leaking blood.

"The ball went through," Thor said. "That is good, right?"

The doctor nodded. "Except for the blood loss. At least we won't have to go in and try to dig it out."

"What can we do?" Lindsey asked.

"If we can get the bleeding stopped, he might have a chance. Even so, he'll face the problem of putrefaction."

Lindsey fought a wave of despair. It seemed so hopeless. And yet she was determined. "Can we sew him up? Will that help stop the bleeding?"

"The ball didn't hit an artery—he'd be dead by now if it had. But we need to find a way to lift him up so we can deal with the other wound as well as the one in his chest."

"I can rig a sling," Thor said. "But I will need some help." He looked over at Tommy, whose eyes were wet and his face the color of ice. Clearly, the young groom had grown to love the stallion as much as they did.

"Get my brother," Thor instructed. "Tell him what has happened and ask him to hurry." Thor gave the lad directions to Leif's town house in Berkeley Square and Tommy shot out of the stable, headed in that direction.

Using lengths of heavy rope tossed over the rafters, Thor worked to build a device that would lift the horse enough to sew up the wounds and get a bandage in place. Still, they didn't want to move him so much that the bleeding would increase. They would need to be very careful.

Lindsey watched Thor at work and her heart filled with love for him. She knew the pain he barely held in check. Saber meant so much to him…so very much.

God, if there is anything you can do to help save this beautiful horse…

She could barely finish, though she prayed with all her heart that He would answer her silent prayer. For it was clear to one and all the stallion's fate rested in God's hands.

It was well past midnight. Though a lantern burned not far away and another had been lit, only a dim yellow glow warmed the interior of the stable. Thor glanced up at the sound of heavy footfalls, felt something move inside him as he watched his brother approach.

When he walked over to thank him for coming, Leif put an arm around his shoulder and gave him a fierce man-hug. "I am so sorry, brother. What can I do to help?"

Thor released a shaky breath. His brother had always been there when he needed him. He'd had no doubt Leif would come tonight.

And yet it meant so much.

"We need to lift him," Thor said. "The ball went into his chest and out through his side and we need to tend that wound as well as the first. I have built a sling, but I need your help to make it work."

Leif just nodded. His jaw worked as he looked down at the beautiful stallion. Thor introduced him to the doctor, Leif spoke a gentle word to Lindsey, then he and his brother set to work.

They lifted Saber carefully, a little at a time, just enough to get the sling beneath his belly, then Leif took hold of the rope while Thor controlled the stallion and they hauled the animal slowly to his feet.

Saber fought, but only for a moment, settling again as Thor spoke to him softly and Leif lowered him until his hooves touched the floor. He tied the rope to a wooden support to hold the sling in place.

As soon as they were finished, the doctor came forward to examine both wounds. "Drawing an imaginary line from entry to exit," he said, "I would say there is a good chance no internal organs were hit. The bleeding has nearly stopped. The problem now will be putrefaction. With this kind of injury, that, rather than the injury itself, is often the cause of death."

"Is there any way to prevent it?" Lindsey asked.

"Not that medical science has found thus far." Working with quiet efficiency, the doctor prepared the needle that would close up the wounds, a larger hole where the ball had torn its way out.

Saber's head hung down and his eyes were glazed and cloudy. He was weak from loss of blood and it was clear the doctor believed that disease was sure to set in.

Thor clenched his jaw against a rush of despair and felt Lindsey's hand searching for his. She laced their fingers together.

"He's going to make it," she said. "We aren't going to let him die."

But he knew the stallion was suffering and Thor felt the pain as if it were his own.

"Let's get this done," the doctor said, "then we'll lower

him back down and let him rest for a while, try to recover some of his strength."

A noise sounded in the doorway. Thor looked up to see Krista sweeping into the stable, the skirt of her simple blue wool gown flaring out as she hurried toward them. "Wait a moment, Doctor!"

Carlson paused.

"What is it?" Thor asked.

Krista cast a pleading look at the doctor, silently begging him to wait. "I went to see Corrie and Gray. I told them Stephen tried to kill Lindsey and that Saber was shot trying to save you. I thought Samir might be able to help."

And then he saw the others rushing in behind her, the Earl of Tremaine and his wife, Coralee, and with them, the wiry little dark-skinned man from the country called India who was Tremaine's valet.

Thor could read the worry in each of their faces, the concern for him and the horse they knew he loved. He swallowed against the knot that swelled in his throat.

"I am a fortunate man to have such friends," he said gruffly.

Gray cast him a sympathetic glance, tossed a brief look at the blanket-covered body in the shadows, then urged his wife toward the silver-haired doctor. "How is he, Doctor?"

"Is he going to be all right?" Coralee asked anxiously, her fiery, sleep-tangled hair tucked behind her ears.

"The bleeding has stopped and I am preparing to close the wounds. I've told Mr. Draugr that putrefaction will be a very large obstacle in the animal's recovery." He turned to Thor. "I'll need you to tend the horse while I sew him up."

But before he could move, Samir shuffled forward, his shoulders slightly stooped. Garbed in white, his dark, thin body outlined in the glow of the lantern, he paused in front of Thor.

"I have brought a potion. I will need to apply it before the wound is closed."

The doctor frowned. "What sort of potion? This horse has been gravely injured. I'm doing everything in my power to save him. I won't have him destroyed by some… some foreign witch doctor."

Thor stepped forward. So did Lindsey, Corrie and Gray.

"Samir is a great healer," Thor said, remembering how he had once saved Coralee. "He has worked miracles before."

"If anyone can save this horse," Corrie added, "it is Samir. Please, Dr. Carlton, you must let him try."

"She's right, Carlton," said Gray. "The man can work wonders."

"Fine," the doctor said with obvious disapproval. "But I take no responsibility for what happens from here on out."

Samir shuffled in front of the horse, poured the potion into the wound in his chest, drawing only a soft whinny from Saber, then did the same to the wound in the stallion's side.

"Thank you, my friend," Thor said to Samir.

The little man bowed. "I will say a prayer for your beautiful horse."

Thor's eyes burned. "Thank you."

Vowing to return, the little Hindu disappeared into the shadows as if he had never been there. Meanwhile Thor soothed the stallion while the doctor sewed up the wounds, working with speed and efficiency. He tied bandages in place around the injuries, then went to collect his instruments and the leather satchel he had brought with him.

"I appreciate all you have done," Thor said, digging into his pockets, hoping he carried enough money with him to pay the man's fee.

"You needn't worry about that tonight. I'll come back tomorrow to check on him."

Thor just nodded.

"The next few hours are critical," Dr. Carlton finished. "If he is still alive in the morning…" He let the sentence trail off since no more words were needed.

Carlton left the barn, Saber still in the sling. Thor and Leif untied the rope to release the tension and without the device to help him stand, his legs too weak to hold him up, Saber crumpled onto the bed of straw they had laid down for him. He rolled onto his side and his head went down.

He looked at Thor and his big brown eyes slowly closed.

Thor's heart squeezed.

As if she knew what he was feeling, Lindsey walked toward him. She slid her arms around his neck, pressed her cheek against his, and simply held him.

Thor had never loved her more.

As soon as the doctor left, the police arrived—two uniformed officers, one young and fair, the other older and ruddy-complexioned who seemed slightly battle-weary.

"Here, now—what the devil is going on?" The young policeman surveyed the chaos in the barn, his gaze going from the injured horse to the blanket-covered body lying a few feet away.

"I think one of you had better explain," said the older policeman.

Thor left Saber, walked over and lifted the blanket.

"This man is the killer you have been seeking. The Covent Garden Murderer."

"It's true," Lindsey confirmed. "His name is Stephen Camden, Viscount Merrick. He killed those three women in the Covent Garden district, as well as a woman in Foxgrove."

Leif, Gray, Krista and Coralee all came over to verify the story of what had happened in the stable, how the viscount had followed Lindsey and tried to kill her. The older policeman walked over and crouched down beside the body, saw the pitchfork Lindsey had used and one of Stephen's spent pistols.

"I think we'd best get Constable Bertram," the officer said. "He's the man in charge of the murder investigation." He tossed the blanket back over Stephen's face. "I'll send a wagon to pick up the body."

The men left to fetch their superior and didn't return for several hours. After they'd gone, Krista, Leif, Corrie and the earl went home, Krista and Leif promising to stop by Lindsey's to tell her parents what had happened, where she was, and that she was safe.

Lindsey figured they probably hadn't even known she was missing from the house, but they would certainly be happy to learn their son would soon be free.

Stephen was dead, the case of the Covent Garden murders finally solved.

And Simon Beale, Lindsey discovered the following morning, was alive. A message was waiting at the house when she returned to bathe and change into fresh clothes, addressed to her from Mr. Beale. According to the note, Stephen had overheard his conversation with Thor and confronted him. Afraid for his life, Beale had fled the viscount's town house and gone into hiding. She penned a return note, telling him Stephen was dead and that he was safe.

With the statements taken from Lindsey, Thor and Beale, Constable Bertram had no choice but to search Stephen's town house. Simon Beale helpfully showed the police the drawer where Stephen kept his scarves, long pink silk ones that were certainly not the sort a gentleman would wear. And there was blood on one of them.

The scarves by themselves weren't proof enough, but combined with the attack on Lindsey and the information the investigator, Harrison Mansfield, had collected in the disappearance of Penelope Barker, there was sufficient evidence to obtain Rudy's release and the dismissal of charges against him.

The matter of the Covent Garden murders was resolved.

Only the life-and-death struggle of Thor's magnificent stallion remained.

Wearing a drab brown woolen gown, Lindsey settled herself in the straw next to Saber. She hadn't slept in three days, not since the beautiful stallion had been shot. Neither had Thor.

Lindsey looked down at the horse, stroking his long, smooth neck, whispering words of encouragement and trying to will him some of her strength. Saber made a soft rasping sound and his velvet brown eyes slowly closed. A long, deep breath whispered out.

"Saber!" Lindsey's heart constricted. The stallion was so weak and he had been in a great deal of pain. Her hand shook as she reached out to touch him, felt the warmth of his slick black coat beneath her fingers. "It's all right, boy. Everything is going to be all right." But her chest ached at the thought that the breath he had just released might be his last.

Then the stallion dragged in a lungful of air, and relief washed through her, so potent she felt dizzy. She glanced up at the sound of footsteps and saw Thor striding toward her, his brilliant blue eyes filled with pain and fear. When he looked at her, sitting in the straw with his precious horse, there was something in his face she had never seen before.

"How is he?" Thor asked.

"I don't know. I thought he was…I thought—"

Just then Saber snorted. He looked at Thor, lifted his proud head and began struggling to get to his feet. Thor ran for the rope that controlled the sling, pulled hard enough to give the stallion the help he needed, and Saber managed to unsteadily regain his footing.

"He's standing!" Lindsey cried as Thor secured the rope to the post just tight enough to provide the support the horse needed. "Is he…do you think he's going to be all right?"

Thor hurried back to Saber. He made a quick check of his injuries and examined the pupils in each of his eyes.

"He's better, isn't he?" she asked. "He isn't going to die. He's going to get well."

Thor smiled so brightly her heart squeezed. "Aye, I think he is."

And as the animal stood unsteadily but now securely on all four feet, his breathing more even and his eyes no longer glazed, it was almost certain that he was going to live. Saber snorted and blew and tossed his magnificent head, sending his thick black mane into the air. He nickered long and deep, and the sound was so sweet that tears filled Lindsey's eyes.

Thor pulled her into arms. "He is going to be all right. You helped save him, sweetheart. I will never forget what you've done."

"I just…I love him, too, Thor."

He took a deep breath, looked as if there was something important he wanted to say, but couldn't quite find the words. Reaching out, he took hold of her hand and led her out into the sunshine. Standing beneath a brilliant blue sky, he looked incredibly tall and impossibly handsome, and her heart clenched with longing. His gaze found hers and where pain had been only moments ago, hot need burned, and something deeper, more fierce.

Lindsey tried to smile but she was too nervous, too hopeful of what he might say. "I'm…I'm so happy for you, Thor."

Instead of speaking, he cupped her face in his big dark hands, bent his head and softly kissed her.

"It is you who makes me happy, Lindsey. You and no other."

The words wrapped around her heart and hope expanded inside her.

"It is time I spoke to your father. Much has happened. There is much to be discussed. Soon we will wed and all will be put right."

Lindsey just nodded. They would marry as he had said. Her parents didn't approve her choice of husband. But they didn't know him.

"I suppose it is time. In a couple of days, we can speak to them—"

"Today," he said firmly. "Tommy will stay with Saber. I will go to my house and change into proper clothes. I will meet you at your parents' house. I will talk to your father as I should have done before."

"But—"

The fierce look in his eyes cut her off. "I want you in my bed, Lindsey. I am tired of sneaking about as if what we do when we are together is wrong. I am tired of hiding what I feel for you."

She looked up at him, a soft pulse beating in her throat. "What is it you feel for me, Thor?"

His gaze remained fierce and intense. "I love you, Lindsey Graham. More than my own life."

As if at last, he had found what he needed to say, the tension faded from his big hard body and his mouth curved into a smile so filled with love, her heart simply melted.

"You are sweet and you are kind," he said. "You are smart and you are determined. You are the most courageous woman I have ever known and though you are sometimes pigheaded, in your own way you are wise. You are my life-mate, the woman the gods have chosen for me, and I will love you for all of time and beyond."

Her eyes welled. "Thor…" Tears rolled down her cheeks as he hauled her into his arms and very thoroughly kissed her. "I love you," she said softly. "I love you so much."

There were problems to solve. She shuddered to think of the coming confrontation with her parents. She prayed that in time they would accept Thor as a member of the family, but it was really of no consequence. Thor loved her and she loved him and that was all that truly mattered.

Thor nibbled the side of her neck. "For a time, I did not have the courage to tell you the way I feel, but no more. I love you, Lindsey, and I promise to be the husband you deserve."

Lindsey looked up at him, into those blue, blue eyes and knew that this man she loved with all her heart was a man who would keep his word.

Epilogue

Two months later

The house echoed with the clink of glasses raised in toast, the sound of laughter and well wishes. After their wedding, a simple service attended by a small group of friends in the chapel of St. Mary's Church, Lindsey's parents had provided a wedding feast at their home.

Her father still grumbled, but in the end, he had accepted Thor as the man she would wed. Her mother was gradually succumbing to her husband's not-so-subtle charm. Thor was, after all, an extremely handsome, very masculine male—one even her mother could not remain immune to for long. In his own way, he was sweet, and he was caring, and it was clear how much he loved their daughter.

As for Rudy, her brother practically worshipped him. Thor had helped prove Rudy's innocence. Without that help, he might well have hanged.

Other problems had also been solved. Lindsey had ex-

plained her situation to Michael, apologized and asked
him to forgive her, which amazingly, he had. She had
helped Krista find a new editor for the women's section of
Heart to Heart, though she hoped to continue writing
articles from time to time.

Lindsey's husband of four brief hours tugged on her
hand. "I have waited long enough. It is time for us to leave."

She looked back at the cluster of people laughing and
talking in the drawing room. "At least let me make my
farewells."

He nodded grudgingly. "I will wait here. Do not take long."

She cast him a look. He was still not completely comfortable at social gatherings but she didn't really mind.
Lindsey gave him a last warm smile and made her way
across the room to the circle that included her friends.

She spoke to Krista and Leif. "Thank you for everything. You are both the dearest of friends."

Krista squeezed her hand. "I am so happy for you."

Leif bent and kissed her cheek. "My brother is a very
lucky man. Welcome to the family."

Her eyes misted. "Thank you."

She turned to Corrie and Gray. "Tell Samir we will
always be grateful for what he did for Saber."

"We'll tell him," Corrie promised.

"And I want you to know how thankful we both feel to
have you as our friends."

Gray lifted his champagne glass. He flicked an affec-
tionate glance at his wife, who had discovered two weeks
ago she was definitely carrying his child. Gray had been
over the top, which was obvious by the protective way he
kept Coralee by his side.

"You married a good man, Lindsey," Gray said, "though I'll deny it if you tell him I said so."

She laughed, glanced to where her husband impatiently waited, his eyes dark blue and hungry. She knew he was thinking of the night ahead and her stomach lifted in anticipation.

"I have to go. I shall see you all in a couple of weeks."

Leif chuckled. "You'll be lucky if my brother lets you out of bed before the end of the month."

Lindsey blushed.

Thor joined her for a few more brief farewells, including a quick goodbye to her parents and Aunt Delilah, who had returned to London for the wedding.

"What did I tell you?" Aunt Dee whispered with a conspiratorial glance at Thor. "I knew it would be impossible to remain *just friends* with a man who looked like *that.*"

Lindsey grinned.

Aunt Dee's escort, Colonel Langtree, arched a silver-blond eyebrow. "How difficult do you think it is going to be, my love, to remain merely friends with me?" He slanted Delilah a possessive glance that made very clear his intentions; Aunt Dee's cheeks went pink, and Lindsey thought there would probably be another wedding soon.

Thor took Lindsey's hand and they walked away smiling. A few minutes later, they were finally able to escape.

"We are still more than an hour's ride from home," Thor grumbled. "I intend to consummate this marriage in our own bed." She couldn't miss the heat in his eyes and her body warmed at the promise of what was to come.

They hadn't made love in weeks, Thor insisting they be properly wed before he claimed his husbandly rights.

Lindsey wondered if he would truly make it as far as the house before he took her.

But Thor remained stalwart as the carriage rolled toward Greenbriar, the property in the country he had purchased to start his Thoroughbred breeding farm. His control was admirable, except of course, that he touched her, caressed her, teased and kissed her all the way home, and by the time they got there, Lindsey was consumed by a fever of lust.

"It isn't fair," she muttered as she tried to coax him into making love to her on the plush velvet seat.

"Soon, my love," he promised, kissing her deeply again. "This is one night I mean for you to remember."

Lindsey inwardly groaned. She had never endured such torture. Yet every hot look, every heated touch, promised pleasure she would never forget.

And so when they finally reached the lovely manor house and he led her inside, she barely noticed the rose petals strewn across the polished wooden floors, trailing up the staircase to the master's suite. She scarcely saw the soft pink petals strewn over the white linen sheets on the big four-poster bed, or realized the fragrant scent of lilacs came from the pillows.

Instead, the moment Thor carried her over the threshold into the candlelit bedroom, she reached up and pulled his mouth down to hers for a deep, scorching kiss. Thor made a sound low in his throat and returned the fevered contact. In minutes, he had stripped her naked and then himself and carried her over to the big bed they would share from this night forward.

"I meant to undress you slowly," he said between burning kisses. "I have a strong will, wife, but I am only human."

Lindsey laughed as his lips moved from her mouth to her breasts. Searing kisses ringed her navel and traveled lower, teased the inside of her thighs. He ran a finger through the tawny curls above her sex and she gasped as his mouth found her most private place and he began to taste her.

Pleasure washed through her. Lindsey peaked in moments, gripping his powerful shoulders, crying out his name and convulsing wildly. Thor did not stop. He had promised her a night she would remember and it was clear he meant to keep his word, continuing his tender assault until another climax shook her.

She was limp and sated by the time he moved above her, kissed her hotly, found her softness and guided himself inside her. Her body responded with a will of its own and desire surged to life once more.

"Please…" she whimpered, beginning to writhe beneath him. "Thor…please…"

A sound of triumph rumbled from beneath the muscles across his chest. He bent his head and suckled her breasts, then he started to move, taking her with penetrating strokes that had her gasping for breath. Pleasure rushed through her, wild and intense. Deep thrusts carried her higher, urged her toward the pinnacle of sweetness and light.

"Thor!" she cried out as she reached fulfillment, wrapping her legs around him, her head falling back at the fierce sensations pouring through her. Thor reached release a few moments later, his muscles tightening, his jaw clenched as waves of pleasure rolled through him.

For long moments they seemed suspended in a world without time. Then he eased himself down beside her and drew her into his arms.

"You belong to me, Lindsey. You are the wife of my destiny, and my heart." His eyes found hers in the flickering light of the candle. "Tonight, if the gods will it, I will give you a babe."

Lindsey thought of Samir's potion, lying unused in a drawer, and the woman's time she had missed some weeks back.

A soft, secret smile curved her lips. "There is a very good chance, my darling, that is a task you have already accomplished."

Author's Note

I hope you enjoyed *Heart of Courage,* the third book in the Heart Trilogy that started with *Heart of Honor,* Leif and Krista's story, followed by *Heart of Fire,* Gray and Coralee's. If you haven't had a chance to read them, I hope you will look for the books and that you enjoy them.

Up next for me is *Royal's Bride,* the first in the all new Bride's Trilogy, tales of the three handsome brothers and the fiery women who win their hearts.

Hope you'll watch for *Royal's Bride,* coming soon!

All best wishes and happy reading,

Kat

The second book in the deliciously passionate
Heart trilogy by *New York Times* bestselling author

KAT MARTIN

As a viscount's daughter, vivacious Coralee Whitmore
is perfectly placed to write about London's elite in the
outspoken ladies' gazette *Heart to Heart*. But beneath her
fashionable exterior beats the heart of a serious journalist.

So when her sister's death is dismissed as suicide, Corrie vows
to uncover the truth, suspecting that the notorious Earl of
Tremaine was Laurel's lover and the father of her illegitimate
child. But Corrie finds the earl is not all he seems…nor is
she immune to his charms, however much she despises his
caddish ways.

**"The first of [a] new series,
Heart of Honor is a grand
way for the author to begin…
Kat Martin has penned
another memorable tale."**
—Historical Romance Writers

*Heart of
Fire*

*Available the first week of January 2008
wherever paperbacks are sold!*

www.MIRABooks.com   MKM2452

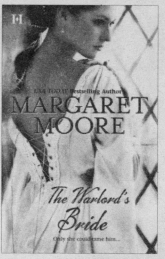

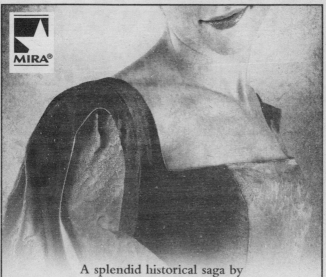

REQUEST YOUR
FREE BOOKS!

2 FREE NOVELS
FROM THE ROMANCE/SUSPENSE
COLLECTION PLUS 2 FREE GIFTS!

YES! Please send me 2 FREE novels from the Romance/Suspense Collection and my 2 FREE gifts (gifts are worth about $10). After receiving them, if I don't wish to receive any more books, I can return the shipping statement marked "cancel." If I don't cancel, I will receive 4 brand-new novels every month and be billed just $5.49 per book in the U.S. or $5.99 per book in Canada, plus 25¢ shipping and handling per book plus applicable taxes, if any*. That's a savings of at least 20% off the cover price! I understand that accepting the 2 free books and gifts places me under no obligation to buy anything. I can always return a shipment and cancel at any time. Even if I never buy another book from the Reader Service, the two free books and gifts are mine to keep forever.

185 MDN EF5Y 385 MDN EF6C

Name	(PLEASE PRINT)	
Address		Apt. #
City	State/Prov.	Zip/Postal Code

Signature (if under 18, a parent or guardian must sign)

Mail to **The Reader Service:**
IN U.S.A.: P.O. Box 1867, Buffalo, NY 14240-1867
IN CANADA: P.O. Box 609, Fort Erie, Ontario L2A 5X3

Not valid to current subscribers to the Romance Collection,
the Suspense Collection or the Romance/Suspense Collection.

Want to try two free books from another line?
Call 1-800-873-8635 or visit www.morefreebooks.com.

* Terms and prices subject to change without notice. N.Y. residents add applicable sales tax. Canadian residents will be charged applicable provincial taxes and GST. Offer not valid in Quebec. This offer is limited to one order per household. All orders subject to approval. Credit or debit balances in a customer's account(s) may be offset by any other outstanding balance owed by or to the customer. Please allow 4 to 6 weeks for delivery. Offer available while quantities last.

Your Privacy: Harlequin is committed to protecting your privacy. Our Privacy Policy is available online at www.eHarlequin.com or upon request from the Reader Service. From time to time we make our lists of customers available to reputable third parties who may have a product or service of interest to you. If you would prefer we not share your name and address, please check here. ☐